# CHRISTMAS IN THREE RIVERS

THREE RIVERS RANCH ROMANCE BOOK 9

LIZ ISAACSON



AEJ
CREATIVE WORKS

ISBN-13: 978-1-953506-15-3

# THE NINTH INNING

# SCRIPTURE

"Blessed is that man that maketh the Lord his trust, and respecteth not the proud, nor such as turn aside to lies."

PSALMS 40:4

# CHAPTER ONE

Sundays had never felt so problematic for Andrea Larsen. Of course, she'd been enjoying her day of rest for years, sitting by her mother at church, attending the picnic, and basking in the one day off she had each week.

Now, with Mama gone, Andy sat alone during the sermon, didn't like lingering afterward, and escaped inside her boutique just to pass the hours until Monday.

Today, she unpackaged a new shipment of blouses perfect for the upcoming holiday season while the winter wind in Texas tried to get in through the shop window's cracks.

She nursed a mug of hot chocolate, her mind far away—at Three Rivers Ranch, where Lawrence Collins worked. She couldn't help thinking about him during the Thanksgiving season, as that's when she'd broken up with him. But now, the tall, sandy-haired, bright blue-eyed cowboy dominated her thoughts.

Regret lanced through her heart, and once again, she contemplated calling him and apologizing. After all, she'd been wrong. He hadn't been dating another woman in Amarillo, but going there to visit his younger sister who'd gotten pregnant and was afraid to tell her parents.

As quickly as the remorse had settled, her pride pushed it out. She could never tell him she'd been wrong, though in the quiet moments—like today—she fantasized about what life would be like if she could muster the courage to apologize.

Would he forgive her?

Could they start over?

Her phone chimed, a peculiar sound for a notification she didn't recognize. At least it drove Lawrence from her mind. When she checked her device, she saw she'd received her first online order. Her brand spanking new system had just been implemented a month ago in anticipation of the holiday season, and a brief balloon of joy lifted her spirits.

Carly Sanders apparently needed a new black pencil skirt and a blouse in "green, white, and black."

Andy didn't stock everything, but she *had* just gotten in a selection of items in holiday colors—including green. She turned on her Internet radio as she browsed her boutique, some of the disquiet of this lonely Sunday drifting into the rafters.

Monday morning, before she usually left the loft above her shop, Andy armed herself with Carly's purchases and set her car on the road. Almost an afterthought, she checked the delivery address.

Her stomach fell to her shoes when she saw she needed to drive all the way out to Three Rivers Ranch. A river of trepidation wound through Andy, mostly because the possibility of seeing Lawrence existed. Of course, she'd seen him at church and around town—it was a small place, after all. But she'd managed to put people between them and keep their paths from fully crossing.

Embarrassment ran with the anxiety. She really just needed to clear the air between them. Then she wouldn't have to worry about seeing him at the grocery store, or the picnic—or the ranch.

She dialed Carly. "You want these clothes out at Three Rivers?"

Scuffling came through the line. "You've got them already?"

"Yeah, I just got a new shipment of holiday things over the weekend. You're going to love the blouse I picked out for you. The stripes are fantastic and will look great on you."

"That's great." But Carly didn't sound like it was great. She seemed distracted.

"I was heading over to your place now." Andy watched a pair of boys walk in front of her, clearly on their way to school. "But then I realized you set the delivery address to the ranch. Have you left for work yet?"

"Yeah. Yes, I'm here." A door slammed on Carly's end of the line. "I want to model the clothes for...uh, a Christmas party we're having here at Courage Reins. That's why I need them out here." Murmurs came through the line, and Carly said, "I know," to someone else.

"Is that okay?" she asked Andy. "If you can't make it here and back by the time you need to open, you could come tomorrow."

Andy frowned. If Carly didn't need the clothes until tomorrow.... She shook her head. She was up, already sitting in the car. "I'm on my way." Even driving eighty minutes round-trip was better than puttering around the shop. Again.

Carly emitted a tiny squeak before she hung up. Andy swung through a drive-through for a cup of coffee and set her car north. The gray skies complimented her mood as she drove.

She usually enjoyed the quiet, quaint atmosphere of Three Rivers. But she felt unsettled now that Mama had died. Now that she was all alone. Just her and her building now. She hadn't had much romantic luck after Lawrence.

"Maybe because you compare every man to him," she

muttered to herself as she tried to take some measure of calmness from the beauty of the landscape. The blowing trees only satisfied her soul for a moment. Then she felt like those trees, being whipped and pushed whichever way the wind happened to blow.

Andy didn't want to be ungrounded. Not anymore. She wanted to take control of her life, the way she had her business. She turned onto the dirt road leading to the ranch, a swift gust of wind knocking into her car. Tightening her grip on the wheel, she glanced into the sky and watched the swirling storm.

She urged her car to go a bit faster on the bumpy road, hoping to make it inside the building before the skies opened. Her teeth knocked together as she rounded the last corner. A new building, nearly complete, sat just on the corner, with fenced in arenas and another barn.

A dark haired woman Andy had seen a couple of times at church pushed her whole weight against a barrel, inching it along the dirt. She dusted off her hands and glanced at the sky, then at Andy as she passed.

She raised her hand in a friendly greeting, and Andy struggled to recall her name. She hadn't come into the boutique before, and she'd rented the old Johnson house that had been empty for years.

"Brynn," Andy said, proud of herself for remembering that much. She'd heard Brynn was starting a horse training facility at the ranch, and it looked like the rumors held truth.

Thunder rumbled the sky, and Andy focused. But the paved parking lot in front of the Courage Reins administration building was full.

*Full.*

She bypassed it, lightning flashing against the front windows of the building, and pulled down the lane where a variety of ranch vehicles crowded together. One space remained, and she swung into it and grabbed the bag containing Carly's new clothes from the passenger seat.

She'd opened her door and stood when the deluge of rain came. Yelping, she cradled the bag in her arms and ran for the closest building to wait out the downpour.

Her shoes ate up the few yards to the horse barn, but they couldn't escape the water. By the time she found refuge, mud had splattered her ballet flats and splashed up the calves of her slacks. At least the clothes were dry. Mostly.

"Wet out there." The man spoke so quietly, Andy barely heard him. At least with her ears. That voice, though, was ingrained in her mind, buried deep in her heart. Had been since she met him at the rodeo and been charmed by his subtle strength. Had been for six months while they dated.

She turned as if in slow motion toward Lawrence, who stood a few paces away in all his glory. Black cowboy hat. Dark leather jacket. Jeans that stretched down his long legs to his boots. Her eyes traveled back to his before her vocal chords remembered how to work.

If only she could think of something to say. Her brain threw suggestions at her: *Hey.* Or maybe *Good morning.* Even *How's everything?* would've worked.

Nothing came out of her mouth.

"You look great," he said, taking a careful step closer.

"Thank you," misted from her mouth, though nothing about her looked great. But she'd always been polite, even when confronted with difficult situations. One sweep of Lawrence, and she knew she'd hurt him badly. Unintentionally, but the breakup still sliced at her every time she thought of it, and she hadn't been wrongly accused.

He kept coming forward, stopping only a few feet from her, and leaned against the railing. "Those Miss Carly's clothes?"

Andy dropped the bag like it was crime scene evidence and she didn't want to be seen with it. She combed her fingers through her sopping hair, wishing she didn't look and feel like a drowned rat.

He bent to pick up the bag. "Looks like 'em." He glanced at her. "You've lost your voice or something?"

Andy blinked and then pressed her eyes closed for a long moment. "Good morning, Lawrence."

He grinned, that sexy, soft smile she'd fallen in love with the first time she'd seen it. Her heart hammered against her breastbone.

"Mornin' to you too, Miss Andy." He stepped forward—again—and handed her the bag. She took it with numb fingers and waited for him to fall back against the rail. He didn't.

He swept his hand down the side of her face. "I miss you."

Her throat squeezed. Squeezed against the emotion in his voice. Squeezed against her own desire and longing to be with Lawrence again. Squeezed against the apology crowding her chest.

"It's good to see you again," she managed to say. Her arms itched to wrap themselves around him and hold on tight. Her feet urged her to leave, and leave now. The rain pounded the ground outside the barn, and she couldn't escape. She peered into the atmosphere, wishing she could.

"Andy—" Lawrence started.

"I'm sorry," she blurted. "Okay? I'm sorry I accused you of cheating on me." Andy looked up, right into his dazzling blue eyes. "I was wrong."

His eyes blazed, first with heat, then with forgiveness, and finally with happiness. "Yeah, you were." He sighed. "But at least now I don't have to ask Miss Carly to lie for me again."

As lost as Andy felt inside his gaze, she still comprehended his words. "What?"

"She didn't order those clothes."

"She didn't?" Andy realized she'd been leaning forward, and she righted herself before she did something she couldn't undo.

"I did," Lawrence said. "Wanted to get you out to the ranch so we could talk."

Andy didn't know what to say, what he could possibly want to talk about. She glared at him, conversation topics they used to enjoy completely off-limits.

Despite the way her mind whirred, trying to think through what he needed to say, the heavy load she'd been carrying for the past year dissipated, eased from her shoulders.

*Thank you, Lord, she thought, for giving me the courage to apologize and for allowing Lawrence to accept it.*

He paced away from her, and a blip of fear stole through her. He had forgiven her, hadn't he?

---

LAWRENCE MOVED AWAY FROM ANDY, THE intoxicating scent of her beachy perfume overwhelming his rationality. Plus, after he'd told her that he'd lured her out to the ranch with an online order from her boutique, she carried a violent edge in her eye, and Lawrence liked his nose whole, thank you very much.

"You can be mad," he said. "But I was tired of avoiding you at church and in town."

"All those cars in the parking lot...."

Lawrence turned and leaned against a post, a healthy distance from her. He kicked a smile in her direction. "You'd be surprised how long it takes to get enough people to move their vehicles." Especially because they all wanted an explanation. Thankfully, Carly could charm a cat to give up its catch, and she'd been able to fill the parking lot before Andy arrived. Barely.

"So you left me that one spot." Andy gestured toward the door, where the rain still fell. "Did you order up the rain too?"

"No, that was just lucky."

She cocked her hip and folded her arms, and Lawrence wished the sight of her didn't drive his pulse into overdrive. He watched her as her mind bent around his set-up. So much of Andy was reactionary—like the first time they'd met and she'd slid her hand into his during the barrel racing—but she also had a side of her that took time to process. Time to think through what she should say.

"Well, now what?" she asked, smoothing down her festive crimson sweater. She'd paired it with a pair of black slacks, which hugged her petite frame, and a pair of ballet flats, which bore the muddy evidence of her escape into the barn.

"Now nothing," Lawrence said, though a dinner invitation sat on the tip of his tongue. "I just wanted to see you and tell you I'm not upset with you." He wanted more than that, but he buried the words deep. Couldn't speak them too soon.

She combed her fingers through her coffee-colored hair and trained her tea-colored eyes on him. He'd lost himself to her beauty before, and he felt himself falling again. He glanced away.

"Sorry about your momma," he said.

She inhaled sharply, sending a hiss through the barn. "You came to the funeral. You already paid your respects."

"Not to you." He stuffed his hands in his pockets as they tingled in anticipation of holding hers. "You doin' okay?"

"Fine."

Which meant no. He wondered if she'd holed herself up in her loft, lost herself in her boutique, spent too much money and too many hours shopping online. One look at Andy, and he knew she'd done all of that.

"What are you doin' for Thanksgiving?" he asked.

"Baking pumpkin pie and roasting a turkey."

"For one?"

She lifted her chin. "Yes."

"You shouldn't do that." He couldn't stop himself from

moving a little closer. Maybe not within arm's reach, but near enough to smell that blasted perfume. "Come on out here. Kelly and Chelsea are preparing a feast fit for kings." He nodded to the bag of clothes she still held. "Carly will probably need to order a bigger size after what they have planned." He chuckled. "Don't you tell her I said that, though."

A ghost of a smile crossed her face. "It'll be our little secret."

Surprise jolted through him at the familiar words. A game they used to play during the months they'd dated.

*"Don't tell anyone I let you in my storeroom." She gives him a flirtatious grin as she pushes open the door. "I never let anyone in here, not even Mama."*

*"It'll be our little secret," he tells her as he enters, pulls her with him, and closes the door. He kisses her in the privacy of her storeroom, away from the window shopping ladies on the sidewalk. Their little secret.*

Lawrence shook the memories from his head, but the fantasy that he and Andy could play such games again remained in full force.

She seemed to remember what the words represented, and her face turned to stone. "I can't come for Thanksgiving." She spun and faced the weather.

He joined her at her side. "Of course you can. You have nowhere else to go." He put his hand on her arm for barely a breath. There, then gone. "You shouldn't be alone at the holidays."

"Will you go home to Amarillo?"

"Not this year." He focused on the rain too, watched the wind drive it sideways. "My folks are goin' on a cruise. I'm staying here. Maybe I'll even help with the baking."

Andy gave him the response he wanted—she threw her head back and laughed. "I'll eat before I come out, then."

"Hey, who says I haven't improved since last year?"

She tossed him a smirk. "Have you?"

"Not even a little bit." He nudged her side. "Does that mean you'll come?" He didn't dare to hope, yet the feeling swelled inside him, expanding until it filled his whole body.

She drew the silence into long ribbons, until the unease inside Lawrence threatened to tear him apart. He hadn't dated anyone since Andy. He couldn't. He believed her to be the only one for him.

Now he just needed her to believe it too.

He tilted his head toward the barn's rafters. *How do I make her believe it too?*

He'd been asking God the same question for months, and finally he'd had the idea to use her online shopping service to get her to talk to him. But now he didn't know what else to say, and the Lord was silent on the matter as well.

# CHAPTER TWO

Andy drank in the warmth from Lawrence's body, inhaled the spicy scent of his aftershave and the comforting smell of leather and horse that accompanied him everywhere. Something about leaning her head against his shoulder would be natural, but a layer of awkwardness existed between them as well.

"You still have my number?" His question shattered the ice between them.

Her stomach squirmed. What would he think if she said no? What would it imply if she said yes?

She decided to be truthful. "Yes."

"Great," he said, his tone unreadable. "Text me and let me know what you decide." He flipped up the collar of his jacket, took the bag from her hand, and stepped into the downpour. "By this weekend would be nice," he called over his shoulder as the rain concealed him in misty grayness.

A keen sense of loss accompanied his absence, and Andy struggled to make sense of it. In the end, she turned back to the barn, reasoning away her feelings as a side effect of her lingering loneliness. She just missed her mother. Missed having days where the world felt right, like things made sense.

Because nothing right now made sense. Lawrence shouldn't have lured her out here. He shouldn't be so happy to see her. He should be upset with her. The fact that he wasn't ignited a fire in her belly she didn't know what to do with.

She wandered down the aisle in the barn, a bit startled when a horse nosed her on her way by. "Hey, there." She stroked her hand down his nearly black cheeks, pleased with the serenity of the animal, the lazy way he closed his eyes halfway.

The alarm on her phone went off, and Andy headed toward the exit. She knew she'd sit and visit with Carly, and she'd set the alarm to let her know when she needed to leave so she could get back to the boutique and open on time.

The rain had let up a little bit—not enough to go traipsing around in, but enough for her to tiptoe-run to her car without much more damage to her shoes and slacks.

The damage to her heart, however, seemed to multiply as she drove by the packed parking lot and found Lawrence leaning against one of the trucks, the rain dripping off his cowboy hat, watching her.

---

THE WEEK PASSED, WITH ONE DAY BLENDING INTO another. Andy swept her store, played lilting music, sold a handful of dresses to a few people. She expected a rush next week before Thanksgiving, and of course, on Black Friday. But the calm before the storm brought nothing but mind-numbing boredom.

She used to play games on her phone, but having the device so close—with Lawrence's number still programmed in and his invitation to Thanksgiving dinner ringing loudly in her ears—had proven dangerous.

She'd had an acceptance text all typed out before she realized what it could mean. Or maybe it wouldn't mean anything. Maybe she just didn't want to roast her own turkey. Maybe spending time with a big group was just what she needed to get out of the slump she'd fallen into since she broke up with Lawrence and then lost her mother.

On Friday afternoon, the bell on her door tinkled, bringing her attention from the fashion magazine spread before her. A smile bounced to her face.

"Carly, hey."

"Okay, so you're not mad at me." The blonde woman strode toward her as best as she could in her high heels. "Because you haven't called, or demanded payment for the clothes, or texted Lawrence about Thanksgiving."

Andy moved around the counter at the same time Carly arrived, and she embraced her friend. "I'm not mad." She stepped back. "But I do need you to pay for the clothes." She glanced at what Carly wore. "Oh, they look great on you. Spin."

Carly obliged, and satisfaction slipped through Andy at the exact fit of the skirt, the way the black and white stripes—with a green one every third line—slimmed Carly at the waist.

Her friend pulled out her debit card. "So about Thanksgiving...."

"I'm still thinking about it." Andy started the transaction as a way to keep her hands and eyes busy.

"It's just one dinner," Carly said. "There will be loads of people there. Kelly invited her parents. Kate and Brett are here from North Carolina while he builds Brynn Bowman's facility." Carly frowned faintly. "But I think they're going to Oklahoma City to visit his family. But there will still be lots of people there."

"Sure," Andy said, sliding the receipt across the counter. "So it's not like Lawrence and I will be on a date." She leaned her elbows on the counter. "But everyone *will* be staring at us.

Wondering. Rumors will fly afterward." This was Three Rivers, after all. Large enough to not know everyone, but small enough that everyone seemed to hear about everyone else's business.

"Who cares if they do?" Carly pushed the signed receipt back. "It's Thanksgiving." She put her hand on Andy's. "Your first one without your mom. Come hang out with me. Just don't stay here by yourself."

The barriers Andy kept employed around customers, around everyone, crumbled. She dropped her eyes to the counter, the cracks in her heart spreading as she let the hurt inside.

"Okay," she said.

Carly squealed and tucked her card back into her wallet. "Okay, now text Lawrence and let him know. I promised him I wouldn't badger you about coming."

Andy's gaze flew to her friend's. "But you *are* badgering me about coming."

"Shh." Carly grinned. "Don't tell him I stopped by." She pulled on Andy's hand until she moved around the counter. Carly tucked her elbow in Andy's as they strolled toward the door. "You should see the poor guy. He's moping all over the place, shooting dark glares at Reese like it's his fault you haven't texted. He eats lunch with me everyday. Just sits there, eating silently. At the end, when he gets up, he says, 'Do you think she'll come?' It's sad."

Honey flowed through Andy's veins as she listened to Carly tell her about Lawrence's behavior. "What do you tell him when he asks?"

"I tell him I'm sure you'll come. That you don't really want to be alone, here in your loft, with a turkey dinner for one." They reached the door, and Carly dropped Andy's arm. "Now don't make a liar out of me."

Andy promised Carly she wouldn't, said goodbye, and returned to the counter. She'd left her phone upstairs in her loft and the shop wasn't set to close for another hour. She glanced toward the boutique's entrance, then to the stairs leading to her loft.

She strode toward the door, flipped the open sign to closed and dashed up the steps to retrieve her cell, knowing if she waited, she'd talk herself out of texting Lawrence, out of closing early, out of going to Thanksgiving dinner completely.

---

LAWRENCE'S PHONE WENT OFF AT THE EXACT MOMENT Gwen walked into the barn. Frustrated and curious and unwilling to get in trouble for texting while with a client, he didn't remove it from his pocket.

He hugged Gwen instead, glad he'd made the right choice as Pete started across the road. "Hey, Gwen," he said. "After you ride, Reese wants to see you in the office. I guess Carly found something you can put on your medical forms."

"Sure thing." She smiled at him. Pete tipped his hat to them both and continued through the barn and into the outdoor arena, where another client rode.

Lawrence took Gwen to the tack room. "Who do you want today?"

"Who needs the exercise?" She pulled down a saddle and gathered a blanket from the cabinet.

"Raven hasn't been ridden yet today. Neither has Hank. Or you could go with Chocolate. I know you like him."

She chuckled and finished collecting her supplies. "I do like Chocolate."

"Chocolate it is." Lawrence waited for her to go first, his first instinct to reach for his phone and just see if Andy had texted. He chastised himself for even thinking it could be her. She hadn't messaged once this week, though she'd admitted she still had his number. He couldn't lie; knowing she hadn't deleted his number from her phone when she'd removed him from her life had made him happier than he'd been in months.

It meant he still had a chance.

Her days of silence spoke a different story, but Lawrence refused to listen to it.

He couldn't take another moment of not knowing who'd texted. As Gwen saddled Chocolate, Lawrence pulled his phone from his back pocket. A quick swipe, a fast glance.

*Andy.*

His heart softened into a puddle as a grin graced his face. She'd texted. He stuffed his phone back in his pocket. He could wait an hour to see what she said. At least she'd texted.

Coaching Gwen through what to do became easy after he'd checked his phone. He found he could think about something besides Andy, besides stalking into Carly's office and silently begging her to reassure him he hadn't ruined any and every chance with Andy by ordering those clothes.

He enjoyed his time in the arena for the first time in a week. Gwen accompanied him back to the building, where Reese sat with his head bent over something at his desk.

"Carly said she had something for Miss Gwen," Lawrence said.

Reese glanced up, his eyes glazed. He blinked. "Oh, yeah." He shuffled some papers around on the desk. "She said your insurance company was giving you trouble about the sessions. She said this code should cover it."

Gwen took the papers with a smile. "Thanks. Is she here?"

"No, she had to run into town for a few minutes." Reese glanced at Lawrence, which caused his throat to tighten. Carly had gone to town?

And Andy had texted.

Lawrence clenched his jaw, determined to keep his comments to himself until Gwen had left.

"Well, tell her thanks for me." Gwen said before she limped toward the exit.

"There's a number on there," Reese called after her. "If they give you any trouble, Carly said to give them that number."

Gwen paused at the door, peering at the papers. "Great. Thanks, Reese." She pushed out the door, and Lawrence waited until it settled closed.

"She went to talk to Andy, didn't she?" he asked Reese.

The cowboy blinked. "I don't exactly know." He slid back in his seat, his expression neutral.

Lawrence appreciated Reese, had always liked him. "I know she did. She promised me she wouldn't."

"Sometimes women just need an extra push," Reese said, standing and stretching his back. "Who didn't get ridden today? I have to wait for Carly to come back, and I can't stand bein' at this desk for another second." He studied Lawrence. "You wanna join me?"

"Raven and Hank." Lawrence looked out of the front of the building, made entirely of windows. "And a horseback ride sounds great. Can we get out of the arena, though? Maybe go out on the range a ways?"

"Not far," Reese said. "I'm tired. It's been a busy week."

"No, not far," Lawrence agreed. But he wanted to go really far. Maybe far enough to escape everyone and figure out what to do next. "I'll meet you over there." He pulled out his phone to properly read Andy's text.

*Lawrence, it's Andy. I'd like to come to Thanksgiving dinner out at the ranch, if the invitation is still available.*

Smiling because she felt like she needed to identify herself—as if he'd purged her number from his phone—he tapped out a response. *It's still available. Chelsea is hosting this year.*

He wanted to add so much more, but he stilled his fingers and waited for her to text back. When she didn't, he sent, *Lunch will be served at 1 pm on Thanksgiving Day. You can come anytime that morning. Stay as late as you want.*

He gave her a few more seconds, then stuffed his phone in his back pocket and headed out to the horse barn. Maybe if he rode far enough, he'd be out of cell phone range and he wouldn't have to obsessively check his messages. But he'd never get her sweet voice telling him she was wrong out of his head.

# CHAPTER THREE

Andy changed her clothes at least four times on Thanksgiving Day, unsure of what one wore to a dinner party.

"It's not a dinner party," she told herself as she headed downstairs to find something from the boutique. "It's lunch on a ranch. Black tie is not necessary."

She wanted to look cute, but casual. Friendly, but not flirty. Touchable, but textured. She pushed hangers holding sweaters and jackets to the side, searching for the right thing. She was sure she'd seen it come through the storeroom, she just didn't know what it was. Yet.

Andy glanced toward where she kept the extra inventory, remembering the first time she'd let Lawrence come back there with her. Her hand drifted toward her lips, lightly touching them before shaking herself out of the trance and focusing back on the clothing racks.

Her eyes caught the black and white striped blouse with the third green stripe. She called Carly. "What are you wearing to lunch today?"

Carly laughed. "Oh, girl. Are you that worried about it?"

Andy fingered the silky cotton. "No," she scoffed though her insides were rioting. "I was thinking of wearing that blouse you bought. Don't want to be twinsies though."

"I'm not wearing that."

"What are you wearing?"

"Jeans and that brick red peasant shirt you sold me last month."

"I've never seen you actually wear jeans." Andy paused in her clothing perusal and cocked her head to the side, as if she could detect Carly's lie that way.

"They're denim," she defended.

"Jeggings? That peasant shirt was really long, wasn't it?"

"Yes, okay. There're jeggings." A beat of silence passed. "Am I too old for jeggings?"

Andy laughed. "No, Carly, you're not too old for jeggings." But she would be more dressed up than Andy in such an outfit. She pulled the blouse off the hanger and headed for the stairs as she said goodbye to her friend.

"Maybe I have a skirt that would look good with this...."

A half hour later, she was in danger of being late. She didn't want to arrive too early, but in enough time to mingle and thank Chelsea and Kelly for having her. Half her wardrobe littered her bed, and she'd settled on a pair of faux leather pants to go with the blouse. Her makeup done just-so, and her hair in a crown braid, she finally felt ready to leave the loft.

Lawrence had said she didn't need to bring anything, but she'd run by the bakery and picked up a couple loaves of pumpkin bread anyway. She couldn't show up empty handed.

Nerves assaulted her the entire way out to Three Rivers Ranch. Only a couple of cars sat in Chelsea's driveway, and Andy pulled into the parking lot of Courage Reins. Then she could leave whenever she wanted to.

She gripped the bread like a shield as she walked to the door.

She didn't need to knock. Lawrence leaned in the doorway as she ascended the steps.

"Hey." He reached for the bread. "I said you didn't have to bring anything."

"I know," she said. "I wanted to, though."

He didn't move out of the way, and the space to slip by seemed impossibly small for her to navigate.

"You look fantastic." He scanned her from head to toe and back before offering her his arm. "C'mon in."

Inside the house, warmth radiated from every wall, every person. Chelsea stood in the kitchen with Kelly, as well as Heidi Ackerman. The two of them seemed to be getting a lesson from Heidi about something. Another older couple—Kelly's parents —sat on the couch talking with Frank Ackerman.

Lawrence introduced Andy, though Ivory Armstrong had been her third grade teacher.

"So good to see you." Ivory got up from the couch and hugged her. "How's things since your momma passed?"

Heat gathered behind Andy's eyes, but she willed it away. She'd spent too much time perfecting her makeup to cry now. "I'm okay," she said honestly. "More lonely than anything else." At that moment, she remembered how close Lawrence lingered. His eyes hooked hers, a sense of determination darting across his face.

Mrs. Armstrong patted her hand, and a sense of understanding passed between them. Andy smiled at her, then leaned in and hugged her. "Thanks, Mrs. Armstrong."

"I've told you for years. Call me Ivory."

Gratitude welled in the back of her throat. "I just keep trying, and I can't." As she moved away from the living room, she offered up a prayer.

*Thank you for getting me out here today.* She pressed her eyes closed, the same words bobbing against her vocal chords. She stretched up and said, "Thank you, Lawrence."

It wasn't exactly the same as her prayer, but she spoke it with just as much sincere emotion.

He brushed his lips along her forehead, a whisper of a touch. But it ignited a fire along her skin that trailed down into her belly.

"Andy brought bread," he told the ladies in the kitchen, and Chelsea turned.

"Andy." She embraced Andy, and another sigh radiated through her body. When she'd broke things off with Lawrence, she'd lost several of her friends too. Namely these women out here at Three Rivers. They didn't get to town much, and she didn't come to the ranch very often, so their socializing had dwindled to the picnic after church.

She glanced between Andy and Lawrence. "Which one of you wants to take over making the gravy?"

Andy stepped forward. "If you trust him in the kitchen, we'll be heading to town to find an open Chinese restaurant."

Lawrence laughed and Chelsea joined in. "Well, my mother has great cooking lessons, Lawrence." She nudged him. "And we all know the way to a woman's heart is through a homecooked meal."

Some of the joy flowing through Andy turned to ash, but Lawrence kept his smile hitched in place. "I thought it was the other way around, Miss Chelsea."

"No, sir," she said as Pete came down the stairs with their daughter. "Isn't that right, Lieutenant? Women love men who can cook for them."

He handed her the little girl. "Porter's still asleep. This little miss wants juice." He appraised Lawrence and then Andy. She felt small under the commanding cowboy's gaze, but he softened it with a smile.

"That's how I won over Chelsea. Banned her from the kitchen completely. After that fire—"

"There was no fire!" she yelled from her bent-over position inside the fridge. "Just smoke. *No* fire."

"She used a fire extinguisher."

She rolled her eyes as she poured juice into a sippy cup.

"Anyway," Pete said, chuckling. "Women do like it when you cook for them."

"How about you make the gravy, then?" Kelly stepped next to him and slapped a whisk into his chest.

"That's just fine." He glanced around. "Where's Squire?"

"Waiting for Libby to wake up."

"Carly just texted," Chelsea announced. "They'll be here in about ten minutes."

"Then we'll almost be ready to eat," Chelsea's mom said. "Want me to go get Squire? I can sit at your place until the baby wakes up."

Kelly shook her head. "No, I'll just call him and tell him to wake her up. It's Thanksgiving. We should be together." She moved a few feet out of the kitchen, a phone to her ear.

Andy felt useless loitering in the kitchen, the table already set, with nothing to add to the conversation. She drifted to Lawrence's side, who'd retreated near the steps, out of the way, but still involved.

The hustle and bustle of the house reminded Andy of growing up in their small farmhouse on the edge of town. Or what used to be the edge of town—Three Rivers had grown a bit over the past two decades. She and her two older brothers crammed into two bedrooms and used one bathroom. Mama always had food for whoever needed it, not just her own family, and they hosted someone for dinner almost every night.

A powerful wave of missing rolled over Andy, and Lawrence must've noticed because he slipped his fingers into hers.

"I'm glad you came," he said, low and through lips that barely moved. "You okay?"

A zing shot up her arm at his touch, the gentleness in his voice. "I'm just missin' Mama."

He squeezed her fingers. "Where are your brothers this year?"

"In-laws," she said. And Daddy had passed away a decade ago, leaving only Andy—and her boutique—in Three Rivers.

Lawrence released her hand as Squire entered the house with Finn at his side and a still-sleepy eyed Libby. "Carly and Reese just pulled up."

He left the front door open for them, and Andy got swept away in Carly's hug and Reese's smile. "You came," he said.

"I did." Andy glanced at Lawrence, who looked like he might shoot lasers at Reese. "I'm glad I got invited." And she was. Lawrence had been right. She shouldn't be at home today, alone. So while she wasn't sure where she stood with him yet—if she even *wanted* to stand with him—she knew she'd been led to Three Rivers Ranch for Thanksgiving dinner.

---

LAWRENCE GREW MORE ANTSY WITH EVERY PASSING moment. Andy seemed to blend into the group flawlessly, and why shouldn't she? She'd grown up here, knew these people. He was the outsider, the transplant from the equine therapy center in Amarillo.

Only Pete knew his family owned and operated the Heart Warriors Center—Courage Reins' biggest and closest competition. After all, Lawrence hadn't picked up equine therapy in just a few months. Oh, no. He'd grown up with it in Amarillo.

And he didn't want anyone else to know. He wasn't sure why; just thought they might look at him differently, ask him why he'd chosen Courage Reins over his family's facility. He didn't want to explain that he needed to live his own life, and even if he chose to do the same thing as his father, at least he'd made his own way.

"Time to eat." Chelsea directed people to their spots at the table, and Lawrence sat on one side, sandwiched between Andy and Carly. He exhaled, finally able to relax. He wasn't sure what had kept him so on-edge—besides Andy. But she giggled at something Kelly had said and then took the one-year-old for her while she dashed back into the kitchen for the salt and pepper shakers.

Watching Andy hold the child brought warmth to Lawrence's chest. He'd supported his sister through her pregnancy, held her daughter, loved them both. But the level of admiration flowing through him now, as he saw Andy press a soft kiss to Libby's hair, couldn't be matched.

Kelly returned, took the little girl, and strapped her in a highchair between her and Squire.

"Okay," Chelsea said as she too finished with her children and sat down. "Let's start by going around and saying something we're each thankful for."

Panic squeezed Lawrence's chest. He had a lot to be grateful for—and he was thankful, and he let other people and God know. But what could he say in this group?

The things he could say—*I'm grateful for Three Rivers. I'm grateful for a job. I'm grateful for my friends*—rotated through his mind. He tried to listen to Frank and Heidi, who expressed gratitude for their family.

Reese said, "I'm grateful for my wife."

Carly leaned into him and snuggled close. A flash of jealousy struck Lawrence. He wanted Andy to cuddle with him like that—the way she used to. He sat as straight and still as possible, refusing to look at her.

"My turn," Carly said. "I'm grateful for government grants."

Every eye turned to Lawrence. He cleared his throat. "I'm grateful for old friendships and hope they can become new again." He didn't even know where the words had come from. He hadn't planned to say them. He shifted his attention to Andy, who stared at him like he'd said he was grateful for pneumonia or the grim reaper or something. He slid his hand onto her knee and she jumped.

"Your turn," he said, a smile forming as he felt the tremble in her leg.

She gave a nervous laugh. "I'm grateful for…." Andy glanced around the table, her gaze settling on Lawrence. "An invitation to this meal." She smiled, but he felt the ice in it. She leaned forward and shifted her leg from under his touch, giving him a private glare as Kelly spoke.

Lawrence should've felt frustrated at her rejection. Should've wondered what he should've said besides what he did. Should've done just about anything but push Andy when she clearly wasn't ready.

Instead, he scooted a tiny bit closer to her and leaned forward, almost touching her, in the pretense that he was trying to see and listen to Squire. But honestly, Lawrence had no idea what the man said. Pete went last, and then Chelsea declared it time to eat.

Andy leaned back and bumped into him. "Excuse me." Her voice could've lanced him with icicles.

"No problem." He didn't move away.

"Back up," she hissed through clenched teeth as she spooned creamed corn onto her plate.

Lawrence chuckled, sure he'd made his intentions for the invitation to dinner clear, and gave her the distance she wanted. What he wanted, he couldn't quite have. He leaned over to Carly. "How can I get Andy alone to talk to her?"

She heard him, but she didn't answer right away, instead contributing to the argument Reese was having with Will Armstrong about the Dallas Cowboys. In fact, she didn't answer him at all through the rest of the meal. It ended, and the group moved into the great room on the opposite side of the stairs. Pete produced a stack of games, and laughter and fun passed the next hour.

"How about a walk before pie?" Carly asked, glancing around. She lingered on Lawrence as she tucked her arm into Reese's. "We'll go slow."

"Good idea," Squire said. "Let the kids run for a bit."

Jackets slid over shoulders and shoes were found for children, and Lawrence waited until everyone had left just to make sure Andy went with them. She positioned herself with Chelsea and Kelly while the men took the kids farther down the road and into the Ackerman's bigger backyard.

Carly and Reese, Heidi and Frank, and Ivory and Will climbed the steps to the Ackerman's deck and sat down.

Lawrence tagged along behind the women, desperation flooding him. How could he talk to Andy now? She wouldn't like him pulling her away, wouldn't want to be seen going off with him alone—though she used to love to sneak away with him for a stolen kiss in the barn.

Another of their little secrets.

Instead of trying to do something he didn't know how to do, he joined Squire and Pete as they threw a football back and forth. Lawrence kept his focus there, and where Andy disappeared to, he didn't know.

Pete tossed the ball to Finn. "So, Lawrence, you gettin' back together with Andy?"

"No." The word came automatically and sounded a tad on the defensive side. He didn't like the look Pete exchanged with Squire.

He expected Pete, ever the observant lieutenant, to press the issue, find out the truth. But he just said, "Oh, okay," and caught the ball Squire threw his way.

Several minutes later, Carly called, "Lawrence! I need you up here."

"Duty calls." He left the game and mounted the steps. "Yeah?"

She pointed across the road, down toward Brynn's new facilities. "She went that way two minutes ago. Alone."

Lawrence could've hugged Carly. Instead he said, "Thanks, Carly," and bolted down the steps.

"Go slow!" Reese called after him, but Lawrence couldn't make his heart go slow, or his legs, or his ideas.

He found Andy around the back of the arena, the barn between her and everyone else on the homestead. She stood facing the open range, her back to him. Her dark hair blew in the winter wind, and she clutched the throat of her jacket closed with tight fingers.

"Mind if I join you?"

She shrugged and he leaned against the fence next to her, looked out in the same direction she was.

"You okay?" he asked.

"Why didn't you ever tell me about your family?"

Her question caused fireworks to explode in Lawrence's brain. He knew the answer, but didn't want to say it out loud.

"I mean, if we're going to make this old friendship new again, I think you should be more forthcoming." She didn't sound mad, or happy, or teasing. Lawrence couldn't figure out how she felt, and unease tripped through his body.

"Also, had I known you had a sister in Amarillo—a sister at all—I might not have assumed you were dating her." Folding her arms, she shifted her weight away from him, her message clear.

Lawrence watched the dead grasses lean in the wind. "I didn't tell you, because I didn't want you to know what a failure I am."

She finally turned and looked at him. "Why would you be a failure for having a family?"

He didn't expect anyone else to understand. "They don't

know where I am," he said. "They don't know what I do. If they did…trust me, I'm a disappointment."

Cheryl, five years younger than Lawrence, didn't work with horses. She'd never wanted to, and somehow that was okay. But if Lawrence didn't want the equine therapy organization his parents had dedicated their lives to, suddenly he'd committed the crime of the century.

"My sister, Cheryl, by the way. Her name is Cheryl. Her baby's name is Ruthann. She moved to San Antonio right after she had the baby." He looked at Andy, really let her see whatever she wanted to see. "My parents didn't treat her well."

She reached up like she'd touch his face, but her hand dropped to her side and she tucked it in her jacket pocket. "Do your parents treat you well?"

"They wanted me to take over the family business." Lawrence looked away. "I didn't want to."

"What was the family business?"

"Nothing." He turned and started back toward the homestead. He didn't want to have this conversation. This was why he hadn't told her anything about his family in the six months they'd dated.

"Lawrence." She hurried to catch him, pulled on his arm to get him to stop from entering the barn. Sparks raced through his body, though her skin hadn't touched his.

"Come on," she said.

"Come on, what, Andy?" He made himself as tall as he could. "You made it real clear you aren't interested in getting back together. I'm not gonna bare my soul now." He yanked open the barn door and went inside, half-hoping she'd follow him, demand he tell her more, confess that she *was* interested in getting back together.

She didn't; the barn door banged closed behind him. He continued past Pete and Chelsea's, across the parking lot where

Andy had left her car, and between the silos and the chicken pens.

His cabin sat third in line, and he dang near tore off the door when he entered. He paced the small living room, trying to decide what to do. His temper rarely made an appearance, but if there was one thing that could drive him mad in less than a heartbeat, it was talk of his family.

So what if he'd left his parents and their equine therapy unit?

So what that he hadn't been able to find anything else that he liked nearly as much, even after years of trying?

So what that his pride had prevented him from ever going home again? Ever apologizing? Ever making things right?

His parents didn't know that he'd made practically nothing of his life.

No one knew. No one needed to know, especially not the beautiful, successful Andrea Larsen.

# CHAPTER FOUR

"Are you sure about this?" Andy looked at the pie plate as vipers bit their way through her system. "He was really mad."

She'd never seen Lawrence get mad, ever. In their six months together, he'd been calm and collected and soft-spoken and soothing. He'd made her feel special by coming to her store and helping her with inventory, or just watching her hang clothes after she'd flipped the sign to closed.

She'd come out to the ranch and watch his therapy lessons, and they'd walk through the fields, and he'd taught her about horses. True, he'd never said anything about his family, and while Andy had wondered at the time, she hadn't found it odd. He was mysterious, and handsome, and she'd assumed he'd tell her when he was ready.

"Of course I'm sure." Carly's voice pulled Andy from her memories. "Every man loves pie, and this is chocolate cookie pie." She straightened Andy's blouse. "Right, girls?"

Kelly nodded, and Chelsea stepped forward. "I brought Pete a pie once. It seemed to work, because he came to dinner the next day."

Andy didn't want Lawrence to come to dinner with her. Or maybe she did. Everything jumbled inside her, and she didn't know what she wanted.

"So you march over there," Kelly said.

"And you knock nicely," Chelsea added. "No banging."

"When he answers, you give him the pie, and say you missed him at the house and thought he might want this." Carly smiled. "Then you say that you could barely eat because you can't stand the thought of him upset, and ask him if he'd like to share it with you." She brandished two forks. "Ask him to walk out on the range. He likes that."

"And you won't have to go in his cabin," Kelly added. "He might not want you in there if he's…a tiny bit upset."

"He's mad," Andy said, eyeing the forks like they'd stab her on the way to Lawrence's cabin.

"Don't beg him to go with you," Chelsea said. "If he doesn't want to come, take both forks and head out on the range alone. That'll get him to come."

"Why will that get him to come?" Andy wondered how these women knew so much about how to win over a man.

"Because, silly, he won't want you out on the range alone." Chelsea smiled and squeezed Andy's shoulder. "And there's a storm comin' in. He definitely won't let you wander off on your own."

"Okay, ready?" Kelly took a deep breath, and Andy mimicked her.

"Ready as I'll ever be." She took the forks from Carly and headed outside. The sky had turned a threatening shade of navy blue, and by the time she knocked—nicely—on Lawrence's door, the air held the promise of rain.

Lawrence whipped the door open and stared at her.

"Hey," she started. "I brought you some pie, since you missed dessert." She held the plate, which held half of a chocolate cookie pie, toward him with one hand. She'd forgotten what to say next, but the presence of the silverware in her other hand reminded her.

"I didn't get to eat any either," she said. "I was too worried about you. Want to share?"

His blue eyes sparked lightning in her direction. Sometime during lunch she'd decided to give Lawrence another chance. Give *them* another chance. Or maybe she'd been stewing over a second chance with him since he'd lured her out to the ranch and invited her to Thanksgiving dinner. She wasn't sure.

When he didn't move, or invite her in, or speak at all, she said, "Well, okay. I'm going to take a walk and find a place to eat my pie." She adjusted the plastic wrap on the plate, turned and moved down his steps, pivoted to go between the cabins and onto the range. Her throat tightened with fear. Everything looked exactly the same out here. What if she really got lost?

"Where you goin'?" he called after her.

"Pie." She lifted the forks and kept walking. The wind nearly stole the dessert from her, but she plowed on. She spied a tree in the distance, and she thought she could make it there and back safely enough.

"Andy, this is insane." Lawrence ran up beside her. "It's going to rain any second."

She looked at him and couldn't look away. "Well, I can't go back to Chelsea's now. It'll be too embarrassing."

"What do you mean?"

"I mean I had to tell them about you stomping off and leaving me, and I can't do that again."

"Like how you rejected me at dinner?"

"I wasn't ready for what you said." She stopped, her anger overshadowing her embarrassment and fear. "And you shouldn't have touched me like that. It really put me on the spot."

Thunder broke the sky; lightning flashed above them.

He stared at her, and she couldn't figure out how to feel. Should she just tell him she missed him, the way he had?

Confess that every time she'd considered deleting his number from her phone, she got physically ill? Confide in him and say she imagined kissing him every time she opened the storeroom?

"You are a maddening woman." He strode forward again, breaking the spell between them before Andy could decide what to do.

"You're just as frustrating," she said as she rushed to catch him. But his long legs made her have to take three steps for every two of his.

"I have one sister. That's all. We get along great. My parents are another story."

Andy didn't know what to add to the conversation; she just wanted him to keep talking.

"They run the Heart Warriors center in Amarillo. I didn't want to do that. I left when I was eighteen. Haven't been back in a decade." His short sentences were punctuated by his long strides. "I thought I didn't want to work with horses and patients. I thought I wanted something else. When Courage Reins opened…well, I got a job here, and I realized I loved it. What I didn't love was being told what I had to do with my life."

He stopped suddenly and faced her. "I should go home. I should take over the program for my parents. But I don't want to. I don't want Reese's job, or Pete's job. I don't want the responsibility. I just want to work with the horses and the patients. That's enough for me. It won't be enough for my dad."

"That doesn't make you a failure."

He gave a short, barking laugh. "No, it doesn't. You're right. What makes me a failure is everything else I tried until I figured out I'm just a horseman." He stomped off again, leaving Andy to wonder what was so wrong with being a horseman.

---

LAWRENCE COULDN'T BELIEVE HE'D TOLD ANDY everything—well, maybe not everything. But he did trust her, and she did deserve the truth. He hated that he'd gotten angry when she'd asked about his family. She'd given him an hour to cool off, and if anything, seeing her on his doorstep with pie had kicked his desire for her into a new gear.

She caught up to him just as the first raindrops fell. He paused, judging the distance to the tree. Too far. He turned and looked back at the row of cabins.

"We're going to get soaked." He looked down at her. She wore her jacket and those sexy tight pants. No hat. No gloves. At least the pie was covered with plastic wrap.

"I don't care." She put the pie on the ground and stepped into his arms.

He welcomed her into his embrace, surprised at this turn of events but not complaining. "You don't?"

The sky opened and water poured out. They were both soaked through in seconds. She tilted her head up, taking partial refuge under the brim of his cowboy hat. "I do want some of that pie. But I guess it can wait."

"Hmm." He wasn't sure why it needed to wait, but he couldn't look away from Andy, from the raindrops on her eyelashes, from the pinkness of her lips. She licked them, and he reacted by pressing his mouth to hers.

She melted into him, threaded her fingers through his hair, and kissed him back.

Hours could've passed and Lawrence wouldn't have known. Kissing Andy had always possessed a bit of magic, and this time felt downright divine. With the rain pounding down around them, he kissed her and kissed her, hoping this was only the beginning of what they could have together.

When he detected a wobble in her chin, he pulled back. "Cold?"

"Just a little." She brushed her lips along his. "We should go back before we freeze, though."

He bent to retrieve the pie, tucked her hand in his, and ran toward his cabin. She came with him, which caused joy to punctuate the perfect kiss.

Once under the safety of his porch, he looked her up and down. "Uh, you're going to need dry clothes."

"I'll wear something of yours while you run the dryer."

"Uh, Andy? My stuff is way too big for you." He opened the front door and ushered her inside the cabin. "Maybe you can borrow something of Juliette's." He didn't want her asking Kelly or Chelsea. He might never get her back if she went over to one of their houses to borrow clothes.

"Aren't they in Montana?"

"I have a key to Garth's place." Lawrence plucked it from the drawer in his kitchen. "Stay here. I'll be right back." He hurried out the door and down the path. Surely she'd wait, right? She wouldn't kiss him the way she had and then disappear into the night.

He dashed into Garth's cabin and hurried into the bedroom. He grabbed the first thing of Juliette's he saw in the closet—a sundress—and hightailed it out of there. When he got back to his cabin, Andy had the inklings of a fire going in the hearth.

"Grabbed the first thing I saw," he said. "I felt weird doing that."

She took the dress. "This is fine. I'm not good at making a fire. I'll change, and you finish that?"

She disappeared into the bathroom, and Lawrence stood staring at the closed door. When he'd invited her to dinner, he didn't think he'd end up kissing her. Never in his wildest—okay, maybe in his *wildest* dreams, he thought she might let him.

She came out of the bathroom holding her wet things, the pink sundress complementing her dark hair and skin. He sucked in a breath and focused on what he should be doing. He took her clothes and ducked into his bedroom to change and start the dryer.

With that all done, he got the fire going properly, and pulled two blankets from the front closet. He gave one to Andy, who wrapped herself in it before settling on his couch. "Got any movies?" She yawned. "All that turkey is catching up to me."

"No napping until after pie." He put his blanket on the other end of the couch, nudged up the heat, and moved into the kitchen to collect the pie. "Movies are in the cabinet next to the hearth."

He grabbed silverware and returned to the living room. "Can I sit here?" He indicated the spot right next to where she'd been sitting. "Then we can share the pie."

"Yeah." She held up a case. "This one okay?"

He didn't care what they watched. Excitement to simply be with her made his nerve endings dance. "Yeah, fine."

She slid in the disc, handed him the remotes, and took her place on the couch. He passed her a fork, adjusted the volume, and started the movie. They ate in silence, Lawrence's mind spinning through where this could go next.

He'd never told anyone about his family, and it felt good to get the weight off his tongue. Andy hadn't asked him about what he'd done in the past eight years before landing at Courage Reins, nor had she seemed to judge him for leaving his family just to become what he'd already been.

He felt insignificant next to her, and a pinch started behind his heart. Could she really want someone like him? The constant struggle, the familiar battle, raged as strongly now as it had the first time they'd been together.

"You done?" she asked as she scooped up another bite. "You've stopped eating."

"Just thinking," he said.

"About what?" She abandoned the movie in favor of him.

"Kissin' me again?" Her playful tone and twinkling eyes sent heat through his core.

"*Now* that's what I'm thinking about." He leaned over and tasted her whipped cream lips.

"Mmm, tasty." Her whispered words caused a shiver to shake his spine.

He touched his lips to hers again. "I was thinking about why you want to be with me."

She pulled back a couple of inches to look into his eyes. She searched and searched, and he didn't know if she found what she wanted or not. "Why wouldn't I want to be with you?"

"Why did it take me ordering something from your boutique to get you to apologize?"

"Same reason you haven't gone home in ten years."

Pride. He understood that. Couldn't blame her for it, though they probably should both get over being too proud to apologize to those they loved. Not that she loved him. Lawrence cut off his thoughts before they could derail.

"And you really want to be with a horseman? Someone like you…." He trailed off, unsure and unwilling to let her see how weak he felt, how inadequate. He kissed her again, grateful when she returned the gesture.

Grateful he didn't have to explain anything else.

Grateful she stayed in his arms through the rest of the movie, long after her clothes had dried.

Grateful God had brought her back to him, at least for one day, though Lawrence prayed for a lot longer.

# CHAPTER FIVE

Andy puzzled through Lawrence's words as she bustled around the shop, the two other ladies she'd hired just for Black Friday as busy as she was. No matter how often she circled the store, she found more tops that needed to be refolded, additional tissue paper that had fallen from inside sweaters, hangers that needed to be straightened.

She didn't complain, instead pressing her eyes closed for a brief moment of gratitude with every sale. The holiday season kept Andy afloat during the slower winter months. Still, her mind wandered to Lawrence as she selected sizes and styles and colors.

The bitterness and longing in his tone when he mentioned he was just a horseman. The way he pondered why she wanted to be with him. She obviously wasn't the only one who had her eye on Lawrence, whether he knew it or not. But she couldn't believe he missed the constantly vulturistic women at the church picnics.

She'd just gotten him out of her mind when her phone blared, bringing him right back in. Because the ringtone belonged to him. Silencing it, she flashed an apologetic smile to the woman preparing to purchase two pairs of slacks and a trio of holiday sweaters. She shoved the phone in a drawer behind the cash register, determined to focus on her boutique until she could afford to donate some brain cells to Lawrence.

Her holiday hours extended well past normal, and by the time she locked the door, her feet felt like she'd walked across live coals. She heaved herself upstairs before she realized she'd left her phone in that blasted drawer downstairs.

Too tired to go retrieve it, she fell into an Epsom salt bath, knowing she had to redo what she'd done today all over again tomorrow. Though Sundays had been a source of loneliness for her, she suddenly couldn't wait until she could have her day of rest.

Sunday came, as Sundays always did, and Andy took her usual seat near the back of the chapel. She'd almost skipped church today—surely God would've given her a pass because of the exhausting nature of the last forty-eight hours.

If she were being honest with herself—something she'd been trying to do more recently—she hoped to see Lawrence at church. She'd even sat down from the end of the pew so he could slide in next to her whenever he happened to arrive. She'd even come early so he'd see her.

Her patience was rewarded when a warm arm settled across her shoulders, and the leather and horse scent met her nose, and the handsomeness of Lawrence's face filled her vision. "This seat taken?"

"It is now." She leaned into him, satisfied when he cupped her shoulder and pulled her a bit closer.

A group of women slid onto the bench next to Andy right when the service started, but she didn't pay much attention to them. They whispered through the first fifteen minutes, and it wasn't until one of them spoke a little too loudly that she turned toward them.

But she heard the word "boutique," and she owned the

only boutique in town. Suddenly, her ears went into owl-mode, flicking and zeroing in on the conversation. She couldn't hear much, because the choir got up and began singing.

But those women were definitely talking about her. Her and Lawrence.

Andy straightened under his arm and lifted her chin. If they wanted to gossip, she'd let them. In fact, maybe she should give them something to talk about.

Wicked thoughts ran through her mind, but she didn't act on any of them. She already had enough on her plate this holiday season; she didn't need to add more to it.

The service ended, and she stood.

"You in a hurry?" Lawrence asked, peering up at her from under his cowboy hat.

"Well, no."

"Did you make anything for lunch?"

She hadn't even thought about lunch. Andy usually grabbed something from the fridge or called in take-out during the busy season. At the moment, she couldn't remember what, if anything, her fridge held.

"What did you make?" she asked to save herself from admitting anything.

"I'm sure you don't want food poisoning going into the busiest time of the year." He grinned and added a chuckle to his statement.

"I probably have a frozen pizza."

"I was just gonna say I'm really craving a frozen pizza." He leaned back into the bench and grinned.

A flush rose to her face. "Are you inviting yourself to my place for lunch?" She wondered if he'd stay for dinner too. The man was hopeless when it came to cooking.

He finally stood. Most of the other churchgoers had already left the chapel, including the gossipers. "I haven't been to your place for a while," he said. "Seems like a good time to check it out."

Stepping into the aisle, he offered Andy his hand. She slipped her fingers into his, a thrill trailing down her back. The storeroom dominated her thoughts as he followed her to the boutique, as they parked in the narrow driveway behind the building, as he captured her hand again and they moved up the back steps.

The storeroom sat just inside the door, but Andy refused to look at it. She continued into the shop and swept her hand toward the area. "It's kind of a mess right now," she said. "I'll come clean it up later." She sighed just thinking about it. But she couldn't open on Monday morning without clean floors and crisp folds in the clothes. She'd spend an hour this evening straightening and creasing, and everything would be set for the next day.

"It's so festive." Lawrence admired the set of Christmas trees Andy had set up late on Thanksgiving night, after one of the most perfect evenings she'd ever spent with a man. She'd also trailed lights along the check-out counter, around the mirrors on the west wall and lining the windows on the east.

A pine-scented candle warmer sat next to the front door, and another next to the till. Her mannequins wore the most festive and spirited holiday items, and if she flicked on the stereo system, Christmas music would complete the picture-perfect atmosphere.

Lawrence paced a few steps away, fingered a red bow skirt on a mannequin and twisted back to her. "I didn't see the shop at Christmas last year. It's fantastic." He beamed at her, and something in Andy's gut jumped.

He adored her. She could see it, right there on his face. Anyone would be able to see it. Suddenly self-conscious, she turned away, unsure if she deserved such adoration. He hadn't seen the shop last Christmas because she'd freaked out before she'd gotten the facts and broken things off with him.

"Let's see about that pizza." She headed upstairs, all fantasies about the storeroom shelved for now.

---

THE FOLLOWING SUNDAY, ANDY ARRIVED LAST TO church, grateful Lawrence had saved a sliver of space for her on a pew near the back. Seemed like more and more people were coming out for services, probably because of the approaching Christmas season.

She enjoyed Pastor Scott's sermon, which focused on living more like the Savior. Andy wanted to do that, wanted to be as forgiving and loving as the Lord. She tried to be kind to those she came in contact with, but they usually were potential customers. She thought of the twittering women who'd sat next to her last week. Would she be as kind to them after knowing they'd been speaking about her?

Frustration sparked at the truth flowing through her mind. She probably wouldn't be. And it had taken a ruse to get her to apologize to Lawrence.

A frown buckled her eyebrows. *Why did it take me a year to apologize?* she wondered.

The service ended, leaving a multitude of questions in Andy's mind, and she stood with Lawrence.

Pete stepped up to them. "Lawrence, I need you for a second." He nodded toward someone exiting the chapel. "That's Bobby Haskins."

Lawrence obviously knew who Bobby Haskins was, and why he was important, because he turned and said, "Give me a minute, okay, Andy?" He didn't wait for her to answer before he moved down the aisle with Pete and Reese.

Andy assumed their business with Bobby had something to

do with Courage Reins, and she moved a little further into the chapel to help Chelsea clean up after her kids. By the time they toddled down the aisle with the littles, Andy assumed Lawrence would be finished with his business.

Nobody waited in the lobby, but Pete came through the door and swept Julie onto his shoulders. "You good?" he asked Chelsea, and they stepped out of the church.

Andy followed in their wake, freezing as soon as she moved outside. The door bumped her, pushing her forward. She stumbled as her brain tried to make sense of the scene before her.

Lawrence stood several feet away, far enough to keep his words from Andy. But his mouth moved, and he grinned at the group of women who'd gathered around him. The group of single women.

She and Lawrence hadn't made lunch plans, but Andy had assumed. Assumed he'd be coming over for something to eat—she'd even run to the grocery store last night to have a variety of frozen meals on hand. He hadn't seemed to mind the pizza from last week, though it bore the marks of some freezer burn and she didn't have any extra cheese to add to the top.

He'd eaten a lot of it, stayed for a movie, kissed her until her legs couldn't hold her weight. She'd been hoping for a repeat today, but now, the sight of all those women blurred her fantasies.

She blinked and shook her head. She'd seen Lawrence talking to, laughing with, and helping another woman once. She'd jumped to the wrong conclusion that his sister was his date, just because he paid for dinner. Was she destined to repeat that same mistake now?

Jealousy roared through her, making her stomach turn and her throat burn. The real question became: Did she trust Lawrence or not?

*You have to trust him,* she told herself as she made her way down the steps on wobbling heels. *Help me trust him.*

She feared, though, that all the self-talk and all the prayer in the world couldn't make her do something she didn't know how to do.

---

LAWRENCE CHUCKLED AT NATALIE, THE WOMAN FROM the Three Rivers women's association. She wanted him to bring some of the horses from Courage Reins to a family carnival the group was planning for the spring.

He'd told her he didn't have the authority to say yes or no, but that he'd ask Pete. He liked Natalie and played golf with her brother from time to time. He wanted to support the women, and he made easy conversation with them while he waited for Andy to come out.

Movement caught his attention, and he found her coming toward them, her face a quivering mask of emotion. He couldn't decipher how she felt as she neared and smoothed over her true feelings with a smile.

"Ladies, do you know Andy Larsen?" He drew her into his side, clearly claiming her as his. Every woman there catalogued the movement, Lawrence made sure of it. "Andy, these ladies are from the Three Rivers women's association." He named them all, pleased at his own memory.

"Well, let me know, Lawrence," Natalie said. The ladies made themselves scarce after that, leaving Lawrence to practically drag Andy to her car.

"You okay?" he asked as they neared. "You don't look so good."

"I don't feel so good," she said. "I hope you weren't planning to come for lunch."

"Of course I was." He leaned against her car, noticing the glassiness in her eyes. "What's wrong?"

She shook her head and caught the tear as it fell from her eye. "Nothing. I just need to lie down. I feel sick."

Lawrence had the sick feeling he'd done something wrong. But he didn't know what. "I'll follow you home. Make sure you're okay."

"No." She reached for the door handle. "I'll make it."

"I can heat you up some of that canned soup you have in your cupboard."

She managed a slight glare. "How do you know I have canned soup in my cupboard?"

He gave her a slow grin. "Saw it last week." Stepping away from the car, Lawrence pulled out his keys. "I'll follow you home."

She might have argued, but Lawrence didn't quite hear it as he strode toward his truck. She could lock him out if he didn't arrive close to the same time as her. Thankfully, Andy wasn't the fastest driver in the world, and he pulled in right after her. She let him in the shop, but he sensed something was still off.

The door had barely closed when he asked, "Are you going to tell me what I did wrong?"

"Nothing," she said, bending to remove her heels. "You didn't do anything wrong."

He moved closer and took her into his arms. She came willingly, a good sign. "Then why were you cryin' at the church?"

Embarrassment stole across her expression. "I don't want to tell you." She squirmed to get out of his grip, and he let her go. "It's just something I need to work on," she said. "It honestly has nothing to do with you." She moved toward the stairs that led to her loft.

"Honestly?" he asked as he followed.

"Cross my heart," she tossed over her shoulder. At the top of the stairs, she pushed into her living space, which consisted of the entire second floor of the building. Everything Andy touched had an air of sophistication about it, and the sitting room at the entrance of her loft was no exception. Lawrence barely knew how to exist in such a refined space, and he wondered what she thought of his simple, country cowboy cabin.

He also knew she owned this building, had inherited it from her daddy when he'd died. Andy had no debts, and a heap of success. Lawrence felt seven shades of inadequate standing in her loft.

Why now, he wasn't sure. Last Sunday, he'd been okay. Fine, he'd shaken off the feelings of self-loathing and charmed his way into staying for lunch, a movie, and a passionate embrace that had ended too soon for his liking.

"You comin'?" she called from farther inside the loft. "I'm not making these pot pies by myself."

He gave himself a mental and physical shake, removed his jacket and hung it on the antique iron coat rack, as if he could remove his shortcomings as easily, and followed her into the gourmet kitchen.

If she could pretend like she was fine, so could he.

# CHAPTER SIX

"You like that Natalie Cooper?" Andy couldn't help herself. She'd been stewing over the other women for the last hour since seeing Lawrence talking to her. While she drove home, while he asked her if she was okay, while the turkey pot pies browned and bubbled and baked.

He glanced up as if a gunshot had sounded. "What? Definitely not." He stuffed a forkful of green beans—canned and heated in the microwave—into his mouth. His face reddened as he chewed and swallowed. "I mean, I like her just fine. She's nice. But I'm not…you know. I don't *like* her."

Andy pushed her food around inside the pie shell. "What did she want?"

Lawrence stared at her for several moments past comfortable. Andy finally lifted her eyes to his. "What?"

"You think I was—" He set his fork down, his food forgotten. "Well, what exactly did you think, Andy?"

She didn't like the resentment in his tone, the piercing slice of his gaze. Though he had every right to be upset, Andy wished he wasn't. Wished she hadn't said anything. Wished she didn't automatically assume the worst about him.

"Nothing," she tried, but Lawrence scoffed.

"You think I want to be with one of those women more than you." He pushed away from the table and stood. "You think eventually I'll cheat on you with one of them. Is that it?"

Helplessness made her stomach quake, her bottom lip tremble. "You're awfully handsome," she said. "And hardworking, and honest, and—"

"Are you tryin' to pay me a compliment or tell me you don't trust me?" He sat heavily in the chair again, his voice a mere ghost of itself, but his eyes as penetrating as ever.

*Both,* Andy thought, but kept the word contained in her mind. Thankfully.

Emboldened by her decision to start being more truthful with him—and herself—she looked at him. She put both her hands on one of his, wishing she could erase the anguished expression from his face.

"I—I want to be with you." The admission rang with truth, though it wasn't the one she needed to say.

"But you don't trust me." He kept his hand under hers in a fist, unwilling or unable to soften it and let her hold his hand.

She dropped her eyes to the table. The small table he could barely fold himself under without crowding her. The small table where she wanted to eat breakfast with him. And lunch. And dinner. The strength of her thoughts surprised her, and she didn't know how to make them line up with the jealousy and bitterness she'd felt at the church.

"All right." He slid his hand out from under hers. "I'm gonna head home."

"No," she said. "You don't need to go."

"I think I do, Andy." He stood, and she couldn't argue with the quiet strength in his voice. Couldn't get up and follow him through the living room. Couldn't make her voice say, "Don't go. Stay and let's talk about this."

The door closed and she heard his cowboy boots clomp down her stairs. The old building shuddered as he left the shop, and Andy dropped her head into her hands. Why had she said anything? Or at least phrased it like, "Hey, what did Natalie Cooper want?" instead of making it an accusation.

Eyes brimming with tears, she set about cleaning up the remains of their lunch. She'd barely eaten two bites, and yet her stomach waged war against her. She'd felt like this for the whole holiday season last year. She didn't think she could survive another one. To keep her hands as busy as her mind, she moved from the eat-in kitchen into the living room and vacuumed the rugs she'd special-ordered from New York. She dusted the shelves holding the pictures of her and Mama. Tears trickled down her face while she completed the long overdue chore.

But this time, they didn't belong to Mama.

This time, they trailed tracks down her cheeks for Lawrence.

She flung down the duster and rushed across the room and into the entryway. A sob choked her as she yanked open the door and flew down the stairs. Outside, her chest heaved. Lawrence's truck was long gone. Of course it was. She'd been cleaning for a good twenty minutes.

She hated this feeling. This feeling of waiting for something to happen so she could stop feeling so anxious. Of constantly searching for him in crowds so she could either worry when he wasn't there or relax when he was.

Andy didn't know what to do, short of getting in her sedan and driving out to the ranch. But too many eyes and ears existed out there. Too much of an audience for her private business.

She returned to her loft and snatched her phone from the kitchen counter. Her fingers fumbled over the screen as she brought up Lawrence and pressed call.

It rang once. Twice. Three times. Her heart stalled its beat. He had to answer. Four rings. Why wasn't he answering?

His voicemail picked up, a sore disappointment to the real timbre of his voice. She hung up, defeated. Familiar anxiety and worry and absolute tension gnawed at her until she shook with the effort it took not to collapse on the couch and cry.

Her phone buzzed before it rang, and she startled. Her hopes soared when she saw Lawrence's face.

"Lawrence," she breathed into the line.

"You called?"

"Please come back," she blurted. "You can't be far. Just... please come back." She glanced into the kitchen, though she'd cleaned up his lunch. "You didn't even finish eating."

"That's what you're worried about?" He didn't sound like he was driving. Maybe he'd pulled over to call her. "That I didn't get enough to eat?"

"That's what I always worry about." A nervous giggle escaped her mouth. "I know you can't cook, and yes. I worry about what you eat everyday. I'm scared you'll get tired of me really fast." The floodgate on her insecurities and fears dropped. "And I'm absolutely terrified that I'll never figure out how to trust you."

She took a deep breath, the weight of her words out in the open, where he could possibly help shoulder them.

"Well," he started. "I get along just fine in the food department. You realize I live next door to Juliette, right? And Chelsea and Kelly aren't bad, either." Something changed on his end of the line, because his voice sounded farther away when he said, "I don't think I'll ever get tired of you, but we can talk about why you'd think so. If you want."

A door closed; her building trembled. "And you do need to figure out how to trust me, Andy. I can't really help you in that department."

A knock sounded on her door, and she spun and crossed the distance to it in the time it took to breathe. She opened the door and lowered the phone when she found Lawrence on the other side.

"But I'll try," he said, stepping into her entryway and sweeping her into an embrace that felt like home.

---

Nervous energy punctuated every breath Andy took while she waited for the last customer of the day to make her selections. Lawrence had been waiting upstairs in her loft for twenty minutes. He said he didn't mind, and he probably genuinely didn't.

"I think I like this one." Sandy twisted to look at the back of the jacket.

"It looks fabulous," Andy said, smoothing her fingertips across Sandy's shoulders. "Going somewhere special for Christmas this year?"

Sandy made a face. "Do I ever?"

Andy forced a laugh. "Christmas in Three Rivers isn't the worst."

"I know." Sandy sighed. "I'm just...done here, you know?" She looked at Andy with such honesty, her heartstrings sang.

"You bought the pancake house, didn't you?" Andy asked. "You can't be done here now."

Sandy shrugged out of the jacket and handed it to Andy. "I'll take this and those jeans. And that reindeer sweater. My mother will love that." She flashed a grin at Andy. "And no, I know. I'm not done bein' in Three Rivers." She turned and headed back into the dressing room for her own jacket. "Just done with the men here."

Andy understood that more keenly than she'd like to admit. Once she'd ended things with Lawrence, the men she'd dated had been dull, brash, or just plain annoying. She rang up

Sandy's purchases and had them wrapped when the woman came out of the dressing room.

"Saw Lawrence's truck outside," she said as she added her signature to the receipt. "Am I keeping you from something?"

Andy took the slip of paper and tucked it in the till. She gave Sandy a warm smile. "Not at all. We're just goin' to dinner in a bit."

Sandy took the bag with her new clothes, her own unassuming grin in place. "He's a nice guy."

"Yeah," Andy agreed, beyond relieved when a rush of jealousy didn't threaten to unseat her. "He is."

"Well, Merry Christmas." Sandy headed for the door, and Andy went with her. Once she'd given the proper holiday salutation, she locked the door and flipped the sign to closed. She should stay and clean up for the Saturday crowd. After all, only three weekends left to shop for Christmas.

But she could get up early. Right now, she wanted to see Lawrence, smell Lawrence, kiss Lawrence.

---

"BUSY WEEK?" LAWRENCE TRACED LAZY CIRCLES ON her upper arm as he cradled Andy in his embrace. It had been five long days without her, and now that he had her in his arms, he didn't want to let her go.

"Not bad, actually," she said, snuggling closer. "Thanks for dinner."

"Mm." He'd taken her out to dinner after asking her what she wanted. She'd said, "All the bread and pasta I can get."

Since they'd gotten a later start on dinner, they'd missed the movie he'd been planning to take her to see. So now, they laid on her couch, a movie on but Lawrence wasn't really watching it. He wondered if Andy was.

After last Sunday's situation, he'd been thinking about how

he could convince Andy he was trustworthy. He'd spoken true—he couldn't really help her with that. She either believed he wanted to be with her and no one else, or she didn't.

But he had thought he could tell her everything. Be one-hundred-percent honest about his life, lay open his soul, and see if she still wanted him.

The idea had kept him awake at night, and everyone from Juliette to Pete to his patients at Courage Reins had noticed.

Taking a deep breath, he reached for the remote. "You watchin' this?"

"Not really." She sat up and tossed him a guilty grin.

He switched off the TV and ran his hands over his face. "I want to talk to you about something."

"Okay." She held perfectly still, her expression unreadable.

"Remember I said I left home when I was eighteen?"

"Yes."

"I tried to start a business that failed. Cost my folks a lot of money. That's one reason I can't seem to go home and face them." Familiar guilt coated Lawrence's throat, but he swallowed it away. "Don't have much of a head for business."

She blinked at him. "All right."

"Don't you see?" He leaned forward. "You're like, this successful businesswoman, and I couldn't even hack it in the feed industry for more than a year."

Andy sat there, an utterly perplexed look on her face. "I don't get what that has to do with anything."

"I have a lot of debt, that's what." He exhaled sharply. "Maybe this was a bad idea." he studied the swirling pattern in her rug. "I just want to—I think we—" Why couldn't he get his tongue to cooperate with his brain?

"I guess I just wanted you to know." He didn't add that if they were married, his debt would become her problem too. He didn't want to scare Andy away with declarations and proposals too soon. And by the deer-in-the-headlights expression she now wore, he would if he said much more.

"How much debt?" she asked.

"Thousands," he said darkly. "Doesn't help that my ex-wife —" He sucked in the rest of the sentence, his body recoiling from the word—just like Andy's was.

"Ex-wife?" she choked out. She got up and moved into the kitchen, where she filled a glass with water from the tap and gulped it. She leaned against the countertop a good twenty feet from him. "Tell me about her."

Dread filled Lawrence from top to bottom. His legs felt like cement, his heart like dynamite. "I told you I'd done a lot of stupid things. That was one of them."

"Getting married is stupid?"

"Most of the time, no. In my case, it was. Jenn—well, we were only married for two weeks before I had it annulled. But that was enough time to do a lifetime of financial damage."

"Annulled?"

Lawrence didn't like the pitch of Andy's voice.

"Jenn wasn't legally divorced when we got married," he said, practically to himself. "She said it had gone through, but well, it hadn't." Luckily for him. "The charges she put on my credit card during our 'marriage' have been ordered to be paid back. But I'm still waiting for the first check."

Andy folded her arms. "How long ago was this?"

"Five years. I bounced around Texas and Oklahoma for a while until I settled at Three Rivers." Contentment ballooned in Lawrence's chest. "I'm finally getting things together. But I still have some hurdles to overcome. And if you and I—" He cleared his throat, unwilling to say more.

"That's why you were worried about me liking you," she said, some of the stoniness on her face melting away. "Of you just being a horseman."

Lawrence nodded, his voice too knotted to work.

"Well, don't worry about that," she said.

A scoff burst from his mouth. "Right. I'll put that at the top of my to-do list. Don't worry about what the gorgeous, successful, has-it-all-together Andy Larsen thinks of me." He made a slashing motion with his hand. "Check." He shook his head, his tone harsher than he intended. But come on. Did she think it was just that easy to do?

She took a calculated step toward him. "You think I'm gorgeous."

"Uh, yeah."

"Successful?"

"Every woman I see is wearing something that came from this shop."

She invaded his personal space, practically forcing him to meet her eye. "I do not have it all together. Most days I'm hanging on by a thread."

He wanted to argue. Wanted her to take his concerns more seriously. Wanted to ask if his confessions had helped her to trust him more.

Instead, he leaned down and kissed her, relieved and reassured when she kissed him back.

---

LAWRENCE BOOSTED HIMSELF ONTO THE BOTTOM rung of the fence surrounding the indoor arena. "Make 'im go right."

Sariah Swanson, the teen riding Chocolate, nodded, her mouth in a grim line. Sariah came from a town about thirty minutes east of Three Rivers, the victim of a severe fire that left seventy percent of her body covered in scars. Working with the horses gave her a confidence and strength she hadn't possessed six months ago when she'd started.

Lawrence watched her bring Chocolate around again, this

time muttering at him and pulling harder on the reins. He obeyed at the last moment, stubborn horse that he was. Or maybe he just wanted Sariah to work for her successes.

She beamed at Lawrence, who gave her a thumbs up and a grin.

"Lawrence?"

He glanced toward Reese, barely taking his eyes from Sariah. "Yeah?"

"There's someone here to see you."

"I'm with—"

"Pete said I should take over."

A pit formed in Lawrence's gut. "Who is it?"

Reese shook his head. "Just go see."

"It's not my mother, is it?" Lawrence couldn't get his feet to move toward the offices of Courage Reins.

"No." Reese didn't take his eyes from Sariah. "She's younger than that."

"My sister?" Urgency flowed through Lawrence now. He'd told her to call him if she needed anything. His phone hadn't rung in months, since he'd helped her move to San Antonio with her baby girl.

Reese shrugged, but the tight set of his mouth suggested Lawrence wouldn't like whoever he met. Besides Cheryl, he couldn't think of a single person who would come looking for him at Three Rivers Ranch.

The walk to the lobby seemed to stretch for miles and he paused at the corner. A woman stood near the front wall of windows, her back to him. She had dark hair and wore jeans and a leather jacket.

Nothing remarkable about her. Maybe she was a new patient.

"Ma'am?" He moved forward. "You asked to see me?"

The woman turned, and still Lawrence found nothing familiar in her face. She had dark eyes to match her hair, and when she smiled, it was a bit crooked like his.

"Are you Lawrence Collins?"

"Yes." Snakes writhed through his veins. "What can I do for you?"

"I'm Gina Collins." She grinned at him, her eyes watering now. "I'm your half-sister."

## CHAPTER SEVEN

Andy had barely closed the store after an exhausting Monday—a Monday! Usually one of her quieter days—when her phone sang from inside the drawer. It was Sandy.

"Hey," Andy said. "What's up, Sandy?"

"Okay, I don't normally do this, but I think you better get over to the pancake house."

Andy punched in the code to open the till, none of her nightly chores complete because of the flurry of sales she'd had in the last half hour. "Why?"

"Lawrence just came in."

"Okay." Andy didn't see why this mattered, though an undercurrent of urgency rode in Sandy's tone, something Andy hadn't heard before.

"He's with another woman."

Andy's blood turned to ice. She took a second to force herself to be rational, to trust Lawrence. "Does she have short hair? Sort of chopped like it was an accident?"

"No—"

"Because that's his sister," Andy practically yelled over Sandy.

"This woman has dark hair. Curled." Sandy's voice dropped to a whisper on the last word. "It's not my business, and like I said, I don't normally do this. But I know y'all were dating last year and then weren't, and now are again, and...I don't want you to get hurt again, Andy."

Fire raced through Andy's system at the same time her thoughts seemed frozen. "Thank you, Sandy," fell from her mouth and she hung up. She looked around her festive shop like Mama would appear and give her some advice.

Last time, she'd jumped to conclusions.

Last time, she'd trusted what someone else said more than she trusted Lawrence.

Last time, her decision had cost her a year of happiness.

"Not this time," she vowed as she grabbed her keys and headed for the door. "Not this time."

---

TEN MINUTES LATER, ANDY SAT IN HER CAR IN THE pancake house parking lot, seriously questioning her sanity. *What are you going to do?* she asked herself. *March in there and demand to know who he's eating with?*

She could see them through the front window. Her beautiful Lawrence and that dark-haired beauty.

Taking a deep breath, and without a plan in place, she slipped out of the car. She made her steps even as she entered the pancake house. Sandy met her eye and twitched her head toward where Andy had already seen Lawrence.

*Now or never, she thought. Help me, Lord.*

She slid into the booth next to the woman. "Lawrence," she said. She'd thought about pretending to just stumble upon them, but had dismissed the idea. She'd been aiming for truth, and he was going to get it.

"I don't know who this woman is, and I'm sure you're going

to tell me. It doesn't really matter who she is. What matters is that I love you, and I trust you." Her words hit her square in the face at the same time they hit him. She found she didn't need to say anything else.

"Yeah. That's it. I love you, and I trust you. When you finish up here, come on over and you can tell me all about her." She cast a look at the woman, who wore a look of pure surprise.

Andy slid out of the booth, her heart thudding in her chest like it was about to go belly up. She paused next to Lawrence, reached out, and grasped his fingers as he reached toward her too. Satisfied and relieved and still beyond curious, she held her head high as she left the pancake house.

Back in the safe darkness of the driveway behind her building, she let herself collapse. Without the adrenaline, Andy felt like she had no bones to support her body. But somehow, she managed to make it upstairs to her loft, half-hoping Lawrence would be waiting there for her.

Of course he wasn't.

---

LAWRENCE STARED AT GINA—HIS FATHER'S DAUGHTER from a relationship before his dad had met and married his mom. She'd been put up for adoption as an infant, had the birth certificate, his father's eyes, and Lawrence's crooked smile. Once he'd verified who she was, he'd suggested dinner. Gina claimed to want only to know where she came from, who her blood relatives were. She'd only be in Three Rivers for the night.

"You should go after her," Gina said, spearing a chunk of her whole wheat pancakes.

"I should, shouldn't I?"

Andy's words rang in his ears. *I love you and I trust you.*

He fumbled for his wallet. "I'll leave you some money. I'm so sorry, Gina." He threw some cash on the table and stood. "You have my number?"

"I have it," she said. "Go talk to whoever that was."

Lawrence grinned. "That's my Andy." He hurried toward the exit.

"Better tell her you love her back next time!" Gina called after him.

He'd wanted to tell Andy he loved her since the day he met her. The past couple of weeks rekindling their relationship had only increased that desire. He drove too fast through town, arriving at her loft after only a few minutes. He pulled into the back driveway, directly behind her car. The lights along the top floor indicated she was home, though he knew she sometimes walked the downtown area.

He went up the back steps only to be met by a locked door. He'd come to Andy's shop after-hours enough to know where the bell was. His fingers searched for the bump on the wall, finding it after several agonizing seconds. He pressed it, satisfied when the peal resonated through the building.

Lawrence stepped back so Andy could look out the window and see him—a dance they'd perfected in the months they'd dated. Sure enough, her shadow passed by the window. Then drew nearer.

She lifted the glass and leaned her elbows on the sill. "Who are you and what do you want?"

He tilted his head back and laughed. "Andy, let me in."

She regarded him, her head cocked adorably to the side. "You never said what you wanted."

She seemed playful, yet serious at the same time. His heart raced.

"You," he said. "I want you."

She ducked back inside, and a few second later, the door opened. She didn't come out to meet him, but hung back in that sexy, shy way she had.

"So that woman is Gina Collins," he said as he crossed the threshold into her boutique. "She's my half-sister, put up for adoption before my dad met my mom."

Andy blinked at him. "Wow."

"Yeah." Lawrence's gaze flitted to the storeroom and back to Andy. "Care to show me your new arrivals?" He dashed off a grin.

She returned it and hipped her way into the storeroom. This time, he didn't even wait to close the door before kissing her.

"I love you, Andy," he whispered against her lips. "I've loved you forever."

# CHAPTER EIGHT

Andy hurried down the stairs when she saw Lawrence's truck turn the corner. She switched on the built-in speakers and *Silent Night* filtered through the space. The grin she'd been trying to contain spilled onto her face as she unlocked the shop's door and opened it.

"Merry Christmas," she said as Lawrence appeared. She flew down the stairs and into his arms, though he had to practically throw the groceries he'd brought in order to catch her.

"Merry Christmas to you too." He chuckled and she held onto his broad shoulders even tighter.

"You sure you don't mind coming here over being at Kelly's?" Andy pulled away so she could see his face, read the lie in his eyes—if there was one.

But she couldn't find one. He kept one of her hands in his as he bent to grab the grocery sacks he'd been carrying. "Andy, I'd rather be alone with you, trust me."

And alone they were. Just the two of them. It was the greatest Christmas present Andy had ever had. All she'd ever wanted.

"Did Santa come?" he asked as they made their way into the boutique.

She sighed and pressed further into his side. "You already know he did." And the microscopic box had been taunting her since he'd left last night.

"I know of no such thing." He'd tried to hide the fact that he'd stood in front of her Christmas tree for at least fifteen minutes, even kneeling to examine her tree skirt, exclaiming over her mother's lace work. She'd found the small, gold-wrapped box tucked into the boughs after he'd left.

"Sure." She locked the shop's door behind them, satisfied there wouldn't be any interruptions this Christmas.

"So you're sayin' you didn't get me anything for Christmas," he said as she started up the steps leading to her loft.

She turned, up a stair from him, now at the same height as him. "That's not what I said."

His hands snaked around her waist. The last few weeks of sneaking kisses in the storeroom and spending most of her awake time on Sundays with Lawrence had made her happier than she knew she could be, especially after Mama's death.

But the sting of her absence had lessened, and the loneliness that had threatened to crush Andy just a month ago had ebbed into a memory.

She leaned forward and kissed Lawrence, beyond grateful that she could, grateful that he loved her, grateful that she'd found a way to make things right between them. Overcome with emotion, she ducked her head and rested her cheek against his. "Thanks for coming."

"Mm." He turned and pressed his lips to the spot just behind her ear. "Nowhere I'd rather be."

They continued upstairs, and Lawrence hadn't taken two steps through the door when he said, "You made a ham?"

"It's Christmas," Andy said. "And it's about the only thing

Mama taught me to make before she died." She went into the kitchen ahead of him. "Ham and cheesy potatoes."

"You've been holdin' out on me."

She turned and found him leaning against the couch, a delicious half-smile on his face.

"I know how to cook," Andy said. "I just don't do much of it during my busy season."

He stalked a step closer. "So you're sayin' when it's not busy, we can eat like this every Sunday?"

She shrugged, though a zing of delight pulsed through her. He came closer and closer still. "Should we eat first or open presents first?"

"Presents," Andy said. "The ham has another hour at least." She tipped her head back as he drew her into an embrace. "And it's only ten o'clock in the morning."

"Presents it is." He kissed her, and Andy thought she could lose hours to Lawrence's touch. She thanked the Lord for Lawrence's calming and comforting presence in her life at this precious time of year.

As he took her hand and led her toward the Christmas tree, Andy wondered if every holiday season could be as magical as this one had been. She hoped so.

---

THE ANGRY BEES THAT HAD TAKEN UP RESIDENCE IN Lawrence's chest buzzed louder with every step toward the Christmas tree. Andy had obviously already seen the box he'd left last night. It had taken every ounce of self-control he possessed to stop himself from giving it to her then. But he wanted it to be a true Christmas gift.

He didn't care if she got him anything, though he was sure she had. The four wrapped boxes under the tree hadn't been there last night, and she'd already sent gifts out to the ladies and cowboys at Three Rivers.

"So you sit here." He led her to the couch. "And I'll start." He plucked the box from the branches, his heart beating so fast he thought it might burst.

He cleared his throat, and though he'd already said all these words to Andy at some point over the last several weeks, he somehow couldn't order them now.

"I've known you were the one for me from the day we met," he said, this part of the proposal completely unplanned. "And I want to be with you for the rest of my life." He thrust the box toward her, unsure of what to say next.

She unwrapped the box and took out the jewelry container. Her eyes widened when she looked inside. "Lawrence," she breathed.

"It's an emerald," he said, gently taking the box from her fingers as he sat next to her on the couch. "A real one. For your gemstone." He couldn't get the emotion out of his voice. "And though we haven't been able to share your birthday together, when I saw this ring, I thought it would be perfect for—"

His voice stopped working completely, so he carefully removed the ring and started to slide it on her finger. Her left ring finger.

Her gaze flew to his. "Lawrence." Her voice held a note of warning.

He kept his eyes locked on hers. "I thought it would be perfect for an engagement ring." His throat felt like someone had swapped it with sand and cotton. "I love you, Andy. I want to see you everyday, not just on Sundays. Will you marry me so we can make that happen?"

His body had forgotten how to do all its involuntary functions. She didn't seem to be breathing or blinking either. "Well, now my gift is going to seem really lame," she whispered.

"Not if you say yes," he said. "You're all I need for Christmas."

With her eyes drifting closed and her leaning closer, she said, "Yes, Lawrence. Yes, I'll marry you."

Fireworks popped through his mind, bringing a smile to his lips just before he sealed their engagement with a Christmas kiss.

*The End*

# TEN DAYS IN TOWN

# SCRIPTURE

"Delight thyself also in the Lord; and he shall give thee the desires of thine heart."

Psalms 37:4

# CHAPTER NINE

The dates Sandy Keller had been on hadn't been so disastrous in at least six months. Maybe longer. She'd been out with so many men, she'd lost count. Of course, she hadn't ever had to drive out to Three Rivers Ranch to pick up her date before. That was a new low.

And so was having him say the words "my girlfriend" while *she* paid for dinner.

She fumed as she pulled into the parking lot, the long drive of shame back from the ranch finally over. Sandy didn't want to return to the pancake house, where she'd have to explain to the night manager how utterly ridiculous dating in Three Rivers had become.

"Only for you," she muttered as she turned the corner and headed toward the back building. Her oasis away from everything, her condo sat around the rear of the building, giving her unprecedented views of the western range. Living on the very edge of town had its perks, she supposed.

She pressed the brake too hard, jerking her car to a stop. Someone had parked in her designated space. Again.

Muttering, she backed up and found an uncovered parking

spot, eyeing the red SUV like it had done her a personal wrong. She unlocked her front door and eased into her condo like she was settling into a warm bath.

Coming home had always brought her comfort. So had cooking. She whipped out a batch of oatmeal chocolate chip cookies, slid the tray into the oven, and disappeared into her bedroom to change. She wished she could slip away from the night's horrors as easily as she shed one set of clothes and replaced them with silky pajamas.

She looked at herself in the bathroom mirror, trying to see her flaws. Oh, she had them—a lot of them—but she couldn't understand why everyone around her seemed to be able to find someone to love and she couldn't.

"No more dating anyone from the ranch," she told her reflection.

Sure, she'd been on some fun dates with some nice guys. But she hadn't made it past the third date in over a year. There had to be something wrong with her, but looking at her brown eyes and highlighted brown hair, she couldn't see it.

So, like she'd done dozens of times before, she returned to the kitchen to drown out the memories of her terrible date in ooey gooey chocolate.

The timer beeped once as she came out of her bedroom—the signal that it had been going off for a while. Her adrenaline spiked. How long had she been staring at herself in the mirror?

Thin, white smoke issued from the vents at the rear of the oven. She hurried into the kitchen, grabbed the oven mitts from the drawer, and yanked open the door.

Smoke and heat and vapor smacked her in the face. She cringed and pulled back, her stomach rioting over the loss of the cookies.

She'd barely slammed the ruined sheet of what was going to be her saving grace for the night on the stovetop when someone opened her front door.

Panic poured through her in waves, and she lifted her still oven-mitted hands like she could ward off any attack with them.

"Sandy?" a man asked.

Through the haze, Sandy made out the tall form of her brother, Hank. Relief made her sag against the peninsula. Just as quickly, she straightened and marched into the living room. "What are you doing here?"

Hank lifted his duffle bag. "We're here for the holidays." He peered at her, something he had to do to actually see her through the smoke hanging in the air. "Did you forget Ma was gettin' new floors done this week?" He gestured to someone standing behind him. "You said me and Tad could stay here."

Sandy tried to see her brother's best friend from college, but he lingered directly behind Hank. "I did say that." She stepped back. "Come on in. I haven't gotten the beds made up yet. Weren't you coming tomorrow?"

"Willow's coming in tomorrow."

Of course. Willow, Hank's bubbly, blonde girlfriend. Well, fiancé now that he'd asked her to marry him. Sandy's only comfort all these years had been that Hank hadn't been able to get married either. She hadn't been the only disappointment to her mother. But come June, she would be.

Hank stepped into the living room, finally revealing Tad. He flashed a mega watt grin that made Sandy's heart go flippity-flop and stepped forward. "Sandy, it's so good to see you again."

She stared at his outstretched hand, not quite sure if she trusted herself to shake it. Seconds stretched into awkwardness, which Hank broke by saying, "Don't you own the pancake house now? How is it possible for you to burn cookies?"

Embarrassment flooded Sandy's cheeks, along with a healthy dose of heat. She turned away from Tad's tall frame, his intoxicating dark eyes, which still watched her, his windswept, dark chocolate-colored hair. She'd met him a few times in the past, only for a couple of minutes. But now he screamed *available!* even though she'd just sworn off dating.

*You just swore off dating anyone living at the ranch, she amended as she went to open the windows in the dining room. And Tad doesn't live out at the ranch.*

She gave herself a mental shake, a stern reminder not to be ridiculous. Tad was going to be here for ten days, not forever. And Sandy, owner of the steady and successful pancake house, was a lifetime resident of Three Rivers. The thought had never felt like such a life sentence.

---

TAD JORGENSEN WATCHED SANDY KELLER—HIS BEST friend's little sister—slink into the dining room to open windows. He'd left the front door open, but not because he'd thought it would help clear out the gauzy smoke. But because Sandy's beauty had struck him full in the chest, rendering him slow of thought. It had been a miracle he'd managed to say hello and offer his hand to her.

She hadn't taken it, and now he focused on his fingers, thinking them covered with slime or something.

Sandy's light laugh brought Tad out of his trance. His pulse quickened when she glanced his way, and he needed to pull himself together. Fast. He'd come up with a plausible reason he could go home for Christmas with Hank this year when he'd never been able to before. Mandatory vacation.

Helicopter pilots rarely got vacation, especially in the tourist industry where Tad worked. *Used to work,* he thought as he watched Sandy and Hank banter in the kitchen. His fingers itched to touch her silky pajamas, and he reined in his thoughts.

*She's your best friend's sister, he told himself. And you're unemployed.*

Even if she had burnt the cookies, she wouldn't be interested in a helicopter pilot who was afraid to fly.

Bitterness, now becoming more and more familiar as the weeks passed, coated his throat. He had been asked to take a mandatory vacation over the holidays—usually the busiest time of the year—but it wasn't because he'd stored up too many days.

He forced his mind somewhere—anywhere—else, and the traitorous thing landed back on Sandy.

"Didn't think you'd be here," Hank said when Tad's brain started working again. "That's why I opened the door without knocking."

"Why wouldn't I be here?" Sandy sat at her bar, her back to Tad, but he heard the false note in her voice.

"You said you had a date." Hank pinned her with an older brother look that said *Well, why aren't you out?*

Sandy's shoulders fell, and her chin dipped for half a beat. It could've been Tad's imagination, but he swore she angled her face in his direction when she said, "I'm not really into dating right now. I have the pancake house to whip into shape and...." He let her sentence hang there, and Tad wasn't sure if she didn't know how to finish it or just didn't want to in mixed company.

Hank frowned, his confusion evident. "I thought you liked—"

"Hank," she warned. "So, which of you wants my office?" She stood and faced Tad fully. Again, the subtle strength in her face, the set of her shoulders hit Tad in a way it never had before. An edge of sadness also rode in her expression, barely noticeable. In fact, Tad wondered if anyone else would be able to see it. Or if he could because the same vein of despair had been lingering with him since the beginning of November, when he'd barely made it back to the rim of the Grand Canyon.

In many ways, he was still out there. Still lost in the wilderness. Still radioing for help.

His clients hadn't filed any complaints. Their version of what had happened painted him in a complimentary light. But everything about Tad's confidence had been shattered. He'd thought he understood his helicopter; he'd been flying over the Grand Canyon for years. But nothing had prepared him and no experience could've helped him during that fateful flight.

"Tad?" Sandy stood in front of him now, but he hadn't seen her move.

"I'll take the office," Tad said. "Sure." He glanced left and right, seeing only one door to the right of the kitchen. That would be her room. On the left, an arched doorway revealed a hall branching in both directions, with a closed door at the junction. He stepped that way.

"I can set up my own bed. Or sleep on the couch. The floor. Whatever." He didn't want to add to Sandy's load. She looked and sounded a bit worn down.

His attention came back to her when she said, "Let me clean up in there first," with a tremor of trepidation in her tone.

He paused upon entering the hall. Her office obviously existed to his right, but he didn't want to enter it unless she approved. "Sure. Is this the bathroom?"

"Yeah." Sandy squeezed behind him and entered the office. "I'll just be a minute." She closed the door, that panicked edge in her eye kicking Tad's pulse into a new gear.

He turned away, frustrated with himself. He could not be attracted to Hank's little sister, even if she was twenty-seven years old. Tad joined Hank in the kitchen, where he stood at the sink, staring out the window.

"Three Rivers," he said, though darkness had fallen an hour ago and not much could be seen.

"So much sky," Hank added, and Tad appreciated being able to see something in a way Las Vegas had never allowed. He could see the stars without straining. Coming into town, Tad had felt the smallness of it, and something about it sang to his soul.

He hadn't told anyone about the flight that had almost ended his life, and had definitely stalled his career.

"So what's here?" he asked Hank.

Hank shrugged and turned away from the window. "Small town stuff." He spoke as if small towns had nothing to offer. But Tad craved the tranquility and peace of a place like Three Rivers. Somewhere where no one knew him, no one thought of him as a helicopter pilot, no one assumed anything about him.

*Stay,* he thought, and the feeling spread through him slowly, like honey dripping from the hive. Tad closed his eyes and drank in the peace emanating from the very air in Three Rivers.

He was going to stay—and not just for the ten days with Hank. But for good.

His decision made, and approved of by the Lord, Tad couldn't wait to spend some time alone. Because now he needed to figure out what he could do in Three Rivers to make a living.

# CHAPTER TEN

Sandy opened the bottom drawer in her desk and shoved in anything that would fit inside. The computer and desk dominated the room, but she'd also put in a deluxe sleeper sofa that would accommodate Tad's height just fine. She just didn't want him to see the mess she worked in. She'd been planning to clean her office before the New Year, but owning and figuring out and running the pancake house took a lot of her time.

In short, she needed a vacation. She fired off a text to Gail, her front-of-the-house manager, asking her if she could manage the pancake house alone the following day. Sandy had unfolded the couch and set the air pump to blow up the airbed before she got a response.

*Definitely,* Gail said. *It'll be slow until the New Year's Eve pancake fundraiser. Take all the time off you want.*

Every muscle in Sandy's body sighed. She wanted to take off the next eight days until New Year's Eve, but she knew she wouldn't. But she would sleep in tomorrow, and go to lunch with her brother, and welcome Willow, and eat dinner with her family. The thoughts comforted her, brought a smile to her face where one hadn't been in a while.

With the natural disaster that had been her desk contained, and the bed ready, she stepped into the hall to get sheets. She couldn't see Tad, but his presence filled her condo. And it called to her.

Confused, she opened the linen closet and collected the things she needed. She'd flapped the fitted sheet once when Tad said, "I'll help you."

The hair on the back of her neck stood at attention as he moved behind her and around to the other side of the bed.

"Thanks for letting us stay here," he said, taking one corner of the sheet.

"Sure, yeah." Sandy wanted to pull the words back into her throat. "You still flying?" She tugged her corner over the edge of the mattress and glanced at him.

He'd frozen completely, his gaze that same faraway, here-but-not-here, look she'd seen in the living room several minutes ago. Sandy had seen this look before, usually on the face of Pete Marshall or Reece Sanders. Men who had seen horrific things and somehow survived. But Tad hadn't served in the military.

Sandy sidestepped down to the other corner, glad when Tad moved with her.

"I'm…." He exhaled as he pulled on his end of the sheet. "Yeah. Still flying."

She detected something strange in his voice and glanced up. His gorgeous eyes hooked hers. She sank into them even though she commanded herself not to. The air in the room turned charged and something sparked between her and Tad in a way it never had before.

She imagined climbing into his helicopter with him and just flying. Flying anywhere but here. Flying fast and furious until they ran out of fuel and had to land. And wherever that was would be amazing, because it wasn't here.

Startled by the depth of her fantasy, Sandy blinked and reminded herself of her reality. Sure, she could take a few days off work. She would. Maybe she'd be able to find her center. Restart her passion for the restaurant business. Rejuvenate herself for another year of solitude.

Tad tossed the flat sheet onto the bed, and Sandy used the distraction to force herself to focus on the situation in front of her. She couldn't afford to let herself slip into daydreams and self-depreciating thoughts. Hank rivaled her mother in his detective skills, and he'd know something was bothering Sandy before bedtime.

"Fly anywhere fun recently?" she asked.

"Just the Grand Canyon."

Sandy grabbed the pillows and placed them on the bed. She reached for the quilt and together, she and Tad finished making the bed.

"Thanks," she said. "You still live in Vegas?"

He dropped to the bed and studied the floor. "Yep."

Sandy suddenly found the conversation too one-sided. He hadn't asked her a single question, and he didn't seem terribly forthcoming about his answers. "Okay." She took a step backward. "I'm going to make sure Hank's room is ready, and then I'm going to try those cookies again. You're welcome anywhere."

He lifted his hand as she left and went in the guest room opposite of his. This room held a queen bed, already made up for guests. Sandy didn't have anyone stay very often, but everything here was clean and ready. She returned to the living room to tell Hank and found him fast asleep in the recliner.

He had come from a different time zone, but eight-thirty was early for bed no matter what. Sandy admired her brother, her heart full at his presence. She lifted his duffle and placed it inside the guest room before heading into the kitchen to recreate the chocolatey treat she desperately needed.

*Help me get them right this time,* she prayed as she whipped butter and brown sugar. God surely didn't care how her cookies turned out, but Sandy recalled the thought. Pastor Scott had said that God was interested in their lives, even the little things. That He wanted us to be happy and to pray for what was important—even if that was a batch of cookies.

Sandy calmed as she added eggs and vanilla, then flour, oats and baking soda, and finally the chocolate chips. She sat at her dining room table while they baked, her thumbs firing off texts to Gail and a couple other key members of her staff.

"Can I join you?"

Sandy startled, though Tad's voice vibrated gently against her eardrums.

"Sure, of course." She placed her phone face-down on the table so she could give him her full attention.

*Don't ask him another question, she coached herself. Do not ask him anything.*

But he didn't speak, and the clicking of her oven and Hank's steady breathing almost drove her mad.

Just when Sandy was about to blurt the first thing that came to her mind, Tad said, "So I was looking at something on my phone." He tilted it toward her. "What's this Bowman's Champion Breeds?"

Being a small town, having someone new in town piqued everyone's interest. And Brynn Bowman, a world champion barrel racer, had caused quite the stir when she'd moved to Three Rivers over the summer.

"It's a horse-training facility," Sandy said. "Brynn Bowman is a champion barrel racer. She's going to be training champion horses for the rodeo."

"This says they're gearing up to open."

"Yeah, that's probably right." Sandy didn't want to pry, but she didn't understand why Tad cared about a horse-training facility out on the ranch. He was about as far from a cowboy as a man could get—and her attraction to him ratcheted up another notch because of it.

Tad cocked his head and stared at her. "You working tomorrow?"

She squinted at him. "I was actually planning to take the day off."

That delicious grin spread his lips, causing her to focus on his mouth. Her fantasies ran wild, all of them ending with a kiss with Tad.

"Maybe you can take me out to the ranch to see this place." He glanced at his phone and back to her. "I want to check it out."

Sandy's heart settled like a stone. The last thing she wanted to do was return to Three Rivers Ranch, especially after tonight's disaster. Never going there again sounded like a better idea.

"Really?" she asked. "What do you think you're going to do at a place like that? What if it's not even open?"

"I just want to check it out," Tad said, his voice that false airy type that Sandy had heard a lot of people use when they were lying. "I'm sure there's an office or something, at least."

"You don't seem like the cowboy type," she said, pushing the issue.

"I don't?" He lifted his eyebrows before smiling. "Yeah, I guess not. Maybe Hank will let me borrow one of his old hats."

"I've got a couple," Sandy said, pushing her chair back.

"You've got a couple of men's cowboy hats?"

Sandy froze, halfway turned toward the front entrance closet. What could she tell him? That yes, she had a couple of men's cowboy hats because she'd purchased them for gifts and then the guy had broken up with her? That she was too busy serving coffee and pancakes to return them?

She might as well outline how pathetic she was.

Thankfully, the timer went off on the oven, signaling the

cookies were done. She turned that way instead, and forced a giggle through stiff lips. "Oh, right. Mine are for ladies." She pulled the cookies out of the oven, the desire to eat the dozen by herself raging within her.

"So, will you take me out there tomorrow? Willow is coming in, and I'm sure Hank will want to be here to introduce her to your parents."

"I'm sure," Sandy murmured as she finished moving the cookies from the sheet pan to the cooling rack. "And why not? I'll take you out to the ranch tomorrow." She twisted and jabbed the spatula toward him. "But I'm sleeping in."

Tad's grin nearly melted her insides. Sandy thought she'd never need to find comfort in the arms of another chocolate chip cookie if she had him to come home to every day.

"This says they don't open until ten," he said. "Does that work?"

She picked up a warm cookie, pleased at how perfect this batch had turned out. "As long as we *leave* at ten. It's a forty-minute drive." She pointed to the cookies. "Want one?"

"These do look better than the last batch."

"Ha ha." Her natural instinct was to slap playfully at his impressive bicep, especially after his flirtatious statement and delivery. But she snatched up another cookie instead. She couldn't flirt with Tad.

Could she?

Her feelings swirled like a tornado, and by the time they'd eaten their way through most of the cookies, the conversation lighter and easier, Sandy felt wrung out. She escaped to her bedroom at the same time Tad did, Hank still snoring softly in the recliner.

She fell into bed since she already wore her pajamas. And though her mind felt bruised from all it had been through today, the one shining ray was Tad.

---

THE NEXT MORNING, TAD FELT LIKE HE WAS GEARING up to take a group of tourists over the deepest part of the Grand Canyon. Though he'd been flying for a decade, the nervous buzz of bees in his gut never went away. Not until he brought them all back to the rim safely.

But he was nowhere near the canyon now, and he'd already decided to give up piloting completely. So as he brushed his teeth and combed his hair, he couldn't quite figure out why he felt like he could fall off a cliff at any moment.

He stepped out of the bathroom and put his toiletry bag in his suitcase. Behind him and around the corner, he heard the low warble of Sandy's voice as she bustled around the kitchen. His nerves rioted, and everything became clear.

Tad had always craved an adrenaline rush—it was what got him into flying helicopters in the first place. He actually enjoyed the tremors in his stomach, lived for the rush of hovering over the Green River and doing a buzz by Hoover Dam.

And now, everything in him wanted to see Sandy, smell Sandy, and get closer to Sandy. He smoothed his palms down his jeans as he went into the kitchen, expecting to see her fresh from bed, maybe without makeup and just getting ready to shower.

Instead, she stood in front of the French doors that led to her small balcony, her back to him. Her dark hair cascaded down her back in soft curls he wanted to run his fingers through. He fisted his hands, wondering if his attraction to her would be approved of by her brother.

Tad glanced over his shoulder, but Hank's door stayed shut. Maybe what Hank didn't know didn't need to hurt him. And why would Tad dating Sandy hurt Hank? Tad was a good guy, even if he was currently unemployed and not telling anyone why.

She wore a long-sleeved, green sweater and a pair of jeans that hugged every curve. Tad cleared his throat and forced his attention to the coffee maker. Sandy turned and nearly sent his adrenaline to the moon with her dazzling smile.

"Morning," she said. "You just put in one of those pods." She pointed to the counter. "Choose the flavor you want. Pop it in, hit brew."

He reached for one of the disposable pods she'd indicated. He chose a regular roast and stuck it in the machine. He selected one of the mugs she'd set on the counter so he wouldn't try to touch her and set the coffee to brew. "Thought you said you were sleeping in."

She sighed and added a little giggle at the end that made a thrill squirrel up Tad's spine. "I can never sleep in. I used to work the breakfast shift at the pancake house." She met his eye. "Old habit."

"So you don't go in for breakfast anymore?"

"I'm really that transparent, huh?"

"It's eight o'clock," he said. "You said we couldn't even leave till ten." He shrugged and added a scoop of sugar to his coffee.

"Yeah, I'm usually at the house at six," she said. "I stay through lunch, because my night manager comes in at three."

Tad returned her natural smile. He'd already asked her if she liked owning the pancake house. She'd claimed to love it, and going in at six a.m. testified further of that. Standing there with her, sipping coffee that desperately needed a shot of hazelnut cream, Tad couldn't think of a single thing to say. He just liked being with Sandy. The quaking in his gut had gone out, and he didn't feel the need to stuff this silence with awkward questions.

The urge to tell her he'd quit flying surged to the front of Tad's brain. The words sat on the edge of his tongue. But she'd already asked if he was still flying, and he'd said he was. He'd been in Three Rivers for twelve hours. Talked with Sandy for maybe two. He barely knew her, even if he felt comfortable with her.

"Maybe we can go get some pancakes," he said. "Since you didn't want to leave until ten and all. I'd like to see your house."

A sparkled entered her eye. "You really want to?"

Tad took a step closer, his eyes seemingly unable to look anywhere but into hers. Dozens of lines ran through his mind, but he managed to say, "Sure, why not?" casually, like he wasn't aching to see what the pancake house had to say about Sandy Keller.

"I'll wake Hank."

Tad's spirits fell, and he hid his emotion behind his coffee mug. Sandy flounced out of the kitchen while Tad wondered—again—why he thought getting to know his best friend's little sister was a good idea.

He'd barely swallowed another mouthful of coffee when Sandy returned. "Hank's picking Willow up in Amarillo at eleven. He can't come." Her fingers worried themselves around each other. "Then he's taking her to lunch in the city before coming back out here." Her gaze flitted around the room. "I guess he'll be back around four. My mother's making Christmas Eve dinner, something she's never done before." A measure of bitterness accompanied her words.

"Ham, I heard," Tad said, cursing himself for not saying something more soothing, more comforting. "It's totally overrated. Turkey is a much better Christmas meat."

*Stop talking!* he commanded himself, but Sandy smiled at him.

"I totally think turkey should be eaten at Christmas," she said. "My mom always dries out the ham."

An opportunity bloomed in Tad's mind. "Well, let's eat as many pancakes as we can now." He offered her his arm, surprised at himself and even more shocked when she slipped her hand into the crook of his elbow. Though he wore his jacket already, fire came with the weight of her arm in his. He tucked her close, unsure of what the heck he was doing.

"And then we can get lunch too," he finished. "You need your purse or anything?"

"It's in my car."

"You leave your purse in your car?"

"It's Three Rivers." She opened the door. "You grew up in a small town, Tad. You know how it is."

He did, so he nodded, but he was drunk on the sound of her voice saying his name. He went with her down the steps and to a red sedan.

"Someone parked in my spot," she said, glancing down the row of cars. "Looks like they're gone now."

"Does that happen a lot?"

"More than I'd like."

"And yet you leave your purse in the car." He scoffed and chuckled at the same time. "Sounds like Three Rivers isn't all it's cracked up to be."

She swatted his arm, and he pulled her closer to his side. She paused, and he did too, and time seemed to as well. Sandy looked up at him, and he looked down at her, and Tad knew in that moment that the attraction he felt for her wasn't one-sided.

"Tad," she said.

He waited for her to continue. When she didn't, he took a deep breath and forced reason into his thoughts. Adding a smile to his actions, he stepped away from her, veering toward the passenger side of her car. She unlocked it, the sharp sound of the locks breaking the moment—and the awkwardness—between them.

He folded himself into her tiny car and buckled up, keeping his focus away from her by training his eyes out the window. "This is a beautiful town," he said.

"I guess."

"You guess?" He dared a quick look at her but couldn't read her expression so fast.

"I've...." She pulled out of the parking lot and Tad couldn't help himself. He stared at her, troubled by the long pause and the crease between her eyebrows.

She pulled onto the road, pointing the car east. "I've lived here my whole life." Her fingers flexed on the steering wheel.

"Ah." Tad remembered his teenage feelings of being trapped in the small Wyoming town of Stillwater, where nothing ever happened and nothing was worth staying for. He'd left as fast as he could and only returned to visit a couple of times a year. He'd completed his pilot training in Los Angeles, and chosen a job in another big city. He loved the activity, the constant noise, the eclectic mix of people.

Or at least he had.

Now, the thought of six hundred thousand people surrounding him brought a panicked edge to Tad's thoughts he couldn't rationalize. Tall buildings reminded him that he could fall. That he was human. That his life could end with simple decisions like feathering the throttle when he should've given it more gas.

He pushed the memories of that flight from his mind.

"You okay?" Sandy's hand landed on his arm. There, then gone. Quick as a wink. But the weight of it pressed into him, burned into his veins. He wanted to reach for her hand, have skin to skin contact.

"Fine," he forced through a narrow throat.

Sandy frowned, but smoothed over it a moment later. "Okay, well, we're here." She gestured out the windshield.

Tad's stomach revolted. How long had he disappeared inside his memories? Too long. Just like he'd done for weeks now. Months, if he were being honest.

*Be honest.*

The words sounded in his head like a siren, and he shifted so he faced Sandy. "I'm not really okay." The raw emotion in his voice scared him.

Sandy blinked, her eyes softening. She reached across the console and took one of his hands in both of hers. Through Tad's panic and fear, a jolt of electricity came with the touch.

"Well, let's go get a short stack and talk about it." She released his hand as fast as she'd taken it and opened the door.

Tad took a deep drag of her perfume-scented car, unsure of where the conversation would lead but desperate to have it at the same time. He'd only ever really talked about the flight with his boss, and even then it was all logistics. Not how the experience had changed Tad.

But changed him, it had. He stood, glanced around at the brilliant December sky of Texas, and closed his eyes. *Thank you, Lord.*

When he opened his eyes, Sandy waited for him near the hood, her expression concerned but not judgmental. "You ready?"

"Ready," he said. For what, he wasn't quite sure, but his word almost sounded like a promise.

# CHAPTER ELEVEN

Sandy knew something wasn't quite right with Tad. She'd known it last night too. Curiosity tugged at her, and she tried to dismiss it. Just because she was small-town didn't mean she had to enjoy gossip.

The bell on the door rang as she entered, and Gail froze her to the spot with a withering glare. "What are you doing here? You took the day off." Her eyes traveled to Tad as he stepped beside Sandy. A knowing glint entered her expression.

"Two today," Sandy said, sending a strong *don't ask anything. Say nothing* vibe to Gail. She didn't usually bring her dates to the pancake house, but Tad wasn't a date. Not even close. More like an old friend who'd be in town for a few days. Nothing more.

She paraded these thoughts through her mind as Gail led them to the back corner, near the windows she knew Sandy loved. "Coffee?" she asked.

"Yeah," Tad said. "Do you have hazelnut cream?"

"Sure thing, honey." Gail left, taking some of the anxiety Sandy had spooling inside her. She shrugged out of her jacket and sat, pleased when Tad waited until she did to take his own seat.

"Hazelnut cream?" she asked. "That doesn't seem very Vegas."

"Oh, it's very Vegas," he countered, that playful tease back in his voice. "Dirty sodas and every mix-in you can imagine. Soda bars are everywhere. Can't go anywhere and just get a Pepsi. No ma'am. That doesn't fly."

Sandy tipped her head back and laughed. She liked this side of Tad, the one that wasn't burdened with a secret worry. One that didn't censor himself. One that glowed with life.

Amber, one of Sandy's best waitresses, brought their coffee, complete with the hazelnut cream. "Y'all ready to order?"

"Pancakes," Tad said. "Lots of them."

"Two tall stacks," Sandy clarified. "You just want buttermilk?"

"With blueberry syrup," he said. "And bacon. I want a lot of bacon too."

"Bring the man a lot of bacon." Sandy smiled first at Tad and then at Amber. The girl returned the smile and turned away. Sandy's jovial mood went with her.

"So," she started. "About you disappearing in the middle of a conversation...."

A pained expression shot across Tad's face. "Is that what I do?"

"Twice now." Sandy settled her elbows on the table, like she didn't much care what haunted him. The truth was, she needed to know. Needed to help him.

Why, she wasn't sure. Maybe because someone so handsome shouldn't be so troubled. But Sandy dismissed the idea. She'd been attracted to a lot of handsome men. She'd dated many of them. She'd never felt this need to help them, soothe them, smooth out the rough parts of their pasts.

Maybe it was because Tad was Hank's friend, and she knew what kind of man he'd used to be.

"I don't like flying," he blurted. His eyes caught hers and

wouldn't let go. Sandy tried to read what swam in their dark depths but couldn't quite grasp what she saw.

"You've always loved flying." She wished she didn't sound so strangled, but her dreams of jumping onto a helicopter with Tad and jetting off to destinations unknown fizzled.

*They were stupid fantasies anyway,* she scolded herself. She always managed to come up with some harebrained idea of romance, of how a relationship with a particular man would go. And when it didn't turn out that way, she ended up alone again, making cookies and going into work in the wee hours of the morning.

Even though Tad had just come into her life, her thoughts had circled an exciting world adventure with him.

He pulled his gaze from hers and stirred his coffee. "Did Hank tell you why I was able to come visit?"

"No." Sandy didn't even think about why Tad had accompanied her brother this time. Hank came home every year between Christmas and New Year's. He'd been at his restaurant in Vegas long enough to get the prime vacation time.

"It's really busy in Vegas this time of year. Lots of tourists." He looked out the window like he meant the words only for himself.

Sandy frowned, trying to match the pieces up. His glazed look. His admission that he didn't like flying. His presence. "What happened with your job?"

He jolted like she'd stabbed him with her fork. Soon enough, he settled back into a peaceful expression, sipping that hazelnut coffee in silence. Sandy decided to emulate him. He'd talk when he was ready.

Amber brought the plates of pancakes and bacon, and Sandy slathered her butter from side to side.

"There was an accident," Tad finally said once Amber had moved away and he'd swallowed a piece of bacon. "At the beginning of November. Flying hasn't been the same since." He cut his pancake into a couple of bites and drizzled blueberry syrup over them. "I haven't been the same."

He speared the pancake and put it in his mouth.

Sandy copied him, but her usually delicious pancakes tasted like sawdust in her mouth. "What kind of accident?" She managed to keep the interest out of her voice, replacing it with compassion. Something tugged in her chest, right against her heart. She liked this broken side of Tad too.

*Stop it,* she told herself. She'd tried fixing men in the past. All that led to was a heap of resentment and a painful break-up. Besides, she and Tad were friends. Not dating. Not in a relationship.

"My bird malfunctioned. I panicked a little. Did things in the wrong order." The bite he put in his mouth this time would surely choke him. Sandy took it as a sign he didn't want to explain further.

She nibbled on the edge of her pancake—usually her favorite bite because of the crispiness from the grill—and sipped her coffee. She waved Amber away from ten feet so the girl wouldn't interrupt.

"Was anyone hurt?"

He obviously was, but Sandy wasn't quite sure how. He didn't walk with a limp. She'd only seen him in long sleeves, so he could have scars. Or maybe everything that had happened had left trauma on his mind, his ego, his heart.

"No." He sighed. "That's the thing. I got everyone back to the rim just fine. It was rocky, not gonna lie. But we all made it. No blood. No broken bones. Nothing." He set his fork down as that faraway look relaxed his face and tensed it at the same time. He pressed his lips together and exhaled through his nose.

When Tad brought his gaze back to hers, he carried agony in his eyes. "The clients even said I did everything right." He shook his head. "But I didn't. And the real kicker is I don't know what I should've done differently." He picked up his fork again, pushed his pancakes around in the purple syrup. "And that's what keeps me up at night. It's what paralyzes me when I get in the cockpit." He snatched a piece of bacon and took a bite, glancing around the pancake house. "This place is real nice." He looked at her for a split second, a smile gracing his mouth now. "Feels like you."

Warmth gathered in Sandy's face though his compliment hadn't been terribly overt. He hadn't even really said anything nice about her, specifically. She had put her stamp on the pancake house, closing it for a week while she repainted, and installed new carpet, and updated the light fixtures and décor.

"It's sophisticated," he continued. "But comfortable. Like home."

"Thanks," Sandy said, pleased he found her aesthetic to be exactly what she'd been aiming for. She tried not to let herself read more into what he said than just the words. She'd done that before to her detriment. Her pulse sped against her will, and Sandy leaned back in her chair to put some distance between herself and Tad.

"You finished?" He nodded to her mostly full plate.

"I may have eaten a few cookies before you got up." She pinned him with a mock glare. "Lazybones."

He laughed, the sound morphing him from the serious, traumatized Tad into the carefree, handsome man Sandy felt herself falling for.

"Well, let's go." He pushed his plate away. "Though we haven't eaten nearly enough pancakes to sustain us until lunch."

"I don't cook, I'll have you know." Sandy stood, surprised when Tad rounded the table and helped her into her jacket. The weight and heat of his hands through the fabric sent a bolt of heat down her arms. Her fingers tingled.

"You own a pancake house." He lingered so close behind her, his breath drifted across her neck. "And those cookies changed my life."

She turned into his arms, a breathless laugh escaping her throat. Her heart rippled like a flag in a stiff Texas wind. He gazed down on her, his expression heated now, matching hers.

"Well, cookies aren't a meal," she managed to say before stepping away. Gail's gaze on Sandy's back felt like a load of bricks, and Sandy would not do something right here in her pancake house she couldn't take back. Couldn't explain. Couldn't maintain.

Because though Tad had just said he didn't like flying, he hadn't said he wasn't going back. Sandy headed for her car, reminding herself that Tad was only in town for a visit. He wasn't going to stay permanently.

The fact made her heart do a double-beat before it settled into its normal rhythm, completely resigned to only enjoying Tad for a few more days.

---

TAD'S EXCITEMENT GREW WITH EVERY MILE THAT passed between town and the ranch. The openness of the land calmed him, coated his raw nerves in a balm he hadn't known existed. Three Rivers reminded him a lot of Stillwater, but his hometown had never felt so welcoming, or a place where he could be Tad Jorgensen without any strings.

He released a breath and it felt like the invisible band that had been binding his lungs for the past two months had snapped. Finally. A text came just as Sandy turned from asphalt to dirt. He glanced down and caught Chuck's name before the screen darkened. The tension returned, but Tad pushed it back. It felt so good to just breathe, and he didn't want to let that go just yet.

His boss could wait. Probably just checking up on him anyway. Tad wasn't expected to be back until after the New Year.

Sandy rounded the corner, her knuckles so white Tad sensed

a storm beneath her happy surface. "I should've rented a car," he said. "Then you wouldn't have to wait for me."

"I don't mind waiting." She pulled up to a large barn sporting a sign that read "Bowman's Champion Breeds."

But she looked like she minded. Sandy stared straight out of the windshield, seeing something besides the innocent barn in front of her.

"I just want to talk to...what did you say her name was?"

"Brynn."

"Brynn." Tad put the name in his memory, thinking about a girl he knew from Stillwater, whose name was Lynn. Brynn rhymed, and he knew he wouldn't forget. He opened the door and got out of the car.

A winter wind whipped across the range, nipping at his jacket and tousling his hair. He smiled into it. Even the winter in Three Rivers couldn't be nasty. Not really.

A woman opened the door to the barn and leaned into the jamb. "Mornin'," she said. Her dark hair had been contained in a braid that came over her shoulder, and she wore a cowboy hat that threw her face into shadows.

"Are you Brynn Bowman?" Tad stepped forward to shake her hand.

"I am. What can I do for you?"

"I have a few questions about what you do here." Tad glanced around, trying to take in the arenas, the fenced areas, the barns in one single swoop. The inkling of an idea toyed in the back of his mind.

"I train horses to be rodeo champions," Brynn said, looking him up and down. "You ride?"

"Oh, no." Tad chuckled at the very thought. "I'm not into rodeo."

Brynn finally smiled. "I didn't think so."

Tad cocked his head and peered at her as Sandy finally joined him. "What does that mean?"

"It means I can tell who the rodeo boys are," she said. "I can usually peg what event they do." She glanced up. "And you're not even wearin' a hat." She looked at Sandy. "Better hang onto him, Miss Sandy. Three Rivers has a severe shortage of non-cowboys."

Every muscle in Tad's body stiffened. "She's not—we're not—"

Pink stained Brynn's cheeks. "Oh, sorry." She spoke more to Sandy than to Tad.

"I mean, Sandy's great—"

"Better stop while you're ahead." Brynn laughed. "Come on in. If you're not a cowboy, I really want to know what you think I can help you with."

With horror still holding his body hostage, Tad looked helplessly at Sandy. She wore a smile and a mischievous sparkle in her eye. "I *am* pretty great."

"And pretty," he said. "I mean, I think you're pretty and you're great and…." Tad wanted to stuff old socks in his mouth just to get himself to shut up.

Sandy's blush assured him he hadn't messed up too badly. Yet. "So what are you doing here?" she asked as she made to follow Brynn into the barn.

"I need a new job," Tad said. "And my dad raised horses and ran a boarding stable."

Sandy froze. "So you want to work out at the ranch?"

"No." Tad tugged her to get her to move, but she wouldn't. "Not necessarily. I just want to see what Brynn does here. Maybe I can partner with her."

"But you'd still drive out here to work each day."

"Maybe." Tad tried to see further into the barn, but it looked like all hallways. "I don't know anything yet."

"When do you have to be back in Vegas?"

"January third." Tad swallowed back the confession that he was one text away from quitting. "I just want to explore some options." He reached out and tucked Sandy's highlighted hair behind her ear. "I'm not making any major decisions today."

She leaned into his touch, and Tad wondered if she'd let him kiss her. Right here, in this barn that smelled like sawdust and horseflesh. Tad had never wanted so badly to kiss a woman. And that got his feet moving like nothing ever had.

He could not kiss Hank's sister. Not without at least talking to his friend. Not when he didn't have a future to offer her.

# CHAPTER TWELVE

Sandy smiled and smiled and smiled through dinner. She'd never felt more like a Barbie doll. But Willow was blonde and bubbly and bright—she complimented Hank perfectly. If Tad hadn't been there, Sandy would've dissolved into a puddle of goo by the time they said grace.

As it was, the steadiness of the man beside her kept her in the conversation. Lulled her jealousy back into the dark recesses of her mind. Prompted her to laugh at appropriate times and stay engaged.

But, ugh. Engaged. It was the last thing Sandy wanted on her mind.

Willow flashed her diamond at every opportunity—or maybe it just seemed that way to Sandy. Either way, Sandy's mother and daddy had completely fallen for Willow's charms by the time they took their coffee in the living room.

"Hank, can I talk to you for a second?" Tad's question blindsided Sandy. He wasn't going to join them in the living room? She had to go in there with her parents and Willow alone?

She stared at him, silently pleading for him to offer her his elbow like he'd done a few times today. She hadn't realized how reliant on him she'd become.

"Sure thing." Hank kissed Willow before she proceeded into the living room, like they couldn't ever part without exchanging a kiss first. Sandy nearly rolled her eyes.

But her mind lingered on kissing and if she could share one with Tad. She'd spent the day with him, and it had been one of the best days of her life, bar none. By far one of the better dates she'd had in a couple of years.

The man knew how to talk about real things. Things that mattered. Things that she was interested in. Things beyond ranching and horses, though they did speak of those too. She'd asked him about his daddy's boarding stable and if he actually had liked working there.

He'd admitted that he'd felt trapped in his Wyoming small town. Another thing they had in common. Difference was, he'd left his, and Sandy was still dreaming of a day when she could.

Or maybe she wasn't. Tad strutted into the living room, all smiles, and sat next to her on the loveseat. It almost seemed natural for him to lift his arm and drape it over her shoulders. Almost natural for her to snuggle into his side, take a deep breath, and be happy in his arms.

Sandy wasn't even sure she knew what happiness felt like. When she'd bought the pancake house came to mind. She'd been happy then. Happy to be an owner of her own business. Happy to be away from waitressing and more into the business side of things. Happy she had a way to make a good living for a long time.

Even then, though, something had been missing. Sandy felt it as keenly now as she had then. Then, she'd gone home to her dark condo, where she celebrated with an ice cream cake she'd bought at the grocer. Now, she'd go home to her dark condo—where Tad was staying.

She glanced at him and kept her focus there when he didn't

look at her. His striking square jaw and day-old beard called to her. Urged her to touch his face, feel the scruff of his beard as he kissed her.

A flush rose through her like a geyser when he turned and looked at her. The tether that had been winding between them all day seemed to solidify. He leaned closer. "You ready to go home?"

"Could we?" she asked, glancing at the grandfather clock near the fireplace. "I don't know…my mother might get upset."

"Hank said we could, anytime."

"Isn't he coming?"

"He's going to stay until late," he said. "Doesn't want to leave Willow alone until your parents go to sleep." Tad touched her knee, sending shockwaves down to her foot and up to her head. "Said something about your dad being a night owl."

"He likes to watch the eleven o'clock news," Sandy confirmed. A yawn played with her throat.

"You seem like you're ready to go," Tad said. "And I don't care if we miss dessert."

"We can stop by a drive-through and get ice cream cones," Sandy suggested.

"I like the way you think." Tad tacked a flirty smile to the end of his sentence.

*I like you,* Sandy thought but didn't say. Still, she struggled with him moving here and taking up a job out at the ranch. Yeah, she knew the job wasn't exactly at Three Rivers Ranch, but he would be driving out there each day, working with horses. It was only a matter of time before he had the boots and the hat and the Texas twang to go with the new job.

He'd asked Brynn a truckload of questions, and then he'd bubbled the whole way back to town about opening a breeding stable. He'd breed the horses; Brynn would train them. It was a win-win, according to Tad.

He'd spent the next hour and a half on the phone with his

father, while Sandy helped her mother peel, boil, and whip potatoes into a delectable mash of cheese, salt, sour cream, and butter.

"...not feeling well."

Sandy looked up, surprised to see her mom embracing Tad. "Well, you get on back to Sandy's and lie down."

"I will, ma'am."

She scrambled to her feet when Tad looked at her pointedly. "Thanks for dinner, Mom."

"Tad says he's going to get you two dessert." Her mom smiled at Tad like everything he touched turned to gold. Sandy actually wanted to find out if that was true.

"Ice cream," Tad confirmed. He opened the door and ushered Sandy through it. She'd never been more grateful in her life. When they'd escaped the halo of light from the porch, he slipped his hand into hers. Sandy ducked her head and tried to hold back her smile.

But she couldn't.

---

TAD KEPT SANDY'S HAND IN HIS FOR AS LONG AS possible. After she'd pulled into her parking lot—and found her spot empty—they strolled toward her condo hand-in-hand. Hank had actually started laughing when Tad had mentioned leaving with Sandy.

He'd sobered quickly enough, though. "You mean you like my sister? Or you *like* my sister?"

"I like her," Tad had said, not giving anything away. "She was nice to me today. Spent her whole day off with me. I just want to thank her." He'd spoken true. He wanted to thank her. Maybe with a kiss.

When Hank had boldly asked him that, Tad had shrugged. "Don't know that she feels the same."

"You be careful with her," Hank warned. "She hasn't had much luck with men."

That hadn't helped Tad's self-conscious worries about being good enough for Sandy. Sandy, who owned a successful and thriving business. Sandy, who seemed to have every aspect of her life together, right down to automatic lights that switched on when she unlocked her front door and entered her condo.

Tad took a deep breath. He hadn't imagined the connection between them, and he wanted to explore it a little bit. Probe. Push. Prod.

He closed the door behind them, his heart suddenly bobbing in the back of his throat. "Too bad everywhere had closed early for Christmas Eve," he said. "We didn't get our ice cream."

"I have lots." Sandy scooted into the kitchen, where she produced a box of ice cream sandwiches, a container of Ben & Jerry's, and a tub of peanut butter cup ice cream. "I have some of that chocolate topping that hardens, if you want that."

"It's fine," he said, grabbing an ice cream sandwich. "I'll have one of these." He nodded toward her balcony. "Anywhere to sit out there?"

"Sure." She put away the ice cream, snagging an ice cream sandwich for herself, and led him onto the balcony.

The breeze cooled Tad's heated skin. The ice cream helped too. The calm, serene countryside before him further calmed him. "Sandy, I'm going to move to Three Rivers."

She sighed, a sad, defeated sound he didn't understand. "I figured."

"I texted my boss while you were making the creamed peas. I quit." He looked at her and found resignation in her expression. "Tell me why that upsets you."

She shrugged and finished her ice cream. She licked her lips, and the desire to do the same exploded through Tad. "Come on." He reached for her hand and brought her knuckles to his lips. "Tell me."

"I had this wild fantasy," she said, her voice small and low. "You know, of you taking me away from Three Rivers in your helicopter. We could fly anywhere, do anything."

He smiled at the wistfulness of her voice, the stunning innocence of her nature, her dazzling beauty. His mind turned, dampening the rising flame in him that kept yelling, *she likes you! She likes you!*

"You don't like Three Rivers?" he asked.

"I like it okay."

"You own the pancake house," he said.

"I know."

Tad frowned, trying to make the pieces align. "Help me understand."

"I bought the pancake house because I…wanted more."

"Will you help me with my breeding stable?"

She shook her head. "I don't know anything about that. Brynn—"

"Has her hands full with her own training business. You could help me with the financials and stuff. How to deal with a staff, that kind of thing." He squeezed her hand. "Just think about it, will you?"

"I guess."

Frustration boiled through Tad. He'd thought moving here was the right decision—he knew it was. He'd thought Sandy would be happier about it.

"Sandy—"

"Let's go for a walk." She exploded to her feet. "It's not quite dark yet. There's a nice trail around that condo over there. Into a sort of wooded area with a pond."

"Sure." Tad veiled the negative emotions running rampant through him behind a wide smile. "Lead the way."

Thankfully, she pressed her palm to his as she led him through her condo and down the stairs. She turned right and walked behind two more condo buildings before turning right again. Several steps later, the soft glow of muted lamps covered them in golden light. It reflected off the inklings of a stream and soon enough, trees lined the walkway.

"This is beautiful," he said. "So peaceful. That's why I want to move here. I can't feel like this in Vegas."

"It's not always peaceful here," Sandy said.

"Oh, I'm sure." He tugged her a little closer. "Small town. Big rumor mill."

She laughed and finally seemed to relax as she tucked herself closer to his side. "I'm happy here," she said. "I just sometimes dream of going somewhere else."

"You can travel," he said, barely censoring himself from saying *we*. He liked her. Felt comfortable around her. He wasn't ready to propose marriage or anything crazy like that.

"I don't have time to travel."

"Sure you do," he said. "You took today off."

"It's one day."

"I heard you when I came into the kitchen. You told Gail you wouldn't be in until Tuesday."

"It's Christmas tomorrow." Sandy drifted away and came back. "So it's really just one more day after that. It's no big deal."

Tad stopped walking, his heart thundering in his chest. "Will you take me to church with you tomorrow?" He inched closer and slipped his hands around her waist. A feeling akin to joy flooded him when she leaned into his touch.

"Yes." She slid her hands up his arms, resting them lightly on his shoulders.

"And spend Monday with me? Maybe you can show me all around this little town I'll be living in soon."

"Mm, Monday." She tucked her cheek against his chest, and he thought sure she'd hear the galloping of his heart. He pulled back, hoping she'd tip her head back so he could kiss her.

She did, and the moment between them lengthened. Tad

leaned down and pressed his lips to Sandy's. She seemed to sigh against him, seemed to melt into his touch. Encouraged, Tad held on tighter and deepened the kiss.

# CHAPTER THIRTEEN

Sandy woke on Christmas morning, her eyes snapping open as she remembered the way Tad's lips molded to hers, the gentle way he held her close like she should be cherished, experienced.

She giggled and grinned, the giddy feeling in her gut intensifying as she relived the best kiss of her life. Sighing, she slipped out of bed and into the shower. When she exited her bedroom, fully ready for church, the sky had barely started to lighten.

Her heart dropped. It was only seven o'clock. What was she going to do for the next four hours? Tad surely wouldn't be up and awake this early, and she'd gone to bed before Hank had come in. Her brother had never been one for church anyway, and he'd probably spend Christmas day with his fiancé.

Sandy set the coffee maker to brew and took her dark roast out to the balcony. She didn't sip the coffee, just let the scent of it wrap around her, curled her fingers around the hot stoneware to keep them warm.

She watched the sunrise paint the landscape before her in beautiful shades of blue and gold. The shadows shortened, finally allowing the sun to take ownership of the day, and Sandy inhaled the possibilities of this day down into her soul.

"I knew I smelled coffee." Tad poked his head out of the now-open French door. "Can I make myself a cup and join you?"

"Yeah," she squeaked. "Yes. Sure."

He grinned, which coated her insides with honey, and ducked back into the condo. He returned a minute later, stirring his brew.

"Can you grab the blanket from the couch?" she asked. "It's chilly out here."

"We can sit inside if you want."

Inside, where it was actually warm. Inside, where Hank could overhear their conversation and maybe see Tad kiss her good morning.

"I'm fine out here. Just need that blanket."

"Sure." Tad set his mug on the tiny table and went to retrieve the blanket. He extended it toward her, and she pulled it. But he didn't let go. She didn't either. She tugged him closer, closer still, until his eyes drifted closed and he kissed her.

"Mm," he said. "You taste like cream."

"You taste like toothpaste."

"Well, I didn't want to share my morning breath." He chuckled and sank into the chair on the other side of the table.

"So you were planning on kissing me, then?"

"Absolutely." He offered her his hand, and she gladly slipped her icy fingers into his, a zip of energy racing along her skin.

She giggled. "Don't let Hank hear you say that."

"I already cleared things with Hank."

Sandy almost choked on her drink. "You did what?"

"I told him I liked you." He spoke so matter-of-factly, like any man would like her, want to date her.

And fine, yes. Sandy knew she was pretty, and plenty of men asked her out. It was maintaining that interest she couldn't seem to accomplish. Sudden fear gripped her heart and squeezed. Had she kissed Tad too early? Shown her attraction to him too soon? She folded into herself and tucked the blanket around her tighter, trying not to lose herself to the worries. Tad was still here, after all.

They passed the hours with easy conversation, most of it revolving around Hank as a child and then Tad detailing his ideas for a boarding and breeding stable. When Sandy walked into church on Tad's arm, no one so much as looked her way.

The gossips were used to Sandy showing up on the arm of a handsome man. Her friends encouraged her many and varied relationships. Usually.

Andy Larsen, the boutique owner, caught her eye and raised her eyebrows. A moment later, Sandy's phone vibrated in her jacket pocket. She knew who it was from and what Andy wanted to know.

Sandy loved Andy; they'd grown up together in Three Rivers and now each owned a small business in the heart of the town. She tapped out a reply. *Tad Jorgensen. Hank's friend from college. Former helicopter pilot.*

She frowned at the last part of the text, then erased it. She managed to press send before the organ began playing and she stuffed her phone back into her pocket. Tad's arm rested lightly across her back, the weight of it borne by the pew. His hand draped lazily down her shoulder, and she nestled a bit closer to him.

He smiled down at her before focusing back on the pulpit. The scent of him after a shower—all piney and minty and spicy—kept teasing Sandy's nose and urging her to just get a tiny bit closer.

She managed to squash the wicked thought—she was in church, after all—and listen to what Pastor Scott had to say.

"Every decision is important," he said. "But don't spend so much time worryin' about what to do that you don't actually do anything."

Sandy agreed. She'd had some experience there. The pancake house had been up for sale for six months—and survived two failed attempts to buy it—before she made the decision and came up with the cash.

"Some decisions allow future opportunities. And some will close some doors we don't even know about yet. Know where you want to go, and make the decisions that will get you there."

Sandy wondered if she was making the right choices. If she wanted to leave Three Rivers, she wasn't. Tad's arm suddenly weighed ten times more than it had a few seconds ago. If she followed the path with him, she'd never leave town.

*You can travel,* he'd said to her once.

And he was right.

She didn't really want to leave Three Rivers. If she had, she wouldn't have chosen to buy the pancake house. Or her condo.

Satisfied that she could live a happy life in Three Rivers, she stood and joined in singing the last hymn. Tad stayed in his seat, but she could feel his eyes trained on her. Glancing at him, she noticed he didn't sing at all.

She bent down. "You don't sing?"

"Nobody wants to hear me sing."

Sandy reached for his hands and pulled him up. "I do."

"No, Sandy, really."

"Come on." She gave him her best smile. "It's Christmas."

He returned it with a tight-lipped smile that didn't reach his eyes. He opened his mouth, but he didn't sing. Instead, he mouthed the words, ignoring her when she protested. The song ended, and he sat back down, pulling her close as she settled into place beside him.

"I want to hear you sing," she whispered.

"Maybe later."

Later didn't come during the rest of the service as the choir took over with songs about the Savior's birth. When they returned to her condo, they found it empty. A note sat on the counter: *Gone to mom's. Be back late again.*

"So Hank's out," she said, tossing the note in the trash. "I told you I don't actually cook. Everywhere will be closed for Christmas. But I have some stuff we can probably make into something edible. You game?"

A mischievous twinkle entered his eye. "So it's just me and you, all day, alone?" He came around the peninsula and crowded into the kitchen. "What a great Christmas gift."

"Tad," she warned.

"What?" He slid his hands around her waist and traced his lips along her neck. "I just want to kiss you again."

Sandy had a hard time keeping herself upright, what with the fireworks popping in her bloodstream. "One kiss. Then we figure out the food situation. I'm starving."

"One kiss," he murmured moments before he touched his mouth to hers.

Time could've dripped away. Or fallen like a raging river down a mountainside. Sandy had no idea if he'd kissed her once or a hundred times by the time he pulled away. All she knew was that she was falling hard, and fast, and though she should be screaming and searching for a handhold, she really wanted to take another leap.

---

MONDAY MORNING FOUND HER AT THE PANCAKE house ten minutes before it opened. The coffee was hot. The grills steaming. The wait staff and hostess standing by. Sandy sat at her favored table with Gail. They'd exchanged hellos and spoken of the restaurant for a few minutes. Nothing had been said about Tad, though Sandy's mind circled him constantly.

"So I'll be out the rest of the week," Sandy finally said. "You sure you'll be okay?"

"Absolutely sure," Gail said, the same way she had the previous three times. She stood and collected the coffee cups from the table. "Go have fun with your new man."

"He's not my new man," Sandy said, the idea sending cold fear through her veins. "He's just an old friend. We're getting to know each other again."

"I'll bet." Gail smiled and took the mugs into the kitchen. Sighing, but satisfied with her decision—and what doors it could open for her—Sandy headed home. She expected Tad might be awake, but the light in his bedroom remained off.

She entered the condo thinking she might slip back to bed for a couple of hours. But Hank sat on the couch facing the front door. Arms crossed, eyebrows drawn, he watched her enter and close the door.

"You're up early," she said, kicking off her shoes and shrugging out of her jacket.

"I wanted to talk to you."

She curled herself into the couch. "All right. What's up?"

"Tell me about Tad."

Sandy groaned and got up. She headed into the kitchen to make more coffee. This conversation definitely required copious amounts of liquid caffeine. "I thought you were going to ask me if I liked Willow or something."

"This is more important."

"It is?" She practically slammed the lid to her coffee maker, and she winced. The machine cost too much to treat so poorly. "She's going to be my sister-in-law. The only other woman. I'll have to go on, like, girls' trips with her and stuff."

Hank grunted. "So do you like her?"

"Besides, you already know Tad. You guys get along great. There's no issue there."

"What are you saying?"

"I'm not saying anything." She added milk to her coffee and blew on it to cool it down.

"Are you guys dating?"

"I don't know. We…hang out. Talk. It's nice."

"You hang out and talk." He sounded like she'd just told him she and Tad had started a knitting club together.

"Yes, Hank, we hang out and talk. I don't appreciate your tone."

"My tone?" He stood and faced her. "Look, I know what 'hang out and talk' means to a man. There's more to it than that."

"Is there?" Sandy sipped her coffee. "I wouldn't know. I'm not a man."

Hank growled. "You know what I mean."

"I'm sure I don't." Sandy glared at her brother. Why was he being so overprotective? He'd never cared who she dated before. Never.

She'd also never tried to date one of his friends.

"I don't want you to get hurt."

"I'm an adult," Sandy reminded him. "And I know what I'm doing." In fact, she was making conscious decisions about her life. "But I would like to know what 'hang out and talk' means to a man…."

A smile cracked Hank's stony exterior. "He told me he liked you."

"He told me the same thing." The heat in Sandy's face could've come from the coffee. But she knew it didn't. It came because she liked Tad too. Maybe more than she should. Maybe more than was smart.

"You like him too?"

"Yes."

"Did he kiss you?"

"I don't have to answer that."

"Oh, okay. He did." Hank ran his hands through his hair.

"I don't know why you're freaking out about this." Concern

spiked in Sandy. What about Tad had Hank worried? Should Sandy be worried too?

"He lives in Las Vegas," Hank said. "You own a pancake house in Three Rivers."

Confusion needled Sandy. "He's moving here, Hank. He quit his job in Vegas."

"He what?"

Sandy backpedaled, trying to think of what to say next. Tad obviously hadn't been as forthcoming with Hank regarding his life plans and decisions. She didn't want to be the one to tell his private matters.

"You'll have to ask him about it." Sandy sidestepped her brother. "I'm going back to bed for a while."

"Me too." Hank stomped in the other direction, slamming the door behind him. Sandy shook her head as she returned, much quieter, to her bedroom. Tad had said he'd spoken to Hank about her, about *them*.

So what was Hank's problem?

Or did the problem belong to Sandy? She retreated to the mirror, searching, searching, searching for that fatal flaw that would end things with Tad, the way it had ended every other relationship.

She couldn't find it. Frustrated, she fell back into bed, a prayer on her lips that she could find the flaw and rip it out of herself. *Just this once,* she begged. *Please, Lord, just this once, let me be enough for someone.*

---

TAD DIDN'T SEE SANDY OR HANK WHEN HE EMERGED from the office where he slept. He'd planned to borrow Hank's truck and spend the morning at the ranch, walking through Brynn's facilities and drawing up plans to add on a boarding stable. He'd scheduled to meet with the owner of Three Rivers

Ranch, as well as the founder of Courage Reins, an equine therapy program housed at the ranch.

Tad thought he might be able to use existing buildings for his breeding program, and he wanted advice from everyone willing to give it.

He helped himself to Sandy's coffee supply, marveling at her one-cup-at-a-time machine and thinking he needed to invest in such a thing. He doctored his drink up with cream and sugar and turned. A box on the kitchen table caught his attention, especially because his name adorned the envelope leaning against it.

Tad set down his mug and reached for the box. He suspected it was a cowboy hat, and a smile tugged at the corners of his mouth. After opening the card, he found Sandy's handwriting.

*A cowboy needs a hat. ~Sandy*

He took out the dark brown hat, holding it gently by the crown. This was no cheap knockoff. This was pure fur felt, and Tad settled it on his head. The hat felt like it belonged there, and he wondered how he'd managed to walk around Texas for the past few days without it in place.

He'd noticed the cowboys here never took their hats off, not even for church. And now he knew why. He strode into the living room, where Sandy had a mirror hung on the wall. Tad admired the craftsmanship of the hat, the way it made him seem more mysterious, less open to scrutiny.

His pulse sped as he turned toward Sandy's bedroom door. He wanted to thank her. He glanced at his hands like the perfect gift would appear and he could present her with it. He couldn't even think of what she'd like.

Guilt tore through him with the power of a freight train. Here he was, kissing his best friend's sister, and he didn't even know what she'd like for a gift.

He couldn't swallow. Air seemed like the wrong thing to breathe. Disbelief at his behavior made him doubt how he'd felt about Sandy. How he felt about moving to Three Rivers. How he felt about everything he'd done since arriving four days ago.

Leaving his coffee to cool on the table, he scrambled back to the office to grab his wallet and Hank's keys, and then he got out of Sandy's condo before he had to face her.

He wasn't even sure why he didn't want to see her. Shouldn't he want to express his gratitude?

"That's why," he muttered to himself as he hurried toward Hank's truck. He *did* want to express his gratitude—with a kiss. Lots of kisses. The truck roared to life, drowning out his guilty thoughts.

The clear blue sky calmed him, pushed out some of the guilt at what he'd done, what he still wanted to do.

So he liked Sandy, and she just happened to be Hank's sister. Was that so wrong?

He'd even talked to Hank about a relationship with Sandy. Tad didn't know how to feel. Confused? Frustrated? Guilty?

Making a quick decision, he pulled to the side of the road and swiped on his phone. *Are you awake?* he sent to Sandy.

When she didn't answer, he made another choice. He swung around and headed back to her condo. He marched up the stairs and back into the living room right as his phone sounded.

Sandy's name popped up. *Yeah, coming out.*

Her bedroom door opened a moment later, and Sandy stood there, wearing a pink and white plaid sundress with a white sweater covering her shoulders. Her smile made his heart patter harder, and he threw every plaguing worry out the window.

"Thanks for the hat."

"It looks nice on you." She took a step closer, moving close enough to reach out and touch the brim. "Very handsome."

"You didn't need to buy me a hat."

She fell back as if he'd struck her and ducked her head. "You don't like it?"

"I like it fine."

"I thought I heard someone leave already."

"Yeah, that was me. Now I'm going to be late getting out to the ranch."

She fixed him with a cold glare that lasted for one, two breaths before she looked away. "Well, I won't keep you."

Tad didn't know what to say. The words inside his brain wouldn't order themselves to come out his mouth the right way.

"You can go," she said. "And you don't have to wear the hat if you don't want to." Sandy stepped toward her bedroom.

"Why wouldn't—?" he started, but the door closed before he could finish. He didn't understand what had just happened. He'd come back to tell her thanks, show her he cared about her and not just about kissing her. What had he said wrong?

Familiar insecurity bloomed inside him. He couldn't handle a machine, make it do what he wanted. What made him think he could tame a woman? Especially one as beautiful and successful as Sandy.

*She doesn't want you, a voice whispered in his head. The same one that hissed things like, You almost let that family die. You shouldn't fly anymore.*

He tried to push out the poisonous voice, but it only seemed to get louder. By the time he arrived at Three Rivers Ranch, Tad was sure every person he met would be able to read his failures as if they were printed on his forehead.

---

PETE MARSHALL AND SQUIRE ACKERMAN STOOD NEAR the edge of the barn, engaged in deep conversation with Brynn Bowman. A part of Tad died with every second that passed. Though his presentation had gone well, his walk-through had been thorough, and he'd managed to obliterate his insecurities before he came face-to-face with anyone, the serious set of Squire's mouth didn't look promising.

Pete had been more open to Tad's business proposal. He'd even said, "And any horses that you can't train, Brynn, or that you can't sell, Tad, we could absorb into Courage Reins."

Tad had been impressed with the equine therapy program Pete ran. It seemed to operate without a hitch, and their facilities were top-notch. Every cowhand could answer any of Tad's questions, and after spending an hour with Pete, he knew why his men obeyed him.

Tad's biggest opponent turned out to be Garth Ahlstrom, the foreman at the ranch, who'd followed him around wearing a look the color of a winter storm. And he'd put a bug in Squire's ear. Something about having more people out on the ranch, more buildings, less land, more distractions, less peace.

Tad wasn't sure how any more peace could possibly exist out here. Every cell in his body found joy in the whispering breeze, the gentle sound of horses nickering and cattle lowing. The smell of straw and chickens and someone slow roasting meat reminded him of home, of happier times, of the kind of life he craved.

And his anxiety skyrocketed again. His muscles would surely snap from the constant tension. His teeth certainly ached.

Finally, Squire glanced his way, and Tad found the softening he'd hoped for. Squire nodded, and Pete turned toward Tad. The men came forward as a single unit, and Tad wondered at their history, at what could create such unity between them, even when they clearly disagreed. Brynn trailed in their wake, and Tad remembered that she'd just moved to town recently.

"We'd love to have you out at Three Rivers," Pete said, extending his hand for Tad to shake. "Isn't that right, Major?"

"Yeah," Squire said, spearing Pete with a look that said otherwise. "But we can't build any more buildings. My foreman says he'll quit if I allow more construction, and I can't lose him."

"More like you can't lose Juliette's cinnamon rolls on Sunday morning." Pete grinned at Squire and then Tad. "I'll save you one. They're amazing."

Squire grunted. "So Brynn's agreed to rent you stable space for your boarding program. She'll really only have a few horses here at a time as she trains them."

Tad nodded at Brynn, hoping his smile and eyes conveyed his gratitude.

"There should be plenty of room," Brynn said, offering him a friendly smile.

"And Pete's gonna let you use his barn for breeding. Brynn has contacts in that field, as does Pete. You can use his indoor arena if you need to." He glanced at Pete and Brynn. "Did I cover it all?"

"You'll have to live in town and commute," Pete said. "Squire's cowboy cabins are full."

"No problem," Tad said, thinking of enlisting Sandy's help to find somewhere to live. "I won't be ready to start until after the New Year anyway. Even then, it'll be slow at first."

"Not as slow as you think," Brynn said. "I had two guys contact me this morning about boarding. I told them you'd call them back this afternoon." She extracted a piece of paper from her pocket and gave it to him. "So I'd call them back this afternoon."

"And those calls are what pushed Squire over the edge," Pete added. "So be nice to them." He clapped Tad on the shoulder. "I'm glad to have you. My granddaddy had a boarding stable, and I loved going there."

Sudden emotion gripped Tad's throat, so he nodded and managed to squeeze out a "Thank you," before the trio stepped away to continue their work.

His only thought was to get back to Sandy and share his good news. With every mile he drove, though, his excitement fizzled. Would she be happy for him? She'd argued with him considerably when he'd spoken of quitting flying, of moving here and opening a boarding stable.

But then she'd given him the cowboy hat.

Tad couldn't make sense of her actions, but he really wanted to. Before, he might have let her pull back, hide in her bedroom, and then drift away from him completely. He'd never needed a woman in his life, at least not for long. But since the incident where he'd barely made it back to safety, he yearned to have someone to come home to. Someone to share his innermost feelings with. Someone to trust and confide in.

Coming home to his empty apartment had added to his anxiety, and he often found himself going out to eat and staying until the restaurant closed, just so he didn't have to be truly alone.

"I don't want to be alone anymore," he said out loud to make it stick. He just hoped he could find the right words to say to Sandy.

# CHAPTER FOURTEEN

Sandy paced in her kitchen, the peace offering she'd made sitting on the counter, mocking her. She reached for a cookie and practically stuffed the whole thing in her mouth. Tad should be getting back any minute. She had spies out at the ranch, and Chelsea had texted forty-five minutes ago.

*He just left.*

So he should be back any minute.

Any minute.

Plagued by her conversation with Hank, and worried that her gift had been given too soon, she'd retreated that morning, unwilling to have a hard conversation or allow herself to get hurt.

Truth was, she expected to be hurt. To be broken up with. To be kissed and then abandoned. And while she'd known Tad for a few years now, before this weekend, they'd been nothing more than acquaintances. She had no idea how he normally treated women, or if he'd had long-term relationships, or anything.

What she did know scared her. She knew she'd started to fall for him, only four days in. She knew she pictured him by her side next Christmas. She knew she thought of him constantly and—

"Hey."

She spun at the sound of his voice, surprised she'd let her thoughts run so rampant that she hadn't heard him enter her condo.

"More cookies?" he asked, eyeing them with appreciation.

"I'm sorry about this morning." She picked up a cookie and thrust it toward him.

He took it and bit into it, his eyes drifting closed for a moment. "You'll notice I wore the hat all day."

"It looks good on you." She wrapped her arms around herself as if cold, but the smoldering look he gave her warmed her from top to bottom.

"Thank you." He finished his cookie and moved into her personal space. "I'm sorry about this morning too. I wasn't sure of the protocol. And I didn't have a gift for you, and I was worried about how things would go at the ranch, and…." He took her in his arms. "I've been wantin' to kiss you all day to say thank you."

"That's not necessary." Sandy enjoyed the heat of his hands on her back, the delicious scent of fresh air and chocolate that surrounded him.

"Kissing you isn't necessary?" He grinned. "I think you're totally wrong about that. I'm dying a slow death here." He leaned down to kiss her, but the brim of his hat bumped into her forehead.

"Hat," she said, giggling.

He took the hat off and set it on the table. "I need more practice, obviously."

"I'd prefer you don't kiss anyone else." Sandy ran her fingers through his somewhat matted hair.

"Wasn't planning to." He leaned down and touched his lips to hers, hesitant at first. Sandy knew they had a lot more to talk about—including his future at the ranch—but for now, she just wanted to enjoy kissing him.

So she did.

---

"TURN LEFT UP THERE," SANDY DIRECTED. THEY'D escaped Three Rivers to go to dinner, and Tad drove her car into Wellington and turned left.

"Oh, I see it."

The diner ahead on the left wasn't hard to spot. With only a movie theater and a dark office building to make up downtown Wellington, Sandy suddenly appreciated the bustle of downtown Three Rivers.

She pulled out her phone and texted Andy, who had sent a message a few hours earlier, inviting Sandy over for dinner at her loft. And though Sandy loved her friend and normally would've gone, Andy had just gotten back together with her boyfriend, Lawrence, and Sandy didn't enjoy feeling like a third wheel.

*Bring Tad,* Andy had said.

*Sorry,* Sandy texted now. *We decided to go to dinner in Wellington. Rain check?*

She sent the messages as Tad flipped a U-turn and parked in front of the diner. "I gotta say, this place doesn't look open."

"It is," Sandy said. "It's just Monday night, so it's not going to be busy or anything."

He shifted toward her. "Is Monday usually slow?"

"Tuesday night is the slowest night for me," she said. "It's why we have family specials, kids eat free, that kind of thing." She grinned at him, glad everything between them felt so comfortable. "Let's go eat."

They became the second table in the diner, and Sandy settled into a booth with Tad across from her. "So tell me how things went at the ranch." Though the thought of him becoming a full-fledged cowboy made her heart fill with cement, she wanted him to be happy.

"It's going to work out," he said. "I won't have my own facilities, but I'm going to rent stable space from Brynn and partner with the ranch and Courage Reins to use their barns and arenas." Excitement sparked in his voice and brightened his eyes, causing a smile to pull at Sandy's lips.

He continued to speak about all the things he needed to line up before he could really start, but he was planning to spend most of tomorrow talking to his father, who owned a boarding stable in Wyoming.

Sandy nodded and smiled and "mm-hmm"'ed in all the right places. She ate her anxiety away with a cheeseburger and sweet potato fries, unable to identify why Tad's new career made her skin seem like someone had turned it inside out.

"You seem happier," she finally said.

"I feel happier." Tad wiped his fingers on a napkin and set it down. "Just knowing I don't have to go back to Vegas is a huge relief."

"How will you get all your stuff here?" Sandy leaned her elbows on the table and tried to see his eyes under that blasted cowboy hat. As much as it increased his good looks, she'd forgotten that she hated not being able to see a man's eyes when he wore a cowboy hat.

"I'll hire someone," he said. "I'm not going back."

She cocked her head and gave him a teasing smile. "So you're going to live out of my office?"

He reached across the table and took her hands in his. "Yeah, that has to change, even if I like being so close to you." He ducked his head as a smile enhanced his handsomeness. "Will you help me find somewhere to rent? I can look to buy something later."

Curiosity burned through Sandy. How much money did Tad

have? If he could afford to hire someone to pack up his life in Vegas and move it Three Rivers, he certainly had enough to buy something now.

"I'm lookin' to go cheap for now," he said, and the cowboy twang in his speech sent a spike of annoyance through Sandy. She couldn't believe she was on a date with another cowboy!

"Oh?" she said. "Maybe you should get back to Vegas and pack yourself. Save some money." She didn't mean for her tone to be quite so sharp.

Tad watched her, the light in his eyes now more cautious than flirty. "I have an appointment with the loan manager at the bank on Wednesday. Though I don't have any construction costs, I'm going to need to pay Brynn rent, and I need supplies, and funds to pay stud fees." His face reddened, and Sandy wasn't sure if it was from talk about stud fees or because he needed money to start his business.

"But I'm not goin' back to Vegas. I have a severance package I can use to pay for the move and for a cheap apartment." His voice darkened with every word. By the time he finished, Sandy's annoyance had faded and regret had taken its place.

She sighed. "I'm sorry."

"It's fine." He graced her with a quick grin that didn't hold the luster it sometimes did. "You still hung up on me whisking you away from Three Rivers?" The teasing quality of his words told her he wasn't upset.

"Yeah, something like that," she said.

"And this wasn't good enough?" He gestured to the haphazard décor of the diner. "I'm shocked by that."

Sandy laughed along with Tad, the release a welcome change. She needed to get over her fantasy of leaving Three Rivers and living an exotic life on a white-sand beach. It wasn't the life she wanted anyway.

"This was fun," she said as he threw some cash on the table and stood.

"Good." He slid his arm around her waist. "When I'm with you, I don't much care where I am."

Warmth and peace infused Sandy's dark and cold areas. She didn't need to leave Three Rivers to be happy. Maybe Tad moving to town would be exactly what she needed. She snuggled into his side, afraid to speak of such long-term things so soon into their relationship.

Hank's salty attitude toward Tad kissing her revolved through her mind. She needed to ask Tad about Hank, about why her brother wouldn't want them to be together. But after Tad's declaration that he just liked being with her, she decided to clamp her lips shut and save her questions for another day.

She reached for the radio and turned up the volume. "Okay, let's hear your singing voice."

He gave her an incredulous look. "Yeah, right."

"Come on," she begged, glad for the excuse for lighter conversation. "I want to hear you sing."

His grip tightened on the steering wheel. "Okay, but I'm terrible."

"Can't be that bad."

He opened his mouth and sang the next line in the chorus. Sandy gaped at him, sure what was coming from his mouth wasn't even English. She burst out laughing, and he cut off the noise.

"See?" He hunched down in the seat, pulling his cowboy hat lower and hiding under it. "You don't have to laugh so hard."

"I thought you were kidding."

"I rarely joke about my flaws."

Sandy reached over and took his hand in hers. "I thought it was...special." But secretly, she was glad Tad had flaws. They made her more comfortable about him, made him more human, and though she still thought him to be nearly perfect, she could always fall back on his terrible singing when her ideals about him grew too large.

He lifted her fingers to his mouth and kissed them. "So no more singing?"

"No," she said. "We'll leave that to the professionals."

---

By Tuesday evening, Tad's brain felt like it had been taken out of his skull, run over and bruised, and then reinserted. He'd spent most of the day in Sandy's office, his own notes now littering the desk.

His father had been more than generous, giving him advice and emailing him a list of supplies to start his boarding program. He'd called the two men Brynn had referred him to regarding breeding and they were coming on Monday.

Monday!

Tad groaned and rubbed the kink out of the back of his neck. He could be ready by Saturday. He'd have to be.

While he'd only planned to stay in town for several days, everything had changed once he'd actually arrived. He still hadn't done anything about his apartment in Las Vegas, but the thought of making another phone call made a stabbing pain materialize behind his eyes.

*Tomorrow*, he told himself as he emerged from the office. Sandy's living room and kitchen sat empty. Not surprising, since darkness loomed beyond the windows as well. She'd probably gone out to eat, Tad thought, as his own stomach roared.

His phone rang, and he wanted to flush it down the toilet. Though it had been a good day, full of needed information, he didn't want to talk to anyone else.

"Hey, Sandy," he said, trying to make his voice brighter than he felt.

"Are you coming to my mom's for dinner? We're waiting."

A rush of adrenaline seemed to wake his brain. She'd left her car for him and gone with Hank earlier that day. She'd spent hours with Willow, and she hadn't been looking forward to it. And now he was late.

"Yeah," he said. "I'm on my way now. Sorry I'm running a bit behind. Go ahead and start without me."

She sighed. "You don't sound like you're driving." Her lowered voice could only mean she'd called him right from the dinner table. He didn't want to embarrass her in front of her family. In fact, she'd told him on the way home from Wellington last night that she felt like she didn't fit in her family. He'd wanted to provide a refuge for her, a place she did belong. He still did, and he mentally kicked himself for losing track of time, for forgetting Sandy needed him.

"I'm on my way out the door." He searched for his shoes, wishing he had time to change and make himself more presentable for her family.

"Okay, well, get here fast."

He promised he would and then hung up. He grabbed her keys from the counter, slid on his athletic shoes, and flew out the door. He shouldn't have to doctor himself up for dinner at his best friend's house. But for his *girlfriend's* parents....

Tad didn't quite know how to act anymore. He'd eaten and slept at Hank's many times. But he hadn't eaten and slept at Sandy's. The territory suddenly felt a lot more treacherous.

Thankfully, he made it across town in record time, and they'd started without him. He slid into a seat next to Sandy, wanting to lean over and press a kiss to her temple, maybe murmur a heartfelt apology.

Instead, he smiled at her mom and apologized for being late. She grinned at him and handed him a bowl of mashed potatoes. Dinner passed, and Tad noticed Sandy's suffering.

She finally stood. "Well, I'm going into work early tomorrow. So I'm gonna head out."

Her going to work was news to Tad. She'd taken the whole week off—or so he'd thought. Hank apparently thought the same thing, because he pierced her with a glare and then switched his murderous look to Tad.

Tad shrugged and followed Sandy out into the night. "I'm real sorry I was late." He didn't dare touch her—he could barely keep up with her. "What happened in there?"

She marched to the driver's side of her car and held out her palm. "Keys, please."

"I'll drive."

"I'd rather drive."

Tad stopped a few feet away from her and tried to figure out what he'd done wrong. "Sandy, I—"

"I just want the keys."

Determination filled Tad. He lifted his chin. "No." He tucked the keys in his jacket pocket. "Tell me what happened in there."

She met his eyes, and though it was mostly dark, a light from the porch illuminated the fear and anger in her expression. "Were you ever going to tell me about Sarah?"

His heart hammered a couple times before sinking to his shoes. Hank. The scowl made sense now. "Of course," Tad said. "We haven't talked about past relationships yet." It was a painful reminder that he'd been in town for five days, that this relationship wasn't even a week old yet. "That's usually several dates in." He dared to take a step closer. "What did Hank say?"

"That you were engaged."

"True."

"That she was pregnant, and when she lost the baby, she broke things off."

Shame and regret filled Tad. "Also true." He took a deep breath. "And I'm not the same person I was back then. Did he tell you this was years and years ago?"

Sandy nodded. "He did mention it happened right after you first moved to Vegas."

"I'm different now."

"He also said that you haven't really seen the need to have anyone in your life since."

He swallowed. "Mostly true."

"Who?" she asked.

"Just God."

She seemed to deflate with those words, and Tad stepped into her personal space and gathered her into his arms. "Until you, Sandy. Until you."

She relaxed into his embrace, and Tad felt the tiniest bit bad about saying such things. He'd been fine alone until the accident. But since then, even God hadn't been able to soothe him. Nothing had. No one could.

Until her.

So he had spoken the truth, maybe just not all of it. "Let me tell you about it," he said as he unlocked the car and escorted her around to the passenger side. As he moved back to get into the driver's seat, he prayed for courage and strength.

And for Sandy to have an understanding heart. Because if she didn't, he'd find himself on the streets of Three Rivers alone tomorrow, looking for an apartment without the help of the woman he felt himself falling for.

# CHAPTER FIFTEEN

Sandy woke on Wednesday morning to the sound of knocking. Several moments passed before she realized the noise came from her bedroom door. Flinging off the nightmares of her slumber the same way she did her comforter, she jumped out of bed and hurried to the door.

Tad stood on the other side, his handsome face bearing the lines of exhaustion. He painted over them with a smile. "Hey, gorgeous." He hugged her and retreated a few steps. "I thought we were going apartment shopping this morning."

The fact that he hadn't left in the dead of night, that he still wanted to spend time with her, testified of his gentle soul and calm strength. After all, she'd practically poured out every one of her insecurities to him last night as they discussed his past relationships—and hers.

He waited, his watchful eyes refusing to look anywhere but at her. She noticed the slant of the sunlight as it poured through the sliding glass doors in the kitchen. "What time is it?"

"Almost noon."

"Tad, I'm sorry." She ran her hand through her hair, panic welling where her pulse should be.

"Don't." He stepped into her and took her hand in his as it fell back to her side. "I wanted you to sleep. We were up way too late last night."

She didn't try to mask the raw fear, the naked need, in her expression when she looked at him. "Did you get any sleep?"

"A little." He smiled, and she lost herself in his charms, his exquisite patience, his solid strength holding her up. "I heard you sawing logs this morning, so I know you did."

She playfully pushed against his chest, a giggle in her throat. "Let me shower, and we'll go. I printed some listings."

He released her and gestured toward the dining room table. "I got them. I'll make you some coffee too."

She grinned in response and closed the door between them. Leaning against it, she offered a prayer of gratitude that Tad hadn't left. She was so used to the men in her life doing so, she didn't quite know what to do with one who didn't.

*Love him,* came into her mind, and she startled away from the door lest he could hear her thoughts. Still, giddiness swept through her. Could she love Tad Jorgensen?

And even better, could he love her in return?

As she hurried into the bathroom to look at herself in the mirror, she finally saw a woman who could be loved.

*She's always been there.* The thought came from somewhere outside of Sandy, but she knew it to be true. Tears welled in her eyes. "Maybe I just needed to wait for the right man to come to town."

She didn't wait for confirmation from herself or from the Lord. She turned and got in the shower, at peace in Three Rivers for the first time in her life.

---

"I LIKED THAT SECOND ONE THE BEST." SANDY SIGHED as she collapsed on a park bench. They'd been apartment hunting for the better part of five hours, and her feet ached. Though she spent a large part of each day walking and standing at work, the emotional toll of finding Tad a place to live weighed much heavier than getting cakes out to table three.

"Me too." Tad sat next to her and handed her an all-meat calzone. The sun flirted with the horizon as they ate. With darkness falling and winter winds blowing, the park remained deserted except for them.

"I want you to meet my parents," Tad said. He spoke so quietly, Sandy wasn't sure his whispered words weren't part of the wind.

She turned toward him as if encased in quicksand, questions stuck in her throat.

He didn't look at her, but studied his hands. "I'm falling in love with you, and I want to take you to Stillwater to meet my parents." He lifted his head and met her gaze. The penetrating emotion in his dark-diamond eyes amplified what he'd said.

"You're falling in love with me?"

Her first thought was *impossible.*

*Her second was I'm falling in love with him too.*

"More every day." He reached for her hand and dropped his eyes back to the ground. "And I know I've been in town for five days, and it's fast and all that. I'm not asking you to marry me. But I feel good about us. I feel the same way about you that I felt about moving here, about starting the boarding stable. And." He sighed. "I don't know. I need to go home for a few days anyway, and I thought maybe you'd like to come."

"Of course." The words exploded from her mouth. "Of course I want to meet your parents. I want to see the town where you grew up."

Their eyes locked again, and he emitted a nervous chuckle at the same time she released a shaky laugh.

"Okay, then," he said. "We can go tomorrow. I have to be

back on Monday for those two boarders, and I'll need a day or so to get the space at Brynn's ready."

"Tomorrow," Sandy echoed, a sense of wonder floating through her. She actually craved what tomorrow would hold for her, and she'd never felt like that before.

---

TAD FELT LIKE A LONG-TAILED CAT IN A ROOM FULL OF rocking chairs. The flight to Wyoming had only taken a couple of hours, and his mother and father had agreed to pick him up at the airport. He hadn't told them about bringing home Sandy. He figured his mother's questions wouldn't have as much time to accumulate that way.

Plus, he hadn't brought a woman home in well, he'd never brought a woman home. Not even Sarah, when she was going to have his child. They hadn't made it that far before she lost the baby and ran away.

After that, Tad had doubted if she was pregnant at all, though he'd never told anyone that. No sense in talking bad about the woman, and her departure had made him realize how unprepared he was to be a father, to be married. How stupid his actions had been. Eight years had passed since then, and he'd been flying helicopters and going to church. Both had fulfilled him, until the near-accident.

"Is that her?" Sandy's cool voice brought him out of his memories. He looked up to find his mom waving madly from near the baggage claim.

"That's her." He tugged on Sandy's hand to get her to pause. "I didn't exactly tell her you were coming."

She blinked at him, the shock in her eyes not exactly comforting. Her fingers released his. "Why didn't you tell her I was coming with you? I thought that was the whole point of giving me less than twelve hours to tie things up with my busy pancake house and pack my bag and get to the airport." She fell back a step and it felt like a mile to Tad. "I thought you wanted me to meet them."

"I did; I do."

"But you didn't tell them I was coming." She cocked her hip and folded her arms. Tad wished he didn't find her so adorable when she was angry.

"I—"

"C'mon, cowboy." Her tone could've melted metal. "Let's go meet them."

Tad blinked as she stormed away from him, as a squeal erupted from her mouth, as she engulfed his petite mother in a friendly hug. His father stared at the exchange and then switched his eagle eye to Tad. The bewilderment spurred Tad to cross the distance between them and give his dad a quick hug and pat on the back.

Sandy stepped back from his mom, brushing against his side. She slid her hand into his, a movement Tad felt like everyone in the Casper airport catalogued. His mother certainly did.

"Mom." Tad's voice caught against itself. He hadn't seen her in a long time, but he knew the emotion spiraling through his body had more to do with Sandy than with his long absence from Wyoming.

"This is Sandy Keller," he said, glancing at her. The warm smile that came so easily to his face appeared. "You remember my college roommate, Hank Keller? This is his sister."

His mother seemed to have lost her ability to speak, and his dad never had said much. Tad's mouth dried out as the seconds passed.

"Tad wanted me to come meet y'all," Sandy said. "We just have our carry-ons, so we can head to the car."

That got his dad's feet moving, and Tad thanked the stars that Sandy had experience chatting with strangers. She asked his mother about her house, the boarding stable, Tad's siblings, the horses. With her questions and his mother's answers, Tad didn't have to speak until they pulled into Stillwater.

"Tell me about the town, Tad," Sandy said, increasing the pressure on his fingers, which he hadn't let go of once during the hour-long drive from the airport.

"It's pretty in the summer," he said. "The snow makes everything seem dead and deserted." Tad had always hated Stillwater in the winter, which had prompted him to leave town only a few days after his high school graduation.

"The snow is pretty," Sandy said. "You know, I've never actually seen it."

"You've never seen snow?" Tad swung his attention to her. "Well, now I feel like I should've made a bigger deal of it when we came out of the airport." It certainly had blown in his face like it had a personal vendetta against him.

"This is downtown," his father said, turning down Main Street. Tad saw familiar shops—the local deli where his high school crush used to work, the movie theater where he'd sneak up to the balcony even when it was closed, the barber shop where his dad probably still got his hair cut.

Newer additions lined the streets too—a cell phone store, and a fast food restaurant he'd enjoyed in Vegas, and a place where kids could go to jump on trampolines. The street surrounding that establishment was particularly packed.

"This is cute," Sandy said. "I can't believe you didn't like this place."

His mother made a soft huffing sound that Tad chose to ignore. "Snow," he said instead. "Can you imagine driving to work the morning after you get two feet of snow?"

"It can't be that bad."

"Sometimes we don't leave the house for days," he said. "Because it *is* that bad."

She stared at him, horrified. "He's lying, right, Brian?"

"He's not." Tad's father turned to head out to the house.

"We live on the edge of town," Tad said. "Literally. Like right on the border of Stillwater. Most of the boarding stable is technically part of the county, not the township." He did love the drive out to the house. He used to ride his bike down the street, pumping hard to get to town to meet his friends. He'd curse the miles, but when he got home and didn't have to deal with anything but crickets and the wide open sky, he did like it.

The miles went by quickly, and soon enough, his dad pulled down the driveway of the ranch home. "Okay, here we are." A hill of ants crowded into his stomach, and he wasn't even sure why. Probably because as soon as his mother got him alone, he'd get bombarded with questions. But being alone with Sandy—while usually something Tad craved—wouldn't be any better. Her social skills had kept her true feelings from surfacing, but she wouldn't hold back once they could converse privately.

Tad carried her bag up the shoveled walk, hoping his chivalry would win him some points. By her daggered look, he better prepare for an epic battle.

# CHAPTER SIXTEEN

The sprawling home boasted red brick and white pillars. Sandy had never seen a home so beautiful, with so much land surrounding it. In the distance to the west, she found the boarding facilities, and she wondered how Tad could recreate in Three Rivers what his father had here. The barns and buildings at the ranch didn't come close to the operation here.

A coal burned in her stomach. She couldn't believe Tad hadn't told his parents he was bringing her with him. She couldn't understand why he'd do that, and the negative voice in her head hadn't stopped shouting once, despite her continued attempts to keep the conversation going.

*Maybe he's not as serious as he claims to be.*

*Maybe he's embarrassed by you.*

*Maybe he's waiting to see if his mother likes you before committing.*

The maybe's were endless, and they'd started to make Sandy's stomach feel like sour soup.

He led her down the hall. "My mom said you could stay in the guest room. I'll take the basement."

"Is the basement ready for you?" Sandy couldn't help the bite in her voice.

"It'll be okay."

"That's a no, because *she didn't know I was coming*." The end of her sentence came out in a hiss.

Tad's stride didn't falter. "I'm sorry, Sandy. I didn't realize it would be a big deal." He entered the room and she followed him, closing the door behind them. A fissure had started at the airport, and she couldn't figure out how to make it stop cracking.

She folded her arms in a physical attempt to keep herself from falling apart. She'd already shown him some of her worst insecurities, and she didn't want to break down now, when this was supposed to be a fun trip to meet her boyfriend's parents.

*Boyfriend* rang in her head. She hadn't actually said the word out loud, hadn't acknowledged that coming here made him her boyfriend.

"Tad." Her voice broke, and she hated the weakness in it.

He gathered her in his arms, his warmth and scent wrapping around her as effortlessly as his arms. "I'm sorry, Sandy."

She heard the remorse in his voice, felt it in his gentle touch, but something still wasn't right.

"I'm not very good at this," he said. "I've never brought anyone to meet my parents."

An alarm rang in her head. "Never?"

He shook his head, his grip around her firm. "You're the first. There's a lot about you that's a first for me. I don't know how to deal with it. I'm trying."

Panic welled beneath her breastbone. She needed to get away from him, out of the house, so she could think. He let her go when she stepped out of his embrace. "I need to think." She turned, yanked open the door, and fled.

---

"I CAN'T BELIEVE YOU." HIS MOTHER SLAMMED A POT onto the stove. Her method of dealing with her emotions always came down to cooking. That, or scrubbing something really hard. She'd already scrubbed the kitchen counter until it gleamed.

"That poor woman. She looked like you'd dunked her in ice water." She pulled open the fridge and took out two sticks of butter. "Tad."

He looked up, his head almost too heavy to hold up. "What?"

"You need to go after her."

"I don't think she wants me to."

His mother unwrapped the butter and tossed them in the pot before turning to the pantry. "What were you thinking?"

He set his head back in his arms and moaned. "I don't know."

The smell of brown sugar told him she was making caramel popcorn, but he didn't look up at the thought of his favorite treat.

"She probably thinks you're embarrassed of her," his mother said, banging around the kitchen. "Or that you thought it was a good idea to introduce us, then panicked about it for some reason." She continued to muse over how Sandy might feel, but Tad tuned her out. He honestly hadn't thought it mattered. He'd just been trying to avoid his mother's questions. But her wrath and suggestions for how he'd hurt Sandy were far worse.

The tantalizing scent of butter met his nose, then sweet and salty came together. His mom finally fell silent, then she plopped onto the bench next to him. "Go find her," she said, her anger blown out. "Take this and go find her."

She held a zippered bag of popcorn toward him. "I can see you like her, and it was pretty obvious that she likes you too. Are you serious?"

Tad shrugged. "Only started the relationship a few days ago."

He hated saying those words in that order, but didn't love at first sight exist anymore?

"You've always known exactly what you wanted." She smiled at him. "It's good to have you home, Tad." She nudged the bag of popcorn closer and stood. "Now go find her." She left him in the kitchen with unsaid words.

He hadn't told his parents about the helicopter incident. He hadn't wanted to worry them, but now he realized that the people closest to him needed to know. They *deserved* to know. His mom and dad would want to help, the way Sandy did.

"Mom," he called. "I have to talk to you about something...." He grabbed the popcorn and went to find his mom and dad. If Tad wanted to find happiness, he needed to search for it, not just keep hoping it would show up in his life.

---

TAD EXPECTED TO FEEL LIGHTER AFTER HE TOLD HIS parents about what had happened over the Grand Canyon, after he said he was quitting, after he confessed he was moving to Three Rivers. But as he took the keys to his father's truck and headed out into the bitter Wyoming winter, at least fifty pounds had settled on his shoulders.

He needed to find Sandy. Needed to apologize. Needed her to forgive him.

Tad didn't think he could make her understand. *He* didn't even understand why he hadn't told his parents he was bringing a beautiful, talented woman home with him. Or maybe because she was beautiful and talented and successful, he hadn't mentioned her.

And though his mother's caramel popcorn could charm anyone, he wasn't sure it would win over Sandy.

"But it has to," he muttered as he headed down the only road that led to town. He couldn't believe Sandy had walked this road. His fingers ached from the cold and he was in a truck with the heater blowing.

He passed his parents' nearest neighbor, and something screamed in his mind. He slammed on the brakes and put the truck in reverse. After pulling into their driveway, he approached the house.

George, the patriarch of the family, came out on the porch as Tad pulled up and parked. He got out of the truck, wondering how many people needed to know of his mistake before this day ended.

Apparently one more.

"She didn't want to come in." George leaned against his porch railing. "Said she'd walk around the barn."

Tad nodded his thanks and headed around the house to the barn, his steps slowing the closer he got. The barn door stood ajar, and he pushed it open to find warmer air, scented with horseflesh.

He took a deep breath, remembering how much he loved the gentle animals. "Sandy?" His voice came out low, like he didn't want to spook her.

She didn't answer, and he headed down the aisle. Most of the stalls were closed, but a couple down on the end had horse heads poking out of them. He went that way, stepping lightly so as to not make any sound. The horses knew of his presence, but the soft sniffling coming from the tack room testified that Sandy did not.

"Just go back," she said, her voice tinny and small. It made Tad's heart pinch when it pulsed. "He said he's falling in love with you, and that wasn't a lie." She sniffled, and something moved in the tack room. "At least it didn't sound like it was, but—"

"It wasn't." Tad stepped into the doorway.

Sandy startled and looked at him with terror until she realized who he was. Her mouth opened, but nothing came out.

"It wasn't a lie." Tad sighed and moved to sit next to her on a wooden crate. "Would you believe that men are sometimes stupid? That we do things that we don't know matter, and then when we find out that they do matter, well, their mothers make caramel popcorn." He held out the bag of sweets.

"Sandy, I'm sorry. I've said it before, and I'll say it everyday until you forgive me." Tad's hands felt so heavy attached to the end of his arms. They hung between his knees, and his head bent in the same direction.

"Men do stupid things, huh?"

"And we don't even know why." He shook the bag of caramel popcorn. "You really should have some of this. It's amazing."

She took the bag and opened it, selecting a few kernels and popping them into her mouth. She moaned. "Oh, my goodness. This is like magic." She took another bite.

A measure of happiness flowed through Tad. At least Sandy wasn't crying, and she was talking to him.

"Is this a story that we'll tell at parties in a few years?"

The bag crunched as she fisted the top of it. "A few years?"

Tad inhaled, praying for that same strength and courage he'd used to tell his parents about his problems. "Sandy, I want to be with you. Not just today. For always." He exhaled. "So I'm hoping you'll forgive me, and that this will become a story that we'll laugh about as we tell other people about it. Not right now, or anything. But, you know, years from now."

Moments passed, but Tad didn't feel the same level of anxiety he had earlier. "Tad, I have some issues. You know, self-esteem issues."

A chuckle rose through his chest and out his throat. He lifted his arm and put it around Sandy's shoulders. "Honey, I have a lot of issues myself." He pressed his lips to her temple. "What a pair we make, right?"

She snuggled into him. "I've never really been part of a pair."

He inhaled her hair, recalling the bitterness in her voice

when she'd told him about her many dating adventures. "I know, baby. But you are now."

She sighed, and Tad's muscles relaxed. He hoped he wouldn't do anything else that would hurt Sandy for a good, long while. He leaned back and tipped her face up to his so he could kiss her, wanting the way he felt about her to infuse his kiss.

# CHAPTER SEVENTEEN

Sandy walked into church on Sunday by herself, only because Tad had insisted on going out to the ranch to "check something" in the boarding stables he planned to use the following day. He'd promised to be back in time for church, and Sandy checked her watch.

He had four minutes.

She sat in from the end of the pew, her head held high as she tried to ignore the curious looks of the older ladies in town. It mostly worked, though Sandy still needed time to believe that someone wanted to be part of her life. Whenever she doubted, she basked in Tad's beautiful words and lost herself to memories of his heated kiss in the barn. Just thinking about it made her internal temperature spike.

Pastor Scott stood up, and Sandy looked over her shoulder. Tad hurried through the door, spotted her, and slid into his spot beside her. "Hey, sorry." He drew her close to him and pressed a kiss to her cheek.

Peace like Sandy had never known before—at least in Three Rivers—spread through her core, radiating through her whole body, coating each cell.

And though Tad had only been in town for ten days, Sandy knew she was in love with him. Her spontaneous smile could've rivaled the sun in its brightness.

"It's good to see you smile," he whispered.

She glanced up and kissed him quickly. "It's good to have something to smile about."

The End

# ELEVEN YEAR REUNION

## Eleven Year Reunion

## SCRIPTURE

"I will say of the Lord, He is my refuge and my fortress: my God; in him will I trust."

Psalms 91:2

# CHAPTER EIGHTEEN

The sun had never looked so bright to Grace Lewis. Of course, she rarely saw the sun rise, what with arriving at work by three a.m. for the past several years. *The life of a pastry chef,* she thought as she turned out of her driveway and headed north.

She drove slowly, not wanting to arrive out at Three Rivers before everyone else. But she already knew she would. She'd been up since three a.m.—old habits and all that. She'd baked a loaf of bread that now rode shotgun next to her and would become lunch once noon rolled around.

By then, Grace would be ready for her afternoon siesta, but she didn't expect to be done in the kitchen that early. Heidi Ackerman had promised it would be a long day of baking, tasting, tweaking, and testing.

Grace couldn't be more excited.

She eased up on the gas pedal when she realized her enthusiasm over today's adventures had caused her to speed up. She enjoyed the leisurely drive through the crisp fall air, her thoughts wandering.

And when they did that, they almost always journeyed down

south to Dallas. A frown tugged at Grace's mouth, and she did her best to straighten her lips again. So she failed in Dallas. Big deal. Many cupcakeries failed on their first try. At least that was what her instructors had warned the group of pastry chefs that had graduated from the Pastry and Baking School at New York's Institute of Culinary Education.

Still, Grace had thought sure she'd outbake the odds. She'd moved back to Dallas, gotten up at two a.m. for weeks perfecting her cupcake recipes. She painted the shop. Ordered the tables and display cases. Saw to every detail.

She'd made it eight months before admitting she couldn't put another month's rent on her credit card.

"Don't focus on that," she coached herself as she continued down the two-lane highway. She didn't want her thoughts to spiral right before she had to rely on her sharp wit and impeccable palate. If she allowed herself to continue down that particular train of thought, she'd end up obsessing over how she should've chosen a better location or entered more contests or started out of her kitchen before trying for retail space.

As the miles and minutes passed, she refocused her thoughts on the blessings that had led her to Three Rivers. Her friendship with Chelsea Ackerman—now Chelsea Marshall with two kids and a quiet life on a ranch she'd never wanted—made Grace smile.

It also reminded her of the boy she'd left behind in Oklahoma City. She banished those thoughts before they could even take root, beyond relieved when she saw the sign indicating a left turn for Three Rivers Ranch up ahead.

She maneuvered onto the dirt road, wishing she'd considered what the drive out to the ranch would do to her little car before she'd taken the job with Heidi. But it didn't matter. She wasn't in Dallas anymore and she still had the opportunity to work with baked goods. She'd be Heidi's head pastry chef any day, under any road conditions.

Grace pulled around the corner and the homestead Chelsea had described spread before her. Two homes, sprawling yards, a facility with a beautiful sign that read "Courage Reins," and new construction going in on the west side of the road. She passed that first, noticing that the construction workers were already out and busy.

*Of course they would be,* she thought. They didn't want to work in the Texas heat any longer than necessary, though it was October and starting to cool off.

She parked where Heidi had instructed, noting that she was indeed the first to arrive. Not wanting to wait in the car, she got out and took a deep breath of clean, ranch air. Chelsea had told her there was nothing like it—and Grace had to agree.

With a smile flirting with her lips, she headed for the homestead that would be Heidi's test kitchen for the next several weeks. Her son, Squire, now lived in the homestead, but his wife, Kelly, had insisted that Heidi come out and use the large kitchen to test her recipes. After all, Heidi's condo in town wasn't fit for four women to be baking in at the same time.

With no one but the cowhands and the construction crew stirring, Grace skirted the perimeter of the yard, thinking she'd take a short walk out to the fields and back. Someone surely would show up by the time she returned.

She noticed the calving stalls and chicken coops to her right. Beyond them lay the silos and a couple of barns and way down on the end, a large, portable building. Behind all of that sat a row of cabins, presumably for the cowboys who worked the ranch.

To her left sat the homestead, with its sweeping lawn and full vegetable garden, along with an obviously new swing set and shed. The tamed land eventually gave way to the wild range, and Grace paused on the edge of the two pieces. She felt the same as the waving prairie grasses—without shape or form or worry or care. At the same time, she longed to be molded and cultured into something beautiful. Longed to be needed. Longed to be successful.

She turned back to the homestead, wishing she knew how to become the person she wanted to be. She'd prayed for help, for guidance, for answers.

And God had sent her to Three Rivers to test recipes with a retired woman who wanted to open a bakery in town. A woman who had explained to Grace that she'd given up her dream of owning a bakery almost thirty-five years ago.

Grace took another deep breath as she heard Heidi tell her that she hadn't really given up the bakery. God had promised her she'd have it one day. She'd decided to trust in Him, and Grace admired the older woman's patience and faith.

She stuffed her hands in her pockets as she headed for the house. Heidi had told her to take the steps up to the deck and enter through the French doors. As she aimed herself in that direction, something glinted out of the corner of her eye.

Around the steps, under the deck, waited a patio. And on that patio, a guitar rested in a rocking chair.

Her fingers suddenly itched to play. She hadn't taken her guitar to New York with her, and she'd abandoned the instrument completely as she struggled to launch her cupcakery. But now....

Her feet seemed to change direction without instruction from her brain. She picked up the guitar, a small thread of guilt pulling through her, and sat on the edge of the rocker. Her fingers found the strings easily, pressed chords from muscle memory, and she began to play.

She'd hummed her way through her favorite tune, and was gearing up to sing the lyrics when someone said, "What do you think you're doing?"

Grace almost dropped the guitar. She fumbled it, her hands finally finding purchase on the neck and saving it from clattering to the cement.

Good thing, too, because she didn't think the glowering cowboy standing on the steps she'd come down would've appreciated her dropping his guitar. He definitely didn't need to vocalize that he owned it. His offensive stance and folded arms said that.

"I'm—I'm sorry." Grace stood and replaced the guitar in the rocking chair. The man continued to glower, his square jaw boxy and tight. "I was waiting for Heidi to show up, and I just saw your guitar, and—it's a real fine instrument. You must take good care of it."

Of course, leaving it outside in a chair didn't testify of such things, but Grace swallowed those words. She wished she had her own cowboy hat to cover her hair and eyes, or that he would move so she could scamper past him and get upstairs and into her safe place: the kitchen.

"What song was that?" He didn't sound like he was about to snap, and the muscles in Grace's neck relaxed.

"Just something my daddy used to sing."

"I've heard it before."

Grace really didn't think so, but she didn't want to argue with the cowboy. He seemed so tall and imposing, standing on the third step as he did. And she was a tall woman at nearly five-feet-ten-inches.

His arms relaxed; his hands fell to his sides.

"You work here?" she asked.

"Workin' on the new horse training facilities."

Ah, so he was a carpenter. Grace had a soft spot for woodworkers—the boy she'd known in Oklahoma City had been a builder. Or at least his daddy had been, and Jon was set to take over the business once his dad was ready to retire.

Grace once again wiped the memories from her mind. It wasn't uncommon for her to think of what might've been with Jonathan Carver. She'd been infatuated with him, overjoyed to go to the homecoming dance with him, and then devastated when her family moved to Dallas before she could really find out if she and Jon were a match.

She had only been seventeen at the time, but still. Something about him had stuck with Grace through all these years.

Moving forward to go past him, she said, "Well, I should—"

He stepped in front of her. "Grace Lewis?"

She peered up into his face, searching for his identity. His dark blue eyes and strong features could've belonged to anyone. He swept his hat off his head to reveal dark brown hair—with a sliver of white in the front.

Her heart tripped over itself, then catapulted into her throat. "Jon?"

---

JONATHAN CARVER STARED AT GRACE LEWIS, THE GIRL he'd just started to fall for as a senior in high school when her family had moved. A slow grin stretched across his face. "It is you! I knew I'd heard that song before."

Without thinking, without considering, he stepped down to the patio and engulfed her in a Texas-sized embrace. Though she was tall, he still had a few inches on her, and her head fit nicely against his chest, right below his neck.

Suddenly everything about Three Rivers didn't seem so distasteful. He'd come here against his will, because he worked well with Brett Murphy and he needed the money. But he didn't like Texas and wasn't planning on staying once the job was done. Problem was, nothing in Oklahoma City called to him either.

He'd been drifting for a few years, and he knew it. Didn't know how to anchor himself though. Didn't know if he cared to.

Heat bolted through him as Grace laughed and brought her hands sliding up his back. "It's so good to see you."

He stepped away, very aware of how hard his nerve endings

had started firing. It felt as though the temperature had shot through the roof in only a few seconds.

"What are you doing here?"

She pointed up, toward the deck. "I told you. I'm here to test recipes with Heidi."

"Right," he said, listening now. He hadn't before, because his fury at seeing a woman fondling his guitar had deafened him momentarily. "She's startin' up a bakery, right?"

"In the new year," Grace said, her slate blue eyes dancing with light. He wanted to reach out and tug on one of her sandy blonde curls, the way he had in history class all those years ago. He fisted his fingers instead.

"I'm her head pastry chef," Grace continued, a note of pride in her voice.

Jon grinned at her. "You go to school the way you wanted to?"

"In New York and everything."

"That's real great, Gracie."

She stiffened at the childhood endearment, and Jon's smile faltered. His confidence plummeted, and he suddenly wanted to collect his guitar and head inside for his cup of coffee. "Well, I should go."

"Oh." She shuffled sideways. "Okay."

He grabbed his guitar as he passed the rocking chair, all thoughts of bringing his coffee to the patio and playing while his morning off slid on by vanishing with the presence of Grace. He wasn't sure why he was running away, only that he didn't want to play catch-up right now.

He paused at the door leading to the basement, where he temporarily lived with Brett. He turned back to Grace. "It was real good to see you."

She smiled at him, driving his pulse to near erratic proportions. "You too, Jon."

He nodded and slipped inside, his thoughts volleying around

his mind with the speed of a bullet. He couldn't make any of them settle long enough to do more than breathe and walk. The door snicked closed behind him, and he forced himself to move into the galley kitchen to the right.

*Don't look back, don't look back,* he told himself as he reached for the coffee pot and poured himself a cup with slightly shaking hands.

By the time he added sugar and brought the mug to his lips, he allowed himself to glance out the glass door.

Grace had gone.

Relief and regret flowed through his bloodstream simultaneously. *Really?* He aimed the question toward the heavens. He hadn't wanted to come to Three Rivers. Made that clear to everyone. His parents. Brett. God.

But, in the end, he'd come, because he'd felt like maybe in Three Rivers he could find the piece of his life that had been missing.

He just hadn't expected it to be Grace Lewis.

*Is that why you led me here?*

God stayed strangely silent this time, which only unsettled Jon further.

---

A COUPLE OF HOURS LATER, THE SCENT OF CHOCOLATE filled the basement. Probably the whole ranch. Jon had steadfastly refused to leave the couch, where a sports reel had been playing for hours. His coffee had long gone cold and his stomach roared with the want of baked goods.

He'd heard footsteps in the kitchen above him for hours, but now he heard them moving down the stairs. Sure enough, a knock sounded on the door next to the kitchen.

"Come in," he said, thinking of how he would've acted if the person on the other side of the door had been Kelly. In fact, she regularly brought dinner down to him and Brett and neither of them got off the couch for her.

Jon knew, though, as soon as the door opened, that the bearer of delicious food was not Kelly.

"Heidi wanted me to bring some samples around." Grace perched on the edge of the couch, a plate overflowing with three different types of brownies. His mouth watered, and not just from the sight of the chocolatey goodness.

But from the woman holding it. Her skin held the hint of the summer sun's kiss, and he wanted nothing more than to touch it. His gaze settled on her lips as he wondered if she'd taste as sweet as the concoctions she'd brought.

"Jon?"

He blinked and snapped himself out of his fantasies. "Which do you recommend?"

"You should try them all." Her eyes held that mysterious sparkle, the one that had first captured his attention in high school. Memories flooded him now. Memories he'd only been containing behind a thin wisp of plastic wrap because Grace wasn't physically in the room with him.

"Which first?" he ground out through a tight throat.

"The German chocolate is my favorite." She extended the plate closer to him, and he selected a particularly gooey brownie.

As he bit into it, he definitely decided that life in Three Rivers had just improved drastically.

# CHAPTER NINETEEN

Grace watched Jon eat her brownies, supreme satisfaction singing through her when he moaned. "Good grief, Gracie," he said. "These are fantastic. You made these?"

She didn't even mind that he'd used her childhood nickname. She wasn't sure why annoyance had slipped through her earlier, though as she mixed eggs and milk with flour and cocoa she'd figured it out.

"Gracie" was who she'd been in Oklahoma City. Once she moved to Dallas, she'd given up the nickname and hadn't looked back. But somehow, Jon calling her Gracie sang to her soul in a way nothing had since she'd arrived in New York and begun her dream of attending the Culinary Institute.

"It's my recipe, yes," Grace said. "Heidi added a secret ingredient to the mint one." She picked up one of the treats and passed it to him as he licked his fingers. Desire dove through her. She wanted his fingers in hers as they once had been, to pass through her hair as they once had, to stroke the side of her face right before he kissed her—as they once had.

She cleared her throat, relieved Jon seemed absorbed in

devouring the brownies so he couldn't see the rising flush in her face.

"You okay?" he asked, and she flinched.

She nearly threw the plate of brownies at him and fled. "It's hot down here."

Jon watched her for a beat past comfortable, almost like he knew the temperature had nothing to do with the heat spiraling through her core. "What's that last one?"

"Double-chocolate fudge."

He groaned. "That might do me in." Still, he reached for the treat, and Grace noticed the size of his hands. Large, and calloused, and capable. When he drew back, she felt a sense of loss that made no sense.

She needed to go. Head out to the administration building—apparently the portable trailer on the end of the row she'd seen earlier—and pass out the rest of the treats to the cowhands. And come lunch, they'd all come up to the house to sample the cookies that Chelsea, Kelly, and Heidi were now mixing together.

*Go,* she told herself as Jon finished eating. *Go now.*

But she didn't move. Something magnetic emanated from Jon, pulled her in, kept her close.

"How long you in town?" he asked.

"I live here now," she said. "I moved here a few weeks ago to be Heidi's pastry chef."

A frown drew down his eyebrows and his focus slipped back to the TV. "Hm."

"You still in Oklahoma City?"

"Sometimes," he said, an answer that left her unsatisfied. He seemed closed off now that he'd eaten—completely the opposite of how most men reacted after they'd been fed something delicious.

Grace stood. "Well, come on up for lunch. We'll have sandwiches, salad, and more cookies than anyone can eat." She started for the glass door, almost desperate to escape when only moments ago she hadn't wanted to leave.

Her warring emotions almost drowned out Jon when he said, "What are you doin' for dinner?"

She spun, her heart back in her throat, her hope spiraling to ridiculous proportions. "Oh, I'm usually in bed by dinnertime." She gave a light laugh. "Getting up at three a.m. does that to a girl."

He stood now, his lean legs and strong arms more apparent when caged by low ceilings and close walls. "What time will you be done here, then?"

"I don't know. Sometime this afternoon, I suppose."

He moved closer, his blue eyes turning navy as he stalked closer. "I—Let's go grab something to eat whenever you're done. Catch up on our lives."

Grace couldn't help the smile that slipped across her face. Jon saw it, and added his to it. "Okay?"

"Sure, okay." She ducked her head, fumbled for the doorknob behind her, and finally spilled into air that wasn't filled with the delectable scent of sawdust and cotton and all things delightfully Jon.

---

BY THE TIME LUNCH CAME AND WENT, THE COOKIES baked and eaten, and three batches of cupcakes had been mixed, baked, frosted, and taken around for samples, Grace felt ready to drop. She hadn't worked this hard since opening her own shop.

She loved the work though. Realized she'd missed it these past months as she closed things up, sold her lease, and moved to the Texas Panhandle.

"So, we've got the three types of brownies." Heidi bent over a list at the counter while Kelly washed dishes. Chelsea had left an hour ago to tend to her children, and Grace slid onto the barstool next to Heidi.

"I can do a blonde brownie too," Grace said. "And a key lime bar. That will give you five bar options."

Heidi added them to the list. "That should be plenty, don't you think?"

"With cookies and cupcakes, I definitely think so. Remember, it's a bakery. You'll be doing breads and pies too."

Heidi nodded, a worried expression crossing her face. She sucked her bottom lip into her mouth and bit it as she took notes. "So you'll be doing all the sweet stuff. And I'll do the breads. You said maybe five varieties per day?"

"Right," Grace said. "We'll do a pie of the day too. It'll make the workflow easier. Specific cupcake flavors too. And some staples. For example, we'll always have these brownies and cookies. And you'll always make white, wheat, and sourdough bread. The other two can rotate. That kind of thing."

Heidi's pencil flew across the page. "Okay, yes," she said. "All right." She put down her pencil. "It's been so long since I went to school. What would I do without you? I'm so glad Chelsea called you."

Grace smiled at Heidi, a kind woman who had given a lot to others over the years, if Chelsea was to be believed. And Grace believed her. "Me too, Heidi." She stretched her arm over Heidi's shoulders and gave her a side hug. "We'll get everything figured out. We have almost three months before you open."

Footsteps came down the hall, and Grace glanced up in time to see Jon emerge.

"Hey, Jon," Kelly said easily. "Enjoy your day off?"

"Smelled so good up here, I almost went mad." He gave her a playful grin. "Other than that, it was just fine."

She laughed and pointed to the fridge. "Not cookin' tonight. But there's some of that beef and broccoli left over from last night."

He shook his head, and panic poured through Grace. Would he announce they were going out? What would Heidi think then?

Grace wasn't sure why she cared. She was an adult—almost twenty-seven years old. She could go to dinner with whomever she liked, Jon included.

"I'm goin' into town for dinner," he said, his eye catching hers.

"Ooh, do you have a date?" Kelly asked, more interested than Grace thought she ought to be. But she'd learned that Brett and Jon had been living in the basement for going on four months, and she had no idea if Kelly had been trying to set Jon up or not.

"Sure do," Jon said, puffing out his already impressive chest. "And I didn't need your help this time, ma'am."

"Ma'am?" Kelly abandoned her work and stared at him. "Who is it?"

"Someone special," he said, stepping toward the door. "And I'm gonna be late, Miss Nosy."

"Jon," Kelly called after him. "Who is it?"

"I better go too," Grace said so she could walk out with Jon.

"See you tomorrow, dear," Heidi said absently, her attention back on her list. "Was eight o'clock okay?"

"Totally fine," Grace confirmed before she followed a laughing Jon out the door and onto the deck. She'd whip up the blondies and key lime bars before she came out to the ranch in the morning. She'd certainly have time.

She made it to the lawn and started toward where she'd parked her car, Jon at her side. "Thanks for not saying anything about...." Grace trailed off, not quite sure how to finish.

His hand brushed hers, and fire licked up her arm. Another brush, and he held on this time. "I know how to keep important things to myself," he said.

"Oh, am I important?" Grace teased.

He squeezed her hand. "You were once. I'm interested in seeing if you can be again." He paused, making her stall too. "Can we do that, Gracie? See if this could be our second chance?"

Warmth filled Grace from top to bottom from the kindness in his tone, the hope etched around his eyes. She reached up and pulled his cowboy hat down an inch or two. "Sounds good to me, *cowboy*."

He growled, the sound playful and sexy, and Grace giggled as she danced away from him. "When did you start wearing a cowboy hat anyway?"

"'Bout the time I came to Texas, I reckon. The summers here are brutal. The ball cap wasn't cutting it."

Grace floated toward her car, her new life in Three Rivers brighter than ever, despite the darkness she'd brought with her from Dallas.

---

JON'S NERVES SEEMED FRAYED, LIKE HE'D STUCK THEM in a blender on high. He almost turned around and went back to the ranch twice. But the thought of spending the evening hungry and with only Brett for company made his fingers tighten on the steering wheel.

He just couldn't believe Grace had walked right back into his life. He'd barely started to get to know her before her family moved, and he certainly didn't have much to offer her besides a nomadic lifestyle and days filled with long hours.

Happiness sang through him that she'd been able to attend culinary school—something she'd told him she wanted to do the very first time they'd met. Well, she'd told the whole English class—he wasn't special—but he'd felt like she was speaking directly to him that day.

Jon also hadn't been on a date worth talking about in a

while, despite Kelly's attempts at fixing him up with the single women in town. They'd been fine, nice, but not memorable. He wanted fireworks, electricity, excitement.

He'd felt all of that with Grace, then and now. "Doesn't mean you're gonna get married," he muttered to himself as he came to a stop behind her. He'd told her to choose where she wanted to go; he'd follow her.

She turned right, and his stomach tightened. There were only two restaurants to the right, and neither of them appealed to him. He just didn't understand how anyone could think kimchi tasted good. Or at least okay. In his mind, sour cabbage should be given to hogs. In fact, he *had* fed it to hogs in the past.

Thankfully, Grace drove past the Korean restaurant and pulled into the steakhouse. Donna's on Main Street was definitely superior, but at least Jon could get a burger here. Or maybe a steak sandwich.... His mind revolving around food, he forgot to obsess over possible dinner conversation topics or how he could kiss Grace after only a few hours of face-to-face time.

He got out of the car and joined her. "You've eaten here before?"

"Once," she said, peering up at him. "Is this okay? You'd prefer somewhere else."

"This is fine, Gracie Lou."

She made a face and moaned. "I'm okay with Gracie, I guess, but not Gracie Lou."

"Really?" He held the door open for her, his body reacting when hers moved closer, brushed by him, and entered the restaurant. "But you used to like—" He silenced himself before he could bring up the memories she'd rather forget. But how could she forget that he'd called her Gracie Lou right before he'd kissed her for the first time?

Back then, she'd blushed and ducked her chin, just like she had in the basement when she'd brought him the brownies.

His stomach, now a cold stone, weighed him down as the hostess led them to a booth and placed menus in front of them.

"I'm just Grace now." She ignored her menu and added a one-shouldered shrug to her statement. "I don't know why. Just feels like me."

"Just Grace it is." But Jon secretly mourned the loss of Gracie without letting any emotion bleed onto his face. "So you went to New York City. Tell me about that."

Her face lit up and she put her elbows on the table as she leaned forward. She began to talk about creams and puddings and something called a ganache. Jon wasn't exactly sure what she was talking about, but he just liked listening to the sound of her voice. Even after they'd finished eating and he'd given her a hug good-bye and driven back to the ranch, the sweet timbre of her voice rang in his ears.

That was when he knew he was in trouble. After all, he didn't live in Three Rivers and Grace had just moved to town.

# CHAPTER TWENTY

Grace went through the drive-through to get her daily fix of caffeine. A pan of blondies and a jelly roll pan of key lime bars rode in the backseat, the smell mixing with her dark roast coffee and making her mouth water.

She again enjoyed the leisurely drive out to the ranch—until she saw the sign and turned onto the dirt road. Then the coffee she'd finished seemed to turn to tar in her stomach. She'd had a great time with Jon the previous night—he'd starred in her dreams as the heroic cowboy carpenter that would sweep her away to live a fantastic life together—and the thought of seeing him again made her…nervous.

Once around the bend, the new construction came into view. Three men worked on the roof, and Grace identified Jon easily. His tall frame straightened, his gaze fixed on her car. He smiled and lifted his hand in a welcome wave. She did the same, trying not to frantically wave her hand like an excited puppy's tail.

She couldn't be *that* obvious. She'd arrived early again, and she removed the baked goods she'd prepared that morning and balanced them on the roof of her car. She put a few of each kind on two of the paper plates she'd brought and headed for the construction site.

*This isn't too obvious, is it?* she wondered as she tromped through the dust. She assured herself that she'd also planned to take some over to Courage Reins, where the brownies had been well received yesterday. The owner, Pete Marshall, had told her to come back any time with any kind of sweet. When Grace had mentioned his reaction to Chelsea, she'd laughed and said, "I have him on a strict diet right now. His blood sugar is out of control."

She'd just have to keep this early-morning treat a little secret. "Hey," she called up to the boys on the roof. "I have key lime bars and blondies." She glanced around for a place to set the plate. "Should I—?"

"We'll come down," a dark-haired man with a full beard called. She'd met Brett yesterday, and he didn't say a whole lot, which unsettled her. The quiet ones always did.

He greeted her first and took one of each bar. He'd eaten his whole key lime bar before the other two men appeared. "This is fantastic, Miss Grace," he said. "My wife would love these."

Jon and another man, Luis, selected their treats too. Grace wasn't sure what to do. Say "Great, enjoy," and walk away? She should. Anyone else probably would. But she wanted to breathe in the clean, minty scent of Jon's aftershave and press her cheek to his chest to feel his pulse bump against her skin.

"Morning," she said to him as Luis moved away to find a spot of shade.

With his mouth full, he simply nodded. Once he swallowed, he said, "Mornin', Miss Grace."

She indicated the blondie. "You like it?"

He considered it. "It's great, yeah."

Her heart fell to the dirt and rebounded back to her chest like a yo-yo. "You don't like it?"

He put the rest of the bar in his mouth—he obviously liked it. That, or he was really hungry. Or maybe he was part goat and would eat anything. "I think it's great," he said. "I just like chocolate brownies better."

"Yeah, I get that." She flashed him a grateful smile. "Chocolate is the way to go."

"So this is...?"

"Key lime bar," she said. "It's tart and sweet."

He cocked one eyebrow at the dessert and then at her before taking a bite. He moaned and his beautiful eyes closed. "Gracie, you're a genius in the kitchen."

Grace's chest swelled with pride. "Thank you, Jon." She glanced over her shoulder as a couple of trucks came around the bend and pulled into the Courage Reins parking lot. "Well, I better get these over to the people across the street."

Jon's intense stare made her blush, though she wasn't sure why. "All right then."

Grace felt like he was dismissing her, because it wasn't the reaction she wanted. She wanted him to ask her to stay just another minute, or touch her hand before she left, or ask her to come back at lunchtime so he could see her again.

Something tortured passed through his expression before he turned away. "Thanks for the treats, Grace."

"Yeah, thanks Grace," Brett called, and Luis lifted his hand in gratitude. As Jon moved away, another snag of disappointment caught behind Grace's lungs. She turned and hurried across the street, so she wouldn't have to be rejected by him so openly and completely in front of other people.

Her pride had been punched, and she tried to eradicate the pinch in her chest before pushing through the door of Courage Reins. The receptionist glanced up and then nearly toppled his chair as he stood and came around the counter.

"Miss Grace, welcome." Reese beamed at her, and her

wounded pride lifted a little bit. "What do you have for us today?" He stopped and leaned against the counter as Pete poked his head out of the conference room.

"I am so happy Heidi is opening a bakery," he said, a grin gracing his strong features.

She smiled at the cowboys. "Key lime bars and blondies." She passed the plate to Reese, who set it on the counter. "I have more in the car. I just need a couple for Heidi and the other women."

"I'll help you get them," Reese said. He followed her back to the car, his injured leg dragging a little bit. "My wife will be upset she stayed home today."

"Sneak one behind the counter," Grace said.

"Pete'll be able to sniff that thing out by lunch." Reese chuckled. "The lieutenant has the nose of a hound dog."

"I can take it to her on my way home," Grace offered. "Is she not feeling well today?"

A grave look of sadness etched itself across Reese's face. "She's...okay. It's...."

"Never mind," Grace said quickly. She'd only met Reese and his wife Carly a couple of times at church and their personal lives were none of her business. She busied herself with cutting the bars and sliding them onto another paper plate.

"Our adoption fell through," Reese blurted. "Carly spoke to the birth mother last night, and she's...dealing with the loss today."

Grace's muscles tightened and her motions stalled. "Oh, I'm so sorry." She put her hand on Reese's arm. "I didn't know you were trying to adopt."

Anger and hope and regret passed across his face. "Have been for a while." He took a deep breath. "It's okay. I have faith in the Lord. I believe He'll give us a baby when the time is right."

Grace marveled at the strength in him. "And Carly? She believes that too?"

"She does," he murmured as he took the plate of goodies from her. "We just all deal with setbacks in different ways, even if we have faith. Right?"

Grace smiled at him. "Of course, right." She thought about her own losses, the enormous weight of debt she carried on her slim shoulders. She had faith things would work out—just as surely as Carly did—but sometimes seeing the light through the darkness was more difficult than anticipated. Grace knew that better than most.

"Thank you, Miss Grace." Reese tipped his cowboy hat and started across the street. She watched him go, a silent prayer for him and Carly floating through her mind. It felt good to pray for someone else for a change—she'd spent so many months praying for herself, for her cupcakery, for what *she* wanted that she'd somewhat forgotten that others experienced pain and trials too.

She inhaled deeply, taking the fresh scent of ranch air in through her nose to clear her head. *Thank you for bringing me to Three Rivers.* The peace she felt here lifted the weight of the money she owed and the failure she felt so keenly.

Chelsea emerged from the front door of her house, one baby strapped to her body and her toddler's hand in hers. Grace smiled in their direction and collected the remaining treats before glancing toward the construction site.

She wished Jon would be standing on the roof, watching her. But he wasn't. He was bent over, his focus only on his work. Grace sighed, not sure why she'd expected him to act any different, and headed into the house for another day of baking.

---

JON HATED THE DISAPPOINTMENT HE'D CAUGHT ON Grace's face. He'd wanted to hold her, breathe her in, brush his lips along her cheek, but he couldn't. Not in mixed company, and he probably shouldn't at all if he didn't have plans for something more long-term. He didn't want another three-month relationship with Grace. He'd already done that, and been unsatisfied.

With every pulse of the staple gun, a question burst into his mind. *So what do you want to do?*

He placed another tar shingle and pressed the stapler flush against it. *Staple, staple.*

*Move to Three Rivers permanently?*

*What would you even do here?*

Another shingle. Another couple of staples.

*Is there a construction firm here?*

*Maybe you could start your own. And do what?*

He reached for another stack of shingles, the heat even this early in the morning almost unbearable. But it wasn't really. The temperature had skyrocketed since Grace had shown up with those treats, wearing a pair of skinny jeans and a blue flowered tank top.

The shingle made a slapping sound against the roof as he threw it down. He positioned it, the muscles in his back stretching as he placed the stapler along the edge. *Staple, staple, staple.*

*Build sheds?*

*Are there housing developments here?*

*Enough home improvement jobs?*

As the shingles went down in even rows and the minutes passed, Jon tormented himself. By the time Brett called to him to come down to get out of the sun and get a drink, Jon hadn't arrived at a solution yet.

Maybe there wasn't a solution. Maybe he should accept Grace's goodies whenever she brought them, mind his own business, and go back to Oklahoma City when the job ended, just like he'd been planning.

He'd certainly never looked at Three Rivers as a permanent place to put down roots. The very thought actually made him physically ill, and he stumbled on the ladder. Brett lurched forward to help him, knocking Jon's hat off.

"I'm okay," Jon said. "I'm fine."

"Come get a drink now." Brett's commanding tone wasn't lost on Jon, and he actually appreciated it. He'd known Brett since childhood, watched him get married and go off to war, had been there when he'd come home the first time, and the second, and the third.

He obeyed Brett, relishing the icy water as it touched his tongue and flowed down his throat. But he knew he wasn't dehydrated, at least not enough to make him stumble down a ladder, something he'd navigated easily for decades.

He refused to look toward the homestead, instead closing his eyes and breathing deep.

"Eat this."

He opened his eyes to Brett holding a Snickers bar toward him.

"I'm fine."

"Eat it." He shook the candy bar, the plastic wrapper rattling.

Jon glared as he took the bar and unwrapped it. "Commander, it's not the heat."

Brett cocked his head and appraised him in that calculating way all Army men had. Jon had briefly considered following his friend into the Army, but he'd chosen the Marines instead.

"What is it then?" Brett asked.

The water he'd drunk sloshed against his stomach walls. "It's Grace Lewis."

Brett's gaze wandered to the homestead, and Jon could practically see Brett's wheels spinning. "That's Grace Lewis? *The* Grace Lewis? The one you liked in high school?"

Jon pressed his mouth into a thin line and nodded.

"Didn't you take her to homecoming?"

"Yep."

"She moved…." Brett reached up and rubbed his beard, his eyes thoughtful. "Funny how you and her ended up here at the same time, all these years later."

"We went to dinner last night."

Brett switched his shrewd gaze to Jon. "Oh, yeah?"

"Yeah."

"And?"

Jon filled his cup from the orange cooler again, taking a minute to get away from Brett's blazing eyes. "I like her, okay? But…." He looked out over the endless horizon, the undulating fields, imagining he could see the little town of Three Rivers, where he'd never wanted to come.

He turned back to Brett. "But she just moved here to help Heidi open her bakery, and well, I threw a fit about even coming here for a few months to work."

Brett started nodding before Jon finished speaking. "What do you have lined up after this?"

Jon didn't want to say "nothing," but he did anyway.

Brett gave him the courtesy of thinking for several minutes while Jon munched on the candy bar. He did feel new life entering his bloodstream from the sugar, and he took off his cowboy hat and wiped his forehead.

"Maybe God brought you here to reconnect," Brett finally said.

Jon had already entertained that idea, and told Brett so.

He held up his hands. "Okay, I won't counsel you. I'm just sayin' that it's not the first time the Lord has used Three Rivers to help two people reconnect." He stacked his cup on the top of the orange cooler, whistled for Luis, who had wandered out onto the plains, and started up the ladder to resume work on the roof.

Jon took a few extra minutes in the shade, contemplating how he felt and what Brett had said. He mulled over possibilities for a long-term relationship with Grace, but before he could truly come up with one viable option, the woman who'd been tormenting his every waking thought for the past twenty-four hours came walking toward him.

# CHAPTER TWENTY-ONE

Grace had begged Heidi to wait until lunch—when all the cowhands would come to the house anyway—to allow samples of the goods they'd baked that morning. She didn't mind traipsing all over the ranch—it was one way to get in her steps for the day—but she didn't want to face Jon again until they could be alone.

Yet there he stood, alone, in the shadowy doorway of the barn he'd been working on all morning. Yes, she'd taken a peek here and there in between batches of sourdough and honey wheat, and while the cupcakes baked, she'd brainstormed staple flavors of frostings and fillings while she stood at the wide wall of windows in the kitchen.

Jon had been on the roof all morning, his focus admirable, his work ethic second-to-none. Why, oh why, had Heidi timed her delivery of samples with his morning break?

"Hey," she said as she approached with a tray of her cupcakes clutched in her hands. She really wanted him to like them, as if his opinion alone could resurrect her failed business in Dallas.

"Salted caramel chocolate," she said indicating the cupcakes on her left with her chin. "And peanut butter chocolate chip. Oh, and Heidi sent samples of her bread too. Sourdough and honey wheat. She says she'll be making sandwiches out of the bread at noon. Everyone is welcome to come eat lunch at the homestead."

Jon patted his flat stomach. "I just ate."

Her spirits deflated. "I made the cupcakes. You like chocolate." She hated that the desperation in her voice had sounded so loudly.

"Look, Grace—"

"Okay," she said loudly as she moved to the ladder. "Boys, there are cupcakes here."

It took less than ten seconds for Brett to shimmy down the ladder. He took one of the peanut butter cupcakes Grace had presented him with, and the look of pure bliss on his face brought a smile to Grace's face.

"Lunch at noon," she told him and Luis before turning toward the equine therapy center. Kelly and Chelsea had spent the bulk of the morning talking about Pete and his program, who they worked with, and how Pete needed more cowhands to help because his clientele had expanded so much.

"Grace, wait."

She turned at the plea in Jon's voice, but she didn't give him the satisfaction of a verbal answer. Instead, she cocked her hip and waited.

"I want one of those caramel ones."

She made him to come to her, her pulse speeding with every step he took. He selected the smallest of the cupcakes, though they all seemed to be the same size. His eyes didn't leave hers as he took a bite, the whipped cream smearing across his upper lip. Her gaze dropped to his mouth, and everything inside her wanted to lean closer and lick the cream from his lips.

Startled at the strong urge, she stepped back. "Enjoy." She turned before he could see the burning in her face.

"Grace, I don't live in Three Rivers."

A few seconds passed before his words registered in her ears. A few more for her to face him again and set the tray of goodies on the ground, her movement slow and jerky at the same time. "Okay," she said to the top of his cowboy hat, as he'd ducked his head to finish his cupcake.

He licked his fingers and met her eye. "I don't live here, and I don't…." He exhaled and looked away.

"You're not interested," Grace said. "It's okay, Jon. Really." Her heart would recover. He'd only been in her life for one day. Surely it wouldn't take that long to get over him. Certainly not as long as last time. She started to move away again.

"Wait, what?" His fingers landed on her bare upper arm, sending electricity to her fingertips and into her forehead. "Of course I'm interested." His hand slid down her arm and into hers. "I'm really interested in *you*. I'm not interested in living in Three Rivers."

Ah, so there it sat. She blinked at him, not quite sure which part of what he'd said to process first. The fact that he was interested in her? Or that he'd been cold and distant that morning to deliberately push her away because he wasn't a permanent resident of the town where she now lived?

"I—How long will you be here?" She examined the worksite behind him as if the wood could tell her when the barn would be finished.

"Through Christmas probably. I was hopin' to be home for the holidays, actually." He ran his free hand up the back of his neck, disturbing his hat the slightest bit. "I'm sorry about this morning. I don't know if you noticed, but—"

"I noticed." She squeezed his fingers. "And it's okay. We don't have to get married by Christmas." She smiled up at him, leaning into his body a little bit more and taking his other hand with hers. "Right?"

Heat and desire ran through his eyes as he gazed down on

her. She lost herself to the chemistry between them, the current that connected him to her, the shelter of his cowboy hat as he dipped his face closer to hers.

For one breathtaking moment, she thought he'd kiss her right then. Her lips tingled in anticipation of meeting his again. Sure, she'd kissed him before, but it had been a long time and she couldn't quite remember the taste of him, the shape of his mouth against hers. And she wanted to.

His lips skated across her cheek, landing in the hollow just below her ear. "So, what are we gonna do?"

"Do?" She mimicked his hushed tone, her hands sliding up his impressive biceps to hold onto his shoulders. His kiss, though it hadn't landed on her lips, had rendered her weak.

"It's only a few weeks until Christmas."

"It's two and a half months until Christmas, Jon." She giggled, the sound fading into a gasp as his breath coasted across her skin.

"It's too soon," he whispered.

Something clattered above them, and Grace jumped out of Jon's arms, startled and embarrassed at the same time.

"Jon?" Brett called. "Oh, there you are. You comin'?"

Grace had the feeling that Brett had seen their embrace and done his best to spare them the embarrassment of catching them.

"Yeah." Jon didn't look away from her. "I'm comin'."

"See you at lunch."

He took a couple of steps backward and lifted his hand in farewell, before turning and striding toward the ladder. She watched him haul his tall, muscular frame up the rungs and disappear onto the roof.

With giddiness galloping through her veins, a sense of uncertainty also tainted her thoughts.

*A lot can happen in two and a half months*, she told herself as she went to deliver more samples.

Jon adored everything Grace had a hand in creating. The bread was light and fluffy on Tuesday during lunch. The cupcakes on Wednesday possessed just the right balance of sweetness and saltiness and savory-ness. The piecrust on Thursday melted in his mouth. By Friday morning, everything in Jon felt wound tight.

He woke before his alarm, the first time in months, with Grace swimming in his head. The smell of her perfume teased him though it wasn't present. The silkiness of her skin made his fingers itch. The softness of her neck called to him.

He rose, as frustrated with himself as with the situation. He wanted to kiss her more than he wanted to breathe. But he also didn't want to kiss her and start something he couldn't finish. *Not fair, not fair,* floated through his mind. He didn't want to string her along for the next two months only to leave town when the job was done but the relationship wasn't.

*Why start a relationship?* he asked himself as he stepped into the shower. He'd been asking himself the same question for days. He still hadn't found an answer. With a start that made him slip, he realized maybe he should've been asking a different question.

Why *not* start a relationship?

People had long-distance relationships all the time. And Oklahoma City wasn't that far from Three Rivers. And she'd be working a lot anyway, getting the bakery started.

With a lighter heart and muscles that weren't as tight as springs, he headed out to the patio, almost tripping over Grace as he came face-to-face with her sittin' in the very rocking chair where he'd been aiming to enjoy his morning coffee. The hot liquid sloshed over the lip of the mug and onto the back of his hand.

"Grace," he gasped. He switched the mug to his other hand

and licked the coffee from his hand. "Just a sec." He returned to the kitchen and ran cold water over his burning hand. It cooled in only a few seconds—long enough for her to stand and lean in the doorway, effectively blocking his escape from the basement.

Behind him, Brett's alarm went off, and Jon heard the man start to stir. "What are you doin' here so early?"

"This isn't that early," she said by way of answer.

"It's barely six-thirty." He pointed to the coffee pot. "You want some?"

She lifted a travel cup. "Brought my own."

Jon felt trapped, unsure of why she was here and how he could get outside to the fresh air faster. He stepped toward her, taking in the magnificence of her long legs and accentuated curves as she leaned her shoulders into the doorframe. "Want to sit out here?"

She backed out of the doorway and he stepped past her. "You can have the rocker." He took a position on the low wall next to the steps and took a sip of his coffee. "So if this isn't early, what is?"

Collapsing into the rocking chair, she let out a sigh and sipped her own coffee. "My internal alarm goes off at three a.m. Side-effect of pastry school." She leaned her head back and closed her eyes. Jon watched her, his gaze sweeping over the gentle column of her neck, her shoulders. The white top she wore was gauzy and see-through to the aqua tank underneath. Jon's leg muscles bunched and he didn't dare lift his coffee mug to his mouth for fear he wouldn't be able to swallow.

"Did you make anything delicious this morning?" he asked, though she'd brought herself and she was certainly delectable enough.

"No, I took a long bath and read a book this morning." She opened her eyes, smiled, and lifted that lucky coffee mug to her mouth. Jon had never wanted to be an inanimate object so badly.

He hadn't asked her to dinner again. He hadn't made the mistake of holding her in plain sight again. He hadn't done more than get her number and text her for hours after he finished working each afternoon. He wasn't sure why. Indecision, probably. After all, Jon was the king of indecision.

"You want to go to church with me on Sunday?" she asked.

He raised his eyes to her, but she continued to rock in the chair as if asleep. "Sure." Kicking a grin in her direction, he added, "Doesn't start until eleven. Think you can stay awake that long, sleepyhead?"

Her eyes opened, but they didn't focus for a few minutes. When she caught him smiling at her, she rolled her eyes. "Maybe. Maybe not. Could be an adventure."

"I could use a little adventure."

"I'll say. The most exciting thing you do is text past ten p.m."

A flash of guilt stole through him. "I didn't know you got up at three a.m.," he protested. "In fact, I don't know anyone who gets up that early. It's insane."

She yawned. "It's so quiet here."

"I'll stop talking so you can go back to sleep." He watched her eyes drift closed again. "Honest, Gracie, I wouldn't have texted so late if I'd known you got up so early."

She smiled in his general direction without opening her eyes. "It's okay. You can make it up to me by taking me to the picnic after church. I heard it's good."

The thought of being seen in public with a woman as beautiful and kind as Grace made his mouth feel like he'd been sucking on cotton balls. The coffee didn't help. "It is."

"Mm." She seemed to actually fall asleep right there on the patio, and Jon relaxed in a way he hadn't for the past five days. Just being with her, here, alone, felt comfortable. In every other situation, he'd felt like he was playing a part, acting. But when it was just him and her, he didn't need to be anyone but himself.

And for the second time in the past five days, Jon knew he was in big trouble. Because Grace was making it harder and harder for him to leave Three Rivers.

---

Jon held Grace's hand through the service, and while he gave her the opportunity to let go before they stepped out of the chapel, she didn't. In fact, she slid her hand up his arm to the crook of his elbow and held on tight. They strolled to the park along with families and other couples, Brett several paces ahead of them with Squire and Kelly and their kids.

He hadn't become friends with a whole lot of people in Three Rivers. He hadn't seen the need. He lived out at the ranch; he worked out at the ranch. The only time he even went to town was for groceries and to attend church. He'd gone to the picnic a few times, mostly with women Kelly had set him up with. A couple of them eyed him now, with the gorgeous Grace hanging on his arm.

She charmed everyone outgoing enough to approach her. She told them all the same story: she'd moved to town to help Heidi start her bakery. The mere mention of Heidi Ackerman made everyone smile and accept Grace—and by extension, Jon—with chuckles and "welcome, y'all"s.

To his surprise, Grace didn't put any desserts on her plate. "You don't eat sweets on the weekend?" he asked as he picked up two chocolate chip cookies.

"Those aren't homemade," she hissed to him. "I'm picky." She took a cup of lemonade. "And if you must know, I do try to limit my sugar intake sometimes. Not all of us work out all day long for a living." The way her eyes swept the height of his body made a blush burst to life everywhere she looked.

He took the opportunity to once again admire her curves,

though he tried to make it seem like this was the first time he'd noticed her body. "You look fine to me."

"Fine?" Her eyebrows went up with her voice. "You're *so* kind, Mister Carver. I know I have a few extra pounds on me. But you know what they say." She sashayed away a few steps.

Jon hurried to get his own cup of lemonade and follow her. "No, Grace, I have no idea what they say."

"Never trust a skinny chef." She flashed him a flirtatious smile as she sat at a picnic table no one had claimed yet. He sat across from her, thinking he wouldn't be able to control himself if he sat right next to her. The urge to hold her hand had him clenching his fists and the desire to kiss her drove all other thoughts from his mind.

He participated in the conversation with Brett and Squire and Pete, but he wasn't exactly sure what he'd said. He ate, but he didn't know how anything tasted. The picnic began to break up as some families left and others moved to play horseshoes or volleyball.

"You want to go for a walk?" he asked as he stood and collected their plates. "There's a path around the park, and over in that corner, there's a duck pond." He nodded to the farthest corner from the picnic tables.

"Sure." Grace stood too, and when Jon returned, she held hands with Julie, Pete's little three-year-old. "She wants to come."

Jon crouched in front of the little girl. "Oh, yeah? Want to feed the ducks?" The little girl stared at him with wide, serious eyes. "All right, then. Let's go."

They'd taken a few slow steps away when Chelsea said, "Julie, honey. You can't go."

"Mama—"

Chelsea shook her head. "No, Daddy's got to get back to check on the horses." She looked at Grace with an edge in her eye that Jon couldn't identify. "You said you'd help, remember?"

She extended her hand toward her daughter. "Come on. We're going."

Julie looked like she might cry, but Grace bent down and said something to her, which caused the girl to release her hand and take her mother's instead.

Jon claimed Grace's other hand, squeezing it tightly as they stepped onto the path. The noise of the picnic faded the farther they walked, and Grace tilted her head back and looked into the bright autumn sky. "Tell me why you don't like it here."

He took a deep breath, his body filling with gratitude for his health, his job, his seemingly easy life. "I don't know."

She scoffed. "That's a cop-out. You know."

Jon half-appreciated her candor and was half-annoyed at her nosiness. He hadn't had anyone push him like this before. At least not for a long time.

"I'm more of a big-city type of guy," he said.

"You still in Oklahoma City?"

"My father's firm is there."

"Is it still your father's?"

"No."

"So you own it."

"Yeah."

"But you're not there." She finally turned her head to look at him. "How are you living here for this job?" He heard the "why" in the question too.

"I have a foreman and a floor manager who actually run the business," he explained. "I work on projects when I'm in town, if they need me. Otherwise, I take the jobs that are out of town. It's easier."

"Easier?"

Jon felt weary. He wished he had the strength and endurance of the tall trees that lined the path, effectively shading them and blocking this conversation from the rest of the world.

"Most of my men have families," he said. "It's harder for them to leave town. It's not hard for me."

"Even when you have to go somewhere you don't like?"

He nudged her with his hip. "You always this inquisitive?"

She paused and looked back down the path the way they'd come. "I am when I'm trying to find a solution to a problem."

His arms seemed to have a mind of their own as they wound around her waist and drew her closer to him. "Oh? What's the problem?"

"You leaving town." She looked right at him, open and honest and unassuming.

"That's a problem for you?" he teased, though a vein of seriousness rode underneath his playful tone.

She leaned into him and wrapped her hands around the back of his neck. "Oh, it's a big problem." She lifted onto her toes. "I'm going to kiss you now, okay? Is that going to be a problem for you?"

"Oh, yeah," he said, his tone turning deep and husky at the same time his pulse shot to the top of his skull. "It's gonna be a big problem."

Grace gripped the back of his cowboy hat in her fingers and tilted it off his head. "You don't want me to?"

"Grace, kissing you is all I've thought about since I saw you strumming my guitar on the patio." He leaned down to meet her lips with his. A shiver shot down his spine with the first touch, and then he drew a breath and molded his mouth to hers for a deeper exploration of her lips.

"Definitely a *huge* problem," he whispered before kissing her again.

## CHAPTER TWENTY-TWO

Kissing Jon under the Texas trees felt more magical than Grace remembered. Of course, last time, she'd kissed him on her front porch after the homecoming dance. There wasn't a brightly shining sun or a whisper of a breeze through decades-old trees. Or the worry that one of them would leave town in two months.

She didn't want to complicate his life, but at the same time, she totally did. She wanted to kiss him in the middle of the night before she left for the bakery, and then have him wake her with a kiss when he got back from his construction project that night.

The strength of her ideas startled her a bit—enough for Jon to notice and break the kiss. She stood in the circle of his arms and pressed her cheek against his chest to find his heart hammering. She smiled to know she elicited such a response from such a strong man.

"So," she said. "We need to figure out what to do."

He stiffened the slightest bit. "Do we? Can't we just, I don't know, go to dinner and sit by each other at church and kiss by the duck pond every chance we get?"

Grace wanted to, and she sighed into him. "I don't think you get into town much. Seems like kissing at the duck pond is off the table."

His grip along her waist tightened. "I can make the drive."

She laughed at the sexy bite in his tone. "All right, handsome. Let's see if this pond is all you said it was." She slipped out of his arms at the same time she laced her fingers through his. They walked the circumference of the park, the conversation as easy as the fall breeze, but deep inside, Grace harbored worry.

Worry that Jon really meant what he'd said about pursuing a more casual relationship. Worry that Jon didn't want to commit. Worry that Jon wouldn't stay in town, even for her.

She'd just need to change his mind. Filled with determination—especially after he followed her home and kissed her so completely she couldn't think, or breathe, or stand—Grace decided to do everything she could to make him fall in love with Three Rivers.

If only she knew how.

---

"A HALLOWEEN PARTY?" JON GLANCED UP FROM THE invitation Grace had given him. "I'm not dressin' up."

"It's not required." She pointed to the asterisk that said as much. "Heidi just wants to test out her baking on as many people as possible. She claims the cowhands will eat anything she gives them."

Over the past two weeks, Grace had streamlined the menu, the baking schedule, the entire process. And she wanted to experiment. See if she could make an entire bakery's worth of treats in one day and have them be edible. Have them be something people would pay for.

So, yes, the Halloween party had been her idea, though she was more than willing to let Heidi play hostess.

"It's at my house," Grace said. "Since Heidi's condo is too small to hold as many people as she thinks will come."

Jon cocked one eyebrow at her. "You realize the whole town will come."

Grace gave him her best smile. "We're counting on it. If they taste the treats and like them, they'll be more likely to come and pay when we open."

"They'll come no matter what," he mumbled as he swung his head away from her.

"What does that mean?" A sick feeling took root in Grace's stomach.

"It means that Heidi Ackerman is Three Rivers royalty. If she opens a bakery in town, people will come just because it's her."

Grace swallowed down a fresh wave of bitterness, because what he'd said was true. "Well, it's not Heidi's baking."

"Doesn't matter," Jon said. "It has her name on it."

As if the pressure Grace carried wasn't heavy enough. "I need you to come."

He focused on her again. "You *need* me to come?" His eyes sharpened, taking on a dangerous edge she found exciting. So exciting that a grin formed on her face.

"I want you to come, and yes, I need you to come. I...I don't want to be the only one there without someone they know."

"You know people."

"I know three people. And they'll all have husbands and children and other friends there. So I need a friend there too."

He inched closer to her. "A friend?"

Grace shrugged one shoulder. "Sure. We're friends."

He growled, one hand sweeping around her waist in a smooth movement. "No, we're not friends." He touched his lips to her shoulder and a tremor quaked in her center.

"Can I call you my boyfriend, then?" She cocked her head as he stiffened. "I guess not. That has the word friend in it, and we're not friends." She smirked at him, but he stared at her without any hint of amusement.

He brought his mouth to hers with all the urgency of a tropical storm, and she got swept up in the cool touch of his lips, the sweet taste of his tongue, the gentle pressure on her back. When he drew back, he whispered, "Fine, you can call me your boyfriend."

She exhaled, trying to will strength back into her limbs before he released her. "And you'll come to the party?"

"Yeah, all right. I'll come to the party."

She stepped away and pulled the hem of her shirt down to straighten it. "I'm glad we've established some things today." She flounced away while he fisted the Halloween party invitation.

---

A week later, Jon showed up at Grace's house a couple of hours before the party began. He pulled all the way into her open garage, like she'd instructed him to, put his truck in park, and sat in it. Parking here would mean he couldn't leave until the very end of the party. After everyone else had left. Part of him rejoiced at being able to spend so much time with Grace. The other part had been dying for seven solid days.

Because Jon didn't go to parties. Certainly not Halloween parties. He certainly saw nothing worth celebrating about the holiday.

Movement caught his peripheral vision and he reached to unbuckle his seatbelt. "Hey," he called to Grace as he got out of his truck. "I brought the dry ice."

"Perfect." She met him at the tailgate with a rolling cooler. "You need this?"

He pulled the cooler full of dry ice from the truck bed. "No, I think I got it."

"Okay, let's put it in the kitchen. Most of the party will be in the backyard, but I've never trusted coolers to keep things cold."

Jon chuckled as he followed her into her house. He'd never been inside, because they either went out after he finished working, or she stayed out at the ranch for the evening, or he followed her home and kissed her pressed up against her front door.

He kicked the door closed behind him and put the cooler where she indicated he should. Then he took her in his arms and kissed her, his nerves settling and his stomach swooping with her eager response. "I've missed you the last couple of days," he murmured into her hair as he rubbed slow circles on her back.

"Mm, that's nice to hear." She pulled back and grinned at him. "Now come on. You promised to help and well, this isn't exactly helping."

"It's not?"

"Not the kind of help I need right now." She handed him a stack of serving trays and indicated a row of folding tables that had been set up in her backyard. "Put these trays on those tables."

"Yes, ma'am." He allowed her to boss him around, putting brownies on some trays, and cookies on another, and tarts on still more. By the time Heidi arrived, Jon thought Grace had surely done everything worth doing.

But Heidi brought in a basket filled with black and orange decorations, and she and Grace set about placing and adjusting and fixing every witch and each skeleton and all the bats until they were exactly right.

Jon helped at first, but when he caught Grace moving a cauldron he'd placed too close to the edge of the table, he took to carrying things from the house to the yard until the women declared things done.

By then, Chelsea and her family had arrived, along with Kelly and her family. Garth Ahlstrom, the foreman at Three Rivers Ranch, pulled in just as Jon closed Heidi's trunk and pocketed her keys.

He exchanged a hello with the foreman and his wife, a sharp stab of unexpected longing knifing him between the ribs as Garth put his son on his shoulders and headed through the garage. Jon stood stock still, staring after them, unsure as to what he was feeling and why. He'd never thought much about having a family. Never envisioned himself as married. Never even considered being a dad.

But now...his gaze wandered to the glowing square of a window in Grace's house, and he thought he'd like to be a family with her.

Anger accompanied the thought. *So what?* he asked himself—and God—with an edge of fury in the question.

"I'm not moving here," he vowed as he marched through the garage and into Grace's house. "I'm not."

---

JON MANAGED TO ACT HIS WAY THROUGH THE PARTY. He mingled and mixed and played games and ate more than a man should be able to consume. He held Grace's hand, and kept his arm around her waist, and pressed his lips to her temple. If anyone had any doubt about the status of his relationship with her before the party, they certainly wouldn't after.

The last of the partiers finally departed, leaving Grace and Jon with Heidi. Her husband had been smart and driven a separate car.

"Feedback was amazing, Grace." Heidi beamed at her. "I think the recipes we used today are the ones we should go with."

"I still want to try something different with that pumpkin pie tart."

"That will be a seasonal item anyway." Heidi's joviality faded.

Grace sighed and her eyes closed in a long blink. Jon knew she didn't stay up until eleven p.m., and he wondered if she'd be able to sleep past three tonight. "You're right. I'll tweak it as we go."

"Thank you, Grace." She picked up one basket of décor.

"Let me help you, ma'am." Jon collected a box of empty trays, which had held loaves of bread when she'd arrived. It took him a couple of trips, but he got everything out to her car and Heidi on her way in just a few minutes.

When he returned to the house, he found Grace fast asleep, her head cradled in her arms on the dining room table. He paused and watched her, the gentle rise of her upper back as she breathed in and out bringing a smile to his face.

He stepped toward her and crouched. "Grace," he said, but she didn't stir. For the first time—the first real time—he considered relocating to Three Rivers. He brushed her hair off the side of her face, the touch as electrifying as it was soft.

"I don't know if I can do it, Gracie," he whispered. "I really don't like small towns."

She sighed, and he tried to wake her again, this time succeeding as her eyes flew open. He soothed her by rubbing his hand up and down her arm. "Hey, you should go to bed before falling asleep."

She gave him a bleary smile, he helped her stand, and she leaned into him, her eyes already closed again. "Thanks for your help, Jon."

"Anytime, Gracie Lou." She didn't protest at the use of her nickname, simply tilted her head back and stretched up to kiss him good-night. He obliged, a river of guilt flowing through him. He shouldn't kiss her, lead her on, feel things for her when he was planning on leaving by Christmas.

# CHAPTER TWENTY-THREE

Grace leaned in the garage doorway and watched Jon back out of her driveway. She closed the garage door, the rumbling sound matching the quaking in her stomach.

"He's not going to stay," she said as the echoes of sound rattled around the garage. "You heard him." She turned, let the door fall closed, and locked it. She wasn't sure what she'd hoped Jon would do when she pretended to stay asleep when he tried to wake her. Kiss her like Sleeping Beauty? Declare his undying love for her when he thought she couldn't hear?

She shook her head, the danger of crying very real and very close. She certainly hadn't expected him to whisper that he didn't think he could stay in town. She'd stirred the next time he said her name, and she couldn't help kissing him good-bye. She didn't want to have a hard conversation near midnight, when her brain wasn't operational and her heart felt like it had been punctured by a coil of barbed wire.

A tear fell and Grace swiped it away. Would she ever feel successful? Her failed cupcakery hung over her like a thundercloud, and she couldn't hold back the waterworks this time.

After a good cry and a long shower, Grace took a steeling breath and squared her shoulders. She'd just do here what she'd had to do to get into pastry school. Try, try again. She'd dreamed of attending culinary school in New York City, and it had taken three attempts before she'd gotten in.

*Maybe it'll just take a third time with Jon too.* She pulled on pajamas, brushed out her hair, and fell into bed, exhausted. But she didn't want to break-up with him now and hope for a third chance meeting in the future.

*Help me understand,* she prayed. At once, a sense of calmness filled her, and she knew she needed to trust in the Lord's timing. She'd done it before with culinary school. With her cupcakery—although she'd lost her first shop in Dallas, Grace knew it was only a matter of timing before she'd own another bakery.

She'd just have to trust God regarding Jon, too.

---

Rain came with November, and Grace spent days inside, baking. Since Halloween and tasting her treats, the townspeople had been calling Grace and placing custom orders. With the bakery's storefront unavailable, she fielded the calls, managed the payments, and either did the baking herself or called Heidi to get the orders filled.

At first it was a birthday cake for a five-year-old's party. But by the third week, with Thanksgiving around the weekend, Grace found her phone ringing while she was on it.

She hung up with Amy Garrison, who had just ordered a half-dozen pies for her family's celebration the following week. Before she checked her messages, she dialed Heidi.

"Hello, dear. How's the baking going?"

"We have a bit of a problem," Grace started.

Heidi sighed. "What is it now?" Though she sounded tired, she didn't show signs of frustration. Grace admired her for her baking ability as well as her seemingly endless well of patience.

"Amy Garrison just ordered six pies for pickup on Wednesday." Her phone beeped, indicating another incoming call. "And my phone won't stop ringing. When do we cut off the orders?"

A few beats of silence had Grace picturing Heidi's wise face contemplating her choices. "I'd hate to turn people away...."

"We already have sixty-six pies to deliver on Wednesday alone," Grace said. She could only bake four at a time. Heidi could cook an additional four. Without professional ovens and bakery-grade equipment, she'd allocated eight slots of baking time for her and Heidi for a total of sixty-four pies.

"You talked about an assembly line once," Heidi said. "Tell me more about that."

"Well, we make all the pie crusts and fillings—it helps that we're only offering three varieties this season—and send several uncooked but ready-to-bake pies out to the ranch. Chelsea and Kelly could probably bake...sixteen or so pies each." Grace felt bone-weary, and doing the math right now seemed impossible. But if Kelly and Chelsea could take two pie-baking slots each, they could bake sixteen pies in the morning and Grace could get them out to customers in the afternoon.

"So we can take on thirty-two more."

"Only thirty," Grace said firmly. "We're already over by two on our own lists."

"Thirty more then," Heidi said. "I guess I better get to the grocery store—and call Kelly and Chelsea."

Grace agreed and said good-bye. She answered the two messages she'd received and then updated the community Facebook page that only two dozen slots remained for pie orders. A thrill ran from the top of her head to the soles of her feet.

Though backed by the iconic Heidi Ackerman, her baking

seemed to finally be striking the right notes with people. Her mother's voice snaked through her head, eliminating the rising euphoria.

*You should've started in your own kitchen, Grace.* Her mother had been trying to help, Grace knew. But that didn't make her words hurt any less. *You should've gotten established before trying a storefront.*

In the end, her mother had been right. Grace knew it. Her mother knew it. Everyone knew it. And many bakers did exactly what she'd tried to skip—what she was doing now with Heidi, baking from her home kitchen and trying to fill as many orders as possible.

The last pie slots sold out in the next half hour, and Grace headed over to Heidi's to make the master shopping list. Along the way, her phone chimed, igniting a sense of dread in her stomach as heavy as a brick. She didn't want to tell another person no. She'd put it on social media that they were full.

She didn't check the message until she'd parked at Heidi's. Jon had texted, and that sent Grace's stomach toward the heavens. She'd cooled their relationship over the past few weeks, citing her increased workload and the fact that she wasn't coming out to the ranch everyday. He still called, and texted, and took her to dinner sometimes. They sat next to one another at church, but she hadn't gone to another picnic, unable to face that park where she'd experienced the most perfect kiss of her life.

She hit call instead of texting him back. "What's up?" she asked as she got out of her car.

"Nothing's up. Just checking in." Like he was her father or something. Grace couldn't put her finger on why his statement annoyed her so much.

"Busy," she said. "About to meet with Heidi."

"I saw that you filled all your Thanksgiving pie slots."

"Yep." Had he called to talk about her baking? He'd never

done that before, and Grace wondered if they'd hit a new low in their conversation.

"That's too bad," he said. "I was hoping you and I could enjoy a candlelit dinner for two, with a pecan pie for dessert."

She frowned at the flirty tone, at his suggestion that they'd spend Thanksgiving together. "I thought you were going home for Thanksgiving," she said. "You're not working, right?" She distinctly remembered him telling her that Brett wanted to be home to celebrate Thanksgiving with his family, who would then be coming to Texas until the project was finished. Jon had complained about having to move into one of the empty cowboy cabins and "fend for himself."

"Those plans fell through," he said.

"So I'm your second choice, is that it?" Her words flew from her mouth before she could tame them, and they had definite bite.

"Grace—"

She paused on the sidewalk at the base of Heidi's condo. "Look, Jon, I think we should just be done. We've been playing around, and it's been fun, but this isn't serious."

The silence on the other end of the line made her check her phone to make sure they hadn't been disconnected.

"It isn't?"

She almost rolled her eyes. "No, it isn't. You don't live here, and you have no intention of moving here. I do live here, and I'm happy here, and I'm hoping this bakery will be a huge success so I can keep living here."

"It's a—"

"Don't say it's a technicality," Grace said, her emotions spiraling up and out of control. She'd let him console her before, whisper words about how they didn't need to decide anything now. But not anymore. It was time to end this relationship, and she knew it.

"I'm sorry, Jon," she said. "I like you. Given enough time, I'm certain I could fall in love with you. But I'm not willing to do that over the phone or on the Internet." She took a deep breath to subdue the tears, but they wouldn't be tamed. "I have to go."

"Grace—" She heard him say as she hung up. In the next moment, a sob wrenched itself from her throat and tears painted her cheeks. She quieted herself quickly, taking a few precious minutes to make sure she was presentable before knocking on Heidi's door. The woman still saw her distress—or maybe she sensed it. She seemed to have a way of knowing things no one said or exhibited.

"Grace." She rushed forward. "What's wrong?"

Grace wanted to tell someone. She wanted support and encouragement from her friends, from Heidi. So she told her all about Jon.

---

JON STARED AT HIS CELL PHONE LIKE IT HAD MORPHED into a four-headed dog. Had Grace seriously just broken up with him? Over the phone?

*You haven't really given her a reason to stay,* he told himself as he stuffed the phone in his back pocket. Her accusation about being his second choice rang true. So true it hurt Jon's heart to think about.

She had come second these past two months. Second to the job. Second to his own desires. Second to who he'd spend Thanksgiving with. And now that his brother had given his parents a trip to New York for their thirty-fifth wedding anniversary, they wouldn't be in Oklahoma City next week.

Jon suddenly had nowhere to spend the holidays. He couldn't join the Ackerman's festivities, as Grace would be there.

"I'm heading back to get a drink," he yelled up to Brett, who called back to bring him a bottle of Gatorade. Jon stomped away from the construction site, angry at himself, at Texas, at the world.

*What should I do?* he asked as his fury faded, leaving only desperation and helplessness.

*Make a decision,* came into his mind, as loud as if someone had appeared next to him and spoken aloud.

Jon knew he hadn't made a decision regarding Grace. And that his indecision had hurt her, though he'd been trying not to do so. If he were being honest with himself—and there was no better time to be honest with himself—he'd known something was off since Halloween. Grace hadn't inconvenienced herself to see him. She didn't drive out to the ranch when she could've. She arrived late to church and claimed she was too tired to go to the picnic. Even when he invited her to dinner and kissed her good-night afterward, he didn't feel the same level of passion as he had previously.

"You messed up," he practically yelled at himself as he entered the basement. He tore a bottle of water from the fridge and drained it, but it didn't cool the fire raging in his chest. With certain clarity, he knew only one thing would: Grace Lewis.

Even the thought of her name acted as a fire extinguisher, and the flames cooled. He still didn't know what to do short of calling a realtor and then a moving company to get everything he owned from Oklahoma City to Three Rivers.

He plucked his phone from his back pocket, but he didn't call a realtor. He called his brother instead. "Hey, Cam. What are you and Erika doing for Thanksgiving?" He listened while his brother talked about the celebration Erika's family had planned.

"Think they have room for one more?" Jon closed his eyes as he waited for his brother to answer. He wasn't ready to go crawling back to Grace, not yet. If he did that, he knew there'd be no turning back. And that decision required thoughtful prayer—and a talk with his brother, who had always been able to steer him in the right direction.

# CHAPTER TWENTY-FOUR

By the time the last pie got picked up on Wednesday evening, Grace never wanted to see another pecan again. Or another can of pumpkin. Or another dozen eggs. She collapsed in the armchair in her living room, her eyes drifting closed.

A sense of accomplishment flooded her. She'd done it. She'd organized, made, baked, and delivered ninety-five pies in one day.

"Just think what you could do with an industrial kitchen," she told herself as she went to put in a frozen pizza for dinner. Tomorrow, she'd drive out to the ranch for the first time in weeks, and the thought of seeing Jon drove her nerves into a frenzy. He hadn't tried to call her, not once. He hadn't texted. He hadn't liked anything of hers on Facebook.

She didn't know what his plans were now that he wasn't going home to Oklahoma City, but she had to assume he would be at the homestead, ready to eat copious amounts of turkey and mashed potatoes.

Part of her mourned that he hadn't tried harder to get back together with her. The other part argued that Jonathan Carver was Jonathan Carver, and he hadn't tried to stay in touch when she'd moved eleven years ago. It wouldn't have been that hard. She could've done it too, but with him being silent, one year older, and about to graduate, she'd stayed away too.

She'd fantasized that this Christmas could've been celebrated as their eleven-year reunion, the opportunity they hadn't had as teenagers. Her heart hurt thinking about it, so she shelved the thoughts. She'd made it through the busiest day of her life, and tomorrow would be what tomorrow would be.

By the time she arrived at the ranch, lunch was about to start. She'd purposely left late, hoping to sneak in when the crowd wouldn't notice her. Of course, with Heidi there, that didn't work. She parted the sea of bodies and beelined for Grace as soon as she stepped through the French doors leading into the kitchen.

Heidi enveloped her in a motherly hug, and it was exactly what Grace needed in that moment. "Thank you, Heidi," she said as the woman stepped back.

"I was beginning to think you weren't going to come."

Grace swept the people in the kitchen, searching for Jon.

"He left last night," Heidi said. "Went to Wichita to be with his brother."

"Oh." Grace didn't know what else to say, didn't know how to make sense of the relief and simultaneous disappointment threading through her. She put on her happy face, the one she'd employed while she swept out her bakery for the last time, the one she wore while she drove from Dallas to Three Rivers, the one she used whenever she didn't want anyone to know how cracked under the surface she was.

Chelsea must've possessed some of her mother's x-ray vision, though, because after dinner and after pie and after the kids had been put down for naps and after the men had gone downstairs to watch football, she positioned herself next to Grace on the couch upstairs.

"Where's Jon?" she asked as she lifted a steaming cup of coffee to her lips.

"Wichita," Grace said.

"Heard you guys broke up."

Grace cut a sharp look in her direction. "From who?"

Chelsea waved her hand like the living room walls had told her. "He was in a real funk. It was obvious."

The idea of Jon being in a funk over their break-up brought Grace some satisfaction.

"What happened?" Chelsea asked as Kelly sat in the recliner opposite them.

Grace had always liked Chelsea, always trusted her with new recipes and old secrets. "He hates Three Rivers," she said.

Kelly gasped and Chelsea laughed. "I know how he feels."

"What?" Grace stared at her friend from Dallas.

"Remember when I moved here?" She glanced at Kelly. "I think I turned around three times on the way from Dallas. I hated it here...at first."

"I came back after a failed marriage," Kelly said. "Wasn't my idea of a great time either."

Grace had known Chelsea needed to leave Dallas. "I assumed you were...upset because of...you know."

"Danny's death," Chelsea said. "It's okay, Grace. I can talk about it now."

"I didn't know you didn't want to come to Three Rivers."

"Heavens, no." Chelsea laughed. "I left this place as fast as I could after high school. We both did."

Kelly nodded her agreement. "But I love it here now. It's quiet. Peaceful. Exactly where I want to raise my kids."

"All good points," Chelsea said, her eyebrows raised in Grace's direction.

"Jon and I—well, we didn't make it to the family and kids conversation. He wouldn't even talk about anything past Christmas." Bitterness surged up her throat.

Chelsea put her hand over Grace's. "Be patient with him. He probably doesn't know what he wants. Not everyone is as put together as you are."

Grace gave a mirthless laugh. "I am not put together." She felt like she was falling apart at the seams.

"You sure are," Chelsea said. "You went to pastry school, something you've dreamed about since you were ten. Who does that? Actually knows that they want to be when they're a child, and then does it?" She exchanged a glance with Kelly. "He's probably afraid. Worried he's not good enough for you."

"I bet he feels inadequate."

Grace listened to her friends in awe. She was not intimidating. No one—least of all Jon—should be afraid of her. And he was definitely good enough for her. The very idea that he wasn't seemed laughable. "Well, I think I'll go."

Chelsea squeezed her hand. "Okay, but Grace?" She peered up into Grace's face as she stood. "Just give him some time, all right?"

"Sure," Grace said, but she knew: Time didn't do anything. She'd given her cupcakery months to succeed, and all she'd done was dig herself deeper into debt. She drove home, more determined than ever that she'd done the right thing when she'd cut Jon loose.

---

JON ARRIVED AT THE ADDRESS HIS BROTHER HAD given him. The two-story brick house seemed to loom over him, shout at him that he should be in Texas and not Oklahoma. But he hadn't been able to stay, to face Grace. And the thought of spending Thanksgiving alone appealed to him even less.

He'd done that before—spent Thanksgiving with hundreds of other men in Iraq. No family. Just the watered down version of turkey, and the hope that he'd be home in time for Cam's wedding at Easter.

He'd made it then. He could do this now. He got out of the car and walked up to the front door, which opened before he arrived. Cam, his older brother, beamed at him before clasping him in a tight hug. "It's been too long, Jon."

"You're the one who lives in Maryland." Jon chuckled, though he'd secretly resented Cam for years because he'd left the carpentry business for Jon to handle. Now, though, none of those old feelings surfaced, and Jon realized he'd forgiven Cam, moved on.

Cam released him and welcomed him into the house. His wife, Erika, stood in the living room. A petite brunette, Jon felt like he might break her when he hugged her hello. She introduced him to her parents, who Jon thanked over and over for adding him to their guest list so last minute.

"What happened in Texas, anyway?" Cam asked.

Jon flashed him a warning look and smiled. The gesture felt wrong on his face. "I was plannin' to spend Thanksgiving in Oklahoma City," he said. "But *someone* gave *someone else* plane tickets to New York."

That shut Cam up. Thankfully. Jon wanted to talk about Grace, but in private, without the presence of several strangers, no matter how accommodating they were. That moment didn't come until much later that evening, after visiting and dinner and coffee on the screened-in back porch. A humming space heater kept the airy room warm enough, and the hot liquid definitely helped.

Erika swept a kiss across Cam's mouth and headed into the house with her parents and brother, leaving Jon alone with Cam. He enjoyed the silence for a few minutes, searching for a way to bring up Grace without giving too much away.

In the end, he simply blurted, "So I met a woman in Texas."

Cam put his coffee mug down and faced Jon. "Oh, yeah?"

"You might remember her." Though Jon didn't really think so. Cam was three years older than Jon, and Jon a year older than Grace. "Yeah, Grace Lewis."

Cam's blank expression indicated he did not remember Grace. And why should he? He hadn't been the one entranced by the woman's navy blue eyes, or captured by her laugh, or intrigued by her obsession with baking.

So Jon reminded him, though Cam still didn't have any memories of Jon's high school homecoming dance or Grace's sudden removal from his life. "And now she's back." He ran his hands through his hair. He'd left his cowboy hat in Texas, and he suddenly felt naked without it. "What are the chances she'd be in Three Rivers when I am?"

"Probably less than one percent." Cam gazed into the distance, though his degree was in statistics, and surely he knew the exact odds of Grace and Jon being in the same small Texas town at the same time.

Jon stewed, wishing he knew how to articulate to his brother what his problem was, what help he needed. Instead, he told him about Grace, about his hesitation to stay in tiny Three Rivers. He finally fell silent after he said, "Tell me what to do."

"Nope." Cam exhaled and stretched his arms above his head. "Not gonna tell you what to do, Jonny. You always wanted me to choose for you, and I did when we were growing up. But I can't do that here."

"Then what would you do?"

Cam leveled his gaze at Jon. "I'd ask myself if I liked this woman enough to want to see if I could fall in love with her. And if I do like her that much, I'd figure out what to do to keep her in my life long enough to know if we could have a future together."

Jon started nodding halfway through Cam's statement. "I like her enough."

"Do you hate Three Rivers that much?"

"I—" Jon's throat narrowed, and familiar frustration ran through him. "I don't know."

"I think you know what to do, then." Cam stood and entered the house, the screen door slapping behind him as he left Jon alone on the screened-in porch. He stared at the unfamiliar horizon and wondered why he cared where he lived. If Grace was there, he'd be happy. And if she wasn't....

He reached for his phone and dialed her, hoping she'd be forgiving enough to answer. Her line rang and rang, wringing his stomach tighter and tighter. She didn't pick up, and something clogged the back of Jon's throat.

Could he jump in his truck and drive the six hours back to Three Rivers? Show up on her doorstep and beg her to take him back?

He dialed her again, and this time he left a message. "Hey, Grace. It's Jon. I've been...." He sighed and threw caution to the wind. "I've been so stupid. Please forgive me. And please call me back." He wanted to add something more, but he couldn't say, "I love you." So he hung up with extreme exasperation pressing against the back of his tongue.

A half hour passed, wherein Jon pressed the power button on his phone every thirty seconds just to make sure it still had a charge. Finally, it rang. He fumbled it in his haste to answer, especially when Grace's name came up on the screen.

"Grace," he said. "Hey."

"Happy Thanksgiving," she said.

Jon tried to gauge her mood by her voice, but his heart beat so loudly in his ears, he couldn't. "Happy Thanksgiving to you too. Did you get my message?"

"Yes." A door slammed on her end of the line. "I didn't have service on the way back from the ranch. And you're lucky it's Thanksgiving and I'm feeling extra grateful for all I have—which I'll admit, I hope that includes you."

The wave of relief cascading over Jon rivaled a tsunami. He

collapsed back to the chair, not quite sure when he'd stood. "I'm so sorry, Grace. I wish I was there to tell you in person."

"Hearing it in your voice is enough."

"So what now?"

"Well, Jon, we'll need to talk about important things when you get back."

He leaned back in his chair, unwilling to let her go now that he had her on the line. "What about tonight?"

"I'm too tired to talk about serious things tonight." She yawned. "I was up early to make the pies for Thanksgiving dinner. Tell me about your trip."

Jon imagined Grace reclined in the armchair in her living room, her eyes already closed. He smiled and began to talk.

# CHAPTER TWENTY-FIVE

Grace's skin itched with anticipation. With the need to be doing something. She wasn't good at sitting, never had been. But with all the holiday orders fulfilled and nothing to do until Monday—and she wasn't even sure what she'd do then—Grace had a few days to herself.

Problem was, she didn't know what to *do* with herself. She'd driven through her favorite java hut and watched the sun rise over the river on the south side of town. Jon was driving back from Wichita today, but it was a long way, and she wasn't expecting him until at least afternoon.

Black Friday in Three Rivers started later than in other areas—no lines around the block before five a.m. here—and gradually the town came to life. Grace walked down Main Street, ducking into a few shops until she finally found a beautiful clothing boutique. She browsed through the clothes, the scarves, the shoes, looking for something cute to wear to church.

She tried on several things, made her purchases from a kind dark-haired woman named Andy, and headed home. It was only nine o'clock.

A level of exhaustion Grace hadn't experienced since pastry

school engulfed her, and she dropped her shopping bags at the mouth of the hall and dropped to the couch.

She woke to the gentle pressure of Jon's lips against her forehead, the masculine smell of pine trees and wood smoke making her smile and open her eyes.

"Hey," he whispered. "Sorry to wake you. You just looked too beautiful not to kiss."

"Smooth," she said as she lifted her arms to hug him. "I'm glad you came back." She enjoyed the weight of him against her, the electricity zipping down her neck when he kissed her there, the absolute joy coursing through her that he'd called, apologized, come back.

"Are you too tired to talk?" He traced his lips up her throat, and all thoughts of talking fled her mind. By the time he finally kissed her mouth, Grace's muscles felt like warm marshmallows. She twined her fingers through his dark, silky hair, and gave her whole self to him.

She finally put a knuckle of space between them, and his labored breathing indicated he enjoyed kissing her as much as she enjoyed kissing him. But there had to be more to this relationship than hot sparks and great kissing.

"What time is it?" she asked.

"Nearly two." He sat back on his haunches as she came to a sitting position on the couch. "Want to go grab lunch?"

Her stomach answered with a roar. She raked her fingers through her hair, trying to deny she'd slept for five hours and failing. She'd definitely slept for five hours. Jon stood and slid his hand down her shoulder. "You ready?"

"Sure." She collected her purse and followed him out to his truck. Her stomach twisted and untwisted on the drive there. She wanted him to start the conversation, because she felt like she'd said everything she needed to already.

But he told her about his visit with his brother, and the drive from Wichita, and how he wished he'd been able to taste one of her pies. After being shown to a booth, Jon finally fell silent. Grace ordered sweet tea and fixed her gaze on him, almost like she could communicate telepathically with him.

The waitress left to get their drinks, and Jon squirmed. "I'm not great at making decisions."

Grace blinked, unsure of where he was going. "Okay."

"No, it's not okay." He rubbed his hand up the back of his neck and looked away. "It's why I'm still in construction. I couldn't decide if I should go to school and if I did, what I should do."

"You don't like carpentry?"

"No, I do." He let out a frustrated breath. "I don't know how to articulate what I'm feeling." The waitress returned and took their orders, and Jon gulped his soda before meeting her eye again.

"You've always known what you wanted to be. And you went out there and did it." He reached across the table and took her hands in his. "I love that about you. But I'm not like that. I was raised in construction and I liked it. Cam didn't want to stick around, and I didn't have anything else to do...." He shrugged. "It's not that I'm *un*happy. It's just that I didn't *choose* carpentry. I'm not good at making choices. It's like...it's like, if I do, then I might not get what I want. I might be disappointed. I might fail."

Grace's chest heaved with emotion. Here was this handsome, talented man, looking at her with all the vulnerability of a scared boy. She squeezed his hands and opened her eyes wide to try to keep the tears back.

She couldn't quite get herself to speak yet, choked up as she was. He blinked a couple of times, the tendons in his neck tight, tight, tight.

"Do you know why I moved to Three Rivers?" Grace fought against the fear of telling him about all her failures. But at least she had them. Maybe if he knew about them, he'd know life could be great, despite setbacks and disappointments.

"To help Heidi open her bakery."

Grace shook her head. "Yes, because I needed a job after my cupcake shop in Dallas failed." She inhaled, relieved the previous emotion had settled back into her stomach. "And that was after it took me three tries to get into culinary school."

"Grace," Jon said, and she loved hearing him say her name. "I didn't know. I'm sorry." His jaw tightened and he let out an angry hiss. "Here I am crying about failing, and you.... I'm sorry."

She shook her head. "No, don't feel bad. I was just trying to let you know that I've failed. I understand the fear of it. But at least—" She cut herself off before she could say something that would hurt him further, drive him farther from her.

"At least you've tried," he finished for her. His fury faded, leaving behind the scared man again. "I want to try, Grace. With you. Can you give me a few more weeks to try?"

"Of course."

"You didn't even think about it."

"I don't need to think about it." And she didn't. She liked Jon, always had. She wanted to see if they could have a future together as badly as she'd wanted culinary school, as much as she'd wanted her cupcakery in Dallas, as desperately as she'd tried to hold onto it before admitting defeat.

Maybe she was doing the same thing here. She wasn't sure. She just knew she liked him enough to think she might be able to love him, and she didn't want to walk away before either of them knew for sure.

"You're too forgiving," he said.

"That's impossible," she said. "I don't think anyone can actually be *too* forgiving. Can they?"

"In some situations, yes, I think someone can be too forgiving."

"Well, this isn't one of those situations." She pulled her hands back across the table as the waitress appeared with their food. "I want to try too, Jon."

He flashed her a grateful smile, and Grace enjoyed a meal for the first time since she'd told Jon they should be done.

---

A WEEK LATER, JON HAD EXPERIENCED MORE happiness and more heartache than he ever had in his life. He'd realized that he'd never really lived before. Because he'd never *chosen* his life. As he realized his shortcomings, he struggled, but as he made decisions, the joy superseded the tough times.

*How's your day going?* he texted to Grace during his lunch hour.

*Okay, she said. I went for doughnuts this morning, and they didn't have any bacon maple bars.*

Jon wanted to make Grace happy, give her everything she desired. *Sorry, babe,* he texted. Then he called the bakery and asked them about a special order. They agreed to make a bacon maple bar the following day and save it for Grace. They didn't deliver, but Jon would drive to town himself and take the doughnut to her.

When he knocked on her front door, she didn't answer right away. He knew she was awake—the woman rose in the middle of the night. Concern spiked within him when she still didn't come after he'd knocked again.

He didn't want to call her—wanted the doughnut to be a surprise—but he pulled out his phone and paced down her front sidewalk. His thumb hovered above the call button when she came jogging down the road toward him.

She saw him a nanosecond after he noticed her, and he shoved his phone in his back pocket. She pulled out her earbuds. "What are you doing here?"

"You run?"

"I have to do something to keep the sweets I eat in check." She eyed the white bag in his hand. "What is that?"

"Bacon maple bar." He grinned as he held the pastry toward her.

"You didn't." She took the bag and peered inside. When she lifted her eyes back to his, Jon saw admiration in them. "Thank you." She stepped into his arms and kissed him. He didn't care that she was sweaty; he kissed her back.

# CHAPTER TWENTY-SIX

Over the next two weeks, Grace became used to waking up to late-night texts from Jon. He spoiled her constantly, asking her what her interests were, and planning romantic dates to the lesser known attractions in Three Rivers. Once, he'd taken her on an alphabet date—two of them, actually—where they did everything from apple eating contests for the letter A to taste all the types of cheeses at the cheese factory for T. She'd ridden horses, hiked hills, visited the botanical gardens.

Three Rivers had become ingrained in her soul. She loved the shops along Main Street. The friendliness of the townspeople. The close-knit community.

With the bakery only two weeks from opening, she'd started spending her days in the retail space downtown. Heidi had bought the end corner of a building that had suffered fire damage. She'd spent a lot to restore it, and the kitchen gleamed in the early morning light bulbs. Grace arrived at three-thirty and made muffins, brownies, and cookies before Heidi showed up at five to begin the bread.

By six-thirty, when they planned to open, Grace had a tray of samples ready for anyone who wanted to drive or walk by. With the amount of people tasting their toasted sourdough with apricot jam, or the lemon poppyseed muffins, Grace felt sure the bakery would be a success.

She left the bakery just after noon and strolled down the street, her thoughts circling a gift for Jon. With Christmas only days away, she needed something, and fast. She'd gotten to know him better these past few weeks, when they were finally able to talk about real things, their likes and dislikes, their dreams, their worries.

She'd learned that he did love construction, but didn't like being tied down. The freedom for him to travel to job sites was important to him. She'd learned that he loved staying up late, and Neapolitan ice cream, and watching documentaries. She'd already known he was a hard worker, but the fact was driven home as he and Brett labored to finish what she'd learned was a new horse training facility before Christmas.

"One more day," he'd told her yesterday, which meant he'd be done today.

He was planning to stay in Three Rivers for Christmas and the New Year as well as be there to support her and Heidi as the bakery opened on January fourth. After that...he'd promised he'd know by Christmas Eve, only three short days away.

She'd known he loved his family, but she'd learned he also wanted one of his own. She'd known he was smart, but she'd figured out that his preferred wardrobe colors consisted of shades of blue, brown, and black.

She'd already purchased a new shirt for him—in red—and a five-gallon container of Neapolitan ice cream. But she wanted more for him. But what, she couldn't quite put her finger on. She'd already wandered the aisles of the supermarket, the hardware store, and the western wear shop. No luck. Nothing that stood out and screamed *Jon!*

He was planning a private Christmas Eve dinner for them at her house. She'd promised him a dessert he wouldn't forget—she had orange chocolate coffee cake and a coconut panna cotta on the menu. The ingredients had been bought. She'd mailed her parents a present a week ago. A lanyard specially made with the bakery logo Chelsea had designed sat wrapped under her mini tree for Heidi.

Grace ducked into a jewelry store, but immediately regretted the decision. All the diamonds made her think of marriage, and she didn't even know if Jon would still be in town two weeks from now.

Maybe it didn't hurt to look.... Grace examined the cases of rings, finding green and blue gemstones among the purple and white.

"Looking for yourself?" an elderly woman asked.

"No." Grace smiled. "Just browsing." And daydreaming. The woman left her to look while she helped another couple. Grace paused in front of the engagement rings, thinking through what she might like. She'd dated a few men in New York, but chefs often thought highly of themselves and nothing had stuck for longer than a few months. Certainly no one had prompted her to think in diamonds.

She stilled, her heart racing as though she'd just sprinted the last hundred yards of a run. Jon Carver was diamond-worthy. She'd wear his ring with pride. She'd marry him and be happy.

Because she loved him.

A smile moved across her face, stretched down into her soul. She hadn't prayed to know if Jon was the right man for her. Somehow, since she was a junior in high school, she'd known. Now, she prayed that she could be the right woman for him—and that he would know it before it came time for him to leave town.

---

JON ALMOST WENT OFF THE ROAD THREE TIMES ON the way to Grace's. The Christmas Eve wind had brought in a storm, but that wasn't the real reason he couldn't keep his truck aimed in a straight line.

No, that blame fell on the little, black, jewelry box sitting on the seat next to him. He'd never been so nervous to give a gift in his life. Never been so nervous to eat a meal.

*It's Grace,* he told himself, and the nerves faded for a few minutes. But inevitably, they came roaring back. The ingredients for their candlelit dinner sat next to him, and she'd promised she wouldn't bother him while he mashed and basted and sautéed.

She welcomed him with a quick side hug before she took a few of the grocery bags he carried. "It smells fantastic in here," he said, sniffing to identify the scent. "What is that?"

"It's a surprise," she singsonged. "You'll have to be patient." She toted her bags into the kitchen, but Jon paused by the tiny pine tree she'd set up on her end table. Acting quickly, he slipped the jewelry box out of the grocery sack and under the tree. Several other gifts sat there, and he felt certain she wouldn't notice.

He joined her in the kitchen and started unpacking potatoes and green beans and onions.

"Mm," she said. "A man after my own heart."

He laughed as she petted a potato. "You have the oven ready?"

"As instructed."

He nodded toward the front door. "I left the ham in my truck. It's already done. Just needs to be warmed."

"Be right back."

Jon couldn't help watching her walk away, and the feeling he'd been searching for these past few weeks manifested itself —again.

He was in love with Grace Lewis. He smiled at the repeated realization, his heart doing the tango as he thought about moving to Three Rivers.

*You have to do it, he told himself. She's worth it.*

She came back through the front door, laden with the heavy baking dish. She slid the ham into the oven and he slid his hands around her waist. "Grace, I have to tell you something."

She seemed to melt into him, seemed made to fit against him.

For one moment, his brain rebelled. Wouldn't control his vocal chords long enough to get them to produce sound. He swallowed and found his center when she reached up and ran her fingers through his hair.

He gazed into her eyes and saw a life worth having. A life worth having only if it was with her.

"I love you, Grace."

She sucked in a surprised breath and blinked.

"I'm going to move to Three Rivers so we can be together." He hadn't intended to give her his gift before dinner. But he found his feet moving toward the living room, and his hand gently guiding a silent Grace with him.

"I don't know exactly how you feel, because you haven't said anything. I know you've been giving me time and whatever, and I appreciate that. But I've made my decision." He reached for the box and picked it up. "I prayed about it, and the answer was clear. So though I might not like Three Rivers, I love you. And because your life is here, I want to be here."

He dropped to one knee and Grace pressed both hands to her mouth, her eyes shining with what Jon hoped were joyful tears.

"It might be fast, and I haven't asked you when you envisioned your wedding, but Grace, will you marry me?" He flipped open the box the way he'd been practicing for a solid week and held the ring up for her inspection.

She didn't even look at it. She couldn't seem to look away from him, and he gazed steadily back, hoping to be the anchor she relied on in her life.

Worry had just wormed its way under his skin when she nodded, a tear fell, and she said, "Yes," between her fingers.

In a fluid motion, he stood and wrapped her in an embrace. When she stretched up to kiss him, Jon felt sure he was the luckiest man in all of Texas.

"Best Christmas gift ever," she whispered, her lips practically touching his. "I love you too, Jon."

He'd thought "yes" was the best thing he'd ever heard, but hearing Grace tell him she loved him sounded a hundred times sweeter. He grinned as he slid the ring on her finger and kissed her again.

"Well, what'd you get me?"

She giggled but didn't move out of the circle of his arms. "I didn't put it under the tree. It's in my bedroom."

"You gonna make me wait?" He touched his lips to his favorite spot below her ear.

She sighed against him. "I guess not." She stepped away and hurried down the hall. She returned a moment later with a hatbox. "You see now why I didn't put it under the tree." She handed him the gift.

He opened it, expecting to see a cowboy hat—and he did. One of the finest cowboy hats someone could buy. "Grace." He glanced up at her. "This is too much."

She folded her arms. "You bought me a diamond. Go on. Put it on."

He took out the slate gray hat, the weight and texture of it perfect. He placed the hat on his head, and genuine happiness poured through him.

"I noticed you favor blues and grays," she said. "I thought this would match most of what you wear."

He locked eyes with her. “You notice what I wear?”

She flashed him a coy smile. “You are a big, strong, handsome man.”

He growled, pulled her toward him, and kissed the best Christmas present he'd ever received.

*The End*

# THE TWELFTH TOWN

# SCRIPTURE

"For with God nothing shall be impossible."

LUKE 1:37

# CHAPTER TWENTY-SEVEN

The long row of cabins at Three Rivers Ranch had never looked more glorious than they did to Taryn Tucker. She stood at the end of them on a Monday morning, her gaze stretching across all twelve of them, the same way she had last week after she'd been offered the job of cleaning them.

Playing maid was a long way from having a professional makeup artist paint her face and a stylist make sure every strand of hair fell the right way. But Taryn much preferred this life to the one she used to have.

Or at least she hoped she would. With eleven small towns behind her, she desperately wanted to find one to live in for a while. She tucked her newly dyed black hair into a ponytail and then stuffed the ends into a messy bun before stooping for her cleaning supplies. Might as well get started.

She thought about the apartment she'd been able to find in Three Rivers, a town she'd stumbled upon quite by accident the week before. She'd never seen quite such an enthusiastic Halloween celebration before. Not even in New Orleans, where she'd been assigned one October a few years ago—and they knew how to celebrate death in Louisiana.

She'd used the last of her meager paycheck from town number eleven, where she'd worked bagging groceries until she got too nervous to stay, to pay for a hotel for a couple of nights until she found the one-bedroom unit above the barber shop on Main Street.

*They won't follow you this far,* Taryn told herself as she mounted the steps to the first cabin, the one closest to the homestead where she'd been instructed to replenish her cleaning supplies.

At least Taryn hoped they wouldn't. She wasn't even sure who "they" were, only that someone from her former employer wanted to know where she'd disappeared to. As if the public humiliation she'd caused as well as endured couldn't be viewed twenty-four hours a day via the Internet.

Six months had passed. Surely the news station would find another story to focus on, especially in a city the size of Corpus Christi. Taryn had been praying for a hurricane, and though they sat in the thick of the season, God had not granted her requests for such a storm. It was just as well. She didn't want to be responsible for tragedy and death just to get the attention off her messed up personal life.

She mourned the loss of such a life as she fitted the master key into the lock. Still, the owner of the ranch, Squire Ackerman, hadn't seemed to recognize her—*and why would he?* she asked herself.

Corpus Christi television stations didn't broadcast to dinky Three Rivers. But somehow, Taryn carried the weight of who she'd been and it cumbered her shoulders, weighed her down.

She entered the cabin and set her bucket of supplies on the floor so she could return to retrieve the vacuum cleaner. Apparently cleaning the cowboy cabins was a brand-new job; Squire had never hired someone to do it before. According to him, his cowboys right now were of the messy variety.

Taryn lugged the vacuum up the steps and into the cabin,

pausing to wipe the first inklings of sweat from her forehead. She clutched the bucket with one hand and towed the vacuum behind her with the other as she headed for the bedroom in the back of the quiet cabin. She'd mapped out a plan of attack to get three of the twelve cabins done each day, and that started with working from the back to the front. Each cabin would be done in two hours, with fifteen-minute breaks in between.

Squire had agreed to her plan during the second interview, and given her the requested four-day work week. Taryn was really looking forward to a three-day weekend each week, and her spirits lifted as she barged through the bedroom door.

"Hey!" A man stood there, barely wearing a pair of jeans. He fumbled with the zipper while Taryn stared. With his pants securely in place, he folded his arms across his bare chest. His impressively wide bare chest.

"Who might you be?" He grinned at her, an action which made her mortification fall down a notch. He reached for a white undershirt lying on the unmade bed and pulled it over his sandy-haired head. He obviously hadn't shaved that morning—or any morning in the past month. Red and lighter brown salted his beard, which he'd trimmed neatly along his jawline.

Taryn swallowed, unable to find her voice. His blue-gray eyes sucked at her. They seemed filled with lightning, with laughter, with life. She envied him immediately.

"It's no big deal," he said. "I just don't normally have pretty women back here." He pulled a blue and black plaid shirt from his closet and put it on. "My name's Kenny Stockton." He stepped toward her and offered his hand.

She dropped her cleaning bucket and put her hand inside his, and it looked child-sized comparatively. She swallowed and took a calming breath. He didn't seem upset she'd walked in on him. "Taryn Tucker." She cringed at her near-perfect delivery, as if she was signing off one of her newscasts. *I'm Taryn Tucker. Good-night, Corpus Christi.*

"Pleased to meet you, Taryn Tucker." He looked at her curiously, but he didn't seem to recognize her. She glanced around for a television in his bedroom and didn't find one. Her muscles softened, and she allowed herself to smile at the handsome cowboy who still held her hand.

"Sorry I barged on in," she said. "I didn't think anyone would be home. Squire said the cowhands are up early to do their jobs."

Kenny slid his hand away from hers. "Yeah, I got real dirty during the haul this mornin'. Came back to shower before heading over to the admin trailer for my next assignment." He glanced around, as if just now noticing that beds could be made. "Sorry about the mess."

She forced herself to give a light giggle. "That's my job. If you go doin' it, I won't get paid." And she needed the money. Her salary had long dried up, and the hourly-wage jobs she'd been getting by with never seemed to pay enough.

*At least you're not sleeping in your car,* she thought as she searched for an outlet to plug in the vacuum. That night—though it had only been a single night—had been one of the worst of her life. Worse than the night she'd said no to her boyfriend's proposal on live TV.

A chill ran down her back, and she lifted her hand in acknowledgement when Kenny said he was heading out. Relief spread through her when the front door banged closed behind him, and Taryn sank onto his bed. No tears came—she'd cried them all out in the first three months.

Just pure exhaustion. She needed to get out of Texas if she had any hope of living a normal life. But as it always did, the thought of returning home to South Dakota brought on a wave of nausea Taryn had learned to swallow down and breathe through. Her parents hadn't seen the debacle—she doubted they had any idea that she'd left Corpus Christi six months ago—but she didn't want to return to Bottle Hollow and explain why.

After all, she'd vowed never to return when she'd left a decade ago.

She spoke to her mother from time to time, but her father still hadn't opened the lines of communication. Some words took longer to fade to whispers, Taryn supposed. Or perhaps her father was as stubborn as her mother always said he was.

She inhaled deeply to inflate her chest and focused on the closet in front of her. A gray camouflage hint of fabric caught her eye, and she sprang to her feet and shoved the clothes which concealed the uniform to the left.

*U.S. Marines.*

Her chest rose and fell in shallow breaths. *Stockton* sat above the right breast pocket, and Taryn wondered where he'd been stationed, how he'd gotten out of the Marines, and why he'd chosen ranching instead of something like law enforcement the way her brother had.

She took a deep drag of air, expecting to find the woodsy, spicy scent of Collin. She didn't. She hadn't since his death three years ago. Still, something about this desert cammie called to her.

Another breath revealed a new scent, one that wrapped through her soul and wound around her toes. This one smelled like fresh cotton, and outdoorsy dryer sheets, and something deeply masculine.

Kenny's scent.

Taryn closed her eyes and reveled in it, a fistful of his uniform clutched in her fingers. Something beyond the house snapped, and her eyes snapped open. She stumbled away from his personal belongings. Embarrassment flooded her.

"Get a grip," she muttered to herself as she started the vacuum. She attacked the clutter and dust in Kenny's cabin with vigor. After all, she wasn't in town to get involved with another marine, even if he smelled as wonderful as she imagined heaven to be. Even if his eyes carried a twinkle and his deep voice sang to her soul and his muscles testified of his impressive physique.

No, she'd had enough of cops and servicemen. Enough of watching them die, the way her brother had. Enough of dating them and then humiliating them when they proposed to her.

Familiar remorse combined with an inexplicable rage hit her right behind the breastbone. Chris should've known not to surprise her like that. Nothing about their year-long relationship had suggested she'd enjoy an on-air proposal.

Her refusal *was* his fault, and yet she'd lost everything because of it. Taryn left Kenny's cabin in tip-top shape, determined not to let her ex-boyfriend into her thoughts, her decision-making, her life. Not anymore.

As she entered the next cabin, she looked up into the rafters of the porch as if gazing toward heaven. *Help me find what I need here,* she prayed. If only she knew what that was and how to get it.

---

"WHAT'S YOUR DEAL TODAY?"

Kenny looked up at Lawrence's question, his mind still trying to focus on organizing the words into a sentence that made sense. He blinked and looked at the horse he'd been brushing. "No deal."

"I've been talking to you, and you don't respond." Lawrence led his horse into the stall and latched it. "It's like you've got a lot on your mind." He leaned against the fence and grinned. "But you're Kenny, so that can't be true."

Kenny chuckled with his friend. "I suppose I've been distracted today." Distracted by a gorgeous pair of brown eyes and hair he'd been speculating on its true color for most of the day. The black on Taryn obviously came from a bottle.

"You been lookin' at a new horse?"

A twinge of disdain pinched behind Kenny's eyes. But Lawrence wouldn't automatically assume Kenny had been distracted by a woman. He rarely made it past the third date, and the last woman he'd been out with declined his dinner invitation, claiming he was "too happy."

Well, Kenny didn't know how to be unhappy. Didn't really seem to be in his nature, and he certainly wasn't going to apologize about his glass-half-full attitude. His time in the Marines had taught him to see the darkness, the evil, the horrors of this world. He didn't want to exist there all the time.

He thanked God everyday that he'd been able to serve his country without losing his life. So many others didn't. He'd served two four-year terms of active service before leaving the Marines, before wandering the country in search of what to do next, before he'd found Three Rivers Ranch. His father had known Garth Ahlstrom in Montana, and Kenny had come to Texas a few years ago looking for a job. Garth hired him the same day. Another blessing.

"Hello?" Lawrence waved his hand in front of Kenny's eyes. "Must be a beautiful horse."

"Hm." Kenny didn't correct him. So he'd thought Taryn was pretty. Every man who looked at her surely thought that too. She was petite and polite, which led Kenny to believe she'd been raised in the South.

The heat from her hand still burned in his, and he fisted his fingers as he finished his last chore before heading back to his cabin. For one small moment, he fantasized about walking in on Taryn. But the idea was ridiculous. Squire had hired her to clean all the cabins, as well as the administration building. It wouldn't take her all day to clean his cabin, though it was a bit of a pig sty.

Sure enough, when he tried to enter his cabin, the door was locked. He fished his keys from his pocket and entered the quiet cabin. His roommate, Charlie, would be home in a few minutes, and Kenny took the opportunity while he was alone to admire the freshly vacuumed rugs, the straight pillows on the couch, and his crisply made bed.

Kenny wondered where Taryn had come from. He hadn't seen her at church previously, but that was his only interaction with anyone off the ranch. Maybe she didn't go to church. And it wasn't like he went every single week either.

"Wow, this place looks great." Charlie entered the cabin and kicked his dirty boots onto the clean rug. "What're you thinkin' for dinner?"

Kenny hadn't thought of anything but Taryn for hours. He hadn't discovered how to get her number, or what her schedule at the ranch would be, or anything. He didn't want to ask. Didn't want anyone to know of his interest.

The wind shook the windows as Kenny said, "Pizza or spaghetti."

"You cooking?"

"Sure." He stepped into the kitchen and pulled out a stock pot.

"This place smells like lilacs," Charlie commented, and Kenny smiled as he salted the pasta water.

---

THE NEXT MORNING, KENNY DIDN'T SEE TARYN ON HIS way to the administration building. Garth had messaged all the cowhands about a mandatory meeting that morning, instead of just heading out to their usual chores.

"Maybe we'll get our new assignments," Charlie commented.

"Nah." Kenny grinned at him as they climbed the steps to the building. "We just got new ones last month."

"Yeah, you're right." Charlie lowered his head against the wind, his tone resigned. Kenny didn't much care what his chore was, though there were definitely less desirable jobs around the ranch. Kenny was just glad to be out of a uniform, working the hours of the day away, and living a carefree life.

A flash of black hair caught his attention, but he didn't truly have a chance to see if it was Taryn or not before Charlie opened the door and ushered Kenny into the admin building. They took seats and waited for Garth to appear. By the time he finally did, Kenny had listened to Lawrence and Charlie bicker good-naturedly about whose dog was smarter and why.

"Storm comin' in," Garth said as a way to call the cowboys to order. It worked. "I reckon we have today to get the animals secure, get the barns all closed up, and the rest of the week, we'll be working on indoor improvements."

Some of the cowboys shuffled their feet, but not Kenny. He didn't mind working inside any more than he did outside. Someone asked what kind of indoor improvements, and Garth mentioned painting and appliance repair in some of the cabins, maybe laying new flooring in a couple of them, and other home improvement items Kenny had never done. But he could wipe a brush up and down and follow written directions.

The meeting ended with assignments to get the livestock on the ranch secured, and Kenny got assigned along with a half-dozen cowhands to ride out and check on the herd. They'd hunker down next to the tree line for some security, and Kenny labored with the other men to make the field smaller. Keeping the cattle in a group would help them stay calm, and it was only supposed to rain. Buckets, but just rain.

Kenny drove another nail into the plywood back Garth had instructed they build on the existing roof structure that protected the feeding troughs. The cattle wouldn't be able to access the hay from both sides, but the chances of their feed lasting through the storm increased with the additional wall.

"Roof's secure," Lawrence said from the other side of the structure. "This is almost done."

"Great work," Garth said. "The hay'll be here in a few minutes. We'll get that out, and we'll head home."

Kenny nailed faster, swinging the hammer with near lightning speed. He'd had enough of the wind pulling at his hat and whipping through his ears. He wasn't sure Texas ever got truly cold, but with this wind and the threatening gray sky, a chill skated over his arms.

The trucks arrived and the men set to work filling the troughs. Grass still grew in this field too, but no one would be out to check the herd for three days, and Garth wasn't the kind of foreman who took chances. Kenny knew he'd come out in a hailstorm to check on the cattle if he was concerned about them.

He finished up his job and helped get the last of the hay out. With fresh water in the lower trough, Garth called, "Let's get outta here, boys!" He flattened his hand against his head as the wind kicked up, and Kenny started toward his horse. He led two along behind him as a couple of the boys got a ride in the back of the truck.

"You okay there, Kenny?" Garth asked as he leaned out the window of the truck.

"Just fine, boss."

"It's just you and Aaron. Keep an eye on each other."

"Sure thing, boss." But Kenny didn't look up. The weather threw dust and dirt and debris into his face, and he used his cowboy hat to keep himself protected. At one point, he spotted Aaron ahead of him on the horizon, also leading two horses. Kenny whistled a tune he'd learned in the Marines as Orion, his faithful black-and-white horse, plodded on home.

He'd just passed the cabin in section twelve when something floated to him on the wind. He jerked his head up, searching for the source of the cry. Maybe it was an animal—the prairie played home to more than just cattle, he knew.

His pulse pounding and his blood beating through his veins, he scanned the horizon. Nothing.

The cry came again, a high-pitched noise without shape or meaning. He whipped his head left, and there, so far out where the land met the angry sky, he spotted a dark figure.

A human figure.

# CHAPTER TWENTY-EIGHT

Taryn wasn't sure if the water on her face came from her eyes or from the sky. All she knew was that the thunderous gallop of three horses was bearing down on her. An impressive man rode one of the beasts, like a Greek god from the movies she'd loved in college.

"What are you doing out here?" he asked, and her brain registered his voice as familiar.

"Kenny?"

"Taryn?" He swung out of the saddle and hurried toward her. "Why are you out this far?"

"I may have decided to take a walk during lunch and got turned around." She glanced in a near three-sixty-degree circle. "Everything out here looks the same."

He swept an arm around her shoulders and drew her into his wall of a body. The wind chill factor dropped. In fact, the temperature on the plains suddenly rose ten degrees. "You're an hour from the homestead. How long have you been out here?"

"A while," she admitted. She didn't necessarily want to wilt into his arms, but her body acted of its own accord. She gripped the front of his shirt and sampled a breath of his musky, masculine scent. "I'm glad you spotted me."

"I wouldn't have if you hadn't been yelling."

She gazed up at him and locked onto his stormy eyes. She nearly fell at that moment, but managed to keep herself upright with only a slight stumble. "I wasn't yelling."

Concern flashed in his eyes at the same time lightning split the sky. He looked to his right, then his left. "Come on." He secured her hand in one of his and kept his grip on the reins of three horses in the other. "We'll never make it back to the ranch before the rain hits." Even as he spoke, the first drops peppered Taryn's forearm.

"Where are we going?"

"There's a cabin about two hundred yards back this way."

Taryn peered into the murky sky but couldn't see much more than gray soup. "You sure?"

"Dead certain."

Kenny moved with the liquid grace of an athlete, of a man who knew how to keep his body in peak operating condition—and had done so for a while. Taryn had to practically run to keep up with his long strides, a fact she became grateful for when the rain really started falling in earnest.

"Here." He all but shoved her into the cabin before ducking back into the storm to secure the horses. She heard him around the back of the structure, and she hoped the horses at least had some sort of shed to protect them from the weather.

The cabin consisted of one room, with the capability to curtain it into two. A stove sat against the back wall, and Taryn wondered if there was any dry wood to be had. A long counter ran along the wall to her right, and she wandered that way, the single cot on the opposite side of the cabin too dangerous to approach.

Kenny burst into the cabin a few minutes later, water dripping from his cowboy hat. He slammed the door behind him and secured it with two sliding locks, as well as a chain. "Wow! It's comin' down hard out there." He shook his hat off in time to the rhythm of the rain pelting the roof.

Taryn rubbed her arms and pressed herself against the back wall where the counter met wood. "So we're going to just...stay here until the storm settles, right?"

The cabin had two windows in the front, and one on each end, but nothing in the back. Kenny peered out one of the front panes. "Could be a long time." He checked his watch. "It's almost dark as it is."

He turned back to her, a half-smile on his face. "I think we'll probably be here all night."

Taryn's throat turned to dust. "All night?" she managed to choke out. She glanced around wildly, like the cabin would suddenly transform and provide her with a hot bath, a private bedroom, and silk pajamas. "How is that possible?"

Kenny chuckled as he stepped to a wardrobe in the opposite corner that Taryn hadn't seen. "We've got blankets here. Some emergency food. A radio. I'll call in and let Garth know where I am. We'll be fine until morning."

"I can't stay out here all night." She eyed the single cot like it had done her wrong.

Kenny tossed two blankets onto the cot and raised his eyes to hers. "Why not?"

Did he really not get it? There was one bed. Two of them. *Emergency* food—surely that tasted about as good as it sounded. No wood.

"Can we light that stove?" she asked.

"Demanding little thing, aren't you?" He added a genuine laugh to the end of his statement, and Taryn got caught up in the warmth of it. How could he be so cavalier about this? Was he always so good-natured?

"There's wood in the shed out back," he said. "I shoved the horses in there too." He rooted around in the closet. "But here's some pellets for them. I'll go feed 'em, and bring in the wood." He grinned at her. "You can make your bed." He produced a sleeping bag, and Taryn was beginning to think that wardrobe was a cousin of Mary Poppins's tote bag. "I'll sleep on the floor."

He zipped over to the front door, unchained it, and darted into the storm before Taryn could put two words together. The man's energy almost unnerved her. She'd cleaned two cabins today before getting lost, and the weight of her exhaustion had her crossing the room and flopping onto the unmade cot without another thought.

Kenny found her there, and he stopped by the wardrobe before approaching her. "You should eat something." He held out a silver package.

She took it, but the thought of putting whatever it held in her mouth made her stomach revolt.

"You're not goin' into shock, are you?" Kenny crouched in front of her and examined her face. "I totally think you are. You look pale." He reached up and brushed her hair from the side of her face. "You need to eat and drink. And get up. Come help me start this fire." He gently placed his hand in hers, and she let him lead her to the pot-bellied stove. In fact, she would've gone anywhere with him at that moment. Strong, and sure, and smelling so good, Kenny seemed like the knight in shining armor Taryn needed in her life.

She listened to the bass timbre of his voice as he instructed her to place the wood just so, to crumple up the newspaper they kept stored at the cabin, to strike the match. She moved in a methodical way to match his voice, and before she knew it, the heat of the flames licked her face. She grinned and tipped her head toward Kenny's.

With only inches between them, Taryn froze. The happiness in Kenny's eyes brought tears to hers. She'd been happy like that before too. But not now.

"Hey," he said, swiping his thumb under her eyes. "Don't cry, now. I'm no good with beautiful women who cry."

She employed every ounce of self-control she had and willed the tears back into her chest, where they thankfully stayed. "I'm so glad you found me," she said again. "I don't think I would've ever found this cabin, and I certainly wouldn't have survived out here all night." A gust of wind shook the cabin, emphasizing her statement. She shivered with the thought of what would've happened to her had he not seen her.

"It's a miracle," he whispered. "Do you believe in miracles, Taryn?" The earnest way he watched her spoke to her soul, and now the flames in the room weren't only coming from the stove.

"Yes," Taryn said. "I believe in miracles."

Kenny's lips spread into a smile, and Taryn wondered what they'd feel like against hers. Startled at the thought of kissing a near-stranger, she cleared her throat and turned away. "Okay, let's get this place set up for tonight." Already the light was almost gone, and Kenny rummaged through the closet until he found a flashlight with the weakest beam Taryn had ever seen.

Still, it was enough to get the blankets on the cot, and the cot in front of the fire. Kenny gave her two bottles of water and told her to drink them before she fell asleep. He spread his sleeping bag just behind her cot, and if she let her arm slip over the side, she could hold his hand. Thoughts of doing so entertained her while she ate the protein bar he'd given her and drank her water. She watched the flames in the stove play together while she considered what to do with the feelings of attraction sparking between her and this marine cowboy.

No matter what she came up with, she knew she'd end up getting burned.

---

KENNY COULDN'T STAND THE SILENCE IN THE CABIN. Well, it wasn't completely quiet. The rain created a symphony with the fire spitting in the stove.

"How long you been in Three Rivers?" he asked, his curiosity on the matter unending.

"About a week." The sadness in her voice, the fear he'd seen in her eyes, the way she cried so easily, told Kenny to tread lightly and be careful with her. At the same time, he wanted to see if he could make it to a fourth date with Taryn, a feat he hadn't accomplished in a while with any woman.

"What brought you here?"

"I needed a job." She sighed, the sound adding music to the cacophony of nature sounds. "Well, and the town's Halloween festivities lured me in."

"Oh, you like Halloween?"

"Not particularly." She turned toward him, and the fire backlit her face. "But the joy permeating this town.... The way everyone seemed to know everyone else, and the whole community came together." She barely lifted her top shoulder. "I liked how it felt here. So I decided to stay."

Kenny basked in the warmth of her story. "Three Rivers is a magical place," he agreed. "Where'd you come from?"

"Here and there."

He couldn't see her face, but the closed-off tone of her voice probably would've manifested in an icy glare in those luxurious brown eyes. He much preferred them to swim with heat, soften like melted chocolate, the way they had just before a tear had escaped.

"I'm from California originally," he said, deciding to fill the silence with his own story. Seemed like Taryn didn't want to talk much, though he did wonder what kind of woman could roam the panhandle of Texas until she found a town she felt like staying in. "Served in the Marines for almost ten years. I got out of active service about three years ago, and my dad knew the foreman down here. Ranching seemed as good as anything else I might do with my life." He spoke to the ceiling as an overwhelming feeling of peace flowed through him. He hadn't known what to do when he'd graduated high school, thus the enlisting in the Marines.

And almost nine years later when he got released, he still hadn't known. But he knew now—God had led him to Three Rivers. He loved the small town. Loved that some of the roads in the older part of town were only wide enough for one car. Loved the quaint atmosphere of country living. Loved that he could feel things here that he couldn't in the city, because it was quieter and slower and simpler.

"You sound like you love it here," she said.

"I do." He chanced a glance at her, but she'd rolled onto her back too. "You will too, Taryn," he promised. "Like I said, there's something healing and magical about Three Rivers."

Several heartbeats passed, broken when she said, "That's exactly what I need."

Kenny could feel it. Her tension rode in her shoulders, in the tense lines around her kissable mouth, in the way she so easily wandered away from a ranch and couldn't get back.

He woke sometime later, unable to distinguish between having his eyes open or closed. "Taryn?" he whispered.

"The fire went out," she hissed back. "It's freezing in here."

The chill of Kenny's nose suddenly felt like it had been frozen in liquid nitrogen. "I'll get it going again." He got up and felt his way past the cot only to find her kneeling in front of the dark stove too.

"I can't see anything." Something thunked to the ground. "And the flashlight went out five minutes ago." Panic edged her words, and Kenny fumbled his hands through the air until they met her body.

He recognized the shape of her shoulders, her arms, and threaded his fingers through hers. "Hey, it's okay."

She sniffed, and Kenny wanted nothing more than to protect her from everything ugly in her world, both past, present, and future. "I'll take care of it," he said, supremely glad "you" hadn't slipped into the sentence instead of "it."

He felt around on the ground where they'd left the newspaper and matches. His fingers found the right shapes and he struck a match and lit a piece of paper. The flame burned hot and bright—and fast—illuminating the items he needed. He memorized their locations and tossed the burning paper into the stove.

With the precision of a marine, he put in two pieces of wood, stuffed in balls of newspaper, and struck another match. Within a few minutes, a fire blazed in the stove. "There." He sat back on his haunches, pleased with his work.

Taryn sat cross-legged on the floor next to him. "Nice work, Marine."

"Do I detect a hint of sarcasm?" He hoped it wasn't disdain.

"Not at all."

"You wanted a fire. I gave you a fire."

"I want a lot of things." She hugged her knees to her chest.

Feeling brave, the way he had while in active service, he reached for her hand and cradled it in his. "What do you want, Taryn?"

She lifted that shoulder again in a shrug Kenny found sexier every time she did it.

"How about goin' out with me?" he asked, encouraged at the fact that she hadn't pulled her hand away. In fact, she'd matched her fingers to his. "Is that something you might want?"

She turned toward him, and it seemed to take a long time for her eyes to meet his. He didn't look away, though the intense feelings cascading through him evoked more fear than he'd ever felt before—even in Qatar.

"Yeah, sure," she said. "Why not?"

It wasn't exactly the answer Kenny had hoped for, but it would do. He grinned as he focused back on the fire, as Taryn did too, as she leaned her head against his bicep and breathed with him.

# CHAPTER TWENTY-NINE

"Kenny, come back." The tinny, male voice roused Taryn from sleep.

"Kenny, here." His voice came from further away than the sleeping bag he'd used the night before.

"The rain's lightened enough to get back. You should leave right now. Over."

"I'll saddle the horses and be there in an hour. Over."

"We've got the floodlights on. Over."

"Acknowledged. Over." His footsteps came closer. "Taryn?"

She could get used to waking up and having the first thing she saw be his gorgeous face, those cut arms. "I'm awake."

"We need to go. I have everything packed and ready except your blankets."

She scrambled to a seated position and smiled. "I'll take care of these while you get the horses ready." The thought of riding one almost sent her pulse into a frenzy, but she forced the anxiety back. She couldn't let every little thing push her over the edge of panic. Not anymore.

"They go in that closet. You can leave the cot there." He moved toward the door. "I put water on the fire a half hour ago.

We're good to go." He unchained the door and peered into the atmosphere. "It's still raining, but it's more like a drizzle."

"I'll meet you outside."

"Sounds good." He ducked through the doorway and disappeared. Taryn did as she said she would and met him out front, where sure enough, he boosted her into the saddle of a horse. The ride back was miserable, with wind and rain driving into her face from time to time. Conversation couldn't happen, but that suited Taryn just fine. She felt like she'd already revealed too much to Kenny, too soon. But he hadn't seemed turned off. Just the opposite, in fact.

She allowed her thoughts to wander, and strangely they didn't automatically go to the negative events of her recent past. Instead, she contemplated the feelings she'd had while trying to sleep last night. Feelings of contentment of living here—permanently. Feelings of attraction for the handsome marine who'd asked her out. Feelings of uncertainty that she could have this town and this man in her life when so much of it existed up in the air.

Pushing the worries away, she made it back to the ranch, back to her apartment, and into her warm shower.

Her phone rang as she finished toweling her hair, and her blood turned to ice. She eyed the phone like it would be her old boss—or worse, Chris—calling. She didn't recognize the number, and she chose not to answer.

The call went to voicemail—which Taryn had also trained herself to delete without listening to—and the phone immediately began ringing again.

A peaceful feeling reminded her that she'd given her number to Kenny before leaving the ranch. She swiped on the call, the hope it would be him soaring toward the ceiling. When had she last let a man turn her into putty so fast?

"Hello?" she said much more hesitantly than she would've liked. She straightened her shoulders and looked into her own eyes. *Be strong,* she told herself as Kenny said, "Hey, there. Just checkin' to see if you made it home okay. The rain really started up again as soon as you left the ranch."

She leaned against the counter in the bathroom, the smile spreading across her face spontaneous and uncontrollable. "Had to use the wipers on double-time, but I made it."

"That's great." He wore a smile in his words. "So we never planned a time to get together."

"Oh, I'll be out at the ranch tomorrow," she said.

"You will?"

"Yeah, I work there, remember?"

"You can't come tomorrow."

"Why not?"

"The weather, remember?" He chuckled. "Surely you're not going to drive in that."

"It's a little rain," she said. "I have a job to do." And she'd already lost today's hours. She couldn't afford to miss another day. "We can maybe eat lunch together. Do cowhands eat lunch?"

"Usually in a big group, at one of the homesteads. My guess is Miss Kelly will have lunch for us tomorrow."

Taryn's stomach swooped at the mention of a big group. Last year at this time, she would've been on Chris's arm. And he was fun, and flirty, and the life of any gathering. She'd always been more reserved naturally, bringing out the act of perfection whenever the cameras switched on. But she loved being on the arm of the most popular man at the party.

"Oh, well, another day then."

"What? No," he said. "I'd gladly skip if you wanted to sneak off to the barn or something. We can eat in the hayloft, stay out of the rain."

"Ooh, a hayloft. Sounds risky."

Kenny laughed, the booming sound warming her across the

distance between them. "The ladder is a bit rickety. I'll fix it in the morning."

She giggled. "You don't need to fix the ladder for me."

"I'd fix anything for you," he said, his voice serious and quiet. So quiet, Taryn wondered if she'd heard him right.

Her reporter mind thought quickly and she said, "Well, I might just take you up on that, Sergeant Stockton."

A pause on the other end of the line made her think perhaps he didn't appreciate her brand of flirting. Then he said, "How'd you know I was a sergeant?"

"You left the closet door open," she blurted, totally not employing her quick thinking reporter brain. Even something like *Lucky guess* would've been better than saying she'd snooped through the man's closet mere minutes after walking in on him as he got dressed.

"I just saw the uniform. My brother—" She clamped her lips shut two words too late.

"It's okay," he said quickly to fill the gap. "Tell me later. And I did leave my closet open. Thanks for closing that. And, you know, for making my bathroom sink white again." He chuckled nervously and cleared his throat. "I actually have another favor that might send you running for the hills."

"Oh, I don't run," Taryn said, beyond relieved for his kindness in covering up her flub. The man was obviously made of patience—and a little dirt. She smiled at the memory of scrubbing his bathroom. "Unless there are large dogs chasing me. Will there be large dogs involved in this favor?"

His laughter came quickly, and she loved the joy emanating from him. She marveled at how easily he radiated such happiness, even over a phone line. "No dogs," he promised. "Well, maybe a couple of dogs. But they're old, and barely move, and I think even you could outrun them."

"So what's the favor?"

"Since my family is so far away, I usually stay here for the holidays. I go to my friend's house for Thanksgiving dinner, and his mom just asked how many would be coming." He paused, and Taryn's reporter radar went off.

"And?"

"And Charlie has a girlfriend this year, and I don't want to be the third wheel. That, or get seated at the kid's table because I'm a singleton. Believe me, it's happened. And I have a hard time fitting my legs under those tiny tables."

Taryn couldn't help the laugh that burst from her mouth. "I'll bet." She tried to imagine the towering, wide marine squishing himself in with ten-year-olds.

"Wondered if you had anywhere to go for Thanksgiving."

"As a matter of fact, I...don't." Of course, Taryn didn't even know if she'd still be in town in three weeks, when Thanksgiving rolled around. With a fierceness of thought she hadn't possessed since going for the nightly anchor position in Corpus Christi, she determined that she *would* be in Three Rivers for Thanksgiving.

"Great," Kenny said. "So we can go together. His family's in Amarillo."

Taryn swallowed. "Amarillo. Fantastic." But it so wasn't fantastic. She'd avoided cities with more than fifty thousand people, where the newscaster world narrowed and everyone knew everyone else. She tugged at the ends of her dyed-black hair. It was one meal. Behind closed doors. She looked completely different now than she did six months ago.

"You been to Amarillo?" he asked.

"No."

"Perfect," he said, but she wasn't sure why he thought so. "Okay, I have to go. See you tomorrow. Unless it's raining too hard. Then you should stay home."

He hung on the line, and she said, "I'll see you tomorrow, Kenny. Good-night." She pressed her eyes closed and hugged her phone to her heartbeat. If she let this gentle giant of a man into her life, what pain would she have to endure when they broke up? How far would she have to run?

*Maybe you won't break up*, she thought as she snuggled into the couch with a blanket and the television set on low volume. Her first impulse was to scoff at the thought. She'd broken up with every man who'd even gotten close to talking about a long-term commitment. Some very publicly.

Her second thought was, *Have faith*. She seized onto that one, because it felt more hopeful, more helpful, than her usual self-depreciation.

---

WITH ONLY TWENTY MINUTES OF HIS LUNCH BREAK left, Kenny paced in the barn. He hadn't seen Taryn around the ranch that day, his calls went unanswered, and he wasn't entirely sure what her car looked like.

"You're trying too hard," he muttered to himself. "You'll scare her off before you've even had a chance to get to know her." He gripped his phone, but he refused to call her again. Twice was enough. She knew where the barn was. She knew what time his lunch break started and ended.

He checked his phone again, just to be sure he hadn't missed her. That would be easier to swallow than her outright rejection. Hadn't missed her. His chest tightened and his stride lengthened.

The door opened, and he spun toward it, his heart galloping against this ribcage.

A woman moved toward him, and it only took Kenny a few steps for him to recognize Taryn. "You came," he said as she stalled several feet from him.

"I wasn't going to." She scuffed her feet against the floor; the sound reverberated against Kenny's pulse.

"Why did you then?" His words came out with too much bite, but he couldn't help it.

She moved a couple of steps closer. Close enough to see the worried look in her eyes and the tension in her neck. "You're so cute," she said. "I was nervous. Took a while to get over my anxiety and get myself over here."

He simply stared at her. *She* was nervous about spending time with him?

She glanced up to the loft. "So, have you eaten?" Her eyes came back to his, hooking and drawing him closer, deeper, farther than he knew a gaze could transport someone.

He lifted his brown paper sack, the top of which had paid the price of his frustration. "Not yet." His throat felt dry and rough as sandpaper as he gestured her to go first up the ladder. It didn't emit a single creak, and a crack of satisfaction at his handiwork stole through him.

He followed her up, the scent of her perfume barely lingering in the air behind her. When he made it to the loft, she'd already settled her back against the wall, the round window immediately beside her.

Kenny took the spot on the other side of her and flashed her a winning smile. "I can't believe you think I'm cute." He pulled out his turkey sandwich and took a bite.

"Stop it." She smiled and opened a container of yogurt. She flipped the corner and mixed in the toppings.

He swallowed and nudged her shoulder with his. "Here I was thinkin' about how I could tell you how beautiful I think you are."

She blinked at him, her long lashes catching the light and throwing it into his face. "You are, you know. Beautiful." Kenny's fingers tightened and he worked to release them before he squished his sandwich. "I want to know everything about you. Let's start with your family. Yeah?" He examined her face for signs of distress, a warning voice in his head telling him to go slow with Taryn Tucker.

She flinched slightly, and Kenny suddenly remembered the slip about her brother. "Never mind," he said. "Job? I mean, obviously, you're cleanin' out here right now, but...." He shut his mouth, and fast.

This conversation was a complete disaster. Had he really brought up her family again? And was he really going to say she must've had a better job before becoming a maid for two dozen cowhands? He shoved half his sandwich in his mouth, the remaining fifteen minutes of his lunch suddenly too long.

A light laugh started from beside him, causing horror to snake through his gut. "Sorry," he mumbled around bread and meat.

"It's fine, Kenny. My family is...a bit of a sore subject, but I can tell you the basics. Born and raised in South Dakota. My parents are still there." She scraped her plastic spoon around the edge of the yogurt container to get every last bit. "My brother, well, he passed away a few years ago. It's still hard for me to talk about. I was very close to him."

Kenny's hand acted of its own accord, moving up and around Taryn's shoulders, drawing her into the protective shield of his chest. Right where he wanted her to be. Right where he needed her to be.

"I'm sorry," he murmured. "What happened?"

She cleared her throat and remained stiff in his arms. "He was an ex-Marine, like you. Became a police officer and was shot during a drug bust in Philly."

Pieces began to click around in Kenny's head. No wonder she'd snooped through his closet when she'd seen the hint of his desert cammies. He couldn't think of anything to say, just like he hadn't been able to when he'd attended Marcus's funeral, one of his fallen comrades-in-arms. All he'd been able to tell

Marcus's mother was, "I'm sorry," and he repeated the sentiment to Taryn again.

She sagged against him, and he relished the feel of holding her close, inhaling her floral and sunshine scent, and having her company.

"Tell me about your family," she said.

"My parents are divorced," he said. "My dad moved back to his homestate of Montana, where he now lives. He met Garth there. My mom lives in California. She has a boyfriend, but I don't ask her much about him." Kenny's words began to hollow and he forced a measure of happiness back into them. "I have one older sister who's married and lives in California too. One younger brother who works for a software company in Japan."

"Japan? Wow."

Kenny chuckled. "I know, right? He keeps telling me to come visit, but...."

"But what?"

"I don't really like to travel."

She leaned away and cocked her head up at him. "Really? I love traveling."

"Oh, yeah? You've done a lot of it?"

"Yeah, sure, when I was a reporter—" Her eyes rounded and her voice cut into silence. An alarm went off on her wrist, and she frantically pressed the button on the side of her fitness tracker. "I have to get back to work."

"Okay." Kenny watched her scramble away from him and practically tumble down the ladder, wondering what demons haunted her and how he could vanquish them.

# CHAPTER THIRTY

Taryn kicked herself while she cleaned the last cabin of the day, while she drove back to her apartment, while she showered. If Kenny had any skills with a computer, he'd know who she was—everything about her—with a simple Google search.

She wasn't sure how she could ever face him again. And yet, she found her feet taking her to the horse barn the next day when her alarm alerted her that Kenny's lunchtime had started. He wasn't there, but at least neither was anyone else.

A horse wandered closer, and Taryn reached up to pat it. She didn't have much experience with horses, but this eggshell-colored beast seemed about as dangerous as a cotton ball. It snuffled, and Taryn smiled at the gentleness of the animal.

"It's almost done raining," she said. "You look like you'd like a good, long ride."

"Don't promise her it's almost done raining." Kenny's voice widened Taryn's smile and she turned halfway toward him. "It is going into winter, you know. Rains a lot here in the winter."

"Define 'a lot'. Down in Corpus Christi, it didn't rain much."

He leaned against the fence next to her and stroked the horse's neck. "Is that where you're from?"

"I lived there for a long time," she said, her throat closing but not as far as it sometimes did. Progress. "I was a news reporter."

"Like on TV?"

"Yes."

The horse snuffled again, and Kenny laughed. "Okay, Peony. I'll get you some sugar." He moved away from Taryn, and the comfort and peace he seemed to exude went with him. He returned a minute later, several cubes in his hand. He handed them to Taryn. "Give 'er one at a time, and don't be surprised if a big black fellow joins you. Hank adores sugar."

Taryn held out one sugar cube, and a squirrel of delight ran through her when the horse sucked it up with her lips. Sure enough, a tall, black horse stuck his head into Peony's stall a moment later.

"I'm gonna go eat," Kenny said. "It's been a long morning." He moved to the ladder and scaled it in only a few steps. Taryn spent several more minutes with the two horses, also feeling their strength and power give her the confidence she needed to follow Kenny to the hayloft.

She found him in her spot next to the window, so she took his place from yesterday and pulled out her peanut butter sandwich. "Do you have allergies?" she asked.

"Just to penicillin. Makes me throw up."

She bit into her lunch. "Chunky or creamy?"

"Chunky, always." He grinned down at her. "You?"

"Both. Creamy in cookies. Chunky on sandwiches. Also, I found this gourmet peanut butter in Corpus Christi once. It was a blend of chocolate and peanut butter in a jar." Taryn relaxed as she remembered the international shop, which boasted chocolate from all over the world, and soft drinks from all walks of life. She'd found the chocolate peanut butter on a back shelf, along with a hazelnut cream she'd adored.

"Sounds dangerous," he said.

"It definitely was to my waistline," she agreed with a little giggle.

He matched his laughter to hers and slid his hand into hers. He leaned his head back against the barn wall and closed his eyes, that infectious smile still playing with his lips. Taryn watched him, searching inside herself for how she felt here, with him, holding his hand.

She identified peaceful, content, happy. And she hadn't felt anything like those emotions in so long, she could barely recognize them.

She copied him, determined to memorize how right being here with him felt so she could hold onto it for later.

"Thanks for being patient with me," she said, unsure of where the words came from.

His only answer came in the form of extra pressure on her fingers.

---

TARYN MET KENNY IN THE BARN EVERY DAY THAT SHE worked out at the ranch. She did her grocery shopping in person for the first time since leaving Corpus Christi. She even did a little window shopping down Main Street as Thanksgiving approached.

Something about Three Rivers had infected her. Something good. Something she didn't want to leave in her rear-view mirror. It was more than Kenny Stockton, though the handsome cowboy played the biggest part in her love affair with the small town.

She held hands with him, told him about her childhood, even ventured into territory she used to deem dangerous when she spoke briefly about Collin or her travels to various cities around the country.

The weeks passed quickly, until one day, Kenny said, "So I'll pick you up about eleven. Is that okay?"

"Tomorrow?"

"It's Thanksgiving Day tomorrow." He peered at her with curiosity. "Do you even own a calendar?"

She lifted her wrist and shook her fitness tracker at him. "I know what day it is."

"Do you?" He chuckled. "So eleven o'clock tomorrow. I'll need your address."

Taryn startled, unsure if she even knew her address. "Okay, I live above the barber shop."

"You do? Aren't you worried about Old Man Tillman?"

Taryn searched his face but found nothing sinister. "Why would I be?"

"You know, *Sweeny Todd*?" He smiled and tucked her closer to his body. "Never mind. Shouldn't have brought it up."

"Yeah, because now I'll be worried that that eighty-year-old man could climb the stairs." She laughed. "Which he can't, by the way."

Kenny laughed, the sound originating in his chest and vibrating Taryn's body. She loved listening to him laugh. She wished she could bottle the sound and fall asleep to it at night.

"Eleven is fine," she said. "What do I wear?"

"Whatever," he said. "Charlie's mom isn't fussy."

"So jeans would be okay?"

"Sure. That would be okay." He gestured to her disgusting maid clothes.

She leaned out of his arms. "This shirt has holes in the bottom of it."

He licked his lips—completely distracting her—and shrugged. "I like whatever you wear."

"You like whatever I wear?" She tipped her head back and laughed. "All you've seen is raggedy jeans and holey shirts."

"Not true. I saw you in that dress last week at church."

She wondered which one, because she'd left most of her nice clothes down south. "And you didn't come sit by me? I've been sitting alone for weeks. It's...."

"It's what?"

"It would be better if I had a handsome man to hold my hand during the sermon."

His gaze sharpened; he looked at her with all the precision of a predatory bird. A true marine. "Well, if I'd known that, I would've done it weeks ago."

His intense gaze combined with his husky words drove Taryn's desire toward the ceiling. Her eyes dropped to his mouth, her fantasies about kissing him taking center stage in her mind. Could she kiss him here? In a hayloft?

He dipped his head as if he'd meet her mouth with his right this second. She closed her eyes in anticipation, almost desperate for his kiss.

"So eleven tomorrow," he whispered, his mouth missing hers completely and touching just below her jaw. "And church on Sunday." His lips arced up toward her ear. "Yeah?"

"Yeah," she echoed, her voice hardly her own. He straightened, and she released the unconscious grip she had on his collar. He looked at her with desire and knowledge in his eyes, stood, and headed toward the ladder.

"'Bye, Taryn."

"See you tomorrow," she said, glad she knew Kenny wanted to kiss her as much as she wanted to kiss him. An equal measure of fear bolted through her. She knew what came after kissing, and that dating then led to proposals, and Taryn didn't have a great track record with those. Sighing, she followed Kenny's scent down the ladder to the horse stalls, where her newfound friends waited for her with eager eyes. At least they only wanted sugar cubes.

If Taryn could figure out what she wanted, she could at least take a step forward. As it was, she felt stuck. Stuck, with nowhere else to go. Nothing else to do.

---

KENNY MUTTERED TO HIMSELF DURING THE ENTIRE forty-minute drive to town. Charlie had left the ranch last night, so Kenny'd been alone in the cabin. His speeches then hadn't benefitted him any more than his stern self-lectures were helping him now.

He'd coached himself to go slow with Taryn, draw out the details of her life the way he would interrogate a prisoner, let her set the pace with their physical relationship. He'd wanted so badly to kiss her in the hayloft the day before. She wanted him to as well. Why he hadn't done it, he still wasn't sure.

Yes, he was. He hadn't kissed her because he had the feeling he shouldn't. He wasn't perfect at listening to the Lord and obeying, but he'd been trying really hard to do so when it came to Taryn. He prayed for clarity of thought when it came to her, and though his body had been screaming at him to *kiss her!* his mind had warned him to *back off*.

Kenny hadn't made it to kissing ground in a while—that usually happened after the third date with the women in Three Rivers. He could navigate the town's roads without thought, but he didn't know how to map this terrain with someone as complicated as Taryn.

In the end, he knew she needed to come to him. Whenever she was ready. He'd admit he'd prayed for quite a while last night that she would be ready soon. He didn't know how many more lunches he could endure without being able to taste her lips.

"At least one more, Marine," he ordered himself as he eased to a stop in front of the barber shop. He opened the door and stood just as a door to the right of the shop opened and a vision of poise and beauty emerged.

"Taryn," he breathed. No wonder the woman had been on TV. Wearing a denim dress with a wide, mustard-yellow sash, she looked sophisticated and kissable at the same time. He swept her into his arms, where she giggled and lifted her sandaled feet off the ground.

He nuzzled his face into her neck, taking a deep breath of her clean, crisp perfume. A new scent she didn't wear to clean cabins. "Mmm, Happy Thanksgiving, Taryn."

"Happy Thanksgiving, Kenny." She regained her feet and beamed up at him. "You look handsome as ever."

"That wasn't the dress I saw you wearing at church." That one had been black, accentuated all her curves, and accented with bright blue jewelry.

"That's because I just bought it from the boutique." She indicated a building down the block. "The owner there is an amazing woman."

"*You're* an amazing woman." He took both her hands in his, beyond joyful to share this day with her.

She stretched up and brushed her lips across his cheek. "Thank you." Her southern twang pierced him right through the heart, and Kenny felt himself falling.

*Not so fast,* he told himself. Again, and again. He always fell first, and he didn't want to make that same mistake this time. He'd been treading so carefully, because he didn't want to make any mistakes with Taryn. She seemed like the type of woman who'd already seen her fair share of disappointments, and he didn't want to add to those.

"You ready to go?" he asked with a squeeze to her fingers.

"Not quite."

Kenny's eyebrows rose. "No?" He glanced back to the door

through which she'd exited. "Did you need to run back upstairs?"

A playful glint rode in her eyes when he looked at her again. "Nope." She leaned forward, and he encircled her in his arms. She tipped onto her toes again, her eyes drifting closed a moment before Kenny understood her meaning.

Her mouth brushed his, incensing his desire for her. He brought her closer, catching her lips again and keeping them next to his for longer.

His pulse skyrocketed, but he forced himself to remain in the moment. Because it was the single best moment of his life.

# CHAPTER THIRTY-ONE

Kissing Kenny took the number one spot on Taryn's Best Experiences list. Previous to the uniting of their mouths, her trip to Iceland had claimed that spot. But now, standing with his muscular arms around her and his scent tantalizing her and his mouth so perfectly molded to hers, Taryn knew Iceland didn't hold a candle to Kenny Stockton.

Nothing ever would. No one ever could.

She finally broke the contact between them, her calves tense from having to stretch up to reach his face. He held her up easily, and she relaxed against his chest.

"Well…what was that?" he asked.

"Oh, I'm sorry. You didn't want me to kiss you?" She tipped her head back to look at him. "You sure acted like you liked it."

"Oh, I liked it." He ducked his head as if he'd kiss her again. But he didn't, and a knife of disappointment cut through her chest. "Just didn't know that had to be done before you could go to Thanksgiving dinner."

She stepped out of his arms, taking a careful moment to make sure her legs could support her weight. She smoothed down her skirt and adjusted her sash, which had been slightly displaced because of his grip on her waist. "Well, it did."

He stepped to her truck door and opened it. "So if I did that again, you wouldn't mind?"

Taryn moved into his personal space, her eyes caught on his. Desire and joy and a sparkling tease adorned his stormy-sky eyes. She lifted one shoulder in a nonchalant shrug. "I guess not."

She climbed into the truck as he said, "You guess not?"

"You'll have to try it and see." She crossed her legs and stared straight out the windshield. His chuckle made her grin as he closed the door and waltzed in front of the truck.

He got in next to her and started the ignition. He fiddled with the heater settings. He leaned across the space between them and tucked his hand behind her head. She turned toward him, letting him guide her mouth to his for the second best experience of her life.

An edge of fear started to wedge its way into her mind, but she forced it away. She was just kissing a man. A man whose chest housed a heart of gold. A man who knew how to work hard, how to sacrifice, how to kiss a woman like he meant it.

He pulled away first this time, a smile already stuck to his face. "Yeah, okay, that had to be done before we go to lunch. But now we're late."

"Your fault," she said. "We had time for my kiss."

He laughed, the booming sound filling the cab. Against her will, she joined him, but her higher, more delicate laughter couldn't match his. She didn't even want it to. She reached over and tucked her hand in his, more content than she'd been in a long, long time.

He filled her in about Charlie and his girlfriend on the way to Amarillo, leaving Taryn to simply nod or agree in single-word sentences. Which she appreciated, but also didn't, because it let her mind wander down dangerous roads. Dangerous roads that reminded her that she wasn't ready for what came after kissing—and she didn't know if she ever would be.

---

THE NEXT TIME KENNY CAME TO PICK HER UP, TARYN let him come to the door and knock. "Come in!" she called as she searched her jewelry box for the pair of earrings she needed to make her outfit come together. She found the fish and put them on as Kenny's bootsteps stalled in her bedroom doorway.

"Hey, there."

The simple sound of his voice made her heart leap and her smile instantly appear. "Hey, yourself." She finished with her earrings and stepped into him for a kiss. He'd left her in her living room completely breathless on Thanksgiving evening. She hadn't seen him since, and though it had only been two days, she felt like perhaps a lifetime had passed.

Maybe she was ready for a new life. A new life in Three Rivers. A new life with Kenny. She pushed the thoughts to the back of her mind to deal with later. She'd met him a month ago; she certainly wouldn't be making any long-term decisions right away.

*But maybe you should,* she thought, which made her freeze.

"What?" Kenny asked.

"Nothing," she said quickly. Taryn certainly couldn't tell him that maybe they should put both feet on the accelerator and see what happened. She ducked her head, embarrassed at her own idea, though a remote corner of her mind kept screaming at her to do something different than she'd done before. And she'd never spent less than two years dating a man before, well, before breaking up with him.

She stole a glance at Kenny, who seemed wrapped up in the artwork above her mantle. Taryn didn't want to break up with him. But she also knew that relationships with men as magnetic and charismatic as Kenny only ended in one other way —heartbreak.

*He's worth it.*

The thought didn't seem to belong to her, but she listened to it anyway. As she led him downstairs to his truck, she realized that her heart hadn't been broken when she ended things with Chris. No, her pride had been wounded. Her reputation called into question. But she hadn't been heartbroken.

The distinction became important as she entered the chapel with Kenny on her arm, as the pastor started his sermon, as she realized that she'd run away from her own humiliation. Not from Chris. Not from her job. But from herself.

---

TARYN SEEMED TO BE LOST INSIDE HER OWN HEAD. When the pastor cracked a slight joke during his sermon, she didn't even smile. Like she hadn't even heard him. As the minutes passed, Kenny realized his assessment was spot-on. She wasn't listening, but she seemed alert and tense, which meant she'd disappeared inside herself again.

Kenny let her drift, though he wished he could see inside her head and straighten everything out. Instead, he focused on what the pastor had to say the Sabbath after Thanksgiving.

"As we move into the season where we celebrate the birth of the Savior, let us remember how He lived, and strive to emulate Him in our own lives."

Kenny found himself nodding along with most of the congregation. The pastor ended soon after, and he nudged Taryn toward the aisle. But she didn't budge, being surprisingly strong for such a small woman.

"Kenny," she said. "Can you come back to my place for a few minutes? I have something…." She swallowed so hard, it required every muscle in her neck to do it. "I have to show you something."

Her anxiety bled into the air surrounding them, and Kenny found himself tensing as if he might be struck. "Sure," he managed to say. "What's up?"

"Just...something I've been thinking about."

He couldn't force himself to make trite conversation on the way back to her apartment, and she certainly didn't contribute anything. Kenny flexed his fingers on the steering wheel and prayed for patience and strength and for the right reaction and words to say.

She unlocked her door and took a deep breath before entering. "Okay, so I just want you to know this is hard for me, but I was sitting there in church, and I had a feeling I needed to be brave and show you why I came to town."

Kenny's heart twisted, ached, at the sight of pure fear on Taryn's face. He wanted to erase it and build a protective wall around her life so it could never come back. He drew her into his chest and wrapped her in his arms. "Whatever you want, Taryn."

She breathed beside him, the rising and falling of her chest matching his. "Okay. I'm going to get it set up, but I can't watch it again."

Kenny's throat felt like someone had poured sand into his mouth, like he was back in Qatar and couldn't get away from the heat and granules and agony. He watched, mute, as she opened her laptop and clicked, typed, clicked again.

"So I left Corpus Christi several months ago," she said, gesturing for him to take her place at the dining room table where she had her computer queued up. "This is why."

He sat, but he didn't look at the computer. "Taryn, I don't really care why you left Corpus Christi."

She graced him with a faint smile that barely touched her lips. "This is the twelfth town I've come to." Another hard swallow. "But it's the first where I actually want to stay. And the only way to do that is to show someone why I've been bouncing around for months."

He glanced at the laptop. She'd opened a YouTube video and paused it. The screen sat black and waiting for him. His stomach squirmed like it used to before a mission, and he steeled himself for whatever he was about to see.

"I want you to stay in town too," he said.

"You're the reason I want to stay," she whispered. "And that scares me more than anything. More than showing you this video. But at least then you'll have a better idea of who I am."

Kenny almost protested, but Taryn turned and left the room, closing her bedroom door behind her. A few moments later, the low beat of loud music shook the floor. Kenny faced the laptop like it was his target, something dangerous and to be feared.

He squared his shoulders and clicked the play button. Taryn appeared on the screen, her makeup and hair flawless, her smile bright, her words delivered with the practice and skill of someone who'd been on live TV for years. She was every bit the sophisticated professional he'd seen exit her apartment on Thanksgiving Day.

She ended the newscast, but the camera didn't fade into a commercial. Her co-anchor, a man named Harry Herbert, grinned as if he'd won the lottery, and said, "We have one more thing tonight, Taryn."

She maintained her professional smile, but Kenny saw the blip of panic in her eyes. "We do?"

Another man appeared on-set behind her, a tall, blond-haired man with blue diamond eyes. "Taryn Tucker." She spun toward him, her practiced professionalism fading as the man got down on one knee.

"Chris," she breathed, both hands pressing over her pulse. "What are you doing?" She shook her head, tiny little movements left and right that told Kenny she didn't want him to propose. Anyone would've picked up on her cues.

But apparently not Chris. He proposed, and Taryn said no.

Right there on air.

Harry's smile dropped. Chris looked at the camera with pain etched in his face. Taryn fled the set, and Harry closed the segment. The video faded to black.

Kenny sat back in his chair, his mind whirling through the three-minute video again. It didn't take long for him to decide he didn't care. He stood, the chair scraping loudly against the floor. His knock was answered with the music cutting off and Taryn opening the door.

"I don't know who that woman was." Kenny hooked his thumb over his shoulder. "But she isn't you." He inched into her personal space, pleased when she didn't shuffle back. "I'm glad you showed me, because it does explain why you've been so hesitant with me." He paused when she flinched like he'd flicked cold water in her face.

He backed up a couple of steps, enough for her to get out of her bedroom if she wanted to. "Talk to me."

"I dated Chris for two years," she said.

Kenny schooled his features into a mask of stone. He'd had many opportunities to keep his true feelings behind a solid wall. "So?"

"I...I have a hard time committing to someone."

"It's not like we're going to get married anytime soon." He crossed his arms. "We just met a month ago."

"I like you," she said.

He quirked one side of his mouth. "I like you, too."

"I don't want to be hesitant with you."

"I don't want you to be that way either." He relaxed, stuffing his hands into his pockets instead. "But I'm okay with whatever you want. If you just want to hold hands and kiss me, that's fine."

She ducked her head. "What if I just want to be friends?"

"No." Kenny didn't mean for his voice to sound like a bark, but it did. He moved toward her and embraced her. "No, I don't want to be just friends. I want to be your best friend, sure. The person who knows the most about you. Who can run to the store and get your favorite juice and that doughnut you like the most. But not *just* friends." He touched his mouth to the spot just below her jaw. "I like kissing you too much for that."

She tilted her head and kissed him. He felt something new in her kiss, something deeper, something more permanent. And he knew she didn't want to be just friends either.

In fact, that was probably why she'd shown him the video. Kenny catalogued the information, the feelings, and then lost himself in Taryn's kiss—something he wanted to do everyday of his life.

# CHAPTER THIRTY-TWO

Taryn enjoyed her work more than she thought possible. It felt nice, easy, relaxing, to just show up, do her job, and go home. She didn't have to be "on" all the time. She didn't have to look perfect, act perfect, sound perfect. It was freeing to just be Taryn, not Taryn-Tucker-of-Channel-Nine-News.

Kenny had taken the video in stride, and she wondered now why she thought he wouldn't. Everything he did he took in stride. The man was unflappable. It was as maddening as it was admirable.

"Hey there, gorgeous." He leaned in the doorway to the barn, delicious-looking in his cowboy boots, dark jeans, leather jacket, and his trademark cowboy hat.

She smiled but went back to stroking Peony. She'd felt something with the horses, a connection she'd never imagined could exist between a horse and a human. She'd done a little research into the therapeutic riding facility housed at the ranch, and she had an appointment with Pete Marshall, the owner, that afternoon after she finished cleaning cabin three.

"I brought you something." Kenny sidled up to her and held out a pastry bag.

"Kenny." She stretched up and kissed him quick before taking the bag. "What is it?"

"You never did tell me what your favorite doughnut is. So I figured I'd buy one everyday until I landed on the right one."

"You drove to town this morning?" She glanced inside the bag and pulled out an apple fritter. "For this?"

"Ah, so it's not an apple fritter." He swiped the pastry from her fingers and took a big bite. "Good, because I love these things."

She laughed and reached for the fritter. "They're not my favorite, but I don't hate them." She took a bite too, a moan stretching from her throat. "Oh, this is fantastic."

"And I didn't drive to town," he said. "Miss Heidi is startin' a bakery, and her pastry chef has been bringing samples to the ranch for weeks."

"This is literally the best apple fritter I've ever eaten."

"I'll tell Grace. She'll be happy." Kenny smiled at Taryn, the gesture more than just movement. It carried adoration and desire, joy and genuine warmth.

"How are you so happy all the time?" She nudged his shoulder with hers and lifted one foot to the bottom rung of the fence.

"Is that a bad thing?" Kenny clasped his hands and let them hang over the railing into the horse stall. His voice sounded measured and even, and Taryn suspected she'd hit a nerve.

"Have other people said it's a bad thing?"

"About every woman I've dated," he said. "The last one said she didn't want to go out with me again, because it was too hard to see me so happy when she wasn't. Said she actually felt guilty when she got home."

Taryn blinked at him, at the stoic expression on his face, at the way he stared down Peony like she was an enemy. Laughter pooled in her stomach and bubbled up through her throat.

"So that's funny to you, huh?" He kicked a smile in her direction.

"A little, yeah. You must not have kissed that other woman."

"Never made it that far, no."

Taryn linked her arm through his and pressed in close. "Good. Because if you had, she wouldn't care how happy you were. She'd just be thinking about the next time she could kiss you."

"So you're saying you can put up with my joviality because I'm a good kisser?" He peered down at her, that cowboy hat casting them both in shadows.

"You are a *great* kisser." She maneuvered into his arms, relieved when he held her tight and close, the way he always did. "And I like your joviality. It makes me think that I can be that happy one day too."

He kissed her forehead, his cowboy hat getting dislodged. He swiped it off to reveal his sandy hair. She traced her fingers along his ears and behind his neck. He touched his lips to the tip of her nose. "Why aren't you?"

Such a simple question, with such a complicated answer. As she thought about it, Taryn realized that happiness was a choice. That she didn't have to let the things from her past haunt her forever.

"I'm trying to be," she finally said. "I'm going to see Pete this afternoon. Maybe I'll be a cowboy like you."

"I like you just how you are." He beamed down at her and then kissed her. As she relaxed into his touch and deepened the kiss, Taryn recognized a definite vein of happiness threading through her.

She knew what she wanted. For the first time in a long time, she knew she wanted to live in Three Rivers. She wanted to spend as much time as possible with Kenny Stockton. She wanted to be happy with Kenny, in Three Rivers.

*Is that possible?* she asked as Kenny led her up to the hayloft so they could eat lunch.

A distinct lesson from her childhood struck her full in the chest. *With God, anything is possible.*

---

Kenny enjoyed his hour-long lunch more over the next couple of weeks than he ever had. Peanut butter and raspberry jam had never tasted so sweet, especially when it was what Taryn packed and he just got to taste it on her lips.

He spent his afternoons whistling and reliving the passionate kisses he shared with Taryn in the privacy of the hayloft. With two weeks until Christmas, he began to stew about what he should get her.

They were exclusive, that was certain. He was falling fast for her. Also certain. She seemed to enjoy his company as well, and she melted like butter over an open flame every time he touched her. He felt certain the feelings between them were mutual.

He'd actually started dreaming in diamonds, but he wouldn't be asking Taryn to marry him for Christmas. The very idea would drive her to another town in the dead of night. He also knew that for certain.

He could be patient. At least he told himself he could. Seeing her and kissing her five days a week helped. Six if he could get into town on Saturdays. But he never saw her on Fridays, so he put his head down, ate lunch alone in his cabin to avoid the ribbing by the other boys, and passed the hours until he could call Taryn and be soothed by her pretty little voice.

Near quittin' time on Friday, Kenny suddenly thought of the perfect gift for Taryn. His pace increased to get the animals fed for the evening so he could head into town and meet with his friend and travel agent, Jeremy Thacker.

Taryn loved to travel. Had done a bunch for her job, but he wanted this trip to be pure pleasure for her. They'd talked about her family, and his, and where she'd like to visit, and where he would, and Kenny practically burst with happiness at his plan.

*Kitty Hawk,* he recited as he threw hay and slopped water into troughs. He headed over to the administration trailer to check out with either Garth or Lawrence, the controller.

When he opened the door, he practically ran into the back of an older gentleman. The man stood in front of Lawrence's empty desk, holding his phone in one hand like he expected it to go off at any moment.

"Hey," Kenny said. "Has someone helped you?" This man had clearly never stepped foot on a ranch. He wouldn't be wearing leather shoes shinier than the sun if he had.

"I'm looking for someone," he said, his deep voice commanding respect with only a few words.

"Is Lawrence helpin' you find them, or…?"

The man slid his appraising gaze from Kenny's cowboy hat to his cowboy boots. "Not yet."

"Maybe I can help you. Who you lookin' for?"

The man sighed like Kenny wasn't worthy of his attention. "I was told there's a woman here who cleans the cabins. Taryn Tucker?"

Alarms blared in Kenny's head. This man hadn't been on the video. He wasn't the co-anchor or the ex-boyfriend. So who was he?

"She doesn't work on Fridays," Kenny managed to say.

"Do you know where I can find her?"

Kenny didn't want to lie, but he reasoned that he didn't know for certain that Taryn would be at home. When he called her on Friday nights, she answered, and she usually said she'd spent the day cleaning or shopping or wandering the town. She could be *any*where.

"Sorry, I don't."

Kenny held his breath, hoping this guy wouldn't ask for her phone number. But someone else in the world must've needed a bigger miracle than his, because the man did ask.

Kenny leaned all his weight on his right leg, trying to figure out who this man was. In the end, he asked, "Who are you? I'm not sure she wants you to have her number if she didn't give it to you."

The man's eagle eyes sharpened, and he glared up at Kenny. "Taryn used to work for me. I'm not going to hurt her."

"In Corpus Christi?"

The man picked invisible lint from his impeccable suit. "You seem to know quite a bit about Taryn."

Kenny put on his mask. "She's worked here for a couple of months. We've eaten lunch together a few times, that's all."

"I'm not going to hurt her," he repeated.

"What do you want with her?"

"I need her back," he said.

A balloon of sub-zero liquid expanded in Kenny's chest. Taryn couldn't leave Three Rivers. He didn't want to be without her.

"She'll be in on Monday," Kenny said, perching on the edge of Lawrence's desk.

The man glared, and Kenny gave his attitude right back to him. It was obvious that this man was used to getting what he wanted, when he wanted it. But Kenny didn't care. He didn't have the right to give Taryn's phone number out to men whose names he didn't even know.

"Very well." The man turned on his designer heel and left the administration trailer. Kenny didn't waste another moment —he hurried down the aisle, his fingers already pulling up Taryn's number on his phone. He could get her a vacation tomorrow, but he wanted her to know about her old boss now. He wasn't sure what the fallout would be—*Please let her stay in town*, he prayed—but it was a risk he needed to take.

Her line rang while he continued a steady stream of silent prayers to keep her in his life. He would propose on Christmas Day if he thought Taryn was ready. But he knew she wasn't. Even with several sessions with Peony, she wasn't ready. And Kenny didn't want to end up like the boyfriend on the video he'd watched.

Pushing his own fears and insecurities aside, he muttered, "Come on, Taryn. Answer."

"Hey, there," she finally said, obvious happiness in her voice.

"Hey," he said. "So there was just a man here...."

# CHAPTER THIRTY-THREE

Taryn had been in the triangle yoga pose when her phone started ringing. She'd almost let the call go to voicemail so she could keep the positive energy she'd been gathering. But in the end, something whispered to her to get up and get the phone.

Now, as she listened to Kenny talk, she wished she hadn't. Well, that wasn't quite true. She was really glad he'd called, she just didn't like what he had to say.

"Thanks, Kenny," she said when he finally finished. She'd never heard him speak so fast, with such urgency.

"What are you going to do?"

"I don't know."

"Do you want me to come in?"

"No," she said. "I'll deal with Stanley."

"Taryn," he started, and a twinge of annoyance twisted through her.

"It's fine, Kenny. I'm fine."

"I don't think you are."

Her annoyance bloomed into full-fledged frustration. He'd been kind to her; patient and gentle; never pushed her farther than she wanted to go. He let her initiate the hard conversations, and he kissed her whenever she felt like her world was about to implode. She'd come to rely on him, something she'd never really done with Chris—or anyone else in her life.

"This has nothing to do with you," she said.

"How can you say that?" Kenny exhaled, maybe the first angry sound she'd heard him make. "I'm in love with you. What happens to you affects me."

"I—" She stalled completely. He couldn't love her after only a few weeks together. Could he? She didn't even love herself yet, though her training with the horses had helped her in more ways than she could enumerate.

"Just tell me you're not going to leave town. That I'll pick you up for church on Sunday, and we'll go together, and then I'll be able to come back to your place and fall asleep on your couch while you make those meatballs I can't get enough of." His voice held a hint of desperation, a ton of anxiety, and his usual level of playfulness.

She found a smile pulling at her lips. "Of course I'll be here on Sunday," she said. "I'm not going anywhere, Kenny."

"Maybe I can come into town tomorrow."

"Don't worry so much," she said. "You'll ruin your perfectly handsome face." She took a deep breath. "I'll call Stanley, and I'll call you back."

"Okay," he said and they hung up. But Taryn didn't call Stanley immediately. She paced from her living room to her kitchen and back, biting her lip while her mind ran down a road she hadn't unleashed it on in months.

She knew why Stanley had tracked her down—he wanted her to come back. Kenny had confirmed Taryn's suspicion. She also knew Stanley was one of the most persuasive men on the planet. What he wanted he usually got. She was actually surprised that he hadn't been able to get her phone number from Kenny.

Her gaze fell on the sheaf of paperwork she needed to sign.

The paperwork for her new house in Pinion Ridge, a new community going in on the southwest side of town. She hadn't told Kenny about it. Had wanted to surprise him on Christmas Day. She'd imagined the look on his face a hundred times.

"You need a plan," she told herself as she gripped her cell phone. "Stanley just won't accept a no."

But though she paced for another ten minutes, she couldn't come up with a plausible plan, an extraordinary excuse, nothing. She only knew she wanted to stay in Three Rivers. She'd fallen in love with the town, and she suspected she could fall in love with Kenny if she'd let herself.

Needing a bit more time, she texted Stanley that she'd meet him for dinner at the steakhouse—he'd be paying—and she stepped into the shower to put on her professional face.

---

SHE SAT IN THE BOOTH, HER RIGHT LEG BOUNCING A mile a minute. She'd waved the waitress away from refilling her water twice now, and she checked her phone again with a scowl. Stanley was almost thirty minutes late.

So typical. She glared out the window, but all she could see was her own displeased face. Five more minutes. And then she'd leave. She didn't owe him anything. She'd given her notice, worked out her last two weeks in the booth, and come back to town to get her final check. So she'd gone to the station in the middle of the night when she knew Stanley wouldn't be there. So what?

She didn't owe him anything.

Seven minutes later, she looped her purse over her shoulder and stood. She turned toward the exit and came face-to-face with Stanley Summers. "You are so late," she growled. "I was just leaving." She brushed past him and held her head high as she strode toward the front doors.

"You know I'm a vegetarian," he said as he matched his stride to hers.

She burst into the night beyond the steakhouse, her breath seizing at the temperature difference. It never got this cold in Corpus Christi, though it still wasn't considered cold by most standards.

"I'm not coming back," she said.

"I need you. Our ratings have tanked since you left."

"I'm happy here."

He tugged on her arm, and she stopped to face him. "You're cleaning cowboy cabins."

"So what?"

"You have a degree in journalism. You're an excellent reporter."

"I'm really good at a lot of things." She folded her arms to protect herself from his penetrating gaze. "I'm not leaving town. I like it here."

Stanley glanced around like he couldn't fathom what she could possibly like about Three Rivers. "There's nothing for you here."

"I have a job here. Friends."

"Friends?" Stanley chuckled. "Taryn, you lived in Corpus Christi for two years before you knew your neighbor's first name."

"I'm not the same person anymore." She liked that Kenny thought she was someone different from the woman on the video. She wasn't that person anymore. She'd only existed in Corpus Christi, and Taryn didn't want to be her again.

"Name one friend you have here."

"Gene."

"Landlords don't count."

"Pete," she countered.

Stanley cocked his head in disbelief. "What about that Kenny cowboy?"

"Yeah, we're friends," she said, almost choking on the word.

"He's an awful lot like Chris." Stanley focused over her shoulder like anything and everything was more interesting than her.

"He is *nothing* like Chris." Taryn started toward her car again. "We're done here, Stanley. Go home." Just because Chris and Kenny both commanded attention didn't make them a lot alike.

"I can't go back without you." He stepped in front of her, effectively blocking the path to her car.

"I am not going with you." His insistence that she return to Corpus Christi only fueled her fire to stay in Three Rivers.

"You've got to give me something. Your city needs a goodbye."

"I don't feel guilty about the way I left," she said. "I put in my two weeks."

"I needed you in front of the camera." He softened, showing his true age of almost seventy. "I still do."

She sighed and focused on the horizon to her right. "Three Rivers has quaint and festive celebrations during the holidays. Let's say, I...I don't know. Do a holiday spec piece for you. Then will you delete my number from your phone and never bother me again?"

A spark entered his eye. "You're telling me you—*the* Taryn Tucker—really wants to stay in this little town? How many people live here? Like five thousand?"

"I don't know," she said. "And I don't care. I like it here, and I'm tired of running." The thought of packing up her car again tied her lungs into knots.

"There's nothing to run from." He quieted his voice into that grandfatherly tone that had won her over many times. "Chris left town shortly after you. He hasn't come back, and no one misses him." He gave her a warm smile. "It's you they want to see."

She shook her head, the image of Kenny's chiseled face, the

memory of his lips against hers too strong to give in. "I'll do the special. You can call it an op-ed piece. Whatever you want. But I'm doing it here, and that's it." She glared at him, though most of her ire had evaporated. "Now, please move so I can go home. I still need to eat since someone so rudely showed up terribly late."

Stanley's eyes burned with curiosity, with intelligence, with acceptance. He moved out of the way. "Send me a proposal for the piece. You can do whatever you want, but it has to include a proper good-bye to your people in Corpus Christi."

"Fine." She wrenched the car door open and dropped into the driver's seat. She roared out of the parking lot, her blood racing like it was trying to win a marathon. After a few blocks of erratic driving, she turned left when she should've gone right. The road out to the ranch had always soothed her, and tonight, as the street lights in town faded behind her, the stars in the wide, black sky twinkled like diamonds.

By the time she pulled up to Kenny's cabin, the peaceful countryside had worked its magic on her overwrought system.

---

KENNY SULKED AROUND HIS CABIN, EATING A FROZEN pizza by himself as Charlie was in town with his girlfriend again. He had the TV on loud, because while he usually enjoyed the serene quiet of the range, tonight the silence felt suffocating. His phone rested on his knee just to make sure he didn't miss a single buzz.

But none came.

He got up and made himself a cup of spiced apple cider and a stack of toast. He realized as he grumped around his kitchen that he was in a bad mood. He hadn't felt this way in such a long time, he barely recognized the anxiety twining through his stomach and the way everything from Charlie's dirty dishes to having to get out more butter made him frown.

His front door opened, and he turned toward the sound, surprised Charlie had returned so early.

But it wasn't Charlie standing in the doorway; it was Taryn.

"Do you even know how to knock?" he asked, his toast and cider completely forgotten. His foul mood seemed to have evaporated at the sight of her.

"I did." She stepped into the cabin and closed the door behind her. "Your TV is so loud, you obviously didn't hear me."

Kenny scanned her, searching for signs of distress. She said she'd call, not show up on his doorstep wearing her flawless makeup and high-quality clothes. Besides those differences, she seemed whole and healthy. Her dark eyes sparkled, and her hair had grown out over the past several weeks, revealing her naturally honey-blonde color.

"Did you talk to your boss?" he asked, maintaining his position in the kitchen.

"He's not my boss." She shrugged out of her coat and collapsed on his couch. After turning off the TV, she leaned back and closed her eyes. "He wants me to come back to the station."

Kenny practically ran to her side. "What—I mean, you're not —" He closed his mouth, wanting to tell her how much he needed her to stay in town until they could see this through, but not wanting to influence her too strongly. She needed to make her own decisions, choose her own path in life. He wanted to be part of that life, part of her decision-making process, but she needed to include him in that on her own.

"What are you going to do?" he asked.

Without opening her eyes, she snuggled into his side. "I like it here." She sounded sleepy and sexy, and Kenny's hand cupped her bicep and kept her close. "I'm not going back to newscasting, but I do need another job. I can't clean cowboy cabins forever."

He caressed her arm, his mind whirling. "Well, I'm not sure there's something for someone of your expertise in Three Rivers."

"Mm." She yawned. "I'll figure something out."

"So you're not leaving."

"No. Stanley really wants me to come back, and I agreed to do a special piece on the Christmas celebrations here in town in order to give my goodbyes to the people in Corpus Christi."

"And that's what you need to do?" He brushed his lips against her forehead. "Will that give you the closure you need?"

"I think so." She opened her eyes and glanced up at him. "So that's what I'm going to do. Stanley agreed to leave me alone after that."

He grinned, glad she'd come instead of called. Glad she was staying.

"Now, I believe we have something else to talk about." Her eyes burned with an emotion he couldn't quite name, and he'd gotten really good at reading her over the past couple of months.

"We do?"

"Yeah, you said something pretty heavy on the phone earlier."

His brow creased and he searched his memory for what he'd said. "Remind me."

She ducked her head and rested her cheek against his chest. "You said you were in love with me."

His heart catapulted to the back of his throat and back. "Well, I suppose I am."

"You *suppose* you are?"

"I shouldn't have said that," he said. "I know you're not ready to hear it, and you certainly can't say it back. I guess…I guess it was just how I was feeling in that moment, because I was worried about you and wanted you to know you had someone in your corner."

He took a deep breath to force himself to be quiet, to allow himself some time to think, to give her a chance to consider what he'd said.

She breathed next to him, her shoulder rising and falling evenly. He enjoyed the silence with her, knowing for dead sure that he did love her. He shouldn't have said it, but that didn't mean he couldn't feel it.

"I have moments of loving you too," she said.

He flinched like she'd shouted. "You do?"

She heaved a sigh and sat up. "You're right—I'm not ready to say it back. I'm barely ready to hear it. But I want you to know that I feel strongly about you. And if you give me enough time, and keep kissing me when I'm unsure, I know there will come a day when we're on the same page at the same time."

"Did you just give me permission to kiss you whenever I want?" He quirked half a smile at her.

She giggled and pushed her palm against his chest. "You already do that."

"Oh, honey, trust me when I say I don't. If it were up to me, I'd kiss you a lot more." He leaned down, his mouth hovering dangerously over hers. Everything in her relaxed, sighed against him, submitted to his will. Her eyes drifted closed and her lips parted slightly, ready and waiting for him to kiss her.

He sat up straight, satisfied that he could keep kissing her—and nothing more—until she was ready to fully commit to him.

"Tease," she said, ducking her head again.

He lifted her chin and brought his mouth to hers firmly and kissed her with every ounce of passion and love he felt for her.

# CHAPTER THIRTY-FOUR

Taryn pulled into the parking lot in front of Courage Reins on the last Friday before Christmas, ready for her therapy. Reese sat behind the desk, looking tired and happy to see her at the same time.

"You okay?" she asked.

"No, but it's Friday."

"Is Carly in today?" Taryn glanced down the left hall.

"No, she's gone to Amarillo for the weekend." Reese's face lit up. "I'm heading out after work tonight. A birth mom called her last night, and she left this morning."

Taryn's heart lifted. "That's great news, Reese." She knew the couple had been trying to adopt a baby for a while now, but had had some disappointments along the way. She felt connected to Reese and Carly because of it. Same with Pete, who came down the right hall, which led to the indoor arena.

"Miss Taryn, I have Peony ready for you." He turned sideways and pointed down the hall. "You ready?"

She smiled at Reese and stepped past Pete. "Sure am." She pushed through the door. "When's that construction going to be done? What are they doing out there again?"

Pete helped her mount Peony. “It’s a horse training facility, and the construction crew should be done tomorrow, I think. They’ve been pulling long hours to get it finished before the holidays.” Pete handed her the reins. “Remember not to pull.”

She appreciated that his entire lecture consisted of four words. She did like to pull on the reins, control the horse instead of working with it.

An idea had been percolating in her head since Stanley had come to town. She needed to film her piece tomorrow night, Christmas Eve. “Pete, isn’t your mother-in-law opening a bakery soon?”

“Yeah. I’ve gained ten pounds since she’s been experimenting with her recipes out here.” He chuckled and patted his still-flat stomach. “Take ‘er around a few times, and then we’re going to gallop.”

Taryn’s heart dropped to her cowgirl boots, and she stayed still. “Can I get your mother-in-law’s number? I want to talk to her about being in my editorial piece on small town Christmas celebrations.” And she wanted to find out if she needed help in the bakery. Taryn liked coming out to the ranch and spending time with Kenny, but she really needed something else to keep her bills paid.

“Sure, I’ll get it for you while you ride.” He gave her a look that said, *Get going*, and Taryn clucked the horse into movement. She loved moving with the horse, talking to her like she could answer and give advice.

Feeling soothed and relaxed, Taryn slid to the ground at the end of her session. Kenny waited for her in the horse barn, where she brushed down Peony and fed her a sack of oats. “You want to go to dinner tonight?” he asked.

“I…can’t.” She didn’t look at him. “I have tons of prep work to do for the piece tomorrow.”

She hated the little fib. She did have loads to accomplish before tomorrow evening, when the camera crew would expect her to be ready to be on live TV—something she hadn't done in over eight months. But she could afford a few hours for dinner with her boyfriend.

Problem was, she already had an appointment with another man—the one giving her the keys to her new house out at Pinion Ridge.

"Can we get together tomorrow night, late, after I film?" She'd be exhausted and stretched thin by then, and being around the perpetually joyful Kenny would be just what she needed.

"Yeah, sure. I'll be at the celebration, so we can just go from there."

She seized. "You'll be at the celebration?"

He chuckled and pulled her into his chest. "Taryn, everyone in town knows about the camera crew coming for the feature. *Everyone's* going to be there."

She groaned, a low, painful sound she didn't tell her body to make. "What if I mess up? I haven't been on live TV for a long time."

"Everyone here loves you, and everyone in Corpus Christi loves you." He kissed her cheek, the corner of her mouth, the crook of her neck. "I love you. No one's going to care if you mess up. Plus." He pulled back and grinned down at her. "It might be nice to see you do something less than perfect."

She swatted at his arms, but he held her fast. "I am not perfect at everything I do."

"Have you seen my cabin after you clean it? Have you tasted your own cooking?"

She cocked her head at him. "Am I really that good of a cook?"

"Phenomenal." He leaned down to kiss her, but she jerked back. He peered at her, waiting for her to explain herself.

"Could I get a job as a cook in town, do you think?"

"Taryn, I think you could do whatever you want to do." He

gazed at her with such love and adoration, warmth flowed through her like a bubbling hot spring.

"Kenny, I have a Christmas gift for you."

His smile was wide and instant. "Oh, yeah? I have something for you too."

"Can we exchange on Christmas morning?" She hoped she wouldn't lose her courage over the next couple of days.

"Of course."

"I managed to get an apple pie from Grace Lewis, and I think I'll make a ham. Is that what you had for your family Christmas dinners?"

"My mom's not much of a cook."

Taryn laughed. "No wonder you think I'm a good cook." She stepped out of his arms, a bit surprised that he let her. "Maybe I won't be able to get a job in a restaurant."

"Sure you will. Like I said, you can do anything you want to do."

---

By the following evening, Taryn could barely remember Kenny's reassurances. They'd gotten her through filling out a half dozen applications that morning. His vote of confidence had helped her finish her preparations for the op-ed piece. The camera crew had arrived two hours ago, and she'd walked them through what she wanted, where she'd move, when they should pan out, and when they should voice over.

The sun had started to set, and the Christmas lights on Main Street gave such warmth to the town that Taryn knew why she'd chosen to stay here.

She tugged at the hem of her new peacoat, another purchase from Andy Larsen, the boutique owner who Taryn needed to become besties with to start saving on her purchases. She fiddled with her ear mic, the way she used to before a broadcast.

Stanley had sent a crew of five for her special. He himself hadn't come, something for which she was grateful. She didn't recognize any of the cameramen either, though they all seemed to know who she was.

The seconds blurred into minutes, and then one of the men said, "And you're live in five, four...." He held up three fingers, two, then one, and Taryn took a deep breath.

"I'm Taryn Tucker, on location here in beautiful, festive, Three Rivers, Texas. This small town has big charm, as you can see from the holiday excitement behind me." She turned, caught a glimpse of Kenny's beaming face, and knew that everything was going to turn out all right.

---

KENNY WATCHED AS TARYN OOZED CHARISMA, AS SHE chatted with townspeople, as she charmed everyone in Three Rivers, the camera, and anyone on the other end of the feed. No wonder she'd been popular in Corpus Christi.

He'd gone online—probably a mistake—and seen dozens of open letters to "Miss Taryn Tucker, the heart of Corpus Christi" on forums and blogs. She'd had a real following. Part of him couldn't believe that she could just walk away from all of that. Another part of him admired her for doing it. A third part wondered if she ever missed being on-camera.

And now, watching her, he knew she did. He also believed she truly didn't want to return to that life. He didn't want her to either. He wanted to keep her as close as possible until the day he could ask her to be his wife.

He drifted away from the scene as she wrapped up the segment. She'd seemed nervous that he'd be there, and he'd tried to stay near the back of the crowd. They were meeting at the pancake house for celebratory hot chocolates, and Kenny wandered in that direction.

Several cowhands from the ranch passed by, each inviting him to join them for the evening. The owner, Squire Ackerman, caught his eye and Kenny stopped to chat for a second.

"You alone?" Squire asked, his right hand holding his wife's and his left clutching Finn's. Another little girl clung to Kelly's shoulder as she balanced her on her hip.

"On my way to meet someone."

"Taryn," Kelly said with a knowing smile. "I know everything that happens out on my ranch."

Kenny's heart skipped a beat as Squire turned toward Kelly with an arched brow. "*Your* ranch? And what do we feed the cattle?"

She nudged him with her shoulder. "Fine, I know everything that happens to the people out on *our* ranch." She slid a mischievous glance at Kenny. "Including where and with whom they eat lunch."

Kenny's face heated, and he tipped his hat to her. "It's no secret I'm datin' Taryn."

"It isn't?" Squire whipped his face back to Kenny's.

Kelly laughed. "Squire, I swear. You're the last to know everything that happens. Even Pete knew."

"Well, Taryn is his client," Kenny said quickly. "Don't feel too bad, Major."

Squire gazed toward the hullaballoo down the block. "She's not gonna stay on much longer, is she?" He wasn't really asking, and Kenny chuckled.

"My guess is no," he said. "Which is a real shame, because I've sure enjoyed her housekeeping."

"Well, you'll just have to marry her," Kelly singsonged.

Kenny's joy tumbled down a notch. "We're in negotiations."

"Negotiations?" Squire burst out laughing. "Women don't like military talk."

Kenny grinned at him. "She's...working through a few things before we get serious enough to be talkin' diamonds."

"And you?" he asked. "You have anything to work through?"

"Just how to keep her happy until she realizes I'm her one and only." Kenny lowered his voice. "And I'd appreciate it if that stayed between me and you, Miss Kelly."

"Of course."

"At least he knows who the gossipy one is," Squire said.

"I am not gossipy." She hipped Squire this time. "But I probably will tell Chelsea."

"Shouldn't have said anything," Squire said as he started walking away. "Once my sister knows, the whole county will know."

"No problem," Kenny called after them, but a jiggle of anxiety wormed through his bloodstream.

---

ON CHRISTMAS DAY, KENNY ARRIVED AT TARYN'S about mid-morning. She wore her hair up in a messy bun, revealing her very kissable neck, and a festive red and white sweater dress that hugged every curve.

Kenny swallowed as he entered her apartment and she locked them in together. "Have you ever had funeral potatoes?"

"Yeah, sure, every time someone dies." He followed her into the kitchen. "Is that what you're making? Because I've never met a potato I didn't like."

She giggled. "You'll eat anything. I could put butter on a brick and you'd tell me it was the best sandwich you've ever had."

"That is so not true."

She cocked her hip and he lunged toward her, catching her up and twirling her around. She squealed and grabbed onto his shoulders. He loved the way she made him feel: powerful and strong and necessary. He loved being with her. He loved that he could offer her shelter from the storms of life. He loved her.

"Let's do gifts now," he said, setting her on her feet.

A blip of panic stole across her face. "Now?"

He pulled out the envelope he'd put her tickets in. "Yeah, now." He held his gift toward her. She took it and retrieved a small, silver box from the top of her fridge. Bigger than a ring box, but it probably couldn't hold more than a can of soda.

She slipped her finger under the envelope's flap and extracted the tickets. "Kitty Hawk...Kenny. What is this?"

"You said you love to travel, but that you didn't get to do much of it for pleasure. I thought, well, I thought we could take a vacation—a real vacation together. They're vouchers, good for up to twenty-four months. So, you know, you don't have to decide right away or anything."

She held them to her heartbeat like they were precious, made of gold. Her eyes seemed a bit glassy when she said, "Thank you, Kenny," and stretched up to kiss him. He enjoyed the feel and form of her lips against his. She was all he needed for Christmas.

But she pulled away and thrust the silver box toward him. He took it and lifted the lid. Beneath a slip of white tissue paper sat a gold key. A regular, shiny, gold key, like he would use to secure the deadbolt on his cabin.

He glanced at her, unsure about what this key unlocked. "Taryn?"

Her hands wrung around each other. "That's the key to my new house. I picked it up last Friday, and I'm moving in a couple of days." She swallowed, that hard, nervous swallow he wanted to eradicate from her life. "I wanted you to have a key, because it represents how I feel about Three Rivers, how I feel about us."

He flipped the key in his fingers, his eyes trained on the shiny metal. "You're stayin' here permanently." Joy he'd never known spiraled through his chest.

"I am. My new house is in that Pinion Ridge development."

Kenny nodded, and his head felt too loose, almost detached

from his shoulders. "That's great news." He finally lifted his eyes to hers. "I love you."

She invaded his personal space, pressing herself as close to him as she could get. "In this moment, I love you too."

It wasn't the all-out declaration Kenny craved, but in this moment, he'd take it. Because he knew she was dangerously close to being able to tell him she loved him all the time.

---

*The next Christmas:*

"Where's Taryn?" Pete entered the homestead, along with a heavy gust of wind. Kenny's already keyed-up nerves rioted again.

"She's comin'." He wished he hadn't told Charlie about his forthcoming proposal. The news had spread like wildfire, and it was all anyone had talked about for weeks. Even when Taryn came out for her riding lessons or just to see him. It was nothing short of a miracle that she hadn't overheard, that she didn't know.

Maybe she did.

Kenny's stomach swooped as the door opened again, but this time Garth and Juliette ducked into the house with their son right in front of them.

"Did we miss it?" Garth asked, glancing around at everyone in the kitchen, dining room, and living area of Squire's house. Kelly had gone all out for this holiday season. She'd had plenty of help from Chelsea and Heidi. Grace Lewis, the best pastry chef Three Rivers had ever seen, busied herself at the stove, stirring something that normally would've made Kenny double-sniff the air and become impatient for dessert later.

Squire consulted with Jon Carver and Lawrence about how to carve the turkeys, while Lawrence's wife, Andy, kept one hand on her bulging belly while she spoke to Sandy Keller, who'd just been the star of autumn with her wedding to Tad Jorgensen.

Bees buzzed in Kenny's blood. Snakes coiled in his gut. What had he been thinking? Taryn wouldn't want her engagement to be a public spectacle. Maybe it wasn't too late to call everything off. He opened his mouth to say something when the door opened again.

"Sorry I'm late." The wind caught the door behind Taryn, but she won the struggle and yanked it closed. "Phew, it's really angry out there." She smiled at Kenny and stepped to his side, her arm sliding around his waist. "Hey."

He pressed a nervous kiss to her temple and glanced around. It seemed like everyone had at least one eye on him, and he focused his attention back on Taryn. "Everything go okay getting the recording off?"

She'd taken a remote job with her old station, and she did three yearly holiday specials. One always fell on Christmas Eve, which she'd just finished the previous evening.

"All set. What did I miss here?"

"Just Ethan braggin' about how he won Rookie of the Year," Garth said. He lifted a mug of coffee to hide his obviously proud smile. "*Last* year."

"Hey," Ethan complained. "I wasn't bragging. Brynn was bragging for me." He beamed down at his fiancé.

"When are y'all getting married?" Carly Sanders joined their conversation as she bounced a beautiful baby boy on her hip. Kenny watched the child smile and slobber, and warmth filled his heart.

"Next month." Brynn glanced at him with love but a touch of wistfulness. "Your baby is so cute," she told Carly.

Reese slid next to her, and together, they made a beautiful family. It didn't matter that their baby wasn't theirs biologically. He belonged to them, and they adored him. Kenny kneaded Taryn a tiny bit closer.

"We ready to eat yet?" Frank Ackerman appeared at the mouth of the hallway, forever wearing his cowboy hat and boots. He'd hired Kenny five years ago, and Kenny still felt a flash of appreciation whenever he saw the man.

"Brett and Kate aren't here yet," Squire said. "They're bringin' the rolls from the bakery."

"See? You weren't last." Kenny smiled at Taryn, who returned the gesture. All his nerves settled. He loved her, and she loved him, and he didn't doubt for a moment that she'd say yes to his very important question.

He retreated a few steps as he watched the people around him. The foreman he appreciated and obeyed. The men who'd gone off to war, come home broken, and found a way to make a life for themselves at Three Rivers Ranch.

The rodeo champions, and the horse boarders, and the pancake house owners. Kenny felt such love for them all, he thought sure his heart would burst.

Brett and Kate arrived a few minutes later, towing their two kids and dozens and dozens of rolls with them.

"All right," Squire said, sending Kenny's pulse into a tizzy. "We're all here now."

"'Cept Tom," Pete said.

"Of course. Except Tom." A moment passed in silence while Kenny pictured the steady, sure cowboy who'd been the controller on the ranch. He'd been gone for a couple of years, but he came back to visit from time to time. He'd been here over the Fourth of July, but wanted to build his own family holiday traditions on the ranch where he now lived in Montana.

"I just want to say how grateful I am for all of you." Squire swallowed, the only emotion he ever showed. "And for God for bringin' you all out to Three Rivers, in whatever way He did." He lifted his mug; Pete whooped; everyone broke into applause.

"And now, I believe we have a program of sorts that's been prepared." Squire's gaze landed on Kenny. Everyone's did. Garth slid the jewelry box into Kenny's hand, but he couldn't seem to move.

"Go on, now." Pete looked like the cat who'd swallowed the canary.

"Kenny—" Taryn started as she glanced around at the obvious audience.

"Taryn." He turned toward her. "I've loved you since last Christmas, when you became the best present I'd ever gotten. Will you do me one better this year by agreein' to be my wife?" He dropped to one knee, but with his height, he barely had to look up into her face.

A single tear slithered down her right cheek. She nodded.

"Make her say yes!" someone called.

"Taryn?" Kenny grinned at her. "You better say yes for the people."

"Yes."

He swooped her into his arms and kissed her. "Best Christmas ever," he whispered as he set her down and rested his forehead against hers. "I love you."

"I love you, too, Kenny."

"Let's eat," Frank said, and the chaos Kenny was used to—the business and liveliness of the ranch he loved—ensued. He felt like the luckiest man in the world, and he closed his eyes and sent a prayer of thanksgiving toward heaven to be here, in Three Rivers, on the ranch, with the people he loved most.

*Especially Taryn,* he thought just before opening his eyes to the spread of what was sure to be the most delicious Christmas feast he'd ever eaten.

# SNEAK PEEK! LUCKY NUMBER THIRTEEN CHAPTER ONE

"Tanner!"

Tanner Wolf turned at the sound of his name in a female voice. A blond man strode toward him, his hand secured in a dark haired woman's.

A smile warmed his soul. "Brynn."

She laughed as he embraced her, and Ethan's grin seemed as wide as the sky over Montana. "Hey, Tanner." He slapped Tanner on the back. "That was some impressive roping."

"Thanks." He brushed some invisible dust from his hands and a lot of very visible dirt from his chaps. "Nothin' like me and you, but Dallas does all right."

"All right?" Brynn scoffed. "You'll take first with that, and from what I hear, you guys won't be beat this year."

Tanner tried to shrug off their compliments. Since Ethan had chosen Brynn over rodeo, chosen Three Rivers over Colorado, chosen his faith over everything, Tanner had searched his soul. It wasn't easy, and he'd found a lot of darkness inside. He still wasn't all the way where he wanted to be, and being humble didn't come naturally to him.

After all, he'd spent the last thirty years of his life trying to be the best and celebrating when he was.

"You're comin' out to the ranch for the picnic, right?" Ethan asked. Tanner had been in touch with him over the past couple of years, and when his manager had added the Three Rivers rodeo to his schedule, Tanner had called Ethan first.

"Yeah, of course. Tomorrow at four. I've been to the ranch before."

"You haven't seen my training facilities," Brynn said as a group of cowgirls walked by. Her gaze followed them, and Tanner wondered if she missed the rodeo circuit. She'd quit and never looked back, but a glint rode in her eye that Tanner recognized.

"I'll come early," Tanner said. "Will you guys be out there?"

"We can go out whenever we want," Brynn said.

"I want to see your place too," Tanner said. "Ethan's been bragging about how he built it from the ground up."

"I haven't been bragging."

"I believe you said, 'with my bare hands, Tanner. I built a whole house with my bare hands.'"

Ethan chuckled, and a wave a gratitude washed over Tanner. He couldn't believe Ethan's forgiveness had come so quickly, had healed him so completely. But it had done both, and though he'd never told Ethan, it was his forgiveness that had set Tanner down the path toward a relationship with God.

Of course, that had meant his relationships with women had cooled considerably as he navigated his way toward becoming the kind of man he wanted to be. In fact, his last date had been over a year ago, and that relationship had fizzled before the end of the evening.

"Mister Wolf, you're up in twenty," a rodeo volunteer said, stepping into their conversation.

Tanner took a deep breath, his nerves blossoming into a hill of ants. "All right, wish me luck."

"Who'd you draw?" Ethan asked.

"Lucky Number Thirteen," Tanner said, his voice a note higher than normal. "I've never ridden him to the bell."

Brynn's dark eyes caught on his and her hand landed on his forearm. "You'll get 'im this time." She added a smile to her statement, and Tanner couldn't detect a hint of falseness in her voice.

He managed to smile, mash his cowboy hat further down on his head, and follow the volunteer to the loading chutes.

He'd ridden hundreds of bulls over his twelve-year career. He'd drawn easy wins and nasty animals. He'd never had a bull he hadn't been able to ride. Eventually, they all succumbed to Tanner and the eight-second bell.

He eyed Lucky Number Thirteen, the black and white bull he'd come up against in San Antonio earlier this year. He'd only made it three seconds on the animal, and that disastrous ride played through his mind as the other riders took their turns.

Finally, he sat in the saddle. He pulled the rope across his palm tight, tight. He drew breath after breath to calm his heart, relax his muscles. None of the calming techniques worked, and he had a brief second to wonder if he should've asked for a helmet before the bell rang and the gate opened.

The crowd blurred as it always did while he rode. He only felt the bull's muscles beneath his body. Only listened for the alarm signaling he'd made it to eight seconds. Only breathed once the ride ended.

Lucky Number Thirteen reared, driving right back into Tanner's chest. He slipped, and he knew he was going off despite his strong muscles and iron will trying to hold him on the bull's back.

His feet didn't hit the dirt first; his back did. Hard. The air in his lungs seized, and he couldn't take another breath. The bright lights in the arena went dark as the bull kicked, loomed above him, and all Tanner saw was dark sky and dark animal flesh, and a horrifying dark hoof as it crashed into his ribs.

He instinctively curled into himself, protecting his most vital organs. Around him, he heard shouts, silence, the announcers, the snuffling of the bull, the call of the clowns. He couldn't breathe, couldn't breathe, and pressed his chin to his chest and kept his elbows up as another lightning hot pain shot through his back, down into both his legs.

Time seemed to slow and everything felt shrouded in darkness.

Finally, everything brightened again, and Tanner relaxed. His brain seemed to be working just fine, but every cell in his body screamed in pain. He groaned as he started to uncurl.

"Don't move," someone said, his hand landing lightly on Tanner's forehead. He said something else, his gaze darting away, but Tanner closed his eyes and focused on breathing. Breathing was good. Breathing was necessary.

Movement happened around him. Men spoke in calm voices. Tanner felt the summer air turn cold as something pooled beneath his head. He tried to reach for it, but someone stopped him.

"Lie still, Tanner." A familiar face, with bright green eyes and that shock of blond hair, filled his vision.

"Ethan," Tanner moaned. *Help me,* he prayed, and though he was new to the whole communicating with God idea, the thought felt natural.

"You're fine, cowboy." Ethan's eyes said otherwise, and Tanner tried to focus on them. But they turned lighter and lighter, going into seafoam and mint before they faded into whiteness.

"Stay with me," Ethan commanded, but Tanner couldn't. He closed his eyes against the pain and let unconsciousness take him somewhere where he wasn't lying in his own blood in the middle of the rodeo arena.

---

When he woke, a pair of eyes the color of the ocean blinked at him. "There you are, Mister Wolf." The woman spoke in a slow cadence, her accent Texan and sweet. She glanced down at his chart, wrote something, and looked at him again. "How are you feeling?"

He couldn't vocalize the words he used to, and his back and arm muscles seemed to have forgotten how to shrug.

"My name's Summer, and I'll be your nurse today. Now Jean said you slept all night, and came through your surgery just fine."

He blinked at her, a searing pain in his throat. He could only think, *Surgery?*

"Now, you'll have to get up in a few hours and take a walk around." She grinned at him, and he thought she had the most wonderful pink lips, the most beautiful white teeth. His first instinct was to smile back, and he tried, but something seemed to be wrong with his mouth.

"I don't want any complaints when I come back," she said, her eyes dipping to his lips. "I'll go get Margie, and we'll get that tube out of your throat." She disappeared from his line of sight, and Tanner found pain in every part of his body. How Summer thought he could answer her questions with a tube down his throat, he didn't know.

She returned lickety split, and before he knew it, the two nurses had removed the tube from his throat.

"He's making urine," the other nurse said. She beamed at him, and he'd never been prouder of his body for functioning the way it should. She was closer to his mother's age, and panic pounded through him.

"My...mom?" His throat hurt, and Summer was there, holding out a glass of water. He gulped it greedily as Margie explained that she'd been notified and that she should be here soon.

"There's a couple of friends out in the waiting room," she said. "Should I send them in?"

"How much pain are you in?" Summer asked before Tanner could answer Margie.

"Is 'about to die' on your chart?" he croaked.

She grinned. "Yes, we call that a ten. I'll bring you something."

"A lot of something," he said as a pain in his leg fired on all cylinders. "Something strong."

Margie met Summer's eye and the two nurses exchanged a glance. "Something strong, Mister Wolf," Summer said, her voice full of fun and flirtation.

Tanner sat back in bed as they left, warning himself to maintain distance from Summer. He didn't live in Three Rivers, and she'd go home—maybe to a husband and a family—later that day.

*She sure is pretty though,* he thought as he waited for his medicine and his friends. The friends came first, and Ethan and Brynn looked like they hadn't gone home to sleep.

Tears tracked down Brynn's cheeks as she leaned over and gave Tanner a light hug. He couldn't help the groan of pain from the movement and she jerked back. "Sorry."

"I'm fine." He pushed himself up in bed, a flash of discomfort spreading through his right leg. "Aren't I fine, Ethan?"

He watched his friend for the signs he needed. Ethan kept his face a blank slate, but the intensity of his swallow told Tanner everything.

"Yeah," Ethan said. "You're going to be just fine, Tanner."

Tanner looked away as emotion surged up his throat. He knew by Ethan's reaction that he'd never ride bulls again.

With that swallow, Tanner knew his rodeo career had ended, right there in the Three Rivers arena.

**Second Chance Ranch: A Three Rivers Ranch Romance (Book 1):** After his deployment, injured and discharged Major Squire Ackerman returns to Three Rivers Ranch, wanting to forgive Kelly for ignoring him a decade ago. He'd like to provide the stable life she needs, but with old wounds opening and a ranch on the brink of financial collapse, it will take patience and faith to make their second chance possible.

**Third Time's the Charm: A Three Rivers Ranch Romance (Book 2):** First Lieutenant Peter Marshall has a truckload of debt and no way to provide for a family, but Chelsea helps him see past all the obstacles, all the scars. With so many unknowns, can Pete and Chelsea develop the love, acceptance, and faith needed to find their happily ever after?

**Fourth and Long: A Three Rivers Ranch Romance (Book 3):** Commander Brett Murphy goes to Three Rivers Ranch to find some rest and relaxation with his Army buddies. Having his ex-wife show up with a seven-year-old she claims is his son is anything but the R&R he craves. Kate needs to make amends, and Brett needs to find forgiveness, but are they too late to find their happily ever after?

**Fifth Generation Cowboy: A Three Rivers Ranch Romance (Book 4):** Tom Lovell has watched his friends find their true happiness on Three Rivers Ranch, but everywhere he looks, he only sees friends. Rose Reyes has been bringing her daughter out to the ranch for equine therapy for months, but it doesn't seem to be working. Her challenges with Mari are just as frustrating as ever. Could Tom be exactly what Rose needs? Can he remove his friendship blinders and find love with someone who's been right in front of him all this time?

**Sixth Street Love Affair: A Three Rivers Ranch Romance (Book 5):** After losing his wife a few years back, Garth Ahlstrom thinks he's ready for a second chance at love. But Juliette Thompson has a secret that could destroy their budding relationship. Can they find the strength, patience, and faith to make things work?

**The Seventh Sergeant: A Three Rivers Ranch Romance (Book 6):** Life has finally started to settle down for Sergeant Reese Sanders after his devastating injury overseas. Discharged from the Army and now with a good job at Courage Reins, he's finally found happiness—until a horrific fall puts him right back where he was years ago: Injured and depressed. Carly Watters, Reese's new veteran care coordinator, dislikes small towns almost as much as she loathes cowboys. But she finds herself faced with both when she gets assigned to Reese's case. Do they have the humility and faith to make their relationship more than professional?

**Eight Second Ride: A Three Rivers Ranch Romance (Book 7):** Ethan Greene loves his work at Three Rivers Ranch, but he can't seem to find the right woman to settle down with. When sassy yet vulnerable Brynn Bowman shows up at the ranch to recruit him back to the rodeo circuit, he takes a different approach with the barrel racing champion. His patience and newfound faith pay off when a friendship--and more--starts with Brynn. But she wants out of the rodeo circuit right when Ethan wants to rejoin. Can they find the path God wants them to take and still stay together?

**The First Lady of Three Rivers Ranch: A Three Rivers Ranch Romance (Book 8):** Heidi Duffin has been dreaming about opening her own bakery since she was thirteen years old. She scrimped and saved for years to afford baking and pastry school in San Francisco. And now she only has one year left before she's a certified pastry chef. Frank Ackerman's father has recently retired, and he's taken over the largest cattle ranch in the Texas Panhandle. A horseman through and through, he's also nearing thirty-one and looking for someone to bring love and joy to a homestead that's been dominated by men for a decade. But when he convinces Heidi to come clean the cowboy cabins, she changes all that. But the siren's call of a bakery is still loud in Heidi's ears, even if she's also seeing a future with Frank. Can she rely on her faith in ways she's never had to before or will their relationship end when summer does?

**Christmas in Three Rivers: A Three Rivers Ranch Romance (Book 9):** Isn't Christmas the best time to fall in love? The cowboys of Three Rivers Ranch think so. Join four of them as they journey toward their path to happily ever after in four, all-new novellas in the Amazon #1 Bestselling Three Rivers Ranch Romance series.

THE NINTH INNING: The Christmas season has never felt like such a burden to boutique owner Andrea Larsen. But with Mama gone and the holidays upon her, Andy finds herself wishing she hadn't been so quick to judge her former boyfriend, cowboy Lawrence Collins. Well, Lawrence hasn't forgotten about Andy either, and he devises a plan to get her out to the ranch so they can reconnect. Do they have the faith and humility to patch things up and start a new relationship?

TEN DAYS IN TOWN: Sandy Keller is tired of the dating scene in Three Rivers. Though she owns the pancake house, she's looking for a fresh start, which means an escape from the town where she grew up. When her older brother's best friend, Tad Jorgensen, comes to town for the holidays, it is a balm to his weary soul. A helicopter tour guide who experienced a near-death experience, he's looking to start over too--but in Three Rivers. Can Sandy and Tad navigate their troubles to find the path God wants them to take--and discover true love--in only ten days?

ELEVEN YEAR REUNION: Pastry chef extraordinaire, Grace Lewis has moved to Three Rivers to help Heidi Ackerman open a bakery in Three Rivers. Grace relishes the idea of starting over in a town where no one knows about her failed cupcakery. She doesn't expect to run into her old high school boyfriend, Jonathan Carver. A carpenter working at Three Rivers Ranch, Jon's in town against his will. But with Grace now on the scene, Jon's thinking life in Three Rivers is suddenly looking up. But with her focus on baking and his disdain for small towns, can they make their eleven year reunion stick?

THE TWELFTH TOWN: Newscaster Taryn Tucker has had enough of life on-screen. She's bounced from town to town before arriving in Three Rivers, completely alone and completely anonymous--just the way she now likes it. She takes a job cleaning at Three Rivers Ranch, hoping for a chance to figure out who she is and where God wants her. When she meets happy-go-lucky cowhand Kenny Stockton, she doesn't expect sparks to fly. Kenny's always been "the best friend" for his female friends, but the pull between him and Taryn can't be denied. Will they have the courage and faith necessary to make their opposite worlds mesh?

**Lucky Number Thirteen: A Three Rivers Ranch Romance (Book 10):** Tanner Wolf, a rodeo champion ten times over, is excited to be riding in Three Rivers for the first time since he left his philandering ways and found religion. Seeing his old friends Ethan and Brynn is therapeutic--until a terrible accident lands him in the hospital. With his rodeo career over, Tanner thinks maybe he'll stay in town--and it's not just because his nurse, Summer Hamblin, is the prettiest woman he's ever met. But Summer's the queen of first dates, and as she looks for a way to make a relationship with the transient rodeo star work Summer's not sure she has the fortitude to go on a second date. Can they find love among the tragedy?

**The Curse of February Fourteenth: A Three Rivers Ranch Romance (Book 11):** Cal Hodgkins, cowboy veterinarian at Bowman's Breeds, isn't planning to meet anyone at the masked dance in small-town Three Rivers. He just wants to get his bachelor friends off his back and sit on the sidelines to drink his punch. But when he sees a woman dressed in gorgeous butterfly wings and cowgirl boots with blue stitching, he's smitten. Too bad she runs away from the dance before he can get her name, leaving only her boot behind...

**Fifteen Minutes of Fame: A Three Rivers Ranch Romance (Book 12):** Navy Richards is thirty-five years of tired—tired of dating the same men, working a demanding job, and getting her heart broken over and over again. Her aunt has always spoken highly of the matchmaker in Three Rivers, Texas, so she takes a six-month sabbatical from her high-stress job as a pediatric nurse, hops on a bus, and meets with the matchmaker. Then she meets Gavin Redd. He's handsome, he's hardworking, and he's a cowboy. But is he an Aquarius too? Navy's not making a move until she knows for sure…

**Sixteen Steps to Fall in Love: A Three Rivers Ranch Romance (Book 13):** A chance encounter at a dog park sheds new light on the tall, talented Boone that Nicole can't ignore. As they get to know each other better and start to dig into each other's past, Nicole is the one who wants to run. This time from her growing admiration and attachment to Boone. From her aging parents. From herself.

But Boone feels the attraction between them too, and he decides he's tired of running and ready to make Three Rivers his permanent home. **Can Boone and Nicole use their faith to overcome their differences and find a happily-ever-after together?**

**The Sleigh on Seventeenth Street: A Three Rivers Ranch Romance (Book 14):** A cowboy with skills as an electrician tries a relationship with a down-on-her luck plumber. Can Dylan and Camila make water and electricity play nicely together this Christmas season? Or will they get shocked as they try to make their relationship work?

## BOOKS IN THE CHRISTMAS IN CORAL CANYON ROMANCE SERIES

**Her Cowboy Billionaire Best Friend (Book 1):** Graham Whittaker returns to Coral Canyon a few days after Christmas—after the death of his father. He takes over the energy company his dad built from the ground up and buys a high-end lodge to live in—only a mile from the home of his once-best friend, Laney McAllister. They were best friends once, but Laney's always entertained feelings for him, and spending so much time with him while they make Christmas memories puts her heart in danger of getting broken again...

**Her Cowboy Billionaire Boss (Book 2):** Since the death of his wife a few years ago, Eli Whittaker has been running from one job to another, unable to find somewhere for him and his son to settle. Meg Palmer is Stockton's nanny, and she comes with her boss, Eli, to the lodge, her long-time crush on the man no different in Wyoming than it was on the beach. When she confesses her feelings for him and gets nothing in return, she's crushed, embarrassed, and unsure if she can stay in Coral Canyon for Christmas. Then Eli starts to show some feelings for her too...

**Her Cowboy Billionaire Boyfriend (Book 3):** Andrew Whittaker is the public face for the Whittaker Brothers' family energy company, and with his older brother's robot about to be announced, he needs a press secretary to help him get everything ready and tour the state to make the announcements. When he's hit by a protest sign being carried by the company's biggest opponent, Rebecca Collings, he learns with a few clicks that she has the background they need. He offers her the job of press secretary when she thought she was going to be arrested, and not only because the spark between them in so hot Andrew can't see straight.

**Can Becca and Andrew work together and keep their relationship a secret? Or will hearts break in this classic romance retelling reminiscent of *Two Weeks Notice*?**

**Her Cowboy Billionaire Bodyguard (Book 4):** Beau Whittaker has watched his brothers find love one by one, but every attempt he's made has ended in disaster. Lily Everett has been in the spotlight since childhood and has half a dozen platinum records with her two sisters. She's taking a break from the brutal music industry and hiding out in Wyoming while her ex-husband continues to cause trouble for her. When she hears of Beau Whittaker and what he offers his clients, she wants to meet him. Beau is instantly attracted to Lily, but he tried a relationship with his last client that left a scar that still hasn't healed…

**Can Lily use the spirit of Christmas to discover what matters most? Will Beau open his heart to the possibility of love with someone so different from him?**

**Her Cowboy Billionaire Bull Rider (Book 5):** Todd Christopherson has just retired from the professional rodeo circuit and returned to his hometown of Coral Canyon. Problem is, he's got no family there anymore, no land, and no job. Not that he needs a job--he's got plenty of money from his illustrious career riding bulls.

Then Todd gets thrown during a routine horseback ride up the canyon, and his only support as he recovers physically is the beautiful Violet Everett. She's no nurse, but she does the best she can for the handsome cowboy. **Will she lose her heart to the billionaire bull rider? Can Todd trust that God led him to Coral Canyon...and Vi?**

**Her Cowboy Billionaire Bachelor (Book 6):** Rose Everett isn't sure what to do with her life now that her country music career is on hold. After all, with both of her sisters in Coral Canyon, and one about to have a baby, they're not making albums anymore.

Liam Murphy has been working for Doctors Without Borders, but he's back in the US now, and looking to start a new clinic in Coral Canyon, where he spent his summers.

When Rose wins a date with Liam in a bachelor auction, their relationship blooms and grows quickly. **Can Liam and Rose find a solution to their problems that doesn't involve one of them leaving Coral Canyon with a broken heart?**

**Her Cowboy Billionaire Blind Date (Book 7):** Her sons want her to be happy, but she's too old to be set up on a blind date...isn't she?

Amanda Whittaker has been looking for a second chance at love since the death of her husband several years ago. Finley Barber is a cowboy in every sense of the word. Born and raised on a race-horse farm in Kentucky, he's since moved to Dog Valley and started his own breeding stable for champion horses. He hasn't dated in years, and everything about Amanda makes him nervous.

**Will Amanda take the leap of faith required to be with Finn? Or will he become just another boyfriend who doesn't make the cut?**

**Her Cowboy Billionaire Best Man (Book 8):** When Celia Abbott-Armstrong runs into a gorgeous cowboy at her best friend's wedding, she decides she's ready to start dating again.

But the cowboy is Zach Zuckerman, and the Zuckermans and Abbotts have been at war for generations.

Can Zach and Celia find a way to reconcile their family's differences so they can have a future together?

**Her Cowboy Billionaire Birthday Wish (Book 9):** All the maid at Whiskey Mountain Lodge wants for her birthday is a handsome cowboy billionaire. And Colton can make that wish come true—if only he hadn't escaped to Coral Canyon after being left at the altar...

**Her Cowboy Billionaire Butler (Book 10):** She broke up with him to date another man...who broke her heart. He's a former CEO with nothing to do who can't get her out of his head. Can Wes and Bree find a way toward happily-ever-after at Whiskey Mountain Lodge?

**Her Cowboy Billionaire Best Friend's Brother (Book 11):** She's best friends with the single dad cowboy's brother and has watched two friends find love with the sexy new cowboys in town. When Gray Hammond comes to Whiskey Mountain Lodge with his son, will Elise finally get her own happily-ever-after with one of the Hammond brothers?

**Her Cowboy Billionaire Beast (Book 12):** A cowboy billionaire beast, his new manager, and the Christmas traditions that soften his heart and bring them together.

**Her Cowboy Billionaire Bad Boy (Book 13):** A cowboy billionaire cop who's a stickler for rules, the woman he pulls over when he's not even on duty, and the personal mandates he has to break to keep her in his life...

**Rhett's Make-Believe Marriage (Book 1):** She needs a husband to be credible as a matchmaker. He wants to help a neighbor. Will their fake marriage take them out of the friend zone?

**Tripp's Trivial Tie (Book 2):** She needs a husband to keep her son. He's wanted to take their relationship to the next level, but she's always pushing him away. Will their trivial tie take them all the way to happily-ever-after?

**Liam's Invented I-Do (Book 3):** She's desperate to save her ranch. He wants to help her any way he can. Will their invented I-Do open doors that have previously been closed and lead to a happily-ever-after for both of them?

**Jeremiah's Bogus Bride (Book 4):** He wants to prove to his brothers that he's not broken. She just wants him. Will a fake marriage heal him or push her further away?

**Wyatt's Pretend Pledge (Book 5):** To get her inheritance, she needs a husband. He's wanted to fly with her for ages. Can their pretend pledge turn into something real?

**Skyler's Wanna-Be Wife (Book 6):** She needs a new last name to stay in school. He's willing to help a fellow student. Can this wanna-be wife show the playboy that some things should be taken seriously?

**Micah's Mock Matrimony (Book 7):** They were just actors auditioning for a play. The marriage was just for the audition – until a clerical error results in a legal marriage. Can these two ex-lovers negotiate this new ground between them and achieve new roles in each other's lives?

**The Mechanics of Mistletoe (Book 1):** Bear Glover can be a grizzly or a teddy, and he's always thought he'd be just fine working his generational family ranch and going back to the ancient homestead alone. But his crush on Samantha Benton won't go away. She's a genius with a wrench on Bear's tractors...and his heart. Can he tame his wild side and get the girl, or will he be left broken-hearted this Christmas season?

**The Horsepower of the Holiday (Book 2):** Ranger Glover has worked at Shiloh Ridge Ranch his entire life. The cowboys do everything from horseback there, but when he goes to town to trade in some trucks, somehow Oakley Hatch persuades him to take some ATVs back to the ranch. (Bear is NOT happy.)

She's a former race car driver who's got Ranger all revved up... Can he remember who he is and get Oakley to slow down enough to fall in love, or will there simply be too much horsepower in the holiday this year for a real relationship?

**The Construction of Cheer (Book 3):** Bishop Glover is the youngest brother, and he usually keeps his head down and gets the job done. When Montana Martin shows up at Shiloh Ridge Ranch looking for work, he finds himself inventing construction projects that need doing just to keep her coming around. (Again, Bear is NOT happy.) She wants to build her own construction firm, but she ends up carving a place for herself inside Bishop's heart. Can he convince her *he's* all she needs this Christmas season, or will her cheer rest solely on the success of her business?

**The Secret of Santa (Book 4):** Ace Glover loves to laugh, and everywhere he goes, luck seems to follow. When the hardworking cowboy volunteers to help with the Poinsettia Festival in town, he meets Sierra Broadbent. He's instantly smitten and loves spending time with her. She's in charge of the whole event, but she seems to disappear the moment everything starts...day after day.

When he learns her secret, the entire festival could be ruined—and so could Sierra's reputation and his new relationship with her. Will he keep his discovery to himself or will Sierra's secret become front-page news on Christmas Day?

## BOOKS IN THE LAST CHANCE RANCH ROMANCE SERIES

**Last Chance Ranch (Book 1):** A cowgirl down on her luck hires a man who's good with horses and under the hood of a car. Can Hudson fine tune Scarlett's heart as they work together? Or will things backfire and make everything worse at Last Chance Ranch?

**Last Chance Cowboy (Book 2):** A billionaire cowboy without a home meets a woman who secretly makes food videos to pay her debts...Can Carson and Adele do more than fight in the kitchens at Last Chance Ranch?

**Last Chance Wedding (Book 3):** A female carpenter needs a husband just for a few days... Can Jeri and Sawyer navigate the minefield of a pretend marriage before their feelings become real?

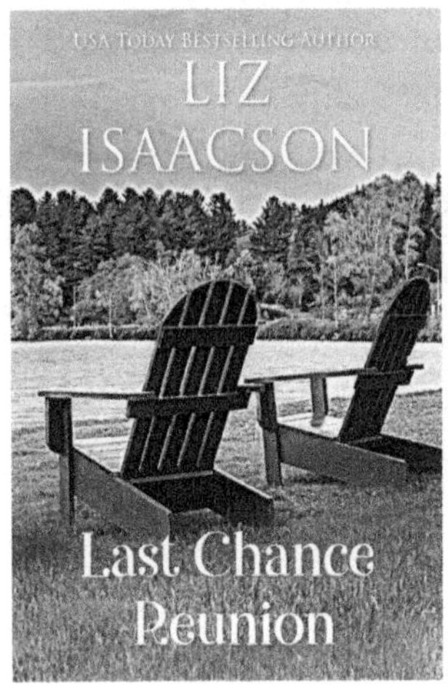


**Last Chance Reunion (Book 4):** An Army cowboy, the woman he dated years ago, and their last chance at Last Chance Ranch... Can Dave and Sissy put aside hurt feelings and make their second chance romance work?

**Last Chance Lake (Book 5):** A former dairy farmer and the marketing director on the ranch have to work together to make the cow cuddling program a success. But can Karla let Cache into her life? Or will she keep all her secrets from him - and keep *him* a secret too?

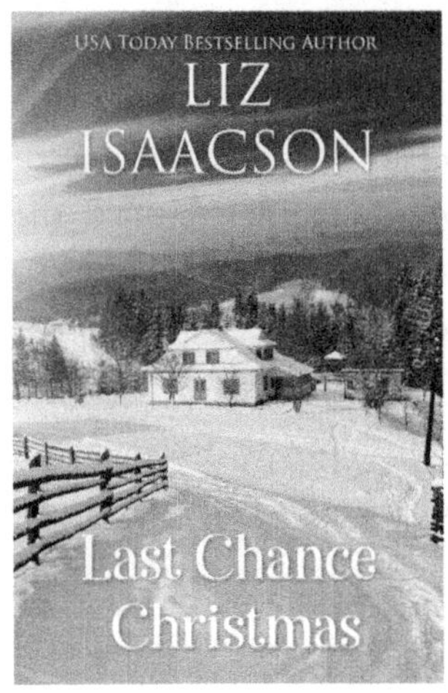


**Last Chance Christmas (Book 6):** She's tired of having her heart broken by cowboys. He waited too long to ask her out. Can Lance fix things quickly, or will Amber leave Last Chance Ranch before he can tell her how he feels?

## BOOKS IN THE GRAPE SEED FALLS ROMANCE SERIES:

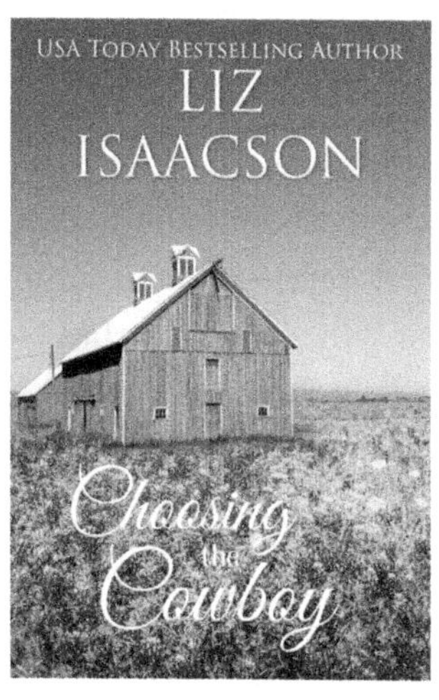


**Choosing the Cowboy (Book 1):** With financial trouble and personal issues around every corner, can Maggie Duffin and Chase Carver rely on their faith to find their happily-ever-after?

A spinoff from the #1 bestselling Three Rivers Ranch Romance novels, also by USA Today bestselling author Liz Isaacson.

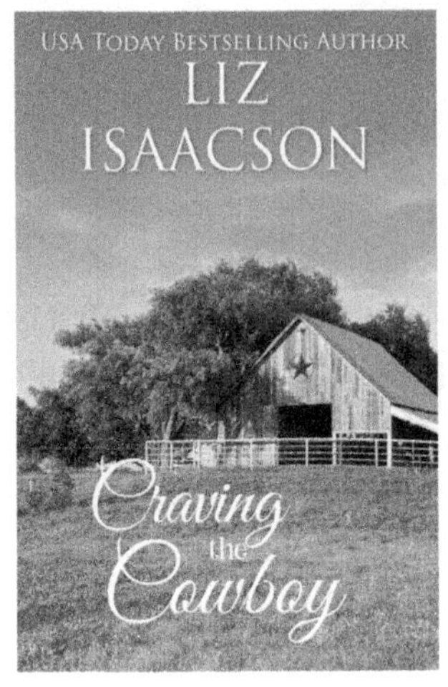


**Craving the Cowboy (Book 2):** Dwayne Carver is set to inherit his family's ranch in the heart of Texas Hill Country, and in order to keep up with his ranch duties and fulfill his dreams of owning a horse farm, he hires top trainer Felicity Lightburne. They get along great, and she can envision herself on this new farm—at least until her mother falls ill and she has to return to help her. Can Dwayne and Felicity work through their differences to find their happily-ever-after?

**Charming the Cowboy (Book 3):** Third grade teacher Heather Carver has had her eye on Levi Rhodes for a couple of years now, but he seems to be blind to her attempts to charm him. When she breaks her arm while on his horse ranch, Heather infiltrates Levi's life in ways he's never thought of, and his strict anti-female stance slips. Will Heather heal his emotional scars and he care for her physical ones so they can have a real relationship?

**Courting the Cowboy (Book 4):** Frustrated with the cowboy-only dating scene in Grape Seed Falls, May Sotheby joins TexasFaithful.-com, hoping to find her soul mate without having to relocate--or deal with cowboy hats and boots. She has no idea that Kurt Pemberton, foreman at Grape Seed Ranch, is the man she starts communicating with... Will May be able to follow her heart and get Kurt to forgive her so they can be together?

**Claiming the Cowboy, Royal Brothers Book 1 (Grape Seed Falls Romance Book 5):** Unwilling to be tied down, farrier Robin Cook has managed to pack her entire life into a two-hundred-and-eighty square-foot house, and that includes her Yorkie. Cowboy and co-foreman, Shane Royal has had his heart set on Robin for three years, even though she flat-out turned him down the last time he asked her to dinner. But she's back at Grape Seed Ranch for five weeks as she works her horse-shoeing magic, and he's still interested, despite a bitter life lesson that left a bad taste for marriage in his mouth.

Robin's interested in him too. But can she find room for Shane in her tiny house--and can he take a chance on her with his tired heart?

**Catching the Cowboy, Royal Brothers Book 2 (Grape Seed Falls Romance Book 6):** Dylan Royal is good at two things: whistling and caring for cattle. When his cows are being attacked by an unknown wild animal, he calls Texas Parks & Wildlife for help. He wasn't expecting a beautiful mammologist to show up, all flirty and fun and everything Dylan didn't know he wanted in his life.

Hazel Brewster has gone on more first dates than anyone in Grape Seed Falls, and she thinks maybe Dylan deserves a second... Can they find their way through wild animals, huge life changes, and their emotional pasts to find their forever future?

**Cheering the Cowboy, Royal Brothers Book 3 (Grape Seed Falls Romance Book 7):** Austin Royal loves his life on his new ranch with his brothers. But he doesn't love that Shayleigh Hatch came with the property, nor that he has to take the blame for the fact that he now owns her childhood ranch. They rarely have a conversation that doesn't leave him furious and frustrated--and yet he's still attracted to Shay in a strange, new way.

Shay inexplicably likes him too, which utterly confuses and angers her. As they work to make this Christmas the best the Triple Towers Ranch has ever seen, can they also navigate through their rocky relationship to smoother waters?

# BOOKS IN THE STEEPLE RIDGE ROMANCE SERIES:

**Her Billionaire Cowboy (Book 1):** Tucker Jenkins has had enough of tall buildings, traffic, and has traded in his technology firm in New York City for Steeple Ridge Horse Farm in rural Vermont. Missy Marino has worked at the farm since she was a teen, and she's always dreamed of owning it. But her ex-husband left her with a truckload of debt, making her fantasies of owning the farm unfulfilled. Tucker didn't come to the country to find a new wife, but he supposes a woman could help him start over in Steeple Ridge. Will Tucker and Missy be able to navigate the shaky ground between them to find a new beginning?

**Her Restless Cowboy: A Butters Brothers Novel, Steeple Ridge Romance (Book 2):** Ben Buttars is the youngest of the four Buttars brothers who come to Steeple Ridge Farm, and he finally feels like he's landed somewhere he can make a life for himself. Reagan Cantwell is a decade older than Ben and the recreational direction for the town of Island Park. Though Ben is young, he knows what he wants—and that's Rae. Can she figure out how to put what matters most in her life—family and faith—above her job before she loses Ben?

**Her Faithful Cowboy: A Butters Brothers Novel, Steeple Ridge Romance (Book 3):** Sam Buttars has spent the last decade making sure he and his brothers stay together. They've been at Steeple Ridge for a while now, but with the youngest married and happy, the siren's call to return to his parents' farm in Wyoming is loud in Sam's ears. He'd just go if it weren't for beautiful Bonnie Sherman, who roped his heart the first time he saw her. Do Sam and Bonnie have the faith to find comfort in each other instead of in the people who've already passed?

**Her Mistletoe Cowboy: A Butters Brothers Novel, Steeple Ridge Romance (Book 4):** Logan Buttars has always been good-natured and happy-go-lucky. After watching two of his brothers settle down, he recognizes a void in his life he didn't know about. Veterinarian Layla Guyman has appreciated Logan's friendship and easy way with animals when he comes into the clinic to get the service dogs. But with his future at Steeple Ridge in the balance, she's not sure a relationship with him is worth the risk. Can she rely on her faith and employ patience to tame Logan's wild heart?

**Her Patient Cowboy: A Butters Brothers Novel, Steeple Ridge Romance (Book 5):** Darren Buttars is cool, collected, and quiet—and utterly devastated when his girlfriend of nine months, Farrah Irvine, breaks up with him because he wanted her to ride her horse in a parade. But Farrah doesn't ride anymore, a fact she made very clear to Darren. She returned to her childhood home with so much baggage, she doesn't know where to start with the unpacking. Darren's the only Buttars brother who isn't married, and he wants to make Island Park his permanent home—with Farrah. Can they find their way through the heartache to achieve a happily-ever-after together?

## BOOKS IN THE HORSESHOE HOME RANCH ROMANCE SERIES:

**The Redesigned Ranch (Book 1):** Jace Lovell only has one thing left after his fiancé abandons him at the altar: his job at Horseshoe Home Ranch. Belle Edmunds is back in Gold Valley and she's desperate to build a portfolio that she can use to start her own firm in Montana. Jace isn't anywhere near forgiving his fiancé, and he's not sure he's ready for a new relationship with someone as fiery and beautiful as Belle. Can she employ her patience while he figures out how to forgive so they can find their own brand of happily-ever-after?

**The Snowstorm in Gold Valley (Book 2):** Professional snowboarder Sterling Maughan has sequestered himself in his family's cabin in the exclusive mountain community above Gold Valley, Montana after a devastating fall that ended his career. Norah Watson cleans Sterling's cabin and the more time they spend together, the more Sterling is interested in all things Norah. As his body heals, so does his faith. Will Norah be able to trust Sterling so they can have a chance at true love?

**The Cabin on Bear Mountain (Book 3):** Landon Edmunds has been a cowboy his whole life. An accident five years ago ended his successful rodeo career, and now he's looking to start a horse ranch--and he's looking outside of Montana. Which would be great if God hadn't brought Megan Palmer back to Gold Valley right when Landon is looking to leave. Megan and Landon work together well, and as sparks fly, she's sure God brought her back to Gold Valley so she could find her happily ever after. Through serious discussion and prayer, can Landon and Megan find their future together?

Be sure to check out the spinoff series, the Brush Creek Brides romances after you read FALLING FOR HIS BEST FRIEND. Start with A WEDDING FOR THE WIDOWER.

**The Cowboy at the Creek (Book 4):** Twelve years ago, Owen Carr left Gold Valley—and his long-time girlfriend—in favor of a country music career in Nashville. Married and divorced, Natalie teaches ballet at the dance studio in Gold Valley, but she never auditioned for the professional company the way she dreamed of doing. With Owen back, she realizes all the opportunities she missed out on when he left all those years ago—including a future with him. Can they mend broken bridges in order to have a second chance at love?

**The Wedding in the Winter (Book 5):** Caleb Chamberlain has spent the last five years recovering from a horrible breakup, his alcoholism that stemmed from it, and the car accident that left him hospitalized. He's finally on the right track in his life—until Holly Gray, his twin brother's ex-fiance mistakes him for Nathan. Holly's back in Gold Valley to get the required veterinarian hours to apply for her graduate program. When the herd at Horseshoe Home comes down with pneumonia, Caleb and Holly are forced to work together in close quarters. Holly's over Nathan, but she hasn't forgiven him—or the woman she believes broke up their relationship. Can Caleb and Holly navigate such a rough past to find their happily-ever-after?

**The Long Way Home (Book 6):** Ty Barker has been dancing through the last thirty years of his life--and he's suddenly realized he's alone. River Lee Whitely is back in Gold Valley with her two little girls after a divorce that's left deep scars. She has a job at Silver Creek that requires her to be able to ride a horse, and she nearly tramples Ty at her first lesson. That's just fine by him, because River Lee is the girl Ty has never gotten over. Ty realizes River Lee needs time to settle into her new job, her new home, her new life as a single parent, but going slow has never been his style. But for River Lee, can Ty take the necessary steps to keep her in his life?

**Christmas at the Ranch (Book 7):** Archer Bailey has already lost one job to Emersyn Enders, so he deliberately doesn't tell her about the cowhand job up at Horseshoe Home Ranch. Emery's temporary job is ending, but her obligations to her physically disabled sister aren't. As Archer and Emery work together, its clear that the sparks flying between them aren't all from their friendly competition over a job. Will Emery and Archer be able to navigate the ranch, their close quarters, and their individual circumstances to find love this holiday season?

**The Love of a Cowboy (Book 8):** Cowboy Elliott Hawthorne has just lost his best friend and cabin mate to the worst thing imaginable—marriage. When his brother calls about an accident with their father, Elliott rushes down to Gold Valley from the ranch only to be met with the most beautiful woman he's ever seen. His father's new physical therapist, London Marsh, likes the handsome face and gentle spirit she sees in Elliott too. Can Elliott and London navigate difficult family situations to find a happily-ever-after?

## BOOKS IN THE BRUSH CREEK BRIDES ROMANCE SERIES:

**Brush Creek Cowboy: Brush Creek Cowboys Romance (Book 1):** Former rodeo champion and cowboy Walker Thompson trains horses at Brush Creek Horse Ranch, where he lives a simple life in his cabin with his ten-year-old son. A widower of six years, he's worked with Tess Wagner, a widow who came to Brush Creek to escape the turmoil of her life to give her seven-year-old son a slower pace of life. But Tess's breast cancer is back...

Walker will have to decide if he'd rather spend even a short time with Tess than not have her in his life at all. Tess wants to feel God's love and power, but can she discover and accept God's will in order to find her happy ending?

**The Cowboy's Challenge: Brush Creek Brides Romance (Book 2):** Cowboy and professional roper Justin Jackman has found solitude at Brush Creek Horse Ranch, preferring his time with the animals he trains over dating. With two failed engagements in his past, he's not really interested in getting his heart stomped on again. But when flirty and fun Renee Martin picks him up at a church ice cream bar--on a bet, no less--he finds himself more than just a little interested. His Gen-X attitudes are attractive to her; her Millennial behaviors drive him nuts. Can Justin look past their differences and take a chance on another engagement?

**A Cowboy Proposal: Brush Creek Brides Romance (Book 3):** Ted Caldwell has been a retired bronc rider for years, and he thought he was perfectly happy training horses to buck at Brush Creek Ranch. He was wrong. When he meets April Nox, who comes to the ranch to hide her pregnancy from all her friends back in Jackson Hole, Ted realizes he has a huge family-shaped hole in his life. April is embarrassed, heartbroken, and trying to find her extinguished faith. She's never ridden a horse and wants nothing to do with a cowboy ever again. Can Ted and April create a family of happiness and love from a tragedy?

**A New Family for the Cowboy: Brush Creek Brides Romance (Book 4):** Blake Gibbons oversees all the agriculture at Brush Creek Horse Ranch, sometimes moonlighting as a general contractor. When he meets Erin Shields, new in town, at her aunt's bakery, he's instantly smitten. Erin moved to Brush Creek after a divorce that left her penniless, homeless, and a single mother of three children under age eight. She's nowhere near ready to start dating again, but the longer Blake hangs around the bakery, the more she starts to like him. Can Blake and Erin find a way to blend their lifestyles and become a family?

**The Cowboy and the Champion: Brush Creek Brides Romance (Book 5):** Emmett Graves has always had a positive outlook on life. He adores training horses to become barrel racing champions during the day and cuddling with his cat at night. Fresh off her professional rodeo retirement, Molly Brady comes to Brush Creek Horse Ranch as Emmett's protege. He's not thrilled, and she's allergic to cats. Oh, and she'd like to stay cowboy-free, thank you very much. But Emmett's about as cowboy as they come.... Can Emmett and Molly work together without falling in love?

**Schooled by the Cowboy: Brush Creek Brides Romance (Book 6):** Grant Ford spends his days training cattle—when he's not camped out at the elementary school hoping to catch a glimpse of his ex-girlfriend. When principal Shannon Sharpe confronts him and asks him to stay away from the school, the spark between them is instant and hot. Shannon's expecting a transfer very soon, but she also needs a summer outdoor coordinator—and Grant fits the bill. Just because he's handsome and everything Shannon's ever wanted in a cowboy husband means nothing. Will Grant and Shannon be able to survive the summer or will the Utah heat be too much for them to handle?

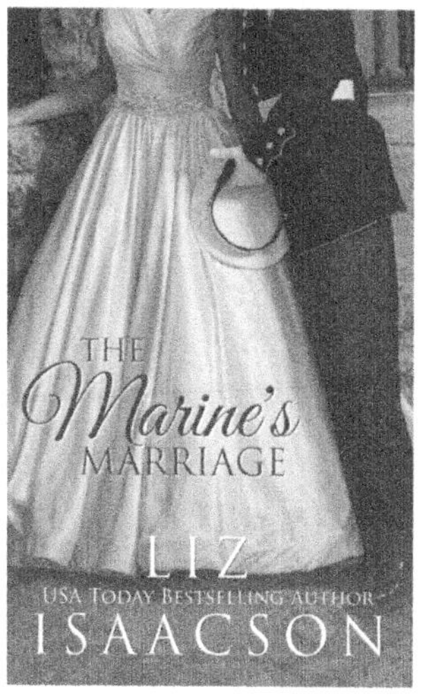


**The Marine's Marriage: A Fuller Family Novel - Brush Creek Brides Romance (Book 1):** Tate Benson can't believe he's come to Nowhere, Utah, to fix up a house that hasn't been inhabited in years. But he has. Because he's retired from the Marines and looking to start a life as a police officer in small-town Brush Creek. Wren Fuller has her hands full most days running her family's company. When Tate calls and demands a maid for that morning, she decides to have the calls forwarded to her cell and go help him out. She didn't know he was moving in next door, and she's completely unprepared for his handsomeness, his kind heart, and his wounded soul.Can Tate and Wren weather a relationship when they're also next-door neighbors?

**The Firefighter's Fiancé: A Fuller Family Novel - Brush Creek Brides Romance (Book 2):** Cora Wesley comes to Brush Creek, hoping to get some in-the-wild firefighting training as she prepares to put in her application to be a hotshot. When she meets Brennan Fuller, the spark between them is hot and instant. As they get to know each other, her deadline is constantly looming over them, and Brennan starts to wonder if he can break ranks in the family business. He's okay mowing lawns and hanging out with his brothers, but he dreams of being able to go to college and become a landscape architect, but he's just not sure it can be done. Will Cora and Brennan be able to endure their trials to find true love?

**The Trooper's Treasure: A Fuller Family Novel - Brush Creek Brides Romance (Book 3):** Dawn Fuller has made some mistakes in her life, and she's not proud of the way McDermott Boyd found her off the road one day last year. She's spent a hard year wrestling with her choices and trying to fix them, glad for McDermott's acceptance and friendship. He lost his wife years ago, done his best with his daughter, and now he's ready to move on. Can McDermott help Dawn find a way past her former mistakes and down a path that leads to love, family, and happiness?

**The Detective's Date: A Fuller Family Novel - Brush Creek Brides Romance (Book 4):** Dahlia Reid is one of the best detectives Brush Creek and the surrounding towns has ever had. She's given up on the idea of marriage—and pleasing her mother—and has dedicated herself fully to her job. Which is great, since one of the most perplexing cases of her career has come to town. Kyler Fuller thinks he's finally ready to move past the woman who ghosted him years ago. He's cut his hair, and he's ready to start dating. Too bad every woman he's been out with is about as interesting as a lamppost—until Dahlia. He finds her beautiful, her quick wit a breath of fresh air, and her intelligence sexy. Can Kyler and Dahlia use their faith to find a way through the obstacles threatening to keep them apart?

**The Paramedic's Partner: A Fuller Family Novel - Brush Creek Brides Romance (Book 5):** Jazzy Fuller has always been overshadowed by her prettier, more popular twin, Fabiana. Fabi meets paramedic Max Robinson at the park and sets a date with him only to come down with the flu. So she convinces Jazzy to cut her hair and take her place on the date. And the spark between Jazzy and Max is hot and instant...if only he knew she wasn't her sister, Fabi.

Max drives the ambulance for the town of Brush Creek with is partner Ed Moon, and neither of them have been all that lucky in love. Until Max suggests to who he thinks is Fabi that they should double with Ed and Jazzy. They do, and Fabi is smitten with the steady, strong Ed Moon. As each twin falls further and further in love with their respective paramedic, it becomes obvious they'll need to come clean about the switcheroo sooner rather than later...or risk losing their hearts.

**The Chief's Catch: A Fuller Family Novel - Brush Creek Brides Romance (Book 6):** Berlin Fuller has struck out with the dating scene in Brush Creek more times than she cares to admit. When she makes a deal with her friends that they can choose the next man she goes out with, she didn't dream they'd pick surly Cole Fairbanks, the new Chief of Police.

His friends call him the Beast and challenge him to complete ten dates that summer or give up his bonus check. When Berlin approaches him, stuttering about the deal with her friends and claiming they don't actually have to go out, he's intrigued. As the summer passes, Cole finds himself burning both ends of the candle to keep up with his job and his new relationship. When he unleashes the Beast one time too many, Berlin will have to decide if she can tame him or if she should walk away.

# ABOUT LIZ

Liz Isaacson writes inspirational romance, usually set in Texas, or Montana, or anywhere else horses and cowboys exist. She lives in Utah, where she walks her dogs daily, watches a lot of Netflix, and eats a lot of peanut butter M&Ms while writing. Find her on her website at lizisaacson.com.

Made in the USA
Monee, IL
16 January 2021

57828747R00246